Venice

Michelle Novak

Olivia,
Enjoy the adventure!
Best Wishes,
Michelle

Printed by CreateSpace, An Amazon.com Company

Cover Design: SelfPubBookCovers.com/Daniela

Author's Website:
inspiredbyvenice.org

For Lita

THIS was a long awaited moment. You have made a very distant fantasy come true, traveling to one of the most romantic and beloved destinations in the world, Venice, Italy. For years you had regarded splendid scenes of this place in the glossy ads of travel magazines, the erudite pages of history books and in browsing the city's rich culture through the abundance of online photography and discourse. You had always heard stories of its exquisite architecture, over 100 little islands separated by scenic waterways and linked by an army of ancient bridges. It is a city born from the sea, the very air damp and brackish from the Adriatic. A place so picturesque and antiquated that it isn't hard to believe it was once one of the most opulent and commanding cities in Europe, brimming over with riotously profitable trade, unprecedented diversity and art abundant. It is a mysterious place. Even on the brightest of days, it is easy to get lost while exploring its narrow pathways, many of which are overshadowed by monolithic *palazzi*. There are secrets, forgotten histories and delicious pleasures amongst its labyrinth of winding *calli*.

This is what drew you to Venice, creating an interest too powerful to ignore, especially considering you had never heard anything but news of this city's irresistible charm. You had to experience it, explore it and fall in love with it for yourself. It had taken some time to put aside the resources you felt would be necessary to truly enjoy your stay, thoughtfully planned out by considering exchange rates, travel fees and hotel costs. You wanted this trip to be unrestrictively savored, thus you diligently saved, devising that when the visit finally came, you could afford every luxury within reason. You wanted to be a discerning traveler able to spoil your senses, better yet to taste the life of an aristocratic Venetian during the eighteenth century, buying what you fancied and living as though life itself was all a decadent dream.

As though traveling to this grand city were not enough, you scheduled this trip around one of the most historic and celebrated festivals known throughout the world as the Venetian Carnival. Annually during the 10 days preceding the Christian holiday known as Ash Wednesday (give or take each year), the *Carnevale di Venezia* is celebrated and this is the year that you will experience every illustrious moment of it for yourself. There was even a period in Venice when this well-known *celebrazione* lasted for months, the spirit of the season fostered by nightly banquets, elaborate theater, exhaustive dancing and disastrous gambling. Additionally, many wore costumes while *everyone* concealed their identity by wearing a mask. In tribute to Venice's sumptuous history, you decided to invest in the construction of several simple, yet elegant eighteenth century style gowns, accompanied by a selection of ornate accessories.

There are many possible delights available to you including musical performances, amusing *caffe* entertainments, soothing gondola rides and panoramic masked balls (all in costume of course). You will decide as your trip unfolds, where you will go, what you will do and in whatever style you wish. This is *your* stay in Venezia and you intend to make it memorable.

You are now just arriving into the city of Venice by way of a sizable *vaporetto*, a slow moving boat with a flat floor and awning. You are among other travelers with overstuffed luggage and everyone is in awe of the view as you approach the docks at the edge of Piazza San Marco or St. Mark's Square. Minutes later, you are pulling along your own two large yet fashionably matching travel cases on wheels, into the square itself. The marble blocks beneath your feet are a new sensation from the cement pathways back home. Inhaling deeply, you note the sea and a hint of ancient mildew.

SHOULD you like to pause a spell to take in the *piazza*, luggage and all, turn to page 27.

IF you believe that it is better to proceed straight to your hotel and explore later, turn to page 5.

V e n i c e

YOU decide that it is better to get straight to your hotel with your things and take care of the business of settling in. It will be a scenic walk and you have booked a room at the Hotel Fato, a short stroll from the Piazza San Marco (where large portions of the festivities take place). You more than once pondered over the name of your accommodations, as *fato* means fate. As you amble along with luggage in tow through one of the many passageways leading out of the square into the great city, your eyes begin to wander to the superfluity of tiny storefronts, lined together one after the other. You stop before one to admire the painted masks in the darkly lit display of a shop centuries old. Lavish emerald green crushed velvet is spread the length of the prominent exhibit. Full-face masks mimicking characters of the past, such as the beak-faced mask of a doctor who fought the plague, are carefully laid out for viewing. There are ghastly smiles and frowns, eye slits slanted like those of a fierce and agile cat, lusciously full lips and many other colorful and flamboyant facial expressions. There are many laboriously painted masks with ornate crystals and shimmer, half and full-faced masks in every hue with delicate silk ties attached to hold them in place around the face. You imagine that hiding your true identity behind these ostentatious characters is liberating. For a time, you could be anyone or anything you wish.

As you wander further, another shop grabs your attention. A brightly lit and more currently renovated retailer presents Italian leather goods in its window. Elegant gloves, shoes and handbags abound in a variety of hides. An assortment of suede wallets look as soft as butter, you imagine smoothing your fingers over a number of pieces just to feel how fine the leather is. A smart briefcase the color of espresso catches your eye, its gold closures glinting in the light. A slim evening purse dyed a purple as dark as eggplant would look very fine as an accessory for a romantic dinner out. Finely handcrafted watchbands and belts in every hue from cream to dark chocolate are thoughtfully displayed and you can imagine how a quality piece or two from this place might find its home with you before your trip is at an end.

Meandering around a corner and over a bridge, you come to a standstill in front of an artist's lineup. Grand and miniature paintings of people and landscapes in the style of the Renaissance are displayed. Sumptuous cupids flying amongst fluffy clouds, ample bosomed women in ethereal foamy gowns and strictly dignified men of religion in shadowy pose, are all for viewing. Such fine detail and realism make you feel as though you could be in the scene. As if you were looking at real people and they are looking back at you from within their imprisoning frames. You want to ask the smirking clergyman why he is so smug and what secrets this copious woman lying out on lush pillows has to tell. You'd even be tempted to ask the plump infant angels if they have been delighting on pastries for all eternity. Apart from the art museum, you have never seen works like this (especially not such fine art) on sale to the public for the purpose of displaying along the walls of your own home. You are sure that owning artwork like this comes at a price.

You continue to walk slowly through the tight street, intimately engulfed on either side by an array of vendors. The appetizing aroma from a *bacaro* (Venetian wine bar) serving *panini imbottiti* (stuffed sandwiches), *tramezzini* (smaller snack sandwiches), seafood risotto, *polpette* (fried meatballs), calamari, strong coffee and more, looks tempting. Your neglected stomach grumbles in confirmation that you have become rather hungry. You haven't eaten anything since just before your plane landed some hours before (and that was just a nibble). You could also use a little caffeine to ward off the jet lag you are beginning to feel. However, the sun is beginning to set and trying to find your hotel after dark could be somewhat challenging in this labyrinth of winding *calli*.

IF you decide that it is better to continue on to your hotel, turn to page 75.
IF it is time to take a meal to appease your hunger, turn to page 9.

Venice

YOU know that when you are getting an appetite, irritability follows not far behind without eating. Besides, it may take you a while to check in to your hotel room, lay out your things and feel settled enough to go out for dinner. After all of that, you would likely have a headache from hunger or be extremely fatigued, and would skip the meal altogether to sleep instead.

As you and your hobbling luggage approach the entry of the bar, you are simply enchanted. You feel kind of silly, but you are experiencing a burgeoning thrill that you haven't felt in a long time. Everything seems so exciting: the compelling storefronts, the sound of church bells tolling the time, the delightful Italian spoken by strangers passing by. The orange glow of a waning sun only gives your current moment a warmer, more captivating frame. You are happy to go unnoticed, as you would feel a little embarrassed to be smiling so avidly to yourself in front of strangers. A cold gust of air bites at you from one side, causing you an unexpected chill and the giddiness ends. Though it is unseasonably warm for February in Venice, you realize that with the setting sun, nighttime could prove to be rather cold. As you approach the little *bacaro*, somewhat reminiscent of a quaint coffee shop back home, a patron leaves and holds the door open long enough for you to make your way inside with your luggage.

You read about bars in Italian cities, how they are liken to a quick serve restaurant, except offering higher quality food and drink. There are dozens of *bacari* saturating Venezia, perfect for stopping in to enjoy a *tramezzino* and a strong, rich espresso. The permeating fragrance of coffee makes you feel comforted, as if you have just walked into your kitchen at home on a lazy morning full of nothing to do but just as you like. You roll up to the marble bar, freestanding without any stools. As space is precious in Venice, table service comes with a fee. Since you were sitting long enough on the flight and boat ride over to the island from the airport, you could stand to stretch your legs for half an hour as you enjoy your first bite of real Italian fare. After arranging your luggage under the bar in front of you, you loosen your scarf a little with one hand while unfastening a few buttons of your coat with the other. Several men standing on either end of the bar are sipping glasses of dark liquid contemplatively, perchance taking respite at the end of their workday. You suspect it isn't only coffee in those tumblers and are half inclined to ask the bar attendant to pour a shot of amaretto liqueur into yours to add a little warmth to your cheeks.

Outside the sun is setting beautifully, beaming crimson and persimmon colored rays on the opposite side of the street while the shadows begin to grow on your side. In moments, the walkways will become dark and you already notice a few street lamps beginning to flicker on. Though they are clearly powered by electricity, the lamps are designed like lanterns that may have lit the streets by candlelight many years ago. You imagine that there may even be a few streets yet lit by candle in Venice; unlikely, but the thought is charming. The lamps certainly add to the antiquated look of the cobblestone streets and mature buildings.

You begin to look over the vast variety of *tramezzini* on display behind a case, which is reminiscent of an oversized breadbox made entirely of glass with its rounded lid on the staff side. All of the sandwiches are made of soft white bread and filled with countless choice fillings: meat, cheese, seafood and a variety of vegetables. All of the *tramezzini* are cut into triangular halves and appear ridiculously creamy and flavorful. You are almost enjoying making a selection as much as you will enjoy eating a few, kind of like staring into a French *patisserie* with its decadent delights and then stuffing an éclair into your mouth. You decide on ham with roasted red peppers and spinach, as well as a tuna with white cheese and tomato. Flagging the barman over takes a while; back home you are used to speedy service otherwise gratuity is in jeopardy. As tipping is largely underrated here (leaving small change from your bill will do), the bar attendant is in no rush to service you. In fact, he may even take his time as a courtesy, purposefully allowing you to catch your breath and relax after coming off the street. You realize you are usually pretty uptight about fast service when you are dining out. Here however, the slower service complements a culture that remembers to enjoy life. You don't mind at all waiting a few extra minutes considering you shouldn't be in any hurry anyway. You are going to enjoy these sandwiches and ignore your innate feeling to rush through a meal as you usually do.

The sandwiches are as delicious as you expected, even better at this point considering how ravenous you have become. You are considerably pleased that you stopped to eat and are enjoying the ambiance almost as much as the food. As tempting as your first authentic Italian espresso sounded, you decided to try a hot chocolate instead. In the 1700s, when the Venetian

Carnival was at its height and filled with celebratory extravagance, hot chocolate was very popular. Aristocrats that could enjoy the imported luxury took pleasure in the beverage while being waited upon in their lavish beds and in fashionable cafés. Unlike the version of hot cocoa that you are accustomed to (a drinkable liquid), this version is so thick that you amusingly balance your spoon on top of the chocolate and watch it slowly sink into a hot, rich pudding.

As you finish the last dollop of creamy chocolate, something in the window catches your eye. A man dressed in baroque costume wearing a long black cloak, has stopped just outside of the glass and is peering in. Though it is not fully dark outside, it is almost so and the man appears eerily mysterious under one of the hanging lamps above the window. One side of his cape drapes back over his shoulder, revealing a vest studded in crystals and a lacy white cravat neatly pinned with a glimmering broach at his neck. The stranger is wearing sleek black breeches and dark stockings and leaning on a silver cane with an ebony knob. The top half of his face is covered in a bejeweled half mask. Atop his head sits a tricorne, a hat liken to a fedora, only fashioned with a wider brim turned up at the edges to catch and dispel rain. You don't want to stare since you aren't sure if the man is looking at the sandwiches on display, or if he is looking further into the bar, directly at you; it is hard to tell. This is the first costumed person that you have seen since your arrival. His clothes are quite fine and historically sound from what you can see at this distance. You wonder if he is a Venetian.

You try to distract yourself for a moment by rustling through your coat pocket for some euros to pay the tab, thankful that you exchanged enough currency for several days' worth of minor purchases while back home. The barman has been animatedly involved in conversation with other locals and hasn't looked up in 10 minutes. You feel comfortable leaving the unbroken bill as payment without getting your change, but as you look over your shoulder and out of the window, you see that the cloaked man is still leaning on his walking stick outside and most certainly staring directly at you. His lips appear to be turned up faintly, a hint of an uninvited smile and you begin to feel a little chill creep under your coat. You can't quite tell the age of the man from the exposed half of his face. Though his smile has a twinge of the nefarious, he doesn't look unattractive, just up to something. You consider that it is somewhat exhilarating that a mysterious Venetian is watching you from the shadows in genteel costume and then quickly come to your senses and remind yourself that only exceptionally rude or disturbed people stare at strangers from out of the darkness of night for more than a curious short moment.

You stall a little longer by moving closer to the other patrons and asking the attendant for a San Pellegrino and your change. You thirstily gulp down a little bottle of the sparkling water, leave the exchange's coin on the marble bar and look again as subtly over your shoulder as possible towards the window. It is now fully dark outside. Beneath the glow of the street lamps, you can't see anyone at the exterior of the bar at all, except for a few random people in everyday clothes walking by. Considering it is much brighter in the *bacaro* than outside, you can't be fully sure that there is no one lurking in one of the alleys between the buildings across the way. Venice is full of dark alleys, waterways and side streets. Even during the light of day, people frequently get lost. You ask the bartender where the Hotel Fato is from here, and he tells you in broken English that you are only a few minutes' walk away and gives you a few lefts and rights to get you there.

IF you feel ready to leave the bar and walk on to your hotel, turn to page 252.

IF you are undecided about leaving the *bacaro* just yet and wish to stay a little longer, turn to page 17.

IF you feel inclined to exit by way of a door at the rear of the bar to avoid the *calle* out front, turn to page 343.

Venice

THOUGH it is likely that you are overreacting by prolonging your stay in the bar, you still feel a bit eerie on account of the onlooker. He watched you more particularly, if even taking the time to admire you as an attractive woman, than what you would expect to be courteous. Furthermore, there was something devious in the way the stranger smiled at you and remained posed just outside of the window for much longer than curiosity necessitates. You have been told more than once that you are a beautiful woman, but your simple travel attire and worn appearance doesn't seem deserved of any particular attention.

Several more locals cheerily walk through the door bringing a cold draft in with them as they enter. You can tell the temperature has dropped since you were outside. The smell of the sea wafts in with the visitors and you consider how unique it is to live in a city where walking and boating are the only methods of transportation. It appears there are as many waterways as there are cobblestone paths. You wonder what it would be like to grow up taking a water taxi to school everyday instead of a big yellow bus. You consider how much more important it must be here to teach young children to swim rather than look both ways before crossing the street! As the attendant wipes away the leftover crumbs and smudges of chocolate you've dripped on the counter, you request a glass of red wine. By the time you are finished you will be feeling warmed and just right to check into your hotel for some much needed sleep. You smile to yourself as you contemplate that drunk driving must be nonexistent here, but wonder what the statistics are on drinking and boating. The bartender lifts your filled glass as if in cheers before pushing a fruity Corvina your way and then continues wiping down the marble after re-corking the bottle.

The wine is strong and fragrant. If you lived in Italy, you might consider taking up wine tasting as a hobby, or for that matter, the tasting of both food and wine. Somewhere from above comes the sound of a guitar in a spicy, slow strumming. You look up and notice two small speakers hinged into the ceiling corners above the bar. The attendant must have turned on the music for a little ambiance for the guests. The chattering begins to get a little louder as the newest visitors huddle around an intimate table and laugh heartily at some story or other. You hadn't noticed a waiter before, dressed in a crisp white shirt, black trousers and a maroon half apron. He brings four glasses of black coffee and sets out a silver bowl of brown cane sugar and a porcelain creamer for the table. You ponder for a moment why you are the only woman in the bar when two lovely ladies in sleek dress coats float in, bringing another cold gust of air with them. They smile familiarly to the barman (whom may also be the proprietor) and squeeze in next to you at the counter. Without their even making the order, the attendant pours two glasses of chilled Trebbiano white wine and produces a plate of white cheese, pitted black olives, salty sardines and some thinly sliced Italian bread.

Though none of the other guests seem to so much as notice you, you realize that your avid people watching experience is turning into the equivalent of being stared at by the darkly dressed stranger earlier. You simply got caught up in the moment of observing the comings and goings of the eatery, but realize it is about time to get to your hotel and rest for the forthcoming events of your trip. A bit of the butterflies stir up in your stomach in anticipation of all of the activities you hope to enjoy during the Carnevale. You swallow your last sip of the wine and feel it warm your throat as it goes down, quelling the fluttering feeling inside. Buttoning up your coat you glance out of the window and see that it is bare of people. You slip a few more euros under the base of your wineglass as payment and after wrapping your scarf around your neck a little tighter to secure your partially exposed chest some warmth from the wind, you pull your luggage back out onto the street.

You can see your breath in the chilly air as you walk with purpose along the route that the bar attendant gave you earlier. You are a little unsure of your first turn considering you can't really differentiate between a street, an alley or a private walkway. Some portions of the walk are dimly lit and with others, only the glow of the moon on this clear night lights your way. Taking what you believe to be the correct next turn, there is a rather extensive length of unlit street leading to a faraway bridge. Though it isn't all that late, the shops all appear to be closed; you really aren't sure what time it is, having lost track of it in the bar. However, there are several storefront displays softly lit, lending some slight illumination to your path. Strolling past a cavernous doorway, your peripheral vision catches a red flicker moving within the shadows. A thin ribbon of smoke, cigarette smoke you smell, smoothly streams out of the darkness from the inlet. A glimmer of moonlight reflects off of a smooth silver staff-like object protruding from the base of the cove. You instantly realize that the object is a cane propped against the dark doorway and that the masked man is most probably the smoker shrouded in darkness.

Your heart begins to thump as fast as that of an animal scampering from a predator. You don't want to bring more attention to yourself by sprinting down the path with your luggage noisily lumbering over the cold stones. However, you are also not willing to pace your steps with a potentially dangerous stranger lurking in darkness only yards away, a man who not long ago was watching you from the street. Stepping it up a notch, you are certain that you must appear as though you are in a speed walking competition, only you are dragging luggage rather than pumping arms with determination on either side of your body. The weight you are toting seems heavier and heavier as you approach the bridge.

In the still night, all you can hear is the soft lapping of the water under the bridge, the clacking of your baggage wheels as you mount the steps and what sounds like the clinking of a cane against stones approaching from behind you. Has the stranger lurking in darkness exited his shadowy cave to follow after you? As you reach the flat walkway at the height of the bridge, you stop and turn around to face the man, before descending the other side. You stand very still while trying not to breath so audibly and peer down the *calle*. You don't see anyone and all is quiet. Squinting your eyes as if it will give you a better view, you scan from the shadows on one side of the street to the other and still see no sign that you are being followed. As still as a statue, you stand moments longer straining to hear any sound of movement. Suddenly you jerk, bumping into your luggage and teetering slightly, from the shock of shrill laughter. You fling your head around to see who is beside you on the bridge, only to find that it is a couple in their winter coats and trappings, glittery confetti in their hair. The merrymakers must be coming from a party to celebrate the beginning of Carnevale. The pair pauses to look over the wooden rail aside of the bridge to the canal below. The woman laughs flirtatiously, a sparkly eye mask over her eyes as the man tries to lean in and kiss her. As the couple lingers, you ungracefully roll past them and down the other side of the bridge hurrying to turn at the next street.

You are beginning to feel uncertain whether you turned in the correct direction when moments later you see a well lit stone enclosed courtyard with a sign reading Hotel Fato. You enter in and follow a quaint *terrazzo* path leading up to the front door and into the lobby. Inside it is warm and bright and a few other guests have arrived just before you. After a smooth check-in at the front desk, a young man carries your luggage up the three flights of stairs to your room. You place a few coins into his hand as tip and lock the door behind him as he leaves. Finally in your room after what seems like hours since you got off of the *vaporetto* in St. Mark's Square, you quickly change into your cozy cotton night clothes and nestle up under the wool blankets on your single bed. Only a large armoire, desk and chair furnish the room, with a bathroom all your own set off to one side. Many European hotels have shared toilets and showers for use amongst guests, but you made sure to reserve a room with its own amenities. You switch off the mounted lamp aside your bed and soon begin to drift, wondering if you weren't acting just a little erratic on the street. After all, it may not have been the cloaked man from without the bar. Perhaps it was another man smoking on the street, owning a cane similar to that of the stranger, and who lives in one of the apartments above a shop. In any case it no longer concerns you. You feel safe and warm with an easy exhaustion as you float away into the realm of sleep.

You slowly awake to the sound of women's voices whispering in Italian. As you begin to groggily open your eyes, a burst of sunlight floods your room and the silhouette of a portly older woman in a cotton dress covered with a full apron comes to your attention. She is standing before your window, pushing open a set of large wooden shutters. She turns and faces you, standing with a smile not far from the end of your bed. As your eyes adjust, you sit up, quickly pulling a blanket up around your neck. Coming out of the bathroom, a chirping, pretty lady just a few years older than you, hands the woman at the window a rug. For a moment, both are silent and simply stand there smiling at you. The older woman says something to you in Italian, which sounds encouraging and cheery, but you are completely oblivious to what she has said. A moment later, the younger woman points to a silver tray perched on the desk which is also equipped with a vanity mirror. A modest yet delicious breakfast is set out for you: piping hot coffee with milk, crusty warm bread with jam and butter as well as a juicy ripe pear cut into slices. You smile for the two women, yet are still confused as to why they came in to tidy your room while you were still in it, and sleeping too! You get out of bed and both ladies return to working in haste, the older woman beating the bathroom rug out of the open window, and the younger one fluffing your pillows. You tiptoe into the bathroom and close the door behind you to freshen up, easily able to hear when the two women exit your room not much later.

When you open the door, apart from the bathroom rug airing on the window ledge, you find things straightened and inviting for starting a new day. Still in your night clothes, you wrap your winter scarf around your shoulders, pour a little milk and sugar into your coffee and take your cup and a slice of buttery bread to the window. It is a beautiful day, bright and refreshingly chilly but not too cold. A few puffy white clouds float by, and you notice several women in the building across the courtyard beating and airing linens and rugs from without their own windows. How fresh it would be to air your linens every morning, but you have only ever added fresh scented soap in the wash to encourage the smell of nature on your bedsheets up to now. Down below, another woman is sweeping the marble courtyard with a rustic looking broom that seems to do the job, while singing a lovely hymn of sorts. The courtyard looks inviting with a number of dainty white metal chairs and tables intimately set between potted trees that line the walls. You could imagine spending hours in a courtyard like that, reading while enjoying the sounds of Venice. Soon you feel awake from the early morning air and the humble breakfast and are excited to spend your first full day in Venezia with the Carnevale officially begun.

IF you decide to dress in costume and explore the streets, turn to page 53.
IF you decide to dress in everyday clothing and see what there is to see, turn to page 33.

Venice

THOUGH you are experiencing fatigue from your long journey, you feel that stretching your legs in a turn about the most famous square in all of Venice will be an excellent way to spend your very first hour in this ancient metropolis. As the wheels of your luggage roll over each crack between marble stones on your path, you notice how very grand the city center is. You stop beside a massive bell tower known as St. Mark's Campanile and shade your eyes to the bright sun as you look straight above into the blue sky to the golden statue of the Archangel Gabriel perched at the very top. The Angel's massive wings catch a gust of wind, turning Gabriel facing a new direction. You had already considered how moderate the temperature felt for February, however the wind feels a bit blustery causing you to secure your knit scarf a little higher around your neck.

A group on tour of the square is huddled just under the *campanile*. Rolling a little closer to the tourists, you overhear their guide explain that within the tower, there are five bells. You only catch the names of two of the bells over the laughter and language of all the visitors and vendors meandering around the square. The first is the Marangona, which tolls in the morning and at night to signify when it is time to work, and when to finish. The second is the Maleficio, which chimes when someone is put to death. You grimace to yourself, though certainly doubting that in this modern day, the Maleficio is ever used.

Looking across from the tower you see the famous Doge's Palace originally built in AD 1340, where the government of Venice resided for centuries. Used as the epicenter for justice, there beside it is built the Piombi prison. Incarcerated were many of the men and women sentenced to the deaths that gave cause to toll the Maleficio. Giacomo Casanova, a very real man and professional seducer of women, was imprisoned within and escaped an indefinite sentence by breaking out in 1756. You had read bits and pieces of Casanova's memoirs and imagine now his dramatically fleeing the city after years of cavorting masked balls, gambling houses and operas. He very likely stood cloaked and powdered, admiring pretty Venetian ladies, from the very spot you are standing in now.

According to a map of the square in your guidebook of Venice, just around the corner is Caffe Florian, notorious as a watering hole for the most illustrious Venetians and the oldest *caffe* in the city. Still serving customers in style, Casanova himself sat within drinking hot chocolate. During the Carnevale, the Florian can pack every table full, brimming over with corseted ladies in billowy gowns and gentlemen in wigs and overdone frippery. Wall-to-wall paintings, mirrors and gilded woodwork (which decorate many of the salons and ballrooms in the *palazzi* of Venezia) allow guests to bask in splendor. People stand outside of the Caffe Florian, many of them photographers, just to peer in through the windows and watch the magnificence of multiple dining rooms filled with costumed patrons. You pass the bell tower and round the corner to your left into what officially looks like the square's center, encased on each side by luxurious buildings. You see that the façade of the Caffe Florian is decorated with detailed woodwork and richly ornamented windows. Lit within by electric lamps reminiscent of candlelit sconces, the intimate tables, upholstered chairs and wall lined couches appear romantic and plush. A few scattered guests are enjoying refreshments: fluffy pastries, finger sandwiches, chocolates and dessert wines. Surveying the square, you see a stretch of shops with costly wares on display behind their glass windows. A marble awning spans out and lines three of the four sides of the square above the ground floor of shops, creating a promenade to walk around and view the luxury (an architectural pass called an arcade). Currently, it is festooned with thousands of golden strung lights, twinkling like a sky full of stars to stroll beneath. At night, the illumination must be enchanting.

You pull your luggage out into the middle of the square and turn to face the entrance from which you came. Directly before you is the Basilica of San Marco constructed alongside the Doge's Palace, making up the fourth side of the square on the eastern border. This is the first medieval church, building even, that you have ever set eyes on. As history tells it, in AD 828, two Venetian merchants pilfered the bones of St. Mark (who was the author of the Gospel of Mark in the Bible), from his tomb in Alexandria, Egypt. They reportedly brought his remains to Venice where the then Doge ordered the building of the Basilica to house his remains. The Doge in those days was the height of leadership in Venice's political hierarchy and held the position from election to the end of his life (unless otherwise murdered or overthrown and stripped of his title). This was Venice's primary leadership for over 1000 years. The façade of the Basilica is majestically built of marble columns, each of different colors and origins, leading to striking archways at the height of the church. Hundreds of reliefs are carved in the portico; angels, men and women carved out in a colossal work of genius. Above the archways there are more than a few golden winged lions with swords, a symbol for St. Mark. Similar lions can be found around every corner in Venice: as statues, in paintings and even on the simplest Venetian paraphernalia such as on the front of a menu.

It is very clear that you have a lot of things to see. Perhaps you will decide to tour the Doge's Palace, sit in reverie within the pews of the Basilica of San Marco or lounge in costume finery at the Caffe Florian. But as it stands right now, you still have your luggage and must check into your hotel sooner than later. Across the square from the Florian, you notice alfresco dining. A number of other tourists are enjoying a coffee and *cicheti* (Italian appetizers), chatting amicably while people watching. You realize it has been quite some time since you've had anything to eat. You are warmly dressed and have several days' worth of euros that you exchanged before you left on your trip, so that you would be fully prepared to begin enjoying the city upon your arrival.

Venice

IF you decide to find your hotel and get settled in before exploring further, turn to page 5.

IF you decide to sit at the outdoor café and get a bite to eat, turn to page 47.

HOWEVER tempting it feels to adorn yourself in costume and parade the streets as a woman of eighteenth century aristocracy, you determine after consulting your watch (yet to be adjusted to local time) and calculating the time difference, that it is merely 8:20 a.m. in Venice. As early as it is, you will likely be only one of a few patrons in historical array and think it will be pleasurable to see some of Venice dressed as yourself. With no certain hurry, you pick out a pair of snug indigo blue jeans, a long-sleeved cotton t-shirt, a baggy cashmere sweater and a lengthy woolen scarf. You want to be warm and comfortable during your current outing, as you will likely spend the remainder of your trip tightly made up in bodice, skirts and wig. Pinning your hair up haphazardly, brushing your cheeks with a bit of blush and placing on some oversized sunglasses, you are ready to play tourist. Before you left home, one of your closest friends gave you a brand new digital camera to document your Venetian days and evenings. You slip it into an oversized shoulder bag and stuff a few slices of sweet green pear into your mouth as you leave your room.

As you walk down the stairs to the lobby, you see that the attendant on duty is a dark-eyed, fresh-faced young man in a crisp white dress shirt and pressed blue trousers. As you approach the front desk, the youthful maid from your room bustles out of a curtained door behind the reception area and sets out a tray of coffee, ham and sliced cheese on a corner table by the desk phone. You can only assume the food is for the concierge, proven when in a bit of playful spunk, the maid tousles the man's hair and exits out where she came from with a flirtatious giggle. Looking somewhat off guard and attempting to ignore his messy hair, he asks with a thick Italian accent how he might be of assistance this morning. You smile while asking where you might go to see something special in Venice and not too far by foot. The pretty maid pokes her head out from the curtains, quickly blurting several words, and then grins at the young man before disappearing again. Slowly looking over his shoulder to the door and then back at you, he begins nervously messing with a pen lying on the guest book before stating that the *pescheria*, due to the early hour, may be the only thing entertaining until after lunch. You guess that this was the maid's idea as you thought you heard her say something that sounded like *pescheria*, the Italian term for fish market. You assume that the maid understood your question, and that perhaps this young man is relatively new to the hotel and without his own touristy opinion, or that the maid was simply putting words in his mouth to provoke his attention.

After drawing for you a reasonably simple map to follow on the back of one of the hotel's oversized business cards, you nod your head gratefully and head out into the courtyard. It really could not be a more perfect morning. Inhaling deeply, the crisp air smells of seawater and a hint of something like moldy library books that haven't been read in many years. You've always liked that smell, not exactly a repugnant decay but rather something that smelled lightly musty and mysterious. The whole of Venice smells of this, in part due to the water, which flows between buildings, around squares and aside walkways. Damp places will ever smell a hint of mildew, a dankness that can especially never be parted with in a city planted into the very sea. A few pigeons peck idly at some dust and pebbles along the courtyard entrance and warmly coo at each other, walking hurriedly to get out of your way as you pass out onto the *calle*.

Though by no means simple, by light of day the streets don't seem quite as daunting to follow as they did the night before. You wouldn't however want to go traipsing about without some sort of street map and can imagine easily finding yourself lost at night, circling the same block for hours. A game of hide-and-seek crosses your mind, imagining that 30 people could easily remain hidden within a short length of street with all of the courtyards, alleys and doorways to sneak about. You would most probably find yourself "it" for an entire game, regardless that other participants were hiding in a shroud of darkness at any given arm's length of you. Taking your time following the route etched out on the little drawing, you stop a number of times to take a picture of an arched doorway, the vines clinging along the side of a marble building, and even of two elderly ladies sharing stories with kerchiefs on their heads. Entering a small square with a fountain in the middle, you stop to observe six or seven little boys playing a game of marbles. Several are laughing and standing over some of the other boys who are lying flat on their stomachs over the cold stones, eyeing their next approach. One very little boy with a scowl on his face begins pushing a few of the older boys as though he wants a turn to play but hasn't yet been given a chance.

As you cross over the middle of the square to the

opposite corner from where you came, you see a man walking in your direction from the lane there. Lying over his shoulder is a giant fish wrapped in paper with only a third of its bottom exposed. Wearing a pair of thick leather gloves, the man is tightly grabbing the tail of the fish to keep it steady. You believe that a fish of that size could feed a family of 10 as you observe the sunlight glinting off of its silvery pink scales. Traversing through the tight lane, you negotiate past a woman with a basket full of brown parcels. Glancing at her goods as you pass, you believe you see a few gooey octopus tentacles oozing from a package that has come loose. You frown a little to yourself, glad that you won't be the one to prepare that dish for dinner tonight. You enjoy a delicious piece of fish now and then, but haven't yet learned the preparation for juicy, squishy sea creatures. You imagine that you'll be trying some new seafood dishes in Venice, perhaps some of the best that Italy has to offer. Just then, you enter your very first outdoors fish market.

This *pescheria* is a long stretch of lane along the Grand Canal (the widest and deepest waterway in Venice) and lined with tables covered by sturdy awnings. Both large crates and shallow trays of sea life are propped up for viewing from before numerous vendors discussing fish prices. Back home, you were only ever accustomed to going to a grocery store with a lacking selection of seafood packed on ice behind a glass display. This freezer section was always a little chilly and slightly smelled of fish, without any of the natural ambiance of the sea. Here however, you watch the bins coming off of the docked boats along the water with great hurry and demand, and consider that the fish are not only just caught from the sea, but will likely all be sold within a few short hours. You didn't notice any grocery stores last night or this morning and acknowledge that the fish in this market will feed many families and premiere on most restaurant menus in Venice today. Slowly walking along, the vendors' selections all appear to be very organized and clean with many fish lying over beds of ice. There are sacks of dried seafood as well to be bought, stored, hydrated and cooked at one's own discretion. You wouldn't have considered dead fish to be beautiful before, but the displays are artful and picturesque in their own way. There are buckets of tiny silver fish and dried shrimp, skewers of white fish steak and freshly cut fillets as well as an abundance of mussels and oysters. There are little blue and red crabs, octopuses and squid and literally fish of every color and kind along the canal.

You see families along the way socializing with one another, mothers sharing news while their children point at interesting creatures being lugged up from boats. Fishermen are mooring their vessels alongside each other for conversation and trading a fish or two, likely for their own houses. The vendors are smiling and working hard to weigh and package up selections, likely consorting with the same shoppers they have provided fish to for years. Many shoppers appear to be restaurateurs haggling the prices for the choices that they intend to put on show for their tables this evening. With Carnevale just begun, you guess that there will be so many more people to feed in the city this very week than any other week all the rest of the year, (though you are told the summer months are very busy too). The restaurant owners are likely vying for the most special and select fish this morning to accommodate the full houses that they are expecting and to fetch higher plate prices than usual. You can't even fathom how many mussels, oysters and cold seafood salads alone that will be consumed over bottles of Prosecco at the festive balls each evening.

Ambling through the entire length of the *pescheria*, you find yourself thinking that this is one of the most amazing places to people watch as the interactions and camaraderie between citizens shows itself. Whenever you go to the grocery store, no one ever really speaks to each other or has any sort of sincere interaction. One politely moves their cart for another person, or impassively waits in line for their deli selections. Mostly, everyone wants to get in and do their shopping and then get out again. You hardly feel that it is culturally exciting in any way, but this market sure is!

You take a dozen or so pictures of vendors and their unique arrangements of sea life. For a few euros, you buy a small paper bag of salty sardines (or at least they look like sardines) to eat with some sliced bread leftover from your breakfast. You are sure you can secure a few other items for lunch back at your hotel and find it special that your meals here will be unique from the repetitive fare you fix for yourself back home. Just before completing your walk back down the canal from where you originally came, you turn to take several photos of the crowd of Venetians browsing the market.

IF you decide to return to your hotel and prepare to go out in costume, turn to page 42.

IF you decide to stay out longer and find something else worth seeing while in your street clothes, turn to page 84.

Venice

THOUGH it is a remarkably lovely morning and you are sure that you could explore Venice all the day long without falling short of an experience, those extravagant costumes are calling for your attention from your hotel room. You imagine them there even now and feel a burst of excitement in your chest.

It isn't difficult finding your way back through the little square and making the other few twists and turns before returning to the courtyard at the Hotel Fato. Along the way, you are sure to slowly pace yourself so that none of the beauty of this morning is lost on you. It was a wonderful decision to plan a visit here and you aspire to be a traveler for life, seeing the rest of the world after a tour of this magnificent city. Upon entering, you find the reception area of the hotel is crowded with newly arriving visitors from multiple countries, judging by the varied languages trickling into your ears. You are pleased to see that it isn't only local Italians that participate in the Venetian Carnevale, but that people come from all over the world to be a part of the annual celebration. You find yourself hastening up the stairs to your room and quickly locking the door behind you once inside. Throwing your bag onto the bed, you walk straight to the armoire.

You had commissioned four gowns to be made with historically explicit expectations from a costume designer at a university close to where you live. It was difficult to find someone that could not only sew well, but also design the historically correct creations that you desired. First researching paintings of women in the 1700s, many of them from Italy's noble class, you could only groan and scoff when you saw the inadequate patterns for dresses at the fabric store. Fortunately your local shop had costume patterns in stock all year long rather than just during the few months preceding Halloween. However, any gowns that remotely resembled what you were looking for appeared inauthentic, silly even. You knew from blog photographs of the Carnival from previous years, that those participants in historic dress looked like real people centuries old. Wearing a gown that looked like a child's Halloween costume would not work; it would be quite humiliating. You pondered more than once where other visitors of the Carnival obtained their costumes and considered that many of them must have sewn them with their own hands, as truly authentic costumes for sale are almost impossible to find (as well as absurdly expensive and rarely made-to-measure). So, you set yourself to finding someone who could rise to the task of making what you needed. There was a handsome fee involved for the seamstress, but seeing the dresses now, each having been perfectly tailored to your body and taste, you know that it was worth it.

Of your four garments, two are day dresses; simple cotton gowns designed for walking around the city during daylight. The other two are considered evening attire and constructed out of silky taffeta and ornamental brocade. Evening gowns were nobly worn during the hours of sumptuous dining and courtly dancing. The lustrous sheen and stitch detail of yours viewed by candlelight will prove enchanting. Of your cotton dresses, one is a bright yellow with linear, thick white stripes and the other is a soft, solid pink. Both of them were hemmed just below the ankle so as not to find your self easily tripping up bridges and along uneven walkways. Before even deciding which of the two day dresses you will don, there is a lot of preparation. Opening up one of the suitcases that you've hauled up from the bottom of the armoire and set upon the bed, you first must decide which wig you will wear.

Gently propping each pompadour up against your erect pillows, you consider between four choices. You have a large round wig with hundreds of tiny corkscrew curls; black and auburn hairs blend to create a beautiful shade of burgundy. Guiding a ribbon to establish a bow on the side of your head over this wig would give you a playfully adorable look. A few false lashes attached to the corner of your lids and your glances will be sweeter than a taste of caramel *panna cotta*. The second wig is grand in height and as white as the sparse wispy clouds reflecting the sun's light outside. You guess that its internal construction includes molded binder's board to make it sturdy. The long synthetic hair is pulled up from the neck and face and laboriously pinned in a complicated mix of plaits and twists at the pinnacle to the back. There are a few loose curls fashioned around the forehead and ears to soften the frame. It is likely the most common of hairdos from the 1700s for women, a tall white wig with complications, curls and panache. The third wig is pitch black and will make a passionate statement paired with glinting jewels and shimmering fabric by the light of a candle or the moon. Originally a wig with long straight hair, all its thick strands have been twisted from the roots and loosely pinned at the back, there creating a French twist beginning at the nape of the neck, working elegantly up to a soft bun at the crown. You consider how ardent fragrant blossoms would look pinned into this coiffure: a Stargazer or a *Calla* lily, perhaps a blushing peony. Your fourth and final wig is a buttery blonde bouffant, soft and puffy around the head with a long curly pony that stretches down to the middle of your back. It is simple, can be decorated with any number of feathers, bows or broaches and the long tresses at the back will look lively while dancing.

IF you wish to dress in your striped yellow gown, turn to page 53.

IF you feel in the mood for pink, turn to page 112.

AS much as you would like to be rid of your heavy luggage and see your room at Hotel Fato (*fato* meaning fate), the fare being enjoyed by the patrons at the outdoor eatery looks too appetizing. You were neither filled nor satisfied by your last airplane meal and figure that eating something sooner than later will keep you from becoming conquered by jet lag and hunger. Rolling over to the first available seat, you position your luggage under the table and take a chair facing into the square to ensure a good view of all the comings and goings. A pleasant gentleman of the wait staff promptly pours a glass of water for you and welcomes you to the Ristorante Gran Caffe Quadri. Glancing behind you toward the buildings, you see that there is a beautiful restaurant that is serving the dining area here and consider whether this *caffe* is of the same historical importance as the Caffe Florian across the way? You cordially return a smile to your server and ask for a sparkling bottle of Valverde and a coffee. As he departs in haste, you retrieve again, your guidebook of Venice.

After looking up the Caffe Quadri, you find that it was first a wine bar by another name, Il Rimedio, which opened in 1638. In 1775, a Giorgio Quadri purchased it (and proudly changed the name to his own). As history tells it, his wife Naxina considered it of interest to invest in this wine bar; how much better for them to serve coffee, then a newer, flourishing beverage (much like hot chocolate). Though cafés in Venice were abundant at the time (and many were serving coffee), wine had always been the Venetian drink of choice. And though many cafés had newly begun to serve the energizing black drink, it was Quadri and his wife that added uniqueness to the trend by serving a strong Turkish variety, the first ever in Venice. You read further that inside, the location flaunts two luxuriously decorated floors (the uppermost of the two is the restaurant and below is the café). The first floor premiers especially enchanting décor: pastel stuccowork, stunning Venetian landscapes and pieces filled with Pietro Longhi style characters, by Italian painter Giuseppe Ponga. Returning with your bottle of water and a cup of steaming coffee, you watch thoughtfully as your server sets the drinks before you. It feels more symbolic that you should enjoy your first Italian coffee sitting here at the Quadri now that you understand the restaurant's history. In light of your discovery, you decide to drink your coffee black and enjoy its strength to celebrate the introduction of a drink that is now so very popular in this city.

You are soon glad to drink your coffee hot and strong with the temperature beginning to drop. As the sun begins its steady decline behind the buildings of the square, the wind feels increasingly more chilling than before. You quickly decide on a grilled *panino* filled with shredded shrimp, crab, cheese, roasted red peppers and lettuce. You have always considered it important to try local specialties while traveling, whether or not it would have been your first menu selection. With the Venetian's roots, reliance and love of the sea and its fruit, seafood was your first choice from off of the menu. Arriving quickly and served up with balls of fried Gorgonzola cheese, you are momentarily in a state of utopia while taking your first delicious bite of crispy bread, fresh flavorful filling and melted cheese. Taking a nibble of encrusted, mouth-watering gooey Gorgonzola, you can't help but appreciate this as one of the most appetizing meals you have ever enjoyed, regardless of the fact that you felt half starved at the moment of sitting down to be served.

Feeling peaceful in your moment of indulgence in the comfort food and awe of the advantageous view of this beautiful square, you idly glance from one place to another, taking in the entire panorama. A couple sitting several tables away appear entranced in each other's company. They are clinking glasses of burgundy colored wine, which is likely keeping them warm and sedated with amorous feelings as they exchange the mysteries of their inner souls. A few paces further, an Italian family is enjoying their evening meal. The father is serving out a portion of vegetables for each of his three small children while the mother is arranging the children's plates around the table. One child, a curly dark haired little girl of about three, places her knees up onto her chair to afford a better situation as she stretches out to dip her spoon into a dish of rice. The mother thoughtfully reaches over to hold back the cuff of the little girl's jacket as she gets her share. In a most endearing moment, the parents kiss while the children giggle at something funny nearby which has caught their notice.

Scanning the square from one side to the other, you listen to the Campanile tolling the evening bell and watch as a dense flock of pigeons rise to gather in the sky and fly over St. Mark's Basilica. In that moment, you cannot think of a more serene city landscape when the sound of shattering glass on the marble stones aside of your seat brings your attention to a pigeon that has flown up from beneath your table. Having knocked over your water glass, he walks further atop, only to begin pecking at the plate of fried cheese. Within moments several more pigeons swoop in seeing that there is food to be had and dropping a partially eaten *panino* half you begin frantically swooshing your arms to scare away the mounting birds. With each swing of your arms, the birds lift and then land haphazardly again, seemingly more dense in number with each effort that you make to frighten them away. Within a matter of a minute, your food is trampled and pecked to mere crumbs, your coffee is spilled and begins staining the tablecloth while the bottle of Valverde rolls off the table, only to smash near your luggage in chunky shards. Almost as quickly as the terribly awkward scene has transpired, it ends with all of the pigeons flying away except for one cooing bird who ruffles its feathers while perching on the backrest of the chair opposite of your own. All of the eyes of the other customers seated outside at the Caffe Quadri are on you and even those of several strolling onlookers in the square. You are sure that they must take pity on your growing embarrassment considering this wasn't a planned debacle. However, you feel that it would suit you to pay your tab and be off just the same to escape your current humiliation. Several employees of the restaurant rush in; one with a hand-held broom and the other with clean white linens to hurry away the mess. Your server sweeps in offering his apology and a replacement spread, should you wish.

IF you decide to finalize your bill and move on to your hotel, turn to page 73.
IF you overcome the fleeting embarrassment and decide to stay on further at the *caffe*, turn to page 124.

YOU decide to debut a yellow gown with bold white stripes on your first turn about the city in costume. It will look smart and bright on such a crisp sunny day and will resemble all of the inner luminosity that you are feeling. To begin your transformation into a noble Venetian lady, you remove your current array, bathe away your modern self and start by pulling on a pair of silky white stockings that reach up to mid-thigh, securing them in place with a lacy garter on each leg. Next you slip a thin cotton shift over your head. It is rather loose-fitting and made of a very thin weave, like a long summer nightgown, and historically would have been meant to protect your skin from your gown's coarse material as well as from exposing your fine fabrics to your own sweat and oils. This was a time before dry cleaners and washing machines made the upkeep of clothing convenient. You would have worn your gown many times over with minimal cleaning and therefore had to wear underclothing that could be washed in its stead. The shift drapes loosely over your shoulders down aside your collarbones, falling rounded above your bosom and exposing the vast delicate skin of your chest.

Next, you step into a pannier (or side hoop), ringed

with durable boning. You tie the contraption in place around your waist and look through the bathroom door into a full-length mirror and laugh lightly at the spectacle. Though far more supple, the wire boning looks reminiscent of an upside down basket jutting out on either hip. The object of this bizarre looking undergarment served two purposes. The first was to create the body silhouette that was fashionable at the time. Over many years spanning the 1500s through the early 1900s, corsets and hoop skirts changed shape dependent on what the style was. During the mid-1700s in Venice and elsewhere in Europe, a hoop that created ostentatiously large hips and thus the appearance of a tiny waist, was vogue. A second principle for a hoop skirt was to support the back and body from the weight of all of the heavy fabric of garments, which could account for an excessive burden in added pounds to a woman's figure. A lady likely felt as though she was floating as weightless as an angel in the clouds once her gown was removed each evening. Furthermore, to say nothing that a corset would actually manipulate the body unnaturally and even damage it, it was as well meant to support the weight of a gown. You ponder what women must have suffered for centuries in the name of style and then consider several pairs of high heels in your bedroom closet back home and admit that many women still suffer for fashion. Sadly in previous centuries, you may have had no choice other than to adhere to rigid dress codes, whereas you are at liberty now to choose whether certain extreme modes of fashion are right for you.

Following the pannier, you arrange a white cotton petticoat over the frame and hook the waistband snuggly at your back. This petticoat, or underskirt, was meant as a slip that protected the fabric of your overskirt from snagging and clinging to your hoop; it now will allow the overskirt of your dress to swing and drape freely. However, it was often the case that ornate petticoats were exposed at the front with the overskirt pulled open; yet another way of flaunting the depths of one's purse, extending luxury to one's underclothing. Next, you disappear into your overskirt by pulling it over your head and then snap securely, the banded waist at your back, then begin pulling into the bodice. The day dresses you've had commissioned, were constructed with boning in the torso of the jacket, therefore you do not need to be bound up in a corset over your shift. This is relieving, as you are able to work your way into the bodice as you would a long sleeved jacket and tightly hook it up the front, lastly covering the seam with a lace placket, without needing anyone else to help you. In the 1700s, it would usually have been the case that your bodice and overskirt would be attached, though for ease of dressing, you had them kept separate. Once buttoned and hooked completely in, the raiment appears almost as seamless as if it were a second skin. At the time that gowns like this were actually worn, if you were rich or a noble, an attendant may have painstakingly stitched your bodice closed instead of using tiny fasteners to secure it shut. Each morning it may have taken you several hours to toilette and create yourself with the help of a lady's maid to dress your hair and sew you in. As would be expected, at the end of the day you would have had to be snipped out of your clothing. This type of excessive attire however was meant only for those wealthy and courtly women who were meant to look stunning and perfectly coiffed at all times. It may have been that many such women moved about very little in the course of the day except for a walk or a dance, their clothing alone giving them exercise in its own arduous way. If you chose to wear a particularly tall or heavy wig on your head to complete the vision, you received a double dose of physical exertion. As it stands, your gown was not built with half the weight, difficulty or ornamentation as truly historic attire, but you look pleasingly the part all the same.

Finally picking out one round and cheery dark-haired wig with tiny curls, you slip a thin nylon cap over your own hair and pin it around your forehead, ears and the nape of the neck with long bobby pins. Carefully you ease the large bouffant over your head and adjust it this way and that until it feels comfortable and assured in place. For adornment, you tie a wide silk yellow ribbon from the bottom up to the top where you create an oversized bow. You sit at the desk, conveniently and femininely outfitted with a mirror like a vanity table, and begin the final stage of completing the look. Since you are going out in the day rather than to an evening soiree, you see no need to powder your face. You apply a few strokes of bright pink blush, darken up your lashes with thick black mascara and create a tiny beauty mark above your lip with a dot of black eyeliner. Next you apply a deep pink lipstick and a coat of gloss. When you smile in the mirror, you look absolutely kissable, terribly adorable. You almost feel like you've played a showy game of dress up where the clothes are too loud and the makeup too tawdry, but it works in your favor instead of against it. To seal the envelope, you choose a white lace half mask that covers only your eyes and tie it by the strings behind your head. The wig is so dense with curls that the mask strings are almost immediately lost to view. For one final splash of panache, you brush a modest dusting of gold glitter over your bosom (which appears considerably lush in your tight bodice) and dab a hint of your favorite scent around your neck and chest.

IF you wish to stroll through the Venetian streets and make your way back to St. Mark's Square where other costumed guests will be amassing, turn to page 59.
IF you would like to float through the city in a gondola, turn to page 119.

YOU are eager to mingle with a richly dressed crowd and know that St. Mark's Square, aside the Doge's Palace, will be the most congested place for socializing. When considering your accessories long before your trip began, you learned that purses were not widely included as a lady's accouterment before the 1790s. Instead a woman's sumptuously large skirts with their full folds of fabric often held discreet pockets. By many, women's pockets were whispered erotic as they held the secret items of the carrier. Perhaps more than once a man indulged in his thoughts, pondering what might be concealed in this hidden compartment of the woman he desired: a missive of love, a corked vial of her sweet perfume? Smiling at the romanticism of the thought, you obscure some currency, your passport, a handkerchief and a small pot of lip gloss, inside the secreted pocket within your own skirt. You ignored the notion of a cosmetic mirror, as this city is full of these reflective pools and there is never a place that you can't stop to view and fix an errant curl or smudged pout. Pulling up a pair of long and soft lacy cream gloves, you take a full and satisfied breath at such finery finally able to be out in the world and swing the thick folds of a half cloak over your shoulders to keep you warm. Liken to a cape, its true Venetian name is a *tabarro*. It is a coat of another time that was usually constructed out of black fabric. However, this *tabarro* is of a pearly cream to enhance your ensemble and also isn't as long as a traditional cape. You are sure that no one will consider the color of the piece considering you aren't really in the 1700s. But if they did, you can just inform them of the historic correctness of your pockets!

Locking the door of your room behind you, you discreet your key with the rest of your hidden personals and assume in the moment how liberating it will feel to walk around with your hands completely free of the usual handbag. You immediately learn however, to pull up your skirts with both hands when you almost trip descending the first step on your way to the lobby. Perhaps your hands wont go as unencumbered as you thought. As you pass down through the entrance, you nod politely in response to several approving smiles from other hotel guests who are pleased to be greeted by such a lovely vision. Perhaps they are soon to join you themselves, in costume amidst a growing crowd in the square. The sun seems also to sparkle in approval at your incandescent array and you beam while listening to the clinking of your embroidered heels, gracing the wise stones beneath your feet. You'd just about skip through the streets if you were sure your bountiful bouffant would stay atop your head or that you wouldn't trip over yourself and fall only to have your hoop skirt rise over your head, exposing your undergarments. Better to take an aristocratic saunter and enjoy the view along the way. You've never felt more like a lady, catching an elegant if not outrageously eccentric image of yourself in the reflection of a passing window. Your eyes cast a mysterious glint beneath fluttering lashes and half mask while your lips appear as lush and sweet as summer fruit with the help of the sun's shine. Your full skirts make passing straight past other pedestrians in the narrow walkways a difficulty. You soon adapt by lifting your skirts just so, while skimming sidelong between this person and the other, as though it were a dance. Though mask makes the view of your partially exposed bosom obscured to you, you imagine the dusting of glitter powder adds a pinch of soft feminine and festive sparkle to your person.

As you approach closer to the square by slowly negotiating the winding *calli*, you begin to see other masked patrons in full disguise and sophisticated attire mingling between those more modernly dressed citizens.

You are in awe of the varied costuming on display, consisting of both noble Venetian garb and historical characters. A gangly sort of man has settled himself on a marble staircase in the corner of a turn of streets, dressed in ratty woolen stockings, gnarled brown boots and breeches, gritty stained chemise and ill-fitting vest with a cap atop his head. A pathetic stringy looking pair of feathers hangs from his hat and he's blackened out several teeth with oily makeup. He frowns, his face an ashen pallor assisted by powder and paste. He looks the exact replica of a Venetian beggar as he outstretches his hands and howls some undecipherable Italian. Should you really have been a wealthy citizen of old, you would have been tempted to drop a few coins in his grimy hands, cupped out in supplication with head bent. Of course, this is all a show. You have taken the approach of simply looking the part, but soon discover that many guests of the Carnevale enjoy acting out their parts as well.

While pausing to appreciate the true likeness of this pitiable beggar, you are startled and then quickly grin at the shrieking of a demon with scarlet horns crowning his head and a ghoulish green mask, which has rounded the corner in a scamper. Clad in red, dripping in crystals the color of blood, you see that he is chasing a chaste maiden all in white. The show is plainly entertaining; a pure soul with flowing blond tresses loosely encased by ribbon, donned in flowing feminine fabric, feigning the frightened look of innocence (ever so tainted with a smirk of mirthful play). The uncorrupted being pursued by a mischievous devil! The juxtaposition of good and evil is likely to be acted out in more than one set of the characters that you should encounter. Continuing along, you find a plump man and woman energetically selling out to the slew of passersby as they stand near the side of a lane. She is evidently the baker and he the butcher. Both are dressed as working class people; her full tan skirts dusted in flour and he in mustard vest, ballooning brown pants and a leather apron smattered in fake animal's gore. Both are effectually painted with rosy cheeks and mussy, frazzled wigs. She seems to be wagging a long thin loaf of bread at her husband and he is waving a wooden mallet back, perhaps the one he uses to tenderize the beef! You are sure that these individuals have paid well to be dressed in these costumes, regardless of the lack of lavishness. It still takes an imaginative costume designer to create a panorama of historic persons outfitted with dirt, flour, faux blood and oily smears. You take a moment to ponder what caricature you may have liked to play had you invested in more than gowns for day and evening pleasures. A searching astrologer, a wounded sailor, or a lawyer carrying scrolls, a fisherman with his net, a gaudy sassing courtesan, a gambling libertine or greedy tax collector? For now, you are in awe of the scene as you walk through one of the numerous marble archways entering an arcade marginal to St. Mark's Square.

Amidst the clamor of the massive crowd within the *piazza*, it is difficult to say where the sound is coming from (perhaps the immense *campanile* situated opposite the Doge's Palace), but a bell tolls three resounding clangs as you enter, as if to announce festivity. A flock of pigeons that seem frightened in response, rise as in a beautiful work of art to fly over the square above the richly situated throng. Slowly working your way in among others entering, you begin to hear deep beat music coming from a massive stage in the center of the square. The reverberation of sexy techno mixed with classical oboe, violin and harp unite with the sounds of many languages and laughter. The scene is wildly exotic for reality. Where else in the world can you go to see a crowd amassed in historic splendor socializing to passionately soul moving music in a place so architecturally breathtaking?

The arcade spans around three sides of the square; a walkway sheltered by a marble awning in front of shops and cafés. There are far less people walking this promenade than amassing in the center of the square itself, with the exception of a handful of modernly attired individuals trying to stay out of the crowd where they have a better vantage point for taking photographs and viewing costumed persons posing beneath the arches.

IF you would like to walk the length of the promenade and regard the crowd from the sidelines, turn to page 136.

IF you wish to mingle with the participants in the core of the square, turn to page 157.

THE wind has become a little blustery and you are somewhat baffled by how dark Venetian city streets are at night. Taking your first turn you find that the only illumination comes from but a few dim sconces randomly scattered above a minority of doorways, bulbs glowing weakly behind their worn and dusty glass encasements. The stones beneath your feet are considerably more bulky and uneven than what you found under foot in Piazza San Marco. It is very possible that the stones on this *calle*, or street have been in place many years longer, pulled up from mainland earth, boated over and sanded by hand, rounded at the corners and anchored in place one at a time with primeval cement. For that, you imagine laborers hauling up baskets of thick dank muck from the lagoon, smoldering under a summer sun. Their feet slip and sink into murky banks as they cut their hands pushing away dense swamp reeds to haul the mud up onto dryer heights. You imagine they're wiping away sweat from their eyes and it stinging the cuts in their hands, their aching muscles abused by the labor, the mosquitoes and the smell of decaying fish and earth. Anyone that labors for a living deserves your respect for his or her struggles and learned handiwork. Even more so do those who didn't have modern machinery and tools and yet accomplished the creation of incredible architectural works. You think it is almost as mysterious that such a spectacular metropolis was built upon shifting island mud and sand, as it was that the pyramids rose up in a vast Egyptian dessert.

You can't be sure when the current street lighting or cobblestones were incorporated, but as you round a corner into a relatively small square, you see a noble structure most evidently derived from some long history. A wooden sign bolted into a building at twice your height at the intersection indicates that you are entering Campo San Fantin. It is an interesting fact that Piazza San Marco is the only square titled as *piazza* or plaza. All other squares are called *campo* or center. Originally squares throughout Venice were plots of land that were securely dry amongst Venice's many islands (islands that today link up to make the city itself). Venice's first settlers were citizens of the Ancient Roman Empire. Over many years the empire was repeatedly assailed by violent tribes, hungrily looking to claim new territories. It was a time of great migration when scores of communities were torn apart by the ravaging visits from intruders like the Huns and Visigoths, from all over what is Europe today. As people fled their settlements seeking a peaceful place to inhabit, some came to travel up the waterways amongst Venice's many islands from the Laguna Veneta (which eventually leads out to the Adriatic Sea). After finding suitable fields, they ultimately built numerous *campi* (plural for *campo*). These squares were where small groups of people built up churches (the center of their social lives), and started life anew. Venice has been known as the Serenissima Republic, or most serene, because it was tremendously complicated to attack and occupy by pillaging forces. This was especially so once these small communities became extremely competent maritime peoples, manning some of the most powerfully crafted ships in Europe. For armies accustomed to attacking by land, approach to this formidable aquatic enemy almost certainly meant failure.

Stopping to stand at the center of Campo San Fantin, you face the façade of a beautiful edifice that you recognize from your guidebook as Teatro La Fenice, the premier opera house in Venice. The original La Fenice completed construction in Campo San Fantin in 1792. It was in concept, the successor of the San Benedetto Theatre (located elsewhere in Venice), which burned down in 1774. Starting fresh, the operatic company moved into their new quarters in a new square (which wealthy opera lovers financed). Thus, La Fenice was a wink to the legend of the phoenix, a mystical bird that sets afire and rebirths amongst the flames to live life again many times over. In 1836 Teatro La Fenice went up in flames. It was rebuilt, yet burned once more in 1996 (this time not by accident but rather at the hands of arsonists). Rebuilding began in 2001, was completed and opened its doors in 2003 in replication of its previous nineteenth century architectural glory. Though many Venetians argue that the current Teatro La Fenice does not pay perfect tribute to its former magnificence, no one can dispute that La Fenice eerily justifies the name of phoenix. It also remains one of the most famous opera houses in all of Europe following its indubitably rich history (owed not to flames, but rather the artists who have graced it). You mentally note that seeing an operetta performed in Baroque era attire at La Fenice may be just the outing. Especially considering Venice has also been called the Republic of Music owing to its elegant opera houses, elaborate church music and *schola cantoruum* or schools for singers that took root in the city as early as the sixth century. Even orphanages were turned into *ospedali* or conservatories where abandoned children became musical prodigies.

Continuing out of Campo San Fantin by an opposite *calle* from where you came, it is only a matter of several more turns before you find yourself facing a nearly hidden courtyard (fortunately sporting a sign) leading into the entrance of the Hotel Fato. Walking under a marble archway between two stonewalls thickly entangled in winter thriving ivy, you feel surprisingly at home. The quiet courtyard is surrounded on all sides by potted trees and shrubs, ironwork tables and chairs, softly illuminated with strings of twinkling white lights. It seems a restful place to take in the morning air with a delicious coffee or a good book. You imagine lunching with friends, or perhaps engaging in a romantic conversation over a candlelit dinner, in this private place.

Soon inside of the hotel, you find the foyer warm and bright and notice that a few other guests have arrived just before you. After a smooth check-in at the front desk, a young man carries your luggage up the three flights of steep stairs to your room. You place a few euros for tip into his hand and lock the door behind you as he leaves. Finally in your room after what seems like hours since alighting the *vaporetto* in Piazza San Marco, you quickly dress for dreams and nestle up under a wool blanket in your single bed. Only a large armoire, desk and chair adorn the room with a bathroom all your own offset to the side. Many European hotels have shared toilets and showers for common use amongst guests, but you made sure to reserve a room with its own amenities for absolute privacy and comfort. You switch off the mounted lamp aside your bed and soon drift into a deep and soothing sleep.

Awaking the next morning to a soft knocking, you groggily throw off your blanket and shuffle over, warily peering through a small crack before fully opening the door. A cheery looking woman not much older than you is standing just outside wearing a crisp white dress and holding a silver breakfast tray. She smiles and nods at the tray while wishing you a, "*Buon giorno.*" You open the door wider and thank her with a, "*Grazi e buon giorno,*" (thank you and good morning). Accepting the tray and closing the door behind you, you walk over to the desk and sit down to see what fare will start your first full day in Venice and the official beginning of the Carnevale. A modest yet delicious breakfast of piping hot coffee, crusty warm bread with jam and butter as well as a juicy ripe pear cut into slices will do just fine! Still in your nightclothes, you wrap your winter scarf around your shoulders, pour a little cream and sugar into your coffee and take your cup and a slice of buttery bread to the window. Stuffing the bread in your mouth, you use your free hand to open and pull the glass inwards and then push the wooden shutters out. It is a beautiful day, bright and refreshingly chilly, but not too cold. A few puffy white clouds float by and you notice several women in the building across the courtyard beating and airing linens and rugs from without their own windows. Down below, another woman is tending the greenery around the courtyard while singing a delightful song in Italian. Finishing the remainder of your breakfast, you consider what should be the first activity on your agenda.

IF you decide to ask for suggestions from the staff of the hotel (being yet so early in the morning), turn to page 33.

IF you decide to dress in costume right away, one as pretty as this new day to venture out in for a walk, turn to page 112.

Venice

THOUGH you could camp out with a freshly laid table, you feel full enough and ready to find your hotel. You ask your server for directions to Hotel Fato, pointing to the address, which you had written at the top of your city map within your guidebook. He takes a pen and draws a route on the map itself leading you out of the square and taking you a few lefts and rights to get to your destination. It seems simple enough, which you are thankful for considering it is getting dark out and colder by the minute. After once again wrapping your scarf more securely around your neck you pull your luggage out from under your table, hand over enough euros to pay your check, nodding a *"grazi"* to your server and begin your walk. You feel yourself smiling at how awkward you must have looked swinging your hands frantically over the flash of pigeons and wonder if that happens often to tourists taking lunch in the square. You recall finding many snapshots of visitors posing with flocking pigeons while you were planning your trip (some people were even throwing fistfuls of birdseed to attract them). You aren't sure however how often the pigeons invite themselves to share a seat at one's table. In any case, it has made a memorable start to your Venetian holiday!

TURN to page 66.

Venice

IT is only a matter of a few more turns through this enchanting maze of *calli* or streets before you find yourself standing before a quaint looking sign reading Hotel Fato, bolted into a stone wall. An imposingly strong wooden door with a giant copper knocker stands majestically in the middle of the wall. You recognize the design of the knocker to be a proud winged lion holding a sword, which is the icon for St. Mark, Venice's patron saint and a symbol that can be found everywhere throughout the city. The entrance is cracked slightly allowing you to push the door open with relative ease. Behind this daunting partition and the dark labyrinth of twisting city streets, you find a most inviting courtyard. Potted trees and shrubs decorated by the warm glow of twinkling white lights surround the marble court on all sides. Amongst them are wooden benches and a few metalwork tables and chairs for taking a private respite. You are convinced that there are likely hundreds of such courtyards and rooftop treasures sprinkled amongst private residences throughout the city and wish that you had more than the days of this vacation to explore each one. Surely courtyards like this substitute for the backyards that you are accustomed to at home, where families gather for meals and fun in good weather. This is most probably a meeting place for chatty neighbors and a charming rendezvous point for socializing.

Pulling your luggage along, you follow a cobble walk into the entrance of your hotel. It has become quite dark outside and the wind a bit blustery with the setting sun. A gust of warm air meets you as you enter a bright cheery foyer filled with more potted plants, a plush couch for two and several ornate chairs. You notice that several other guests arrived for check-in just before you, lending a little excitement just knowing that this week the city will be filled with travelers from around the world here to enjoy the Carnival festivities. Within 10 minutes, a member of the staff shows you to your room on the third floor, carrying your belongings up the narrow staircase and setting them before your door. He hands you a sizeable iron skeleton key as you slip a few crinkled euros into his hand for tip. This is the first time that you have used a cumbersome metal key such as this as your house key is relatively tiny in comparison and you are accustomed to using plastic key cards in hotels. You bend down and peer into your keyhole and see a bit of your modest single bed and smile imagining that the lock cavity is almost large enough to make a house for a mouse.

Entering and securing the door behind you, you are contented to find a desk, chair, armoire for your clothes and a nightstand aside your bed. Attached to your simple room is a bathroom for which you made a strict reservation. It is quite common in European hotels that guests share restroom amenities. However, since you have long planned this trip and are traveling alone, you wanted the luxury and privacy of your own facilities and were willing to pay a little extra for a room that provided such. It isn't long before you are nesting quite comfortably in your room, hanging your costumes and street clothes in the freestanding wardrobe, laying out your toiletries and contemplating a good night's sleep beneath the soft cotton sheets and wool blanket casing your bed. At the moment though, you are quite sure that you are incapable of going another moment without putting something in your stomach. While you were checking in, you were given a list of unpretentious items for order from the kitchen. It is a part of your reservation that you will be served a simple breakfast, whether in your room or at seated dining tables off from the lobby, each morning of your stay. You were also happy to discover that should you need lunch or supper and not wish to forage for a meal elsewhere, you are able to order something for yourself.

Wrapping back up into your outerwear, you descend the stairs back into the lobby, toting your colossal door key. You place an order with the desk attendant for the bruschetta, found on a laminated copy of the menu permanently placed in reception, as well as ask for a hot drink. The gentleman nods confidently as you motion to the front door leading out to the courtyard. He immediately understands that you would like to take your meal out-of-doors and so you go out to find yourself a seat. At first you consider that it is a little quirky to go alfresco after dark on a chilly February evening, but soon ignore the thought when you discover that you will not be alone in the place. Since having settled into your room, a little crowd of visitors have gathered in the intimate quad, pulling together the available seats. If you had been anywhere else but here in Venice at the start of the Carnival, you would have believed that you were transported in time and witness to a ghostly scene of the past as you discover the reason for the small party. Set slightly apart from the gathering guests is a man in a velvety dark costume. Nestled between several hedge plants aglow with strung lights, the bejeweled half cape slung over his shoulder appears like the night sky glinting with speckled stars. He is wearing a plain cap, fitted jacket, breeches and leggings in the style of a merchant class citizen of Venice in what you'd guess to be the 1500s. In fact, he immediately reminds you of a portrait that you were quite taken with from the website for the Gallerie dell'Accademia, an art museum that you had hoped to visit here in Venice on your stay. The piece is Lorenzo Lotto's *Portrait of a Gentleman in his Study* painted in 1530. A pale and noble man is standing at his desk aside an open window where it is evident he has reviewed a letter accompanied by petals and a trinket of love, and is now in the midst of reading. He wears a black velvet doublet with slashed sleeves and ornate ties. The dark jacket along with his raven hair juxtaposes his fair skin and bright white chemise with ruffs at the cuffs. You wondered what it might have been like to go back in time and sit aside him for a while, gathering unique tidbits of information about life during those times, and perhaps even sneaking a peek at his folded missive. The man here in the courtyard of the Hotel Fato holds a striking resemblance to the gentleman in the portrait except instead of a book his study is a lute.

You quietly sit at a patio table and prepare to listen

to his strumming and notice that the rest of those gathered seem quite entranced. As he begins to pluck at his elegant instrument, a slow and moving tune, you also detect the soothing sound of running water, likely streaming from one of the many nearby canals. His soft voice soon accompanies his lute song and you find yourself so distracted by the beautiful melody, as if it were the very music of an entire era long lost, filled with romance and heartache. The minstrel never looks to his audience, as if he is in pure concentration to an unseen muse while looking up to the moon on this crisp night. Your chest begins to ache when a lady in the group starts to sing the lyrics in a sweet and feminine complement to the musician's own deeper tone. You certainly do not recognize the song, which is sung in Italian in any case, but assume that it has been around for generations, owing to the fact that this Italian woman (perhaps even local Venetian) also knows the words. Perhaps it is a love song used for hundreds of years by youths seeking out their lovers as they floated through the canals in gondola by candlelight. You are so taken by the harmonic lute strums and emotional voices that a young female attendant from the hotel almost goes unnoticed as she sets a tray out before you. For a moment you believe that you have lost your appetite while imagining all of the world's broken hearts. But as the song soon draws to a close in exchange for a far happier ditty, you quickly begin gobbling down crunchy slices of Italian bread topped with cold ham and tomato salad. After listening intently to a few more songs and feeling truly fortunate to have been just at the right place at the right time for such an experience, you find yourself growing sleepy on a full stomach and a cup of spiced hot chocolate.

Taking your tray indoors, you set it at the front desk and with some effort, mount the stairs with increasingly heavy feet. It is no difficulty at all finding your room key in your coat pocket and you are soon inside pulling off your clothes while simultaneously searching for your pajamas. Finally ready, you slip into your cozy bed and gather your blanket close around your body. It is hardly a moment before you are drifting asleep to the sounds of a strumming lute that you can hear in the darkness within your room from down in the courtyard below.

Awaking the next morning to a soft knocking, you groggily throw off your blanket and shuffle over unlocking the door with a turn of the giant key from the inside and warily peer through a small crack. A cheerful looking woman not much older than you is standing just outside wearing a crisp navy dress and holding a silver breakfast tray. She smiles and nods at the tray while wishing you a, "*Buon giorno.*" You open the door wider and thank her with a, "*Grazi e buon giorno,*" (thank you and good morning). Accepting the tray and closing the door behind you, you walk over to the desk and sit down to see what fare will start your first full day in Venice and the official beginning of the Carnevale. A modest yet delicious breakfast of piping hot coffee, crusty warm bread with soft cheese and honey as well as a juicy ripe pear cut into slices will do just fine! Still in your nightclothes, you wrap your winter scarf around your shoulders, pour a little cream into your coffee and take your cup and a slice of chewy bread to the window. Stuffing the piece in your mouth, you use your freed hand to pull the glass inside and push the wooden shutters out. It is a gorgeous day, bright and refreshingly chilly, yet not too cold. A few puffy white clouds float by and you notice several ladies in the building across the way holding a quick and jovial conversation while hanging from without their own windows. Down below, another woman is sweeping the marble stones with a rustic looking broom that makes a distinct swishing sound, while scaring away a random pigeon here and there. Finishing the remainder of your breakfast, you ponder what should be the first activity on your agenda.

IF you decide to ask for suggestions from the staff of the hotel (being yet so early), turn to page 33.
IF you decide to dress in costume for a walk out into the *calli*, turn to page 53.

AFTER seeing the *pescheria* on such a fine morning, you are excited to have some other common day experiences such as that a local Venetian might have. After all, there is plenty of time to enjoy the festivities surrounding the Carnevale and it is often the everyday life of a destination that proves to be the most memorable during one's travels. As you are about to exit off of the Grand Canal back into the square from where you came, you see a *vaporetto* making a stop and a number of people getting off with empty sacks, likely to be filled with seafood by the time they depart. In an instant, you have paid for a seat and are sitting in the open air traveling along the waterfront with an exquisite view of the architecture along the Canal. If you were in any other city, it is very unlikely that you would have hopped on the first available bus or subway train for a surprise trip to who knows where. In Venice however, any given water-bus is only going to negotiate one of six major subdivisions that carve up the city map. Though the fish market was located just on the outskirts of the San Polo subdivision, the boat you are on will remain in the San Marco neighborhood where St. Mark's Square and your hotel are both located.

After only a few minutes on the boat, you are lost

for words at the remarkable view. You are riding along the widest canal, much like a four-lane highway with several boats traveling one direction on the opposite side, and your boat traveling up the canal on the other. You immediately note that all boatmen are following the same rules of the road as though they were driving cars. There are massive wooden poles on every bank of waterway where boats hitch up to, often decorated with painted stripes like that of a colorful candy cane. That is usually the first iconic picture anyone ever sees of Venice, ornate gondolas docked at shore in bunches, roped up to their brightly swirled poles. You notice however that most of the poles are not painted at all and there are hundreds of them everywhere, like an aquatic forest of skinny, bark bare tree trunks rising out of the water's edge. They also seem to have a number of purposes: some for parking, some for posting signs like the canal speed limit, some create the median between lanes and others just look like a rest stop for tired seagulls. The canal is quite a fairway of water taxis and speedboats of all sizes and styles, some for personal use and some for business.

As your water-bus pulls into a station to pick up several more people, you watch as an ambulance boat zooms by, ignoring the speed limit with its sirens blazing and red and white lights flashing. Big waves come rolling in from the tide created by the racing boat and your ferry begins to jostle and bounce against the rubber-lined dock at the stop. There are strict rules against breaking speed limits in the waterways of Venice, excepting emergency units of course. One reason is for the safety of drivers, just as it is on any road traversed by cars. Another reason being the waves that are caused by fast traveling vessels. In order to build all of the massive buildings amongst the 118 islands, thousands of colossal tree trunks had to be impounded into the shifting silt as means of foundations. It is a documented fact and matter of constant concern; Venice is sinking. There are a number of contributing factors for this, some of which are: rising sea levels from melting icecaps, the inevitable settling of these ancient foundations over time, and the excessive damage caused by modern day speedboat waves to crackling stonework. For hundreds of years, Venice's boats were fueled by manpower and therefore created far less of a disturbance. With the advent of boats powered by machine, damage becomes far more rampant to buildings made before the invention of gas powered craft. More complicated still are the rules for repair and rebuild on local architecture. Since most buildings are at the very minimum, several hundreds of years old, they are stamped heritage sites and protected from modern renovation. Practically the entire city is considered a historical landmark, and so there are very tight holds on using certain contemporary methods for restoration. Even patching up your waterfront doorway will get you rounds of paperwork and denial notices, not to mention the cost of repairs done in historical fashion should you get your request approved. The dreamlike architecture of Venice is worth restoring, yet increasingly difficult to do.

The *palazzi* are breathtaking; marble balconies decked with potted greenery, shuttered windows, and waterfront entrances. You imagine being a guest for dinner at any one of these divine palaces, taking a gondola from your residence to theirs and being greeted from right off the canal. Instead of car garages, many have boathouses on the ground floor off of the water beneath their homes. As you pass inland channels that would take you deeper into the *sestiere* of San Marco, you see women hanging wet laundry from wires strung between buildings, people accepting boat deliveries from their waterfront porches and uniformed schoolchildren taking lunch on the steps of an ancient church in a small square.

It isn't long before your water-bus pulls up at the same stop that you exited off of when you arrived in St. Mark's Square yesterday afternoon. You disembark with a few other riders at the face of the Biblioteca Nazionale Marciana or National Library of St. Mark's, right off of the lagoon. While pausing to admire an achingly beautiful view of a bobbing cluster of gondolas secured at the edge of the square, you overhear a couple mentioning taking lunch at the famous Harry's Bar. Standing next to the water, you also take notice of a man selling tickets for a tour of the haunted island of Lazzaretto Nuovo.

IF you wish to take a meal at the renowned Harry's Bar, turn to page 104.
IF you want to visit the ghostly island of Lazzaretto Nuovo, turn to page 92.

LOOKING around you, you pause idly for a second as two ladies pass by from out of the powder room, and then walk carefully to the open door and into the room. As you cross the entrance and look to the deeper recesses of the sitting room, you are both surprised and delighted to see an enormous marble fireplace with two identical polished bronze statues guarding on either side; they are the winged lions of St. Mark. The fire is lit and burning strongly. Usually when a fire is blazing, someone is basking in its glow. You figure you should hurry in case they return soon.

Padding over to the painting, you indeed find a piece of art that must have been painted in the 1700s and by a very fine artist. Standing but a yard away it takes you only a moment to discover that the place in which the piece was created, is a frescoed corner of the ballroom below! It hardly looks changed at all and you are in awe of the money that must have been spent in the upkeep of that room for all these centuries past. Shuffling up just a little closer until your nose is at a foot's length from the woman in the painting, you find that it looks unquestionably *just* like Signora Sapienti. A distant relative for sure! As a matter of fact, the woman dripping with rubies that you saw not long ago on that platform looks to *be* this woman! You get the chills and eerie thoughts creep into you mind about immortality. Squinting as you lean down to view the evidence of a date in the corner of the piece, you locate an indecipherable signature of an artist but the year is clear, 1749. She is definitely a distant, distant relative, truly and most quizzically every bit Signora's look-alike. Concentrating heavily on the intimate details of the piece to the crackling sound of the fire's embers, you are earnestly startled to hear a voice and very close to your person too.

What have you found, my darling?

Stunned, you stand as tall and straight as your corset intended and look with the widest eyes that ever knew a half mask, in the direction of the voice. It is a deep voice and robust, a man's voice. From the shadows of a nearby corner in the sitting room, half hidden behind a window's luxurious hangings, a burly shadow comes forth and into the pulsing of the firelight.

I, I...

You blurt with astonishment. It is *he*, the man who accompanying Signora Sapienti on the previous day's promenade delighted you with the invitation to this very ball. This is the man who unbeknownst to himself sent a momentary tingle down your spine when he grabbed your gloved hand with firmness and kissed it. Walking out of the darkness, he looks very much like one of the strong lion statues aside the hearth, ready to pounce unsuspecting prey caught in his lair. Your heart quickens as he moves forward into the light.

TURN to page 470.

JUST before embarking on a tour of the island of Lazzaretto Nuovo, you stop to purchase a bite to tide you over from a street vendor serving the masses of people starting to arrive in the city for Carnival. You quickly ask for the *mesi vovi*, which are seasoned boiled eggs sprinkled with oil, salt and pepper. You also decide on a few slices of bread (you could eat this Italian bread at *every* meal), a small bag of nuts, a sliced tomato and a bottle of water. These items paired with the fish from the *pescheria* will make a fine impromptu snack on the way to your next destination. Comfortably seated in the isle of the boat to avoid any splashing sea mist while you eat, you unfold the several squares of wax paper used to package your items and start to nibble while the tour guide begins to explain the island's history.

It would seem that you are lucky indeed to get the chance to see the island on tour at this time of year as guided walks only regularly occur between the months of April and October. Being February, it is only because of the influx of tourists during the Carnevale that a few trips are opened up to the public. The Island of Lazzaretto Nuovo was known to be inhabited as early as the Roman times, though sparsely and for what purpose is not fully understood. There remains on the island, several stones from an ancient church from that era, leading historians to assume there was once a community of monks living in solitude there. Lying about two miles off the shore of Venice, it became a holding zone for merchants sailing into Venetian ports around the 1400s. To be quarantined meant to spend a certain number of days with your cargo, waiting admittance to your final destination where you could trade your wares. As Venice was once the most powerful maritime community of trade, sailors and merchants were highly esteemed and stayed in respectable enough quarters on Lazzaretto Nuovo, while they waited in quarantine. There was a second island however, called Lazzaretto Vecchio. When someone in quarantine became sick, they were boated over to this second island where conditions were likely much more grim and you were unlikely to return considering you were ill enough to be sent in the first place.

Pleasantly munching on your fresh victuals, no morsel is spared as your ferry makes its approach to a rustic dock on the small island. Your guide continues by explaining the outline of a long singular building that is becoming increasingly visible as you approach. Known as the Tezon Grande, the structure had several uses. The first was to house the quarantined guests. The second was to disinfect the goods from off of their vessels. Ships were coming from all over the known world to trade in Venice, bringing a variety of fevers, bugs and afflictions with them. Though it is possible that the quarantine stopped the spread of some disease by sending away men who had become ill to another island, the methods by which sanitizing wares happened was likely less effective. Incoming merchandise was smoked with herbs or beaten or left to air out. One thing we know about infectious diseases today however, is that it takes a lot more than a fumigation to kill the plague.

Balling up your parcels and wiping any remaining crumbs of food off your clothes, you stuff your trash in your shoulder bag and follow the other tourists off of the boat onto the dock. You are surprised to see that this island seems nothing more than what Venice must have looked like before it was inhabited. It is one giant field with streams of water separating the wild grassland here and there. There are plenty of waterfowl rising up from the meadows, but other than that, Lazzaretto Nuovo seems barren. As your diminutive group slowly ambles along a dirt path leading to the Tezon Grande, your guide continues sharing information.

Here, he points out, is the water well crowned with the Lion of St. Mark, a well that was built capable enough to still collect water today. No one seems willing to look in and see if it has. And there, is where you can still see the foundation for a chapel that has since withered away in time. And over there, he mentions, is the expanse of earth from where the corpse of a vampire was recently dug up. When you decided to enter this tour, you heard nothing about vampires, just that the island was potentially haunted. You were interested in the trip since it is full light out and everyone knows that ghosts only do their haunting in the early hours of the morning. If there are vampires living here too, you only hope that the lore that suggests that they sleep during the day is in fact true. Your guide smiles at all the surprised faces in the group, who are now hanging on his every word.

Continuing, he tells you that Europe suffered many horrible plagues between the 1300s and 1700s. Half of entire city populations from Russia to France were wiped out. Plagues spread quickly from house to house as if they were carried in the very wind, striking and painfully torturing its victims with fevers, oozing boils, excruciating swelling and bleeding. In 1576, the Black

Death came to visit Venice and took with it nearly a third of its human lives, if not half, over the course of two years. Continual screams and suffering and death; it was a miracle if any single home was spared a casualty.

Medical advances allow us to better understand the plague today, of which there are three types documented up until now: pneumonic, septicemic and bubonic. The disease was often spread through infected body fluids of an animal or human carrier. It is no surprise that if an infected loved one is secreting puss and tainted blood, even with the coughing of aerial specks of it into your face, you are probably not going to last long yourself. But the real spreader of the Black Death, or bubonic version of the plague, is the one infinitesimal pest known as the flea, which generally delivered the pathogen from rats. Fleas were a way of life in those days, and not just for your pet monkey, cat or dog. Most people were infested with them, harboring them in their bedding, floorboards, clothing and hair. There were no bug bombs, dry cleaners or effective medicinal baths. People also bathed less and washed their clothes with less frequency. Fleas teeming on your pet, swarming on your livestock, biting under your wig, hopping about your rugs, living on your pillows, on your friend and on you!

There was no escaping it and so people were accustomed to it. There was even a fashion accessory (though some historians believe the piece was *only* for looks), which detoured the pests from biting your skin, the *zibellino* or flea-fur. The tail or pelt of an animal was worn on your person in the trust that the fleas on your body would favor to party on the fur instead. From time to time, you would remove the fur and shake or beat the fleas out of it. Nobles even decorated their *zibellini* with gold and gems; if everyone must know that you're trying to rid yourself of pestilence, why not do it in style? Of course there were some places that were more concentrated with the annoyance than others.

Giacomo Casanova wrote in his diary that while imprisoned at the Piombi in the Doge's Palace of Venice, rats the size of rabbits constantly scurried around his cell. He also spoke that the fleas were so concentrated in the space that he was sure an intense fever, an illness that lasted him over a month, was brought on by them. That he thought he was to suffer severe madness over the rampant creatures that never ceased to torment him. As if it wasn't desperate enough to be imprisoned by the Venetian authorities, when torture and putrid living conditions were common, there was a never ceasing epidemic of bloodthirsty fleas. If they knew what they were to endure, given the chance many prisoners would have chosen death rather than incarceration.

Nearing the Tezon Grande, you see that it is really nothing more than an abandoned building. You are able to nose around the open air cargo hold and walk beneath an awning spanning the promenade which passes the men's quarters. Your guide explains that this walk was made many times a day by the constable in charge for checking in on the conditions of the inhabitants, and who was diligently watching for signs of illness.

Though there were many ill and even plague inflicted people carted off to Lazzaretto Vecchio over the years, the plague of 1576 changed protocol. Initially as people in Venice began to die, their bodies were taken to Lazzaretto Vecchio and buried in mass graves by *monatti* or people employed to dispose of the dead. When the death tolls started to get out of control however, people started to be taken to both islands in droves, as a means of getting the contagion away from Venice as fast as possible. Whether or not you were even dead, if you were very ill, *monatti* began throwing live persons into the ground with the corpses. Hundreds of people were being housed in makeshift huts only to be tossed half dead into the graves. Once covered in sheets and laid side by side, bodies began being abandoned to piles and disposed of as quickly as possible. So it is today that thousands of bodies are buried beneath the meadows of Lazzaretto Vecchio and Lazzaretto Nuovo.

Staring out over the fields, it is chilling to imagine what the scene was here during that time. There were men, women and children (Italians and people of different lands alike) braving painful torment at the end of their days on this island. You are terrified to imagine being a sixteenth century Venetian, living contentedly with your family in joy and prosperity, only to be torn from their side. Tremendously ill and afraid, you would have been boated to an island with other sick strangers to be left lying in isolation wherever you were dropped. Suffering painful delirium, and far worse symptoms, you would have eventually been considered past help and pitched into a hole in the ground with rotting plague victims, despite your weak pleas. Your heart aches envisioning those last breaths of life in a pit of hell, only wishing the agony would stop and that you at the very least, had a loved one's hand to hold as you passed out of this life.

After viewing the Tezon Grande and taking a few pictures, your guide begins to slowly usher the group back towards the ferry stopping along the way to explain the grave of the vampire. The wind begins blowing harder than before and the fields of tall grass are sweeping in their empty vastness, lending some lonely eeriness to the abandoned island. As the fact goes, an archaeological society recently took some particular interest in excavating portions of several of the mass graves here. The purpose was to see how people were being buried and what artifacts might be found for insight into the island's past. One such excavation uncovered the bones of a woman with a jaw that had been dislocated by a large stone jammed between her teeth. It was widely believed that vampires spread the plague during those times and to make matters more confusing, the decomposing of corpses was misunderstood. As bloating bodies began to ooze putrid liquid, those covered in shrouds would get circles of blood around their mouths that would often eat away at the fabric. *Monatti* uncovering shallow graves in order to dispose of more bodies, may have assumed that the corpses with disintegrating shrouds around their mouths were in fact vampires who were recently feasting on the dead around them. If the vampire was left to continue feasting, it would eventually grow strong enough to pull itself out of the earth and begin spreading the plague further. Hammering a brick into the mouth of these supposed vampires was thought to stop them from preying on other bodies.

This is of course a terrible thought, the desecration of already plague-mutilated bodies, and you wonder how these gravediggers had the guts to commit such acts. You suppose it was a time of immense fear and insanity and are thankful that you will never have to be witness to such horrifying atrocities. Waiting your turn to board the boat back to Venice, you feel an uneven bump beneath your foot, partially buried in the dirt of the path. Looking down, and rubbing away the silt a little with the tip of your shoe, you see what can only be one thing. It appears to be the ball joint of a human bone finding its way out of the earth, perhaps from a knee or shoulder. Had you not known what lay everywhere beneath your feet, you would have guessed that it was only a submerged stone. You hastily push some sandy dirt back over the protruding bump and make a silent wish that all buried here and on Lazzaretto Vecchi as well, will rest in peace.

Soon gliding back over the lagoon towards St. Mark's Square, your guide imparts one last bit of information. Most Venetians will not talk about the plague islands, nor will they visit them for any reason. It would seem that fishermen and boaters traveling past the islands frequently hear unnatural sounds carried in the wind from off its shores. Sometimes they even see things, what exactly cannot be said, in the meadows or near the Tezon Grande. You instantly are curious to know what exactly people have seen over the years, though it is unlikely for you to ever find out with everyone remaining concertedly tight-lipped. However, of one thing your guide assures everyone; Venetians say the island is very, very haunted and a place for the dead. A place that isn't right for the living.

Soon you are back in St. Mark's Square and deciding what should be next on your agenda. The *piazza* is beginning to fill up with revelers in historic attire, many in the baroque style that was the fashion at the height of the Carnevale in the 1700s. Others are wearing bright, glittery costumes presenting a variety of quintessential masks and personifying a plethora of strange personalities.

SHOULD you wish to get back to your hotel and don one of your own especially made gowns, turn to page 112.

IF you would like to rest a while at that Harry's Bar you heard spoke of earlier, turn to page 104.

YOU are interested in seeing what makes this Harry's Bar so famous and after asking for directions, discover that it is just a short distance away from the square along the edge of the lagoon. As you make your way in by pushing open a heavy wooden door in what seems the nondescript corner of a large stone building, you find yourself in quite the classy joint. At first you are a little disappointed that the establishment looks more like a fine piano bar that would be found in any big city, than an everyday eatery for the local Italians. Something makes this place great however, and you'd like to find out what that is. A thick bar made of polished timber extends the length of one side of the room while a dining area makes up the other half. Great windows stretch alongside the seated patrons and provide enough sparkling sunlight (aided by its refraction off of the waves just outside) for the entire dining area. You count at least three tidy looking barmen, smartly dressed in black slacks, white dress shirts, dinner jackets and black bow ties, making drinks behind the bar. An ample variety of liquor bottles fill the glass shelves inlaid into the wall behind them as well as a number of silver martini mixers and blending machines.

The restaurant has a full house today and so you'd feel a little guilty taking up a table all to yourself. Bellying up to the bar, as goes the saying, will do just fine. You are given an immediate and rather charming welcome, "*Benvenuto*," from one of the gentlemen as you take a stool at the far end and promptly thank him, adding a polite nod. Your barman evidently knows he doesn't speak your language, likely telling by your choppy accent, and so cordially switches place with another attendant who does. Of course you didn't expect that, but thought it was a nice gesture none-the-less. Your Italian is sparse and you'd have a hard time discovering what Harry's Bar is all about without a lot of translation. Your official barman wants to know, "What does a *lovely* lady like to drink on a *lovely* day like this?" Clearly the barmen at Harry's Bar know how to make a woman blush (it is probably in their training manual along with the drink recipes and house specials). You'd be tempted to make some flattering reply, but instead just ask what's good (with a smile of course). He asks if you have ever had a Bellini. Of course you have! Aren't they the most delicious, fruity, bubbly beverages? He soon tells you that Harry's Bar is where the Bellini was first created and that they make the best! You order one up instantly, the peach Bellini.

You ask him to tell you more about Harry's Bar while he begins cutting flecks of juicy fruit from out of a ripe white peach. He explains that the original owner of Harry's, Giuseppe Cipriani, created the world-famous Bellini when he worked the bar himself. Harry's Bar opened in 1931 and it was Giuseppe's wife Giuletta that chose this location, which used to be a rope repository. Mr. Cipriani had originally worked as a server in a number of cities around Europe, usually in fine hotels, where vacationing celebrities and aristocrats used to lounge over cocktails. Once settled back in Venice and working at the bar in the Hotel Europa, he met a well-to-do American student vacationing and spending countless hours and cash in its bar. This young man's name was Harry Pickering and he was brought to Venice by an aunt, in an attempt to alleviate his insatiable love for alcohol. Alas, Harry's intervention didn't work and he was soon abandoned in Venice alone and broke. Regardless, Mr. Cipriani admired the young man and decided to be a friend by loaning him some money. After some time had gone by, Harry returned to the Hotel Europa and paid Mr. Cipriani back, with a large amount of interest. And so, Mr. Cipriani took the money and opened his own bar, naming it Harry's.

Your attendant pours a little water and fresh squeezed lemon into a champagne flute while simultaneously blending some ice shavings with the peach pulp in a blender. Opening the lid, he also portions in a few spoons full of raspberry juice and sugar, pulses a few more beats and then dispenses the concoction into the glass. Lastly he pours Prosecco into the flute, stirs it altogether while topping it with a fresh raspberry and then pushes it your way. Asking if the Prosecco is champagne, he corrects the mistake by defining that it is actually a sparkling wine only produced in Italy, the Veneto region in fact. He also informs you that the original Bellini only includes peach puree and Prosecco, served in a cold glass; this one is jazzed up a bit! A soft spray of bubbly mist touches your lip as you inhale the fresh peach scent and eagerly take a sip of sunshine. Your first Bellini in this iconic place is full of flavor, refreshing and intoxicating (even from just the fruity fragrance alone).

What else makes Harry's Bar interesting apart from the celebrated Bellini and quaint history, you ask. The barman, who introduces himself as Giovanni, places a menu in front of you and begins explaining a little bit about Venetian cuisine. There are trademark Italian dishes that are recognized all over the world, such as lasagna, pizza, bruschetta and tiramisu. Though the basis of these widespread dishes may have originated in the country, they are usually nothing like the true regional varieties that you will find when you eat *in* Italy. And even within Italy, a bowl of pasta enjoyed in the north will look and taste nothing at all like what you might feast on in the south. True Italian fare concentrates on several things. The first is that one cooks with locally grown, fresh ingredients. Even fine dining restaurants in Venice may not have a freezer in their kitchen except for the purpose of storing ice or gelato, as vegetables, fish and meat are delivered or purchased each morning. Second, Italian cuisine prides itself on regional variety. This means, one region creates a dish *this* way, while yet another strictly believes the dish cannot properly be prepared in any way but *that*. Every region is faithful to their cuisine and will even mock and critique the way a dish is being prepared in other parts of Italy. Additionally, with everyone eating fresh locally grown foods, dishes are hard to replicate anywhere else except from where they originate, as the ingredients just aren't the same. He admits that you can get amazing dishes in

Paris, New York, London, and the like, but the ingredients they use may have been frozen for some time or have been shipped in from all over the world, thus losing their robust, fresh flavors. Italians pride themselves on the flavors that make their dishes special, and which cannot be replicated exactly as the ingredients come from only within the local area of which they are made.

Looking over the menu in more detail than you normally would, you decide on *ravioli con granciola scampi*; an indigenous spider crab, whose light meat is shredded over a salad dressed with lemon juice and olive oil and also stuffed into freshly made ravioli. The ravioli are served over a delicious sauce made from prawns. After ordering the dish, you ask Giovanni to give you a few examples of what ingredients are more likely to be Venetian rather than generally Italian. In Venice, green olives are used in cooking rather than black ones. Polenta, a mush corn prepared with many dishes, is white rather than yellow as it would be in the rest of Italy. Here it is made with a different variety of corn, lighter in flavor and often paired with fish. Rice grains, such as would be used in a risotto, are very small here and called *vialone nano*. Apart from ingredients alone however, it's the unique dishes themselves and how they are prepared that make a regional difference. Venetians have lived off of the fruits of the sea for centuries, and therefore have seafood dishes not so common to other regions. *Folpeti* are little boiled octopus and *sepoine* are tiny roasted cuttlefish. *Peoci gratinai* are mussels baked in the oven with cream and *masanete* are small lagoon crabs that are stewed in their shells. *Bacala* is dried salted cod while *frito de minuagia* are small fish, clams and squid fried in a pan.

Your dish arrives and you find that the freshness of the crabmeat (the little creatures likely pulled up from the sea very recently) lacks the overwhelming fishiness you've often experienced with other seafood cuisine. The salad is light and the ravioli tender and flavorful in its creamy sauce. Giovanni also imparts that because Harry's Bar serves a famous cocktail and truly Venetian fare, celebrated people have consistently visited over the years, making for an interesting atmosphere. Movie stars, writers, politicians and aristocrats alike come to dine at Harry's Bar and so the service and cuisine always models top standards in true Venetian style.

After taking the time to fully appreciate your meal, you thank Giovanni for sharing the history of Harry's

Bar and what makes Venetian cuisine a particular treasure. He tells you that it is his pleasure and mentions that you still have other Bellini flavors on the menu to try, like grape or strawberry. He'll be glad to make them for you any time!

Your appetite satiated and your palate pleasured, you are now prepared to return to your hotel to array in one of your splendid costumes. You'll soon be among many masked and mysterious merrymakers celebrating the Venetian Carnival!

TURN to page 53.

YOU'VE chosen to dress in a pale pink gown finely dotted with delicate cream crystals about the bodice and skirt. The array is simple, yet very elegant and feminine, like a flute of sparkling *rosato*. Your day dresses are structured conveniently enough that you are able to clothe yourself, though this would have unlikely been the case for many noble ladies in the 1700s, who required the assistance of a lady's maid. The clothing worn during the day, as a female aristocrat during that time, would have been called *undress* while only the more excessively ornate attire that you would be presented in at a royal court or important occasion, would be called *full dress*.

After unrobing and bathing, you lightly powder your body with scented talc and begin by pulling on a pair of cream silk stockings to your mid-thighs, keeping them taut and in place with lacy garters. After placing a shift or long shirt of soft cotton the color of butter over your head (it falling down to your knees), you step into your pannier or hoopskirt, which extends several feet out on either hip, clasping its belted closure at your back. Twice more slipping garments over your head, noting that this is why one's wig should be put on last, you button closed both a petticoat followed by the glinting, pink overskirt. Your shift acts as a slip of sorts. It guards your skin against the rougher fabrics of your outfit and also protects your gown from the sweat and oil your body expels. Being a time when washing garments was a more difficult undertaking, having underclothing that could easily be washed in the stead of your attire, was the common practice. The petticoat is a light skirt that hangs over the pannier. It was designed so that the overskirt (made of finer, more elaborate fabric) would be able to hang loosely over the hoop skirt without bunching or even ripping if it were to be caught on any exposed bone, wood or cane (which constructed the basket of the pannier). During the eighteenth century, the overskirt and bodice would likely be attached, though yours are not. With all of your bottom garments in place, you slip into a bodice much like a long sleeve fitted jacket, securing it up the front of your torso with hooks and eyes and then covering the seam with a lacy placket. After everything is in place and fastened, the bodice appears seamless without exposed lace strings, buttons or zippers. The delicate lace running up the front camouflages the part, looking as though simply another flourish of the design. The cotton shift below it all, scoops and edges your bosom just above the low cut neckline of the bodice, exposing a whisper of lace the color of the placket, accentuating the loveliness of your décolletage.

Sitting before the mirror affixed at the writing desk, you begin your toilette. Using a talcum powder puff (synthetic but as delicate as down feathers), you begin dotting it in white talc, pressing it to your bosom, neck and face. Though you are using cosmetic powder that is harmless enough despite a sneeze or two, in the 1700s, noblewomen would have used concoctions that were quite different to whiten their complexions. A paste could be created using crushed white lead, the whites of eggs, perhaps a drop of fragranced oil and other additives depending on the makeup tricks that any apothecary, lady of the night or noblewoman swore by. Lead was also ground into powder to apply over the face. It is known today however, that lead kills. It can make you go mentally insane, cause festering wounds on your skin, halt the ability to successfully bear live children, can cause comas and seizures and traumatic headaches. It is so toxic it can arrest your organs from functioning and be literally, the death of you. However, the European beauties of the eighteenth century were oblivious and many of them gave up their beating hearts to appear paler than they were. This was a trend that had a much more extensive history, as women of leisure who did not work outdoors exposed to the tanning effects of the sun were considered one definition of elegance and nobility, then and for centuries before. You may have crushed precious pearls in oil and spread it on your face to give you a fairylike iridescence. Or perhaps as some women did during the Renaissance period, you may have bled yourself to become pale and listless; the weaker sex stereotype dangerously pursued by women themselves. You may also have used mercury to pale your face, red lead to brighten your lips and cheeks or belladonna (drops of poison from the deadly nightshade plant) to dilate the pupils of your eyes to make them seem large and dewy. But today, some harmless talc will do to replicate the look of a past cosmetic era. Next you place several tiny dots of eyeliner above the right of your lip and under your left eye, to imitate moles, nature's beauty marks. These used to be created using patches made out of fabric that came in various sizes and shapes. They often communicated secret meaning depending on where they were positioned on one's visage.

At almost the final stage of your truncated toilette (much shorter than the numerous hours a lady in history may have had to endure getting ready each day), you gently tuck your hair beneath a nude wig cap, securely pinning it along your hairline. You decide upon one pitch black wig with a French twist ending in a bun at the height of the back of your head, which makes a striking juxtaposition against your pale gown. After adding a few more pins to firmly fix the wig in its place, you select an ornate jeweled hairpin, champagne in color, clipping it on the front right height of the wig.

To complete the look, you curl your lashes with a crimp and apply an ample amount of black mascara, making them appear long and full. After dotting your lips with tinted gloss from a small tin, smelling faintly of vanilla, you use a feathery blush brush to flourish a generous dusting of fine glitter onto your bosom. The sun's reflection off your lips and chest will lend a festive, sensuous appeal to your costume. A sweep of pink blush on your cheeks followed by a spritz of your favorite fragrance, finalize the cosmetic portion of your toilette. You end by choosing a buttery yellow lace half mask that covers only the upper part of your face and tie its silk strings around your black wig to the back of your head. Admiring yourself in the mirror, you almost wonder whom this new woman is staring back at you from the vanity. It is another you, from another time, and you are striking. For one moment, you imagine that you are one of the beauties in Sir Joshua Reynolds' *The Ladies of Waldegrave*, painted between 1780 and 81. Though the three madams are elegantly portrayed in the piece wearing white gowns and ashen bouffants unlike your rosy dress and midnight coiffure, you immediately insinuate yourself into the moment. The ladies are so pleasing and sumptuous, convening around a table, stitching and amusing with a hand of cards. Their bare chests and long necks, though not immodest, are sensual and feminine. Their flushed cheeks, dark eyes and cupid lips, delicate mannerisms and gentle hands are almost deceiving. In your interpretation, the ladies are both graceful *and* powerful. Thus, the affect your costume has on you; the feeling of both being feminine and bold, soft and strong. Pleasing to the eye without immodesty and gaudy excess, you inwardly compliment both your natural loveliness and your seamstress' abilities. You are captivating and acutely looking forward to visually drinking in the images of others as artistically designed as yourself. You feel an exciting anticipation in the outing ahead. You wonder whom you may encounter, what you might learn and what you will see.

IF you wish to stroll through the Venetian streets and make your way back to St. Mark's Square where other costumed guests will be amassing, turn to page 59.

IF you would like to float through the city in a gondola, turn to page 119.

Venice

PREPARING to head out for your first gondola ride, you swing the thick folds of a white mantle liken to a half cape, over your shoulders to keep you warm. You decide upon an elbow length pair of cream silk gloves and into pockets secretly stitched into your plush skirt, you stuff lip gloss, euros and your passport, and after locking the door behind you, your room key. Passing out of the lobby and through the courtyard, you are met with a number of approving smiles by hotel staff and guests alike.

Soon out into the twisting Venetian streets, you begin to capture the essence of being some other woman in another time. You learn that you must slightly lift the folds of your skirts by pinching the fabric just above the knee in order to allow your feet to go uninhibited while walking over uneven stones and up bridge steps. Squeezing past others while negotiating the slim *calli* requires slipping sidelong between obstacles rather than walking straight forward, as your hoop skirt makes your hips far wider than usual. Catching your image while glancing in a passing window, you hardly know yourself under the disguise of mask and wig. You appear sprightly with your alluring array: playful bouffant, glittering eyes behind a lacy cover, glossy lips and feminine sparkle. It isn't long before you discover a trickle of other visitors similarly dressed in magnificent costumes, many concealed under the guise of the most peculiar masks.

Though the geography of the *calli* in Venice is by no means easily understood, you have adopted a loose concept for your surroundings. There are six neighborhoods in Venezia and you are staying in the *sestiere* of San Marco where St. Mark's Square resides. Though the *piazza* is not directly in the middle of the *sestiere* (it is on the right side of the neighborhood), you use it as your point of reference when considering your location. To the immediate west of the square is the Hotel Fato and further in that direction still, the Canale Grand. To the south is the Venetian Lagoon and to the east of the *piazza* is the Doge's Palace and Piombi prison. As you walk through the maze of streets from your hotel in the general direction of east towards the square, you begin to hear the collective voices of an incalculable number of people who are starting to amass there for the day's celebratory events. You have been told that daily during Carnival, people gather in the square to promenade and view each other's costumes, take note of singers and musicians, play games and observe mimes and various street acts. Dancing, paper confetti, bright colors, amusements and acts of all variety engulf the square as guests pour in from every direction.

In any romantic movie scene filmed in Venice involving lovers taking a gondola ride (and in general, almost every gondola photo ever used to promote tourism in Venice) there is one structure premiered; The Bridge of Sighs. The bridge itself connects rooms previously used to interrogate criminals from within the Doge's Palace, to the Piombi prison where convicts were incarcerated. It was a British poet (Lord Byron) who actually gave the bridge its name in the 1800s even though the bridge had originally been built in 1602. The assumption is that as the prisoners walked over the bridge from freedom and into the imminent suffering of imprisonment, they sighed. Whether they sighed from the last enrapturing view of Venice seen through the grates in the windows of the bridge (which is completely enclosed in white limestone) or from the hopelessness of their situation, who is to say? Adding to the romantic ideas about the Ponte dei Sospiri or Bridge of Sighs, locally it is said that should a couple embrace at sunset while passing beneath the bridge in a gondola, their love will never die. Though you are quite sure that a gondola ride through any one of the seemingly numberless waterways in Venice would be just as moving, it only seems right that you pay tribute to this little bit of history and legend, by riding under the bridge yourself.

Since St. Mark's Square is packed with festival seekers (as evidenced by the dull roar of a massive crowd in close proximity to yourself) you decide to stick to a *calle* outside the perimeter of the square, and then walk around the backside of the Piombi. From there, you'll catch a gondola at the head of the Rio di Palazzo, the canal that runs under the Bridge of Sighs between the Doge's Palace and the prison.

Soon just off of St. Mark's Square you stop to admire the view of the Laguna Veneta, the waters of which flow in from the Adriatic Sea. Countless wooden poles line the coast, the gondolas bobbing in the water attached to them with impressively knotted ropes. Along the man-made, stone edged shore, people in costume pose at the waterside to secure the most romantic view for many a photographer's camera. Their dazzling fabrics and glittery sequins catch the sunlight just magnificently while the backdrop of the water appearing sometimes emerald and sometimes turquoise, ushers in wave after wave of salty seawater. The assembly in the square is more thunderous without the buffer of a few back streets between you and the crowd. Several waiting gondoliers are sharing a bag of pistachio nuts while watching each passerby, donning the long sleeved black and white striped shirts denoting their profession. A number of empty boats are ready to embark and take riders down the smooth flowing Rio di Palazzo, but your interest is peaked by the noisy horde and attractive beat of techno baroque music, just around the corner not some forty yards from where you are standing; how magnificent must be the celebration of the Carnevale in the square!

IF you've changed your mind and decide to enter Piazza San Marco, turn to page 157.
IF you continue with your original undertaking and hail a gondola, turn to page 130.

AS quickly as the disturbance took place, the wait staff has cleared away all evidence of any fracas and clean table linens immediately replace the spoiled ones. As efficient as the personnel at the Caffe Quadri are, they must either be exceptionally proficient in prompt customer service, or pigeons are just a normal pitfall of their location. As rejuvenating as your few morsels of food and half a cup of coffee were, you are certainly ready to rest and feel secured at the Hotel Fato. However, the view right here in Piazza San Marco, from this exact spot, could not be any lovelier. Inquiring with a thoughtful smile, your server puts you at ease subsequent to the whole ordeal and asks whether you would have a repeat of your previous order brought to. Allowing your tense silhouette to soften back into your chair, you ask for a cappuccino and something sweet, a local favorite perhaps? With a nod of the head, he leaves to fulfill your order. Though you certainly admire the robust flavors in taking your Venetian coffee black, something a little creamier sounds appetizing with a bite of dessert. One part espresso, a second part steamed milk and a third of milk foam, your cappuccino may still be strong in the way of caffeine, yet a little more smooth on the palate.

Arriving back a few minutes later, the waiter sets a frothy cup nested upon a napkin and plate accompanied by a little silver spoon and a square of milk chocolate. As you pinch the little confection between your fingers and bring it up to your mouth to take a nibble, your server motions to pantomime the placing of the square into your drink and stirring it in. You drop your piece into the cappuccino and swirl away with your spoon, creating a *tink-tink, tink-tink* melody as the white foam takes on a light brown appearance. Setting a small plate of cookies down before you, your server asks whether or not you know where the cappuccino got its name. After taking a sip from the wide brim of the cup and setting it back down again, you shake your head "no". With a half-smile, he points above his lip indicating that you've gotten yourself a little foam moustache. Wiping it away with the napkin from beneath your cup and feeling a little silly, you listen attentively as he tells you that the color of the cappuccino with the coffee and cream swirled together, was named after the Capuchin friars, or more accurately, the color of the brown, hooded robes that they wore. This order of friars originated in the early 1520s in the Marche region, located at about the middle of Italy on the eastern coast. Originally conceived by a

Matteo da Bascio or Friar Matteo, the order was based on the consideration that friars should live very simply, even more so than friars of other orders during that time. He was given permission from the then Pope, Clement VII, to wander and preach to the needy. Later, other friars joined Friar Matteo and the Capuchin Order began, was recognized within the Roman Catholic community and created its own rules of existence. One of these rules was that no member of the Order could own a single coin, thus each friar was forbidden even to touch money and had to beg for the sustenance that he needed to survive.

Assuming that a Capuchin friar never so much as set their eyes on, let alone tasted a cappuccino, you take another sip and contemplate the light foam and whisper of sweet chocolate from the melted square as well as the strong bite from the espresso and imagine roaming the Italian countryside in the sixteenth century, begging for every bite while sharing Christian doctrine and consoling those in need. Your waiter asserts that there is a painting created by an unknown artist in the 1600s of Friar Matteo dressed in the Capuchin hooded robe, holding a crucifix in one hand while resting his other hand atop a skull set upon a bound book; he is not sure which book it is. You assume it might be a Bible or the writings of the Order, as you imagine the painting. Seeing how much your interest is peaked, he continues to describe that Matteo da Bascio's moustache and beard are so full and dark that they blend into the background of his robe in the painting, creating the image that his long facial hair and attire meld together into one dark, serious ensemble. That paired with his poignant, curious dark brown eyes and hood, he seems to be just the person to create a new Order of friars that would yield to completely detaching themselves from worldly comforts. You consider that Friar Matteo's resting his hand upon a skull sounds rather morbid, but also that this may have been the mystery painter taking liberties. After all, did people in history commonly pose for paintings with a skull as décor? You grimace, perhaps they did. Or maybe in this case, it was a representation of taking a stance against worldly pleasure. To finish on the subject, he notes that Matteo da Bascio's soul passed out of this world in Venice and he was buried in a local church. Crowds came to honor him for his life's mission. You are moved to hear this in view of Venetians and their stance on worldly freedoms and passions!

Your server gently pushes the plate of cookies,

which he calls *zaleti*, towards you on the table. Sharing another Italian food fact, your server renders a little information about your plate of treats. He offers that Italy didn't always grow corn (the primary ingredient in these cookies) but that during the mid-1500s, Venice being a wildly traversed trading port, they received corn, which originated in the West (the Americas). Soon, corn ground into a finer cornmeal and then boiled to make polenta, was being used in many Venetian dishes. *Zaleti* are just one culinary item that developed out of the use of ground corn in the north of Italy and are a cookie that uses raisins soaked in *grappa* (an Italian grape derived brandy) and lemon zest. You take a small bite and find that though it is not very sweet, it is crisp, grainy and has just a hint of fruit and citrus. That paired with a little sifting of powdered sugar and you quickly acknowledge that these light, yellow cookies could easily replace the sweeter, flour based cakes and pastries you usually treat yourself to. Picking up a second *zaleti*, you are pleased to discover that this one includes yellow raisins and mild, buttery pine nuts. As these are eaten with your last sips of cappuccino, you take a moment to enjoy the fading light of Piazza San Marco and relax as your server leaves to assist others and tally your expenses.

Paying your bill just as the sun falls below the horizon, the natural light growing increasingly dim, you set out to your hotel. Having reviewed the map in your guidebook with the server, you feel rather confident that your hotel is neither very far away nor that difficult to find. Pulling your luggage behind you, you enter a *calle* off of the square, heading in the direction that the server noted.

TURN to page 66.

AS strong as the magnetic energy is coming from within the square, you feel directed to ease your way into the quickened pulse of a celebratory Venice. What better way to do this than with a soothing, scenic gondola ride up the Rio di Palazzo, in a beautiful gown, glitter and lace mask? To your dismay however, you soon notice that there are clearly marked gondola stations all along the lagoon, but no way to get from this edge of San Marco Square down directly onto either side of the calm Rio di Palazzo. Further still, you start to notice that none of the gondolas are boating in the northerly direction on the Rio di Palazzo, away from the vessel rocking, choppy lagoon. They are all floating south, under the Bridge of Sighs, under the bridge upon which you are standing and out into the open waters where many other gondolas appear to be amassing from different directions.

Looking timidly toward the lagoon, you eye a few of the gondoliers conversing animatedly one to another, using an excessive amount of hand gesturing. Though you generally don't tend to be the nervous type, you do wonder how those gondolas keep from tipping in the surging waves of the Laguna Veneta. You at once experience flashbacks of some scary lake canoeing mishaps during your youth and imagine how frightening a spill into deep seawater would be, weighed down by heavily soaked skirts. You begin tentatively approaching the set of gondoliers coolly noshing on pistachios, hoping that they may have steadier boatmanship than the gesticulating set. As you walk over to their boat station, you remember reading somewhere that gondola fees can often be a matter of negotiation. Though there are standard fees in Venice for gondola rides, you can occasionally haggle the charge. However, and more importantly, though most gondoliers follow the fee guidelines, the rare gondolier may unintentionally overestimate your fee. You feel as though you should have done a little more research to determine about how many euros you should pay, taking into account the time of the ride and the route that you will take.

You wouldn't want this to be one of those situations where your lack of knowledge on the topic is obvious in your demeanor, so you straighten your posture, lift your chin and approach the station in an effort to appear confident. "*Salve bella!*" blurts one of the boatmen with a slanted smile and a wink. "*Buongiorno,*" you return politely, glad that your makeup is sure to disguise the natural blush on your cheeks due to being greeted with,

"Hello beautiful!" You ask about the routes and find that a gondolier can take you from the Laguna Veneta, travel halfway up the Canal Grande and circle back around to where you are now via several smaller waterways. You quickly learn that the entrance from the lagoon that here flows into the Grand Canal is actually called Saint Mark's Basin, not surprising since you are standing on the periphery of Piazza San Marco around the corner from Saint Mark's Basilica. You also discover that the Grand Canal flows in a backward S formation from where you stand in the square, as evident by a small map on a tour brochure that the gondolier shows you for reference. He traces your travel route with the tip of his pointer finger along half of the S and then indicates where you'll veer off down lesser canals to exact a full circle and find yourself here again, completing the journey with a float under the Bridge of Sighs. There are so many wonderful highlights to see along this path. There are the Ponte dell'Accademia and Ponte di Rialto (two of only four bridges that travel over the commanding Grand Canal). There is Ca' Rezzonico (a palace that now hosts a history museum about Venice during the 1700s), Palazzo Cavalli-Franchetti (which proudly maintains an Institute dedicated to Art, Science and the Humanities), Palazzo Grimani di San Luca (where Venice's Appeal Court resides) and the façade of Palazzo Venier dei Leoni (a modern art museum premiering the Peggy Guggenheim Collection). You'll see much of Venice's memorable cityscape with its abundant palaces.

Crunching on a pistachio and flicking the halved shell aside, the gondolier asks what you think as you momentarily scrutinize the miniature map on the pamphlet. You raise your masked eyes and ask about the fee. "For you, such a pretty *signorina*, 100 euros," he says. The tour will take between 45 minutes to an hour and what a more lovely, temperate day than this to enjoy a view of Venice's luxurious architecture from the Grand Canal? You pause to peer once again to the boats in sway amongst the persistent waves, each rhythmically bumping against their mooring poles. The station flag, which reads *Servizio Gondole*, creates a constant cracking noise as it flaps in the wind. Though by no means an inexpensive treat after you consider the exchange rate, you do figure that it is a fair sum.

Just as you are about to ask which boat will be the one you'll be taking, a man in costume which you had not noticed standing so closely before, seems to purposefully interject his body between you and the gondolier. On closer look, he is quite finely dressed in eighteenth century fashion. A knee-length coat in Egyptian blue with a waistcoat to match elegantly stylizes the man. These along with the striking effect of slim fitting navy breeches that tie at the calf with a gold bow, cream stockings and blue-black, buckled and pointed leather shoes, you find that this gentleman has made great efforts to dress historically correct. He wears a tan colored wig, drawn into a ponytail at the nape of his neck with an Egyptian blue bow. He too wears a half mask, though of glitteringly gold painted plaster, rather than lace, bound elegantly around the back of his head with a gold ribbon. A navy tricorne hat nests atop his head snuggly, completing the look.

He asks you to pardon his rudeness in interrupting your transaction with the gondolier but noticed however, that you were without an escort and appeared to be about to take a gondola ride alone. You infer that the man cannot be much older than yourself due to his youthful mannerisms and the smooth skin on his face below the mask line, though you can't be entirely sure considering his noble disguise. Though his thick accent is distinctly Italian, he articulates his English quite well. He further offers that should you be willing to split the cost of the gondola fee, as he was looking also to tour by boat this day, that he would be happy to point out some of the more notable highlights along the route and share what significance he understands of them. Looking amused, the gondolier shrugs his shoulders and chuckles as he crunches another nut. It makes no difference to him as the price will be the same either way and he doesn't mind saving his voice from having to yell out the names of the *palazzi* to you, as he has had to do for hundreds of riders before.

IF you accept the stranger's offer and split the price of a gondola ride with him, turn to page 145.

IF you decide to take this gondola trip alone, turn to page 211.

IF you change your mind entirely and decide to explore elsewhere, turn to page 177.

YOU find the promenade an easy place to traverse and observe the swarming bounty of people. You'll be able to observe all of the creative fashions from steps above the crowd. As you fully enter, you begin to amble along under the marble ceiling of the arcade down its long stretch, soon letting go of the soft hold you had on your skirts, having lifted them enough so as not to trip while squeezing past other visitors in the *calli*. You find yourself relaxing to the hypnotic rhythm of the music, sauntering proudly, passing behind one pillar and the next, taking in views of the crowd and then of the boutiques on the inner side. Your chin high and your gaze thoughtful, you begin to feel more and more like a noble of the eighteenth century and nearly forget that you are not.

An opulent man and wife slowly stroll past you in the opposite direction on your right and both nod an aristocratic acknowledgement, a slight bow with their heads. Lofty, plush white plumes extend from the lady's bountiful, powder blue bouffant. They appear to almost tickle her husband's nose as he touches the tip of his tricorne hat with a flourish of his fingers. You return the gesture with the slightest pause and the softest curtsey. You hardly but bend your knees one inch and arch your neck down so slightly as to have greeted the couple more delicately than with a whisper. As they unhurriedly pass behind you, you look over your shoulder to view a stretch of ornate fabric extending off of her bodice between her shoulder blades, streaming all the way to the hem of the back of her sapphire dress, like a brocaded veil. This was called a sack-back gown (also called a *robe a la francaise*), and was all the fashion for ladies during the Baroque era.

Focusing ahead again, a woman approaches with two small girls on your left. The young ladies appear to be both the same age and you quickly resolve that they are twins at roughly six or seven years. Their silhouettes are exactly like that of their mother, with side hoops extending from their little panniers, tiny fitted bodices buttoned up to the neck and elaborate petticoats exposed at the front of their skirts. The very wealthy ladies of the era sometimes exposed ornate underskirts in an opening at the front of their gowns; extravagant decoration on what was usually an unseen garment. Petticoats uncovered in these instances were no longer considered underclothing but rather another layer of embellishment intended to be seen. Likely, this sort of mode lady would have worn another simple cotton petticoat under the exposed one. As you approach, you notice that there is a forest scene painstakingly stitched onto the front of each of the girls' bodices. Squinting from beneath your lacy half mask, you see deer scampering amongst trees and bush evading a bear on one child, and a bowhunter aiming at fowl on the other. What an excessive delight in the details! Their mother in a chestnut colored dress and the girls both in mint green gowns, they all have beautiful dark brown hair caught up in feminine buns pinned at the back of their heads and thin emerald green ribbons tied high on the neck of them all. Each is carrying a half mask on a stick that they playfully cover their eyes with as they pass with a familial giggle. What a lesson in history this must be for a little girl of the present-day; you commend their mother for exposing them to both the inconveniences and beauty of women's clothing of another era, as well as the peculiarities and historic drama of the pulsing crowd, just steps below. Much better than Halloween and a class lesson on the Baroque period combined!

To your right, a single woman glides forward from some distance away and you are immediately arrested by the view. She is grandiosely, perfectly the image of a peacock, could a woman be transformed into that odd and attractive bird. Behind her, three men are trailing, all in white, gold and foppish manner. The act as it seems, is the majestic beauty and her following. You laugh outright at this exciting show of men courting her in a frenzied, ingratiating, humorous manner. She swats them distractedly with her retracted, hand-held fan as they grasp to entwine their arms in hers to be the companion favorite. They appear to verbally pay homage to her person with clucks and high-pitched, desperate words, occasionally throwing cold stares at their competitors. You wish you could hear exactly what they are saying, but admit that their nonverbal performance is complete. As you come closer to this eighteenth century diva, she stops hard and turns to face the crowd in the square, her monkey entourage collaboratively making a show of bumping into one another at the abrupt halt in their course.

You slow your walk down to almost a tiptoe and veer off closer to the left of the arcade at just the top step that leads down into the square itself. You wish to afford yourself with a better view of this carnal being and her gentlemen. Only a few marble pillars away from her majestic presence, you are thankful for the anonymity of wearing a mask and make your own show of casually scanning the crowds when it appears that she is looking in your direction so as not to be caught blatantly staring. What seamstress in the current day could have made such a costume of luxury, you wonder? Cerulean colored silk sucks tightly to her torso and then flows like the Adriatic Sea over her wide hoop; her skirts appear to be the salty waves of the lagoon turned that tumultuous blue-green just before a storm. You assume that for a price, most anything can be commissioned, as evidenced by her presence.

Scanning again over the crowd, you pause on a woman wrapped in a traditional *zendale*. A *zendale* was an encompassing version of a cape, seamless in that it encircled the torso without ties or clasp at the neck. Dressing in it would require pulling it over the head rather than draping it over the shoulders. The *zendale* came complete with a hood. One most certainly would have worn it with a tricorne hat over the hood and a mask beneath (whether you were a man or a woman), to officiate a disguise out-of-doors. The traditional version of the *zendale* that you are witnessing however is made not of a solid black fabric, but of black lace (also common). Her dress is simple and pitch while the second layer, the *zendale*, creates a smolderingly beautiful effect; the partially transparent lace hanging over her head and veiling just below her eyes. In her arms is an infant who appears to be less than a year in the world, swathed in a blanket edged in white Burano lace, wearing a miniature gold half mask. You are a little surprised that a mother would bring her tiny offspring into such a thick assembly. You are also taken with recalling that historically, mothers did in fact mask their *bambini* during the Carnevale. It was pivotal that every person remained anonymous during the festival. Even beggars wore masks as they bent in supplication asking for coin, as poor, tattered and dirty as they may have been. Furthermore, it was thought rude to try and guess out loud at the identity of persons you met in public. Even if you were sure to identify someone by voice, mannerisms or conversational tidbits, you were not to let on that you did so. This was considered bad manners! In this way, Venetians and foreign visitors both enjoyed traipsing about unknown, as they pleased. Classes of the population mixed at gatherings and public balls. You could forget who you were and pretend to be someone else, at least for a time. Or perhaps, liking just who you were, you could simply be a more socially liberated version of yourself.

You are momentarily startled when looking back to see the play of the noblewoman and her courting fools, you face one of her followers up-close. He is both tall and solid, his face powdered and made-up more prettily than most girls', including a velvet beauty mark and rosy cheeks. His eyes sparkle warmly as he outstretches a hand as if to ask for your own. You tentatively offer the gloved fingers of your right hand, which he firmly grasps and promptly lifts to his lips, delicately kissing the mounds of your knuckles. You are instantly sure that there isn't anything effeminate about this particular man as his eyes meet yours while returning your hand from the arm's-length you had outstretched it a moment ago. Is this an unexpected flirtation or simply a show of courtly manners? Your heart quickens slightly as the gentleman backs up enough to bow forward without coming too close to your person. He leans his weight on a glossy black cane, grasping his hand at the top of it around a golden lion's head, while offering his other hand again, this time to proffer a card. You slowly take it from him, holding it in both hands to examine the thick cardstock cut somewhat larger than a common business card and scripted in gold lettering. It isn't difficult to decipher that it is an invitation to a ball! You instantly feel lighter than before, while determining that it is set for tomorrow evening at 8 p.m., to be held in a *palazzo* unknown to you; the address is indicated. The name of the proprietress (assumably the grand lady) is Signora Romana Sapienti and her estate, the Palazzo Acquarone. Entrance to the event comes at a price, 400 euros. However, you are not at all surprised or offended. During the eighteenth century Carnevale, it would have been very common in Venice to pay for your entry, even into a friend's palace. Some affairs were public and some private (requiring an invitation), however, to most you paid your way regardless and with pleasure. After all, simply to host anywhere from 50 to 500 guests in your home, without also having to cover the expenses for all of their food, candlelight, wine and musical entertainment, was a respected gesture alone. Your entry fee paid for what you enjoyed and likely also stood as insurance should you shatter or stain anything while making masked merriment into the early hours of the morning. An invitation to the estate of the grand lady that you witnessed is a superfluous treat. You had of course expected to purchase a ticket to some public ball of which you would have asked the recommendation from the hotel concierge. You acknowledge that a public ball may cost you half of the price of this one, but also consider that the magnificence of the event itself will likely reflect how much you are willing to spend on entry. To receive a private invitation seems doubly exciting, though you aren't quite sure why since you will not know anyone whether you attend this ball or another public one.

You look up from the card, breaking from your inner imaginations over the anticipated evening, only to find that the lady and her companions have completely vanished out of view (likely into the crowd, which is becoming too dense to filter). The assembly has quickly become an impenetrable mass from one side of the square all the way to St. Mark's Basilica, making you consider what else might be a pleasure to do while strolling around in sweet finery, to both see and be seen.

IF you would like to reenter the *calli* to explore at will, even at the risk of getting lost, turn to page 166.
IF you are a lover of music, turn to page 224.

Venice

YOU acquiesce with a nod directed to the masked man while simultaneously and discretely pulling out 50 euros from your personals, careful to not expose a flash of the sum of the cash that you are carrying. Though you remain confidently poised as both the gentleman and yourself hand the money to the gondolier, you feel the slightest queasiness as your eyes dart over the constant slapping of the waves against the boats into the edge of the marble square and back again to this man. How peculiar was the perfect timing in which he insinuated himself into this transaction. To outwardly assert your coolness, you march behind the boatman as he leads you to his assigned vessel, without hesitation. With one end of his boat secured tightly to a mooring pole, he eases the rest of the craft parallel against the stone, so as to make an easier way of entry into the gondola for you both.

Stepping into the boat with one thick black boot, the gondolier keeps his other foot ashore and with great strength, closes the gap between vessel and land by pulling his legs together. It appears to be an act he's done a thousand times, but which cannot be held for more than a minute as he ushers you forward with a flourish of one hand, while offering you the other to steady yourself aboard. At the same moment that your left hand makes contact with the gondolier's, you find that your right has made it into that of the stranger's, who is standing closely at your other side. He has grasped it to assure your stable footing, a mannerly gesture that lands you quite solidly into the middle of the boat. Carefully balancing your weight, you sit down on a cushioned bench to the rear of the vessel as the man hops in effortlessly behind, sitting to face you from a plush settee nestled into the opposite end. The very back tip of the gondola is outfitted with a deck that the gondolier stands just before. He squats down to retrieve a long, thick oar from the floorboards while another gondolier unties the boat's rope from the mooring pole and casts it into the belly between you and the stranger.

It is merely a sliver in time from when you entered into the boat until you are sailing into the middle depths of St. Mark's Basin, veering toward the entrance of the Grand Canal. This is your very first experience riding in a gondola and you soon become confident in the strength and security of the craft, as evidenced by less frantic rocking in the waves than you had expected. The ride is quite steady and comfortable in fact. Slowly loosening the swollen grip your hands had on the plump velvet cushion billowing up on either side of your skirts, something you hardly even realized you were doing, you begin to ease. Facing toward the ever-distancing square, you gasp at a memorable sight!

Advertised images that you had seen of St. Mark's Square were largely framed from within the place itself or at the edge of it overlooking the Venetian Lagoon. Enchanting social scenes with dining patrons at outdoor tables enjoying a *limoncello*, awkward tourists amidst clouds of pigeons (one or two posing on someone's head), majestic snapshots of St. Mark's Basilica with its oxidized bronze horse statues turned green. Largely popular are photographs of the dazzling masked and sequined anonymous posing as still as Greek marble heroes before the waves. Your most favored capturing of the *piazza* was of dawn breaking over the waters with a dark blue sky. The silhouette of the gondolas and mooring poles were black against the new day. Perhaps you found the picture arresting because of what it made you imagine; the mystique of a nightlong candlelit fantasy broken by the calm of a salty, powerful, sobering daybreak. But now, you are afforded a completely new view, looking into rather than from without.

The scene is one that has surely been replicated a

thousand times throughout history. Gondolas pepper the water's edge, shoring up and launching off in a sporadic dance. There are so many gondolas and rather few modern speedboats in the basin at present, which you attribute to the celebration of Carnival. Currently lasting around 10 days, the festival boasts the best of what tradition has to offer, therefore favoring the historic boats Venice is known for. You assume at the close of the festival, most of the gondola retreat to back waterways, leaving much of the lagoon to their engine driven predecessors. The Doge's Palace prevails to the right of the square, a commanding gothic structure of pale Istrian marble surrounded by traversable walkways at the street level, elaborately worked stone pillars enclosing an elevated arcade at its half and grand windows encased out of the carved marble at its height. The very middle one in the row of enormous windows facing the lagoon is in fact a single balcony protruding from the façade. You read that this was where the Doge, or political leader of Venice, waved in greeting and addressed the throng of Venetians below. You wonder what the view of the square and sea is like from up there and assume how very few today, or perhaps ever in history, will know.

Two towering pillars rise out of the square reaching stories high: the Column of San Marco balancing Venetian's iconic winged lion and the Column of San Teodoro carrying a marble rendition of Saint Theodore, a warrior saint (and beloved patron saint to Venice prior to St. Mark). They each are masculine pieces that represent a metropolis that was once, the most rich and powerful in all of Europe. You can see part of Saint Mark's Basilica nestled behind the Doge's Palace, mainly catching the sun's glint off its multiple domed roofs decorated in enameled gold leaf and a plethora of angel statues sporting gold wings. St. Mark's Church is by many, affectionately called the Chiesa d'Oro, a church of gold. The opulent crowd flowing into and out of the square strikes you, your delight surging as a thousand metallic masks randomly reflect the glory of the sun like the gilded silver tips of sea waves.

A flush of pigeons rise up like a thick of smoke, flying over the left entrance of the Square opposite of the Doge's Palace, landing on top of the Biblioteca Nazionale Marciana or National Library of St. Mark's. The library, designed by the architect Jacopo Sansovino in the 1500s, is a majestic beast of white marble. Carved into its ground level is an arcade guarded by pillars on pedestals, next an elevated second floor of the same leads to proud statues. Sansovino was born in Florence, but also lived and worked in Rome and Venice. He rubbed shoulders throughout his career with other prolific Renaissance artists such as Raphael, Michelangelo, Bramante and Andrea del Sarto. It is intriguing to remember that behind every ancient monument is a great and provocative mind. These talented architects were also artists, mathematicians, sculptors, painters, scientists and astronomers! For most people, it is an accomplishment to establish a single talent or career in a lifetime. You can only begin to imagine the investment of thought, time and passion that great thinkers and doers give to hone their gifts and assume that this aligns with great sacrifice. You wonder how many persons such as these sunk into the depths of madness by blanketing themselves day and night in the aspiration of problem solving and perfection.

You had almost forgotten that you were in the company of an unfamiliar man when the gentleman before you, looking also at the library, begins to speak with his dulcet accent.

That building there is our old library here in Venezia, may it be preserved always from flood and fire.

I am told that there is at least, a million books in that place. But, there are other treasures safely slumbering behind that marble and I do not think that even the annals of the Vatican in Rome could boast much more, though I say that as a proud Venetian. In that library there are collections of illuminated manuscripts from the Middle Ages when there was no printing press and all pictures were painted. Illuminated manuscripts were hand painted with gold and silver. They glow by candlelight. These manuscripts were mostly religious and rare, very expensive when they were created. Common people were in awe to see one. The library also holds stores of documents, drawings, operas, wills and legal writings. If you can conceive it, it is in that place and created at the hand of the most memorable, powerful, saintly and lowly of people from Venetian and European history. If you are passionate for stories, history, art, or even just the beauty and frailty of written antiquity, you could walk into that library, stow away and be captivated eternally.

As the gentleman pauses in his commentary, both of you mesmerized by the view and neither looking to secretly assess the other, you smile to yourself over how smartly the stranger shares his knowledge. He seems sentimental about his city and romantic in the way he expresses it. Inwardly, you are happy to have happened upon someone who could share this tour by adding something to the experience, not to mention the 50 euros you saved in the process. You are eager to hear more.

Here as you see, we are floating on St. Mark's Basin and that way to the right in the square is the Doge's Palace. We began to have doges in the 700s. But I should first preface, Venice is made up of many islands that are now attached by bridges. At the heart of these islands, or a tight cluster of them, there was always a square made of thick stones and a small church built. So before there was a single Venetian leader, the doge, there were principles representing each neighborhood, each neighborhood having a square and a church and their own customs. Even now, there are Venetians who never leave their neighborhoods, their islands, who have never even come to St. Mark's Square, even though they only need walk across a bridge. Some will even tell you that they can note the slight differences in the customs of Venetians from island to island. You probably walked through five or six of these neighborhoods, simply crossing a bridge from one to the next, just to get to St. Mark's Square from where you are staying. Venice has just less than 120 small islands, but from the air, we look like one piece of earth with silver snakes of water slicing and slithering it into pieces. Once there began to be doges, men who remained the leader until their deaths the way that kings do, there began a tradition in which the doge would perform marriage rites every year. The marriage was not to unite common people, but of Venice marrying the sea itself, the water being the very element that sustained and protected Venetian power. And so, on Ascension Day each year, a holiday celebrated by Christians and remembered as the day that Jesus rose to Heaven after his resurrection from the dead, the doge performed a ceremony. From his bucentaur, a boat decked in finery, the doge would throw a ring of gold into the sea while docked nearby. There were 120 doges in all for almost 1000 years from the 700s into the 1700s, and though the marriages didn't start until the 1000s, performed yearly, I can only dream of how many ancient rings are there at the bottom of the lagoon. I have never heard if any have been brought up, but I sometimes dream of finding one washed ashore.

You find yourself delighted with the thought of the masked man aspiring to find one of these gold rings and wonder if it has been an adventurous dream of his since childhood. After all, every youth has had some treasure they'd imagined hunting for and spent some hours or even days, carefully planning a way to go about it. You envision an awkwardly hilarious, if not determined, version of yourself traipsing through St. Mark's Square in scuba gear on a mission to find a gold ring. Perhaps however, some sacred treasures should be left undisturbed. The Piazza San Marco begins to fade from view as the stranger continues.

I would tell you about the palazzi here as we cut up the canal, but I fear there are too many and my memory unclear as to which great family lived in each. Let me just say that there are hundreds of palaces in Venice and I do not know any other city that is made up almost entirely of palazzi the way we are in Venezia. This is the only way I can convince you of how very rich Venice had been during the Middle Ages and the Renaissance. Some of the palazzi are now museums and some are still private homes, many are converted into luxury hotels. Everything here is frozen in time out of ancient marble. It would take you many lifetimes to gather a glimpse of the endless histories, tragedies and fortunes gained and lost here. My city is beautiful. But what is interesting for this masked woman sitting here with me? I am guessing that you come from a distant land but perhaps you already know these stories and I am a fool to think I have anything new to tell you about St. Mark's Square, the doge or our extravagant and decaying palazzi. Perhaps what is hidden is more of interest to you? Things not easily read about in a guidebook?

In all of the time since the stranger began speaking, you have sat delicately motionless, your eyes first fixed on the square and now observing the many *palazzi* beginning to line up along both sides of the canal. Despite the endless and entrancing architecture, you are as equally interested in every word that has come to ear. You had been trying not to fix your gaze on the stranger, so as not to miss the passing panorama or to appear too direct or overly interested. Though it cannot be definite, you find that the man has also made a show of good manners by not speaking to you too directly, but rather more in the style of a reverie as he too looked out over the passing shoreline. As he pauses over his last question however, you feel his gaze turn in your direction for encouragement to forward onto some lesser-known topics. So as to be polite, you turn your head to face and meet his gaze as well, nodding thoughtfully and smiling in silence to prompt the storytelling at hand.

TURN to page 253.

YOU once read that Napoleon himself called the Piazza San Marco, "The drawing room of Europe." It is nowhere documented that he in fact ever made this observation, but you support the anonymous creator of the quote for having made a statement that you can easily imagine being a historically sound reality. A drawing room was originally known as a salon in one's home used explicitly for entertaining guests. It was a place where adults conversed, offered delicate refreshments, played cards and music, told stories, proffered gossip and even performed small private plays. This particular title, the drawing room, was mainly used from the mid-1600s through the early 1800s. However, this room and its purpose have been around since the time of medieval castles and still lives on in common living and formal dining rooms, during holiday gatherings and special occasions today.

At the same time that this term was popular, Venice was also a destination in the Grand Tour. During the seventeenth and eighteenth centuries, aristocratic men spent months abroad after completing their university studies. This tour could last several years and covered many cities throughout Europe. The Grand Tour was considered an educational extension in which refined men learned to dance, fence, become learned horsemen, view ancient art, hear music singularly played in one city or other and to define their courtly manners. In the 1800s it began to be commonplace that ladies too went on their own Grand Tour to hone their cultural sensibilities. Aside from the fact that Venice had always been a magnet for foreign visitors and those with wealth, a place to find a new start and new pleasures, the Grand Tour made it sizzle with rich, stately visitors. Venice and its Piazza San Marco were the place to be! It was an epicenter for fine entertainment, expensive wares and adornments, delectable fare and excessive frivolity amongst the most noble of Europeans.

Entering the swarming crowd, it swallows you instantly into it. Though you have on average five to six feet to negotiate between your body and that of another's at any given moment, you feel sucked into a stuffier environment and a bit jostled about. The high pitch cackle of a woman with thick white foundation blurs over your right shoulder; her bright red lips appear as a bloody streak as she jerks her head at some hilarity. To your left, a portly man with a bulbous nose and beady brown eyes is sweating profusely as he tries to bend over to fetch a wig that has fallen off and gotten away, bumping several onlookers with his rear. An acne-faced young man grins mischievously before you as he strains to get a better look of the bosom of the red-lipped woman, who is now in full screech, grasping her corseted waist as though in need of air. Moving forward, you find a little hand in yours as a nymph of a girl dressed in a white cotton frock with billowy skirts pushes your hand into the air and performs a little twirl under your arm. She lets go with a sweet curtsey and you smile delightedly as she disappears into the crowd, little ribbons in her dark hair flitting behind her. A few small and hard objects beat against your face and breast, raining from above. You fish one from out of the top of your bodice, another from the hip fold of your thick skirt and find that they are chocolate coins wrapped in gold and silver foil. They look like real currency until you dismantle their wrappings in turn and pop them into your mouth, perfectly creamy and sweet. While still savoring the chocolate you stop at a group of people who have turned themselves inward, creating a fairly large circle, and push yourself close against it. Raising yourself up onto the tips of your toes to get a view between high shoulders, you see what cannot be mistaken for any other form of theater but an improvisational scene of commedia dell'arte!

Though not entirely educated about this genre of play, you have read enough to know its basic history and traditions. Around the mid-1500s in Rome, performances sprang up out-of-doors, which included masked and costumed characters played by professional actors. The pieces were executed in settings that were not permanent (such as a Roman amphitheatre or an English playhouse), but were performed most anywhere, set or no set. In fact, emphasis was given to props and the exaggerated acting of the costumed players, rather than to a stage at all. Especially noteworthy, it was first in the later 1500s that female characters in commedia dell'arte were played *by women*, prohibited before or elsewhere. Spanning from the ancient theater in Rome and Greece extending through Shakespeare's era, young effeminate boys played the roles of women as it was considered immodest for any lady to be seen on stage.

It was the commedia dell'arte that brought the very first celebrity actress into the light, Isabella Andreini. Her parents were Venetian, though she was born in Padua, in 1562. At 16 years old, she began her career with the Compagnia dei Comici Gelosi, which was a troupe practicing the commedia dell'arte. The Gelosi toured all around Italy and France, were funded by aristocrats and were invited to play for countless nobles and royal courts, performing even for the King of France, Henry IV. Commedia dell'arte was a unique form of theater in that the same set of recognizable characters played within each performance. These characters can be identified even now, by the theatrical costumes some wear during the Venetian Carnevale in tribute to this form of performance. How would you know who is who? Each character had distinguishing personality traits and consistent attire. By the mask alone, you could often tell which commedia dell'arte character this or that actor was, even without their saying a word!

For instance, there were the *Zanni* who were the servant characters that played tricks on others; some might compare them to medieval jesters. Or the *Vecchi* which were the elderly men in the play; they usually tried to keep the young lovers or the *Innamorati* (the female role of this duo is one Isabella made notorious) from uniting in consummation or marriage. *La Ruffiana* was an old, gossipy woman who like the *Vecchi*, tried to keep the lovers apart. *Il Capitano* was a soldier who outwardly was brazen and arrogant, but at the first sign of trouble, lost all confidence and ran away. There too, were more characters that fell in category with the initial title of each metaphoric persona. For instance, under *Vecchi* might be the *Pantalone* or *Il Dottore*. What better character to play in Venice than the *Pantalone*! He was, as *Vecchi* implies, a man of age. He was also a rich merchant! Apart from the accumulation of great wealth, he usually had in his possession, a youthful wife or innocent daughter that he intended to keep under lock and key. It was up to the *Zanni* to help these ladies as *Innamorata*, to match with their true loves, thus fooling and defying *Pantalone*. The *Il Dottore* was also elderly but rather than a merchant, was erudite, or so he postulated. He interrupted all the other characters with long speeches that claimed a depth of knowledge on every subject. The audience could tell however, that he was hardly an educated man. He was known as the liar, whether playing a politician, lawyer or teacher. He was usually corpulent, having enjoyed wine and feast to excess and loved to hear himself speak, launching off on ridiculous tangents. The audience was happy when at some point, the characters in the play also saw that he was a fool.

Either on the street or in the private salon of a

wealthy supporter of the arts, witnessing a performance of commedia dell'arte felt inclusive as you recognized each traditional character. You felt like an insider in the story, as these were persona that you deeply connected with in daily life. This theatrical was an allegory of everyday happenings that was so relatable, yet far enough removed so as not to be distinctly associated with a real occurrence. Actors were improvisational, in that, they had always performed the same recognizable stories yet they altered them depending on local news and gossip. Therefore the tale felt close-at-hand, changed just so as to protect a troupe from malice. The plays were not fairytale; they were your life or the lives of someone you knew, but funnier! They mostly tended to end well and were comedic from start to finish, thus were a release from the difficulties of real life.

You are charmed with the acting as you determine the scene. Several performers not in immediate use are lined up in a half-moon at the opposite side of the circle from where you are. Within, there are four characters that are easily found familiar. The two *Innamorati* are present and unmasked. They are in fact the only two actors in the commedia dell' arte that ever are, spared the garish, ghoulish, wild expressions brought to life with a disguise. They are instead chosen for their true grace and handsome looks; the love between them is the center of almost every plot and you are sure, always wins in the end. However, the *Innamorati* are not exempt, they are as dazed and ridiculous as all the other characters! This is evident now as they stand center in the circle, facing away from each other back to back. The *Innamorato* is admiring his own attractive visage in the reflection of a hand mirror while the *Innamorata* stares approvingly at her bejeweled and elegant outstretched hands. It is clear that the *Innamorati* are rather vain and as in love with themselves as they should be with each other. Circling the couple is the *Ballerina*, fairylike and dancing effortlessly to a beautiful, stationary songbird that is crooning to the audience, the *Cantarina*. They are both dressed similarly in incandescent, rainbow-colored gossamer bodices, tutu-esque skirts, floral wreaths adorning their long brown tresses and shimmering half masks. Though the couple is silly in their self-admiration, the scene is touching and an artistic rendering of young, romantic love. You are charmed!

The crowd now feels less close as you've grown accustomed to it, but from here, the arched promenade around the square does appear an interesting place to view the fuller scope of all those amassed in the crowd. Looking skywards, you take in a deep breath of crisp salty air and watch a scattering of soft white clouds float along the endlessly beautiful blue sky. You imagine that the heavens and sea here often mirror one another. Scanning the heights of the lustrous marble architecture all around the square, you pause on the exquisiteness of St. Mark's Basilica and consider seeing its mysteries from within.

IF you would like to try a turn under the arcade, turn to page 136.

IF you are compelled to enter the Chiesa d'Oro, Venice's church of gold, turn to page 187.

YOU are elated with the thought of preparing for, traveling to and attending a private ball! In this moment, all of Venice is yours. The entire city is slowly churning a mysterious energy, as if *something* is about to happen, and you can feel it pulsing in your bosom. As if suspended in time for one decadent week, the world outside is nonexistent, and this otherworldly place is all that matters. Walking to the end of the arcade, you turn left and make to head across the *piazza*, leisurely skirting the front of St. Mark's Basilica along the edge of the crowd until you reach a small walkway leading to the *calli* behind the square.

Upon entering the thin walk, you are encased on either side by tall stone buildings that block most of the sun from reaching this alley. The way is only wide enough for about four people to stand shoulder to shoulder and in costume, only two. There is little traffic along this route and as you approach the *calle* ahead, you run your gloved fingers along the wall aside you. The stone is very cold, having pent up the chill of an entire winter. What labor to crack all of this rock from its earthy depths; shaping it with chisel and hammer, boating it to this place in the sea and constructing such beautiful stone monsters as these *palazzi*, churches, bridges and statues. Glancing just below knee level along the wall, you notice on either side of the alley, a green-brown discoloration permeating the stone from the ground to that height and wonder for its appearance. It certainly couldn't be city dogs rubbing their bodies along the walls for centuries. Neither could it be the remnant stains from piles of refuse along this walk before the day public works began to clear such detritus. You are uncertain of the source of the phenomena.

Entering onto the *calle*, you find that much like the streets you used to get to St. Mark's Square from the hotel, this one is lined with shops and restaurants. Turning left, you note a variety of wares sold in these stores that you haven't yet seen. From the first in a row wafts the delicious scent of freshly baked bread. Peering into the tiny shop, you see a few local Venetians inspecting a wall completely covered in hanging baskets, thick like summer ivy. Nestled within the baskets are a rich cornucopia of bagged rice, grain and pasta: polenta, risotto, fettuccine and *bigoli* (a thick Venetian spaghetti), as well as freshly baked, crusty herb bread. Along the back wall are shelves of colorfully shaped dried pastas, herbs, salts, bottled balsamic vinegars and olive oils. Under the shopkeeper's glass, you note today's stuffed ravioli and rolled *gnocchi* sold by weight. You can't read the words on the display cards, but judging by the color, some *gnocchi* is made from pumpkin and some from potato. You can only imagine what is within the surfeit of ravioli, ranging from mini purses the size of a quarter to plump pouches as large as dumplings. You know that ravioli is usually filled with fresh, soft whey cheese ricotta. Here however, others may be secreting spinach, mushrooms, spiced meats and other vegetables.

Passing along front the next little shop, you are awed by the variety of linens and lace within. The room is softly lit like a sleepy dream. White shelves and round tables are blanketed with smoothly folded cottons: tablecloths, bedding, nightgowns and Christening gowns. Much of it is accented with the divine artwork of Burano, Venetian lace.

Burano is an island four miles off the coast of Venice; you can easily get there by *vaporetto* in less than an hour. Though the population of the island of Burano is less than 3,000 people, the isle is so small that it is covered almost entirely with homes. There are two things that are particularly special about Burano: colorful houses and intricate handmade lace. Burano's homes are painted the most vibrant colors of the rainbow! As you pass one abode to the next you'll see red, blue, orange, yellow, green, pink, peach, and more. As with many heritage homes around the world, these lodgings are protected by higher forces, specifically their color. If you own a house in Burano and wish to paint it, the government will tell you what colors your particular dwelling is allowed to exhibit. The effect is like a bowl of brightly colored Easter eggs or a room full of exotic birds, shockingly bright, a rare vivid that is quite beautiful. Historically speaking however, Burano's lace is far richer than its architecture.

There is a legend of how lacemaking began in Burano and it starts with the sea. It is said that in the Venetian Lagoon, a fisherman entered into mermaid territory. There, one of these sassy creatures began to sing her siren's song in an attempt to lure the poor soul. However, the fisherman was very much in love and betrothed to his beloved. He would not be tempted to seek out the source of such a mesmerizing sound, no matter how strong the call to temptation. The mermaid queen was touched by his fidelity and gave him a very special gift to reward him for his loyalty, which he was to deliver to his bride-to-be. She thumped her shimmering tail upon the side of his boat and from the rocking and waves, sea foam formed. When the fisherman took the delicate froth in his hands, it solidified into the most beautiful, transparent material. He gave it to his heart's desire and she used it for her wedding veil. The maids of Burano were in awe of the delicate, ethereal fabric covering the sweet face of the fisherman's bride. From then on, the women of Burano used needles and thread to try and recreate this magical textile from the sea.

Lace is an artful fabric with holes purposefully intended throughout, creating various designs. We don't know who made the first lace, but the oldest piece to ever be found was in a tomb in Egypt and is called mummy lace. How did this craft get to Burano? It is a theory that lacemaking from ancient Assyria migrated to Cyprus. Venice ruled Cyprus from the years 1489 to 1571. It is thought that the art traveled to Burano during the earlier part of this time, which could account for its flourishing during the start of the 1500s. There are many methods available to make lace: knitting, knotting, crocheting, and using bobbins or needles or machines. Burano lace was unique in that women used needles and fine thread without the use of a pillow or canvas behind the lace as support, to create their fabrics of ornate stitch.

It was excruciatingly difficult and time-consuming to construct needle lace, thus it was considered exceptionally refined and very expensive. When the craft first took root in Venice, it was only made within the walls of the homes of the affluent, for the personal use of the rich. That was until a particular woman helped the lacemaking business in Venice become *so* popular, that Burano needle lace was ever increasingly sought-after throughout Europe.

In 1595, Marino Grimani became the doge, or ruler, of Venice. His wife, Morosina Morosini-Grimani therefore, became the dogaressa. She was a very wealthy woman and was crazy for Burano lace. So she created a workshop with over 100 lace makers (130 to be exact) to make the delicate fabric for her own use and to send as gifts to her friends. The show and spread of the lace soon created a demand far beyond Venice. Frenzied ancient Burano maidens envious to recreate mermaid fabric couldn't hold a candle to Europe's desire for it! The daughters of Burano have been making the lace by hand ever since; the art passed down through the centuries, folded into Venice's tremendously rich cultural heritage. Today there is a precious museum on Burano, the Museo del Merletto, which walks visitors through the history of lace in its entirety. One exhibit premieres the Burano Lace School, which opened in 1872 and operated until 1970 in an effort to keep Burano lacemaking alive after a period where the light of that art was growing dim. The museum is in the Palace Podesta of Torcello, the very location of the since closed Burano Lace School! For those who visit the museum as it first opens, you can have the treat of watching ladies at their lacemaking.

Observing how delicate and feminine the items in the linen shop appear, you feel drawn as by that siren's song to enter and see some Burano lace up-close. As you enter, a kindly woman greets you with a smile as she folds soft pink pillowcases edged in cherry blossom pink embroidered lace, tying the pile with a wide ribbon. Perhaps they were especially ordered for a bride-to-be, you fancy. You inhale the gentle scent of rose water as you remove a glove from your left hand and smooth your fingers over the flow of a modest white nightgown hanging on a model dress form. The thread count is evidently very high owing to its buttery soft feel. Around the neck, wrists and hem are thin ribbons of white floral lace. The design appears as delicate and unique as the singular blueprint of every snowflake, impossible to replicate. There is a table topped with velvet globes, each hung with a lace veil. The rounds act as heads; the fabric begins where one's hairline and forehead meet and wash over the back of the head, down to the neck and beyond, leaving the face uncovered. You envision a pious beauty, perhaps Shakespeare's Juliet, with raven hair evident beneath delicate white lace, praying at a church's altar for the return of her Romeo from banishment. The veils are so fine you don't dare to touch them; they are a maze of vines, flowers and delicate shapes. Considering how long it would actually take using a needle and fine threads to construct a piece of fabric of that size and length, you are afraid to look at the price tag and are solidly in the belief that only a very fine occasion would warrant even allowing the lace to be permitted out-of-doors where there is a chance that the elements or wear might mare it. You picture yourself a noble in the 1700s wearing a Burano lace mask with more of the treasured textile flowing over your elbows from the sleeves of your bodice, waving a handkerchief made of it at your friends one gondola over in the canal. Would you jump into the water to save your kerchief if it slipped from your fingers? Would you curse and swat your courtly partner at the ball if they ripped your sleeve during a stimulating *corrente*, a frenzied Baroque era dance? Would you dismiss your lady's maid for knocking over a glass of wine on your lace mask as it rested awaiting your sitting at your dressing table? Well, you just might have!

You pull your glove back on and grin at your imaginings as you walk over to a glass display case. There you slowly admire spools of lace, bookmarks, doilies and precious framed pieces in a variety of delicate shapes. There is also a basket of thin lengths of lace, with ornate buttons sewed at their ends. You look at them puzzling at their purpose for only a moment when the clerk removes the basket from the display and sets it atop for your closer viewing. She lifts a few in turn and you quickly comprehend that she is asking which color and pattern pleases you. You thoughtfully consider and then point to an ornate black ribbon of lace with a ruby colored glass button at its end. Carefully picking it up out of the basket, the clerk comes around the display and ushers you closer to face a mirror on the wall. From behind you, she gently places the ribbon high around your neck and buttons the lace at the back. It is snug enough to remain high on the neck without being too tight to be uncomfortable. It is a decoration of the Baroque; a delicate choker such as Marie Antoinette was known to wear, as did many of the ladies of her court. It is a treat to see yourself with a true ribbon of Burano lace around your neck, worn as many Venetian noblewomen might have in the 1700s. Alas, you nod "no" to the clerk and return to the glass case after she gently removes the collar. You are more inspired by the little shapes of decorative lace encased in tiny frames and would like to purchase a small piece to frame for yourself once home. It will be one of the many things you hope to acquire on your trip to remind you of Venice. You settle on an oval lace not much bigger than a large chicken's egg. Within a solid outline of purple is an intricate design of green vines, leaves and plum colored grapes. It reminds you of abundance, prosperity, health, desire and beauty. After paying the high but most deserved sum, you thank the clerk, secreting the lace in your pocket after it is wrapped in tissue and return to the street.

Outside of the linen shop, there is a spiced wine vendor with her cart. As she opens her kettle to scoop a cup for several patrons, you see the steam rise from the pot and smell the scents of sugar, orange, cinnamon and clove.

IF you wish to rest yourself and enjoy a cup of spiced red wine, turn to page 237.

IF you would like to continue viewing the storefronts to come, turn to page 244.

Venice

YOU glance from the smirking gondolier to the choppy waters to the smiling stranger and decide quickly that this isn't for you. Perhaps you are playing it a little too safe considering you are on an adventure. However, it's your first full day in Venice and you aren't ready to jump in a boat with two strange men on a deep lagoon, wearing heavy clothing and your vision half blurred by your mask. This could be some ploy to kidnap a pretty woman to who knows where. Your vacation would really be ruined then! You'd have to steal the gondolier's oar while kicking his backside, pushing him into the dark waters. Then you'd have to whack the unknown gentleman overboard with the oar and hope that you could paddle the gondola away before either swam back to the boat. After frantically and laboriously rowing back to shore, you'd probably be sentenced a gondola thief and thrown into the Piombi prison. After all, how are you going to defend yourself if you don't speak Italian and look like a crazy woman with your wig half falling off and screaming to all that you were the victim of an attempted kidnap? Of course, this is all very unlikely to be your fate in Venice, but you rather enjoy amusing yourself with your own imaginary tales of peril none-the-less!

You kindly tell the stranger that you are actually, not feeling all that well and will have to wait to enjoy this Venetian luxury on another day. Listening in, the gondolier shrugs his shoulders and walks away, returning to his original post to yell out to other passing patrons, still crunching on pistachios. As he throws his empty pistachio shells to the ground, they create a sound like a handful of tumbling seashells upon the hard marble. A few sporadic pigeons peck at them anxiously but soon walk away when they find no nutmeat is to be had. Looking up from the birds to assess the reaction of the costumed stranger before you depart the edge of the square, you find that he is completely absent. He is nowhere near your person and as you turn your head about to look in several directions, you do not notice him anywhere.

It's very odd that the man could disappear that quickly since you are not within the throng in the square, but rather on the more sparsely populated water's edge. It's not important of course (you didn't even know the man's name). Your best guess is that he must have been offended and slipped off under the cover of other people walking by. However, the speed of his disappearance is strange. Turning back to take one more look at the beautiful lagoon under today's golden sun before you retreat back into the city for further exploration, you are dumbstruck to find that all there is before you, is the edge of a bare marble *piazza*. Still decorated with gondola tied up with rope around wooden trunks, there are many missing items from the vision of literally, a moment before. There are no candy cane striped mooring poles, just plain wooden ones; some are rather decayed and of varying heights. Your stomach turns as you realize this is the least of what is missing. Where is the gondolier's station? Where are the boatmen? You had expected to look out over water that captured the glare of the sun, mirroring the rays in a way that would have caused you to squint your eyes without the protection of sunglasses. Instead, you feel your pupils growing wider as they adjust to a view that is in fact, dusky. Looking to the sky, it is completely overcast and grey and the sun's warmth of a moment ago seems to have left as quickly as though you had been shaken from a pleasant dream. A biting gust of wind assails you and you no longer feel comfortable enough beneath the cozy cover of your mantle.

As you scan out over the lagoon, you see that the waters are now far worse than choppy; they are a sea of treacherous, whitecap waves. The restrained vessels along the shore smack hard against their mooring poles and into one another; the sound is a bit unsettling and you wonder how long these craft can withstand such abuse before they splinter and sink. You are about to whisper thanks for not being in one of the boats out in the depths at this very moment, but then hold your breath from speaking as an eerie feeling begins to grow within you.

Turning back to the square, you immediately notice that the population of ambling walkers cannot be more that 100 people, where as minutes ago, you are sure you would have counted well over 1,000. You are becoming rather cold as you walk briskly to the center, where you pause to look around you. More than people, there is something else missing. There is no music, or at least, the melodic techno beat of before, is gone. You strain your ears and believe you can hear a violin, or several perhaps, carrying on the wind from some distance. It could be coming from a café or the open window from some private residence, but not within the square. You soon notice that the people seem, different. There are so few of them! They are all in costume, which isn't necessarily out of place, but as you squint to examine all along the arcade, you do not see even one lone visitor in regular clothing. There isn't a single pair of blue jeans, winter coat or camera amongst them. Funny too is that the costumes don't look like costumes at all. They look *real*.

As you venture further into the middle of the square, your brow furrowed in confusion, you stare almost rudely as a couple seems to float past. The woman's pannier extends four feet wide of either side of her frame and a mantle covering her shoulders appears to be made of very fine fur. The hair on her head is powdered profusely and elaborately wrapped in a tower, reaching the height of almost two feet. Looking closely, you are sure that it is not a wig or at least that most of it is real hair with faux locks weaved into it. Her visage looks garish; a powered face so white it seems ghoulish and her blush too unnaturally pink. Tint on her mouth only covers the very center of her lips while the rest of her pout is disguised with powder. She's painted a shape to create a minute fuchsia heart there. She is covering just her eyes with an exquisitely detailed plaster mask that has been painted with a night scene, all black and splashed with pearly stars, which is attached to a stick she holds in her right hand. Above the outer corner of her right eyebrow is a large black beauty mark in the shape of a crescent moon. It looks to be made of a fabric rather than penciled on. You can't help paying attention to such detail and register it anxiously into your mind (verification that your nerves not only feel on the defense, but that there is reason). A feel of fright is triggering within you, but you keep it at bay as you try to make sense of your surroundings. As the woman remarks you in turn, she looks puzzled as well and after passing some distance behind you, you stop to turn and look again. She is also peering back at you from over her shoulder and as she walks, she taps her masked companion several times with a fan she holds in her left hand and whispers crisply into his ear. The couple stops to turn back to observe you from some distance away. You want to turn away and run, but you feel nearly crippled in the knees and slightly faint. At this moment, you don't feel disguised in costume. You feel as though *you* are the one out of place in an outfit that isn't quite right, that isn't real.

You slowly pivot in the direction of the exit of the square that you know to be the way to your hotel and begin to walk that course. You pace yourself as you go so as not to draw attention, but also because you do not feel entirely well. As you exit out of the square back into the *calli*, you find yourself trying to get past a rowdy horde that has been rendered helpless against a puppet show. You know this small wooden stall, outfitted with tattered fabric for mini stage curtains and set brawling with foulmouthed jester and harlot puppets, was not here as you passed earlier. The crowd is washed-out in basic grey, black, white, tan and brown, unpresuming street clothing. They seem right out of an illustration in history of common eighteenth century day people, when these ancient streets were in use during the Baroque. In the mix are a few with ornate gems and fine seamless bodices peeking out from beneath fur lined cold weather trappings while many others are clearly dressed in the rougher fabrics of life. Some laugh uproariously while others make a show of modesty, bringing handkerchiefs to their faces with stifled giggles and knowing whispers. Many are spying on one another curiously, as all are masked.

Shockingly, you understood what the shameless puppets were saying, something or other of the sexual misdeeds of the nobility. You were also able to make out some of the commentary coming from the animated observers. This is of course unnatural, as the language being spoken is not English.

Making your way past the gathering, you pick up the pace and begin to toe in haste to the only place that will be able to bring you back to reality; your hotel room filled with your own belongings. You try to comfort yourself by watching your steps and focusing on lifting your skirt high enough to avoid tripping in your hurry amongst these ghosts. You focus on your breathing and think of your family back home, which brings you a small sense of stability. You gather that there must be some explanation for what is happening and begin keenly hoping that it has nothing to do with your sanity.

Soon, you've made your way to a smaller square just a few short moments away from your hotel. You've hardly looked around except to seek direction from your memory and make this turn or that. Almost to your destination, you stop at a horrific sight. From right before your path, an elderly man void of much strength and clothed in tattered rags is slowly pushing a wooden wheelbarrow. What you make out of his face is dirty and his grey hair is shorn unevenly around his head; you detect several sizeable scabs where the one who handled the razor did so with meanness. He wears a half mask, perhaps of linen glued over a common plaster that was once white but is now yellowing with sweat. You pity him, as he must be very cold in his thin chemise, vest and pantaloons. You note the scent of metal in the air accompanied by a far off thundering; a storm is coming. If you were he, caught in an icy rain, you'd surely catch pneumonia and succumb from a burning fever. He however, is not the source of your revulsion. It is the lifeless body he is sluggishly laboring to push across the square in the wheelbarrow. The body is that of a man's, his face completely covered in a full mask that was also once white, but is now stained considerably by putrefaction from illness. You wonder how he keeps from calling out in pain, for as his legs hang over the side of the barrow, wheels creaking and box shifting cruelly over the marble stones in this grim parade, you see festering wounds peering out from holes torn in his breeches. And there, his arms scrawny and useless; the invalid's bloody hands clutching his chest in despair, spotted with decaying lesions. Standing there, you faintly detect the smell of polluted flesh as they pass and simultaneously hold back a surge of nausea noting green-yellow puss and red blotching (the evidence of infectious bleeding), at a growing bloom that is seeping through his cream colored chemise on his upper chest.

Hardly a beat of the heart passes before you are moving again toward your hotel, which now seems like a shining beacon in the midst of a nightmare. You know that what you saw was truly before you, and fully excuse yourself for not having reached out to touch the apparitions to make sure they were concrete flesh. This is further evidence that you are not where you ought to be, or rather, not in the *year* you were presently living.

TURN to page 283.

Venice

IT is but a short distance to the façade of St. Mark's Basilica and not an unpleasant walk as you swim between meandering characters common to the Baroque. When before the front, you find that there is a rather long line to wait in before you will be able to pay your admittance fee and enter the ancient building. You figure this is to be expected since it is one of the most notable churches in Venice and located in such a highly visited square, just aside the doges' great palace. Filing in at the end of the chain amongst other costumed visitors as well as street clothed patrons, you begin noting the architectural details along the building's glorious face while recalling its history.

Originally there was a different church built in this place. It was the first St. Mark's Church and this was where the bones of St. Mark (who wrote the chapter of Mark found in the Bible) were first honored and held in reserve, in Venice. As the story is told, two Venetian merchants whose names were Rusticus and Tribunus were given permission by two monks from Alexandria, Egypt, Theodorous and Stauracius to take St. Mark's remains from their church. Allegedly the monks caught wind of a pending disaster; the Khalif (a Muslim political leader) of Alexandria, had plans to extinguish their church and destroy the Christian relics inside. It is said that Rusticus and Tribunus hid St. Mark's body from Muslim guards while aboard their ship, covering his corpse with cuts of pork (meat that Muslims do not eat and would have avoided). The tale carries on with the merchants claiming they had St. Mark's spiritual assistance after their ship survived rough seas (from which they felt sure they would perish), amongst other miracles. Finally the body made its way to Venice and the doge during that time, Justinian Partecipacius, had a Church constructed to honor the saint and to house his remains. This first church took four years to build, from AD 828 to 832. It was most unfortunately burned down in AD 976 after an angry mob determined to murder the then doge, Pietro IV Candiano, burned him to death in his palace. The blaze crept from the palace to the church and then continued to spread further around the city. St. Mark's Church was resurrected (possibly using what structure remained), completing two years later in AD 978. Approximately 115 years hence, in roughly AD 1093, the construction surrounding the rebuilt St. Mark's had grown out to represent the true configuration that is St. Mark's Basilica today. Over time, there have been many decorative additions, but it is mostly the same structurally as it was then, even after 900 years.

As the line moves along, you wonder over all of the marble columns, etched stone and rich adornments of the façade and how much labor it took artisans to create such an intricate masterpiece. Standing just outside the first of five doorways covered by arches detailed with shimmering gold and colored tiles, you note the mosaic of St. Mark, which illustrates his body being brought forth into the church by Venetians. You begin to wonder what ever happened to the remains of St. Mark.

It is likely a complete myth that Rusticus and Tribunus (who we can read about in a text called the *Translatio* written around AD 1050) brought the body of the true St. Mark home with them. Furthermore, whoever's body it was, it is often said that the cadaver was not given them, but that the merchants were downright body snatchers! Some historians have made claims of other identities the body they believe was brought by merchants from Egypt, could be, including Alexander the Great. Until the remains are scientifically tested, we can't know. Perhaps, the entire story is a complete falsehood and the bones are of some simple citizen of Alexandria, or even Venice, with no historical importance. We do know that these bones were and always have been housed in St. Mark's Church, as they are today under the main altar. However, authenticity is questionable. Even after the fire of AD 976, one might ask, what happened to the body? It was said to have been missing and thus must have been hidden somewhere safely, its presence eluding all during construction of the new church out of the old one (if the body hadn't been destroyed by the flames). It isn't improbable that a body could be entombed somewhere amidst the church as secret places are pervasive in all ancient buildings, places that may be encased in stone or of a depth that will not perish in the flames. It seems to have disappeared until AD 1094, when Doge Vitale Faliero Dodoni claimed to have found the remains in a pillar in the church, a pillar that evidently survived the inferno. In AD 1106, there was yet another fire, which ruined much of the internal decoration, however, the body was safe. Doge Vitale had tucked the bones away in a wooden box in a crypt, just before he himself died in AD 1095, one year after its discovery. As time progressed, others seem to have forgotten the body was in a crypt located beneath an altar, which more than once was opened and closed, but appeared in such disrepair, no one explored carefully, let alone lingered. Hundreds of years later, the box was finally exuded from the crypt in 1811, and there inside were ashes and bones and other religiously valued items. The remains are now resting under the main altar in the Basilica.

Supposing the body of St. Mark never really came to Venice, what would be the purpose of saying that it had? The answer is, out of desire for the fame and wealth that could be brought to the city if one could declare that it contained a holy relic. Since Bible times, people have flocked to churches that claimed to either house a religious item of importance or stated that they had beheld a miracle on the premises. St. Mark's Basilica can claim both of these since it not only houses the bones of a saint, but also, the rediscovery of his body was quite a miracle! Doge Vitale was said to have committed himself to fervent prayer and avoided eating during a devotional fast, in hopes that God would lead him to the body's hiding place. He apparently had his prayers answered when he saw the arm of St. Mark not just hanging out of a pillar, but also pointing out of it as if filled again with life! If indeed, the body of St. Mark was truly brought to Venice by merchants and is housed in the Basilica (not impossibly), then the church does indeed protect the body of a tremendously important person and his very presence within the church would be held sacred and beloved by all Christians. Thus why even when the body was playing hide-and-seek from within a pillar and then again from under the floor within a closed off crypt, its whereabouts unknown to all, the church continued to honor the saint as devotedly as if the body had been laid out for all to see. Not of course in worship to Mark, but rather to God with warm feelings of kinship when acknowledging that one of His beloved saints is lying in rest within the church's walls. Believing that someone or something at hand was present during Biblical times, or in the presence of Jesus, makes people indescribably excitable and devout. They are willing to travel very far and give very much, just to be close to a relic.

As you pay the small fee and enter the church, it takes a moment for your eyes to adjust from the bright sun without. Once you do, you look skyward to the extremely high vaulted ceilings and find it momentarily hard to swallow when you see the completely palatial mosaics, entirely created out of shimmering gold glass tiles. Their reflection splendidly shines as if the entire ceiling was painted in gold leaf and the sun's rays were cast upon them. It is magnificent! It is so glorious that you are at a loss to figure how long it would have taken to complete it. Colored tiles are used to create the images of angels, saints and Biblical stories, among the sea of gold. Certainly, it would take days, months, to admire all of the detail. The gold literally looks as though all the world's treasure was melted down and inlaid within the ceiling of this church. Just considering the devotion, time, love, commitment, money, angst and heartache that would be necessary to create this colossal work in all its transcendence, creates a faintness that directs you to take a seat amongst the pews where you can take it all in.

TURN to page 267.

THE chopine could be called an overshoe. This overshoe was attached to a platform made from wood or cork. These high heels women wear today don't compare to the height that the chopine could have reached. They required several servants to assist their mistress into them! She'd have a dainty pair of shoes on already. She'd then step up and into the chopine with the help of others who would then tie this overshoe into place. I'm sure there were several ways of doing it, but that is one. These chopines, were like clog shoes but much loftier. They could be 15 or even 20 inches tall! Take out a ruler and imagine it yourself, do you believe it? These shoes only had one practical purpose and that was to keep your pretty slippers and the hem of your rich gown from spoiling in the mud and garbage in the street. It has been said, because they were so popular in Venice, that they were invented here for noblewomen and courtesans to keep their feet out of the floods from the aqua alta. But, this is actually unlikely, I told you false! Ha-ha!

You smile at Nicolosa's story and completely understand why it is often said that the shoes were invented for the purpose of walking above flooded streets. This theory makes sense, though you don't believe that chopines would have been as effective as rain boots.

If I were to guess, these ladies didn't walk around in the aqua alta. Chopines may have been tall, but they were richly made, they weren't designed for swimming! Chopines were also very popular in Spain, so who is to say exactly who wore them first? Now imagine women walking about Venice in shoes that were 20 inches tall! They had to lean on the shoulder of a servant in order to not topple over! What was originally useful by helping avoid the mire of the streets soon became a fashion of pure vanity. A noblewoman walking around towering over men and servants, trying to be taller than all her friends! Ha! Some chopines were even embroidered and displayed gems. Occasionally, they even matched the ornate fabric of the wearer's dress. Chopines were not just for noble born ladies but courtesans too!

Courtesans are an interesting part of Venice's history, just as geishas are in Japan. Many people believe that they were only prostitutes who sold their bodies for higher rates than the other local workingwomen who solicited themselves out on the streets. This is only partly true. An honest courtesan or cortigiana onesta was actually a very impressive woman. She would have been very intelligent, even more educated than many women today! She may have been able to speak several languages, would have understood current events thoroughly, had excellent conversational skills and have had a world-view of her own. To add to her intellectual accomplishments, she may have also been a stunning entertainer, being able to act or sing or play an instrument truly well. She also would have been beautiful, wearing the latest fashions and playing up her most elegant features. She would have been sought-after because she made a very nice companion. Courtesans set the fashion trends in Venice and dressed much like noblewomen, even if they were not of the same social status.

Why would a woman have chosen this profession? Freedom I suppose. For most of history and anywhere in the world, women have had to live very strictly. Here in Venice, not a few hundred years have passed since the days when a woman was either married or sent to a nunnery to live her life chaste and enclosed. She couldn't get a university education or choose a career in which she could make her own money. She had to live under the protection of her parents until they found her a husband or sent her to live with the nuns! So some, if they were privileged enough to have a way of getting educated, chose also to learn the graces of the cortigiana onesta, selecting this life path in order to gain enough wealth to become fully independent. Now, not all courtesans had the same plans for themselves. Some were married women who took on a wealthy lover under contract. These women were considered courtesans in that they had a mutual understanding with their clients, either for political gain or social improvement for themselves or their husbands, potentially increasing their entire family's wealth. Their husbands knew of these arrangements and accepted them due to the luxuries that could be afforded to their lives because of them. You might find this horrifying, but as I mentioned before, husbands and wives were not usually in love, but were merely bound to an arranged marriage for the gain of their respective families. This would not have been very common, but it was one lot of the courtesan set. The rest were unmarried women seeking to control their own destinies.

However, living as a courtesan whether married or not was a serious gamble. You could become diseased or socially scrutinized and made an outcast from one day to the next. Most wealthy patrons would pass courtesans they no longer desired, on to other wealthy friends, so that in her career a courtesan needn't necessarily profit from many men. She just needed to keep in good graces and remain beautiful and entertaining to a select few. But, if she caused offense or her loveliness began to fade, her livelihood could be quickly destroyed. You'd have to be a good financial planner, or die penniless in the end, which many courtesans did. They soared the highest echelons of wealth only to crash into penniless exclusion. A courtesan's life should not be romanticized, but neither should it be meanly judged. She was a woman who aspired to survive outside of the, often cruel, social norms of that time and used more than her body to do it. Primarily, it was her intelligence that she used to circumvent the system, as best she could. For those of us who are freeborn women today, and also living in economically healthy countries, we should be very glad to have the choice to mold our lives how we envision them, at least in having the freedom to try. We should be happy that at a young age, we do not have to rush into a career as wife, nun or courtesan!

After this story, you are glad that you do not have to make any fast decisions about your own future. You are thankful to be able to have the liberty to travel alone while enjoying the respite and excitements of your own making. You love being able to take each moment as it comes, fully responsible for your own decisions without pressure from anywhere. With an appreciative spirit, you remember your many blessings, anticipating what happy moments life will bring next.

Having finished your wine, you thank Nicolosa for the delicious spiced beverage as well as her time spent sharing stories. You are glad to have met her and, how nice it was to find such a convenient seat out of the crowd! She returns the thanks for your patronage and is glad to have met you as well. After disposing of your cup and napkins, you both wish each other much luck as you depart.

For a time, you walk the *calli* simply enjoying the fresh air, viewing the elaborate shopfronts and observing the meandering costumed visitors. Before long, you decide to pick up a few *tramezzini* for later in the evening; you'll casually dine on them at your hotel. After removing your dress and all its accompaniments, you'll take a rest in the courtyard for a time, perhaps writing out a few postcards. When it's time, early to bed you'll go. After all, it would be better not to overextend yourself today, with a costumed ball to attend tomorrow!

Turn to page 397.

Venice

YOU retreat back into the belly of the shop and closer to the counter where the spice vendor is in order to hear more about this news of Venice sinking. Of course you had heard this said many times. Even when mentioning to others that you were on your way to visit Venice, you were told that the city was returning to the sea. It was either said as a way to contribute to the conversation by someone who knew nothing more about the city, or one simply shook their head as if mourning a ruined friend, even when they'd never visited Venice themselves. To be polite, you introduce yourself and the gesture is returned. The owner's name is Gasparo and he'd be glad to tell you of the city's ongoing plight.

Here is what most tourists don't know. When they hear that Venice is sinking, they envision our city as one big island and that the whole lot of it is reducing deeper and deeper into the mud, bringing us closer to sea level. They see a single landmass disappearing underwater like the mythical city of Atlantis. I don't blame them for thinking this because it is the media that make it sound this way. If you were to do a quick search on the Internet about it, you'll find several short paragraphs in a few digital newspapers that tell the world that Venice is sinking more and more each year and by about how much. On average, they are telling us we are sinking by one millimeter yearly. Do you know how many millimeters equal one inch? 25.4! So if the entirety of Venice is sinking at a rate of a single millimeter in 1 year, we'll sink a full inch every 25. That is still very serious, but we certainly wouldn't disappear overnight at that rate.

Unfortunately, this is what you read in those articles that amount to one or two paragraphs online. The writers were probably handed an assignment to tell readers about the phenomenon, yet didn't take it very seriously or do much research! The situation is quite different from your single millimeter per year. Venice is not a solitary landmass remember, it is a cluster of 118 islands all connected by bridges. Even with this knowledge alone, it would be clear to anyone that this many islands would not all be sinking just the same. This would be a good assumption, because indeed they are not. The sinking of Venice is a very complicated situation. Some areas are remaining stable, some are sinking at the aforementioned rate and some are sinking at 10 times that speed!

Here is something else most people outside of Venice don't know. Not only are these separately sinking *islands submerging at different rates, but they are also going under because of individually unique circumstances. It is true that our city was all built much the same way. Ancient citizens drove tree trunks into the muddy earth and seawater to create supportive foundations. They then constructed buildings on top of these wood pilings. One may ask how they accomplished this knowing that wood rots when it gets wet. Wouldn't their foundations crumble within years? Interestingly, because these logs are not exposed to very much oxygen, they turn to stone down there deep in the mud below Venice. Petrified wood! All of that wood turned stone is what is supporting these marble palazzi, and quite efficiently for 1,000 years! So, unless there are some very unfortunate problems with your foundation and it is being exposed to air, you aren't likely to sink because your wood is rotting. The real danger is often what is going on above water.*

Venice has many mature buildings that are hundreds of years old. They are so magnificent and so worth preserving, that they have to go under rehabilitation from time to time. You'll never take a walk around Venice without seeing construction on some very grand buildings; the restoration efforts are constantly underway. This work can be quite disruptive to the gentle balance these buildings have with their foundations and there is evidence to show that there are areas on some of the islands where a faster rate of sinking occurs, because of such conservation. Construction is simply disruptive. But that is just the beginning.

Scientists believe that when building began in Venice, long before it looked the way it does today, the height of the city on average was about five meters higher than it is now, or the waters were lower by that much, however you want to look at it. That is 16 feet! How did this happen? How did the sea and our ground level get that much closer to one another? Well, it has been a slow progression but recently in some areas, the sinking is very fast indeed. One culprit is our rising sea levels, and we all know why that is occurring. Global warming! Everyone wants to believe that global warming caused by human pollution isn't really all that bad, that it only affects the polar bears. They couldn't be more wrong. Cities such as New Orleans, Bangladesh, San Francisco, Jakarta, Shanghai, Manhattan and Venice are all being affected by the melting of polar ice, and that is just to name a few. The idea that cities near water, even entire islands, could disappear forever is no myth. As the average temperature of our earth continues to increase, cities will begin to go under.

So some parts of Venice have heavy construction that causes building settlement and foundation disruption, while other areas are being encroached on by the sea. What else is causing our destruction? Tourism! Unfortunately, Venice's glory days of being a wealthy merchant city are over. Instead of maintaining our economy with trade, or say, local production such as salt, we've turned to tourism. This change happened very quickly. Our citizens began turning away from local economy and craft and started working in hotels, as tour guides, waiting tables in restaurants, things of that nature. Thus, tourism continued to increase with all of this open arms hospitality and the price of living began to get out of control, as high prices could be fetched from the daily visitors. Venetians started moving out to the mainland and now what do we have? More tourists than Venetians, a highly inflated market, a loss of our traditional trades and so many visitors, it is destroying the city. Massive cruise ships come to harbor in our lagoon just outside of St. Mark's Square and thousands of people file off of them daily. The waves from ships, *their mass in the lagoon, causes the water to erode our buildings and our foundations. Speedboats carrying needed supplies to host the crowds cause waves, which expose foundations to air and buildings to crumble. At this time, Venice has become reliant on tourism and the city has no other economic fallback. I don't tell you this to say that Venetians are not welcoming of guests, because we are. It is simply the unprecedented amount of tourism, which is squeezing our city to death. If only we could pullback some and rekindle parts of our past trade and stability. After all, balance is everything and a city is nothing without its traditions.*

There are other contributors to the sinking, such as strange weather, which has been increasing in recent years. This can cause flooding and is directly related to our abuse of the environment as well. In any case, the stains that you see here inside of my shop and in the calli outside, that is from the aqua alta. The aqua alta is actually just a tide that is caused by the sun and the moon, regular rising and falling of seawater due to the heavens. There is nothing more normal. However, we are particularly affected by it here due to the shape of our lagoon, our sinking issues and some very intense winds that force the water landward. This is something we deal with for several months each winter, usually on a daily basis. The lowest altitudes of Venice are the most inconvenienced, such as the San Marco district where we are right now. The authorities warn us daily as to what level of flooding to expect and we deal with it; the flood comes and goes within about four hours. That staining you see is seawater that would have made it to your shins. In some places, it will make it to your knees or even your waist. Now, the aqua alta is a natural phenomenon and has been flooding our city for 1,300 years. It's just worse today, because we have come closer to sea level. So, if you look at those stains and wonder why we built this building right in the way of the floods, well, we didn't. And regrettably, the higher the tides of the aqua alta become because of our submersion, the more sinking and destruction that occurs. The worst of these days is when the tide is especially high and it is raining at the same time, HA-HA!

So what are we doing to save our city? Well, there are projects in place that are working to do what they can, if not to stop the sinking, to at least stall and prevent it as much as possible. You should research these efforts if you find it at all interesting. However, as

I said, the problem is very complicated. Not all of Venice is sinking at the same rates or for the same reasons. There are many things that contribute to a problem this serious.

Looking to the level of the stains once more, you ask Gasparo what it's like to manage a business with the *aqua alta* during those months. He tells you that storekeepers such as he always elevate their product at a certain level out of harm's way and that people simply continue to shop. Every Venetian owns several pair of rain boots! Furthermore, they all do what they can to keep things mold free and dry, such as stainless steel display cases and tables that can be wiped down, no carpets out on the marble floors, nothing electrical kept below waist level, plenty of mops and buckets and sandbags, all the things you'd expect when coping with flooding. It can be a pain, but it isn't Atlantis yet!

This gives you much to think about, how hard some people must work to keep a way of life going when greater forces make it daily difficult. You can't imagine what it would be like to have the first floor of your home flooded for four hours each day during the course of several months in the winter! You tell Gasparo as much and he tells you that in fact, many first floors of the local homes are purposely kept vacant in this century as moisture and mildew are not good for human lungs and efforts to keep your possessions out of the path of destruction would be fruitless. With less physical living area in homes in Venice, which were already limited on space to begin with, real estate prices are driven even higher. Living space is precious! However, this isn't entirely due to the *aqua alta* as Venice is built right into the sea. Damp is simply a way of life. And as far as the *aqua alta*, it does not touch every one of Venice's buildings, just the ones in the lowest levels of specifically affected areas (for now). He tells you that his family has been in the spice business for centuries and that he feels quite blessed to own a shop here near St. Mark's Square where business is good. *Aqua alta* or no, he isn't going anywhere yet. You like his spirit! Thanking Gasparo for sharing some of his local wisdom, you tell him that you will be sure to tell others about Venice's current struggles. It is important after all, to talk about how climate change is affecting not just this city, but also all places and all people. Environmental problems and local issues plague all cities, and you tell Gasparo that you hope real solutions will help Venice and fast! He thanks you and wishes you well as you depart.

After touring the *calli* for a long spell, you stop to buy several *tramezzini* to dine on later at your hotel and begin walking back. As for tonight, you must rest and early too, as tomorrow there is a ball to attend!

Turn to page 397.

Venice

YOU take a moment to consider the stranger's offer while the gondolier waits patiently, crunching on nuts and scanning the crowd. The boatman is evidently used to tourists who are trying to make up their minds after considering boat rates, weather conditions and susceptibility to becoming seasick. Considering how long you've been thinking about this day, the day you'd be here in Venice, Italy during the great Carnevale, in costume and riding in a gondola, you are determined that this should be the moment that you take this customary trip. However, following your own best judgment, you don't think sharing an isolated boat out on the deep Grand Canal with a stranger, is the best idea for you. What if he has a criminal relationship with the gondolier and they are plotting to rob you of your money, only to throw you overboard to be sucked below the waves by the gripping undercurrents and you succumb to drowning? It was rather suspicious that the man so advantageously appeared the moment you were asking about the rates. You certainly find it uncommon for a stranger to make an offer to split a public fee and though it isn't quite the same, you begin envisioning creepy scenarios in which people have picked up hitchhikers while driving on dark country roads and were never seen again.

You don't want to appear rude however as the man could have been making a genuine offer out of kindness; the shared ride might have saved you both a little money for this pricey excursion. Also, you acknowledge that your imagination often leads to eccentric suspicions that may be amusing, but have no basis in reality. You smile and thank him while firmly shaking your head "no", also making a fast excuse that you would prefer to take your ride in a gondola alone. Without looking back, you approach the waiting gondolier and count out the full fee into the hand of his that is free of empty pistachio shells. Glancing over your shoulder, the boatman expresses a shrug to the unknown gentleman who is evidently still lingering behind you, then leads you to his boat. Steadying one of your hands firmly while you use the other to lift your skirts out of your path as you embark, he guides you safely into the waiting, wobbling gondola. Almost as soon as you are seated comfortably, the gondolier has untied the boat, pushing it off from shore and is smoothly rowing out into the waves. Glancing over the shoreline of the square, you are unable to identify the whereabouts of the masked man.

Sailing out into a mysterious blue-green sea toward

the direction of entry into the startlingly scenic Grand Canal, the steady boatmanship of the gondolier and the solid workmanship of the craft, stable it from rocking excessively in the waters that you had regarded as irregular minutes before. The wind is a bit more biting out on these reflective waters, thus you melt into the velvet cushions of your seat and shrug comfortably beneath your warm mantle, pulling your gloves that have relaxed, snugly up your elbows.

As soon as the bustling square fades out of sight, the wide-mouthed admission into the Grand Canal swallows your vessel whole and you are soon floating between the copious palaces lining the shores. The agitation in the open waters seem to calm considerably once entering the canal and you find yourself gliding serenely as the gondolier maneuvers his single oar confidently. Your seat is facing the boatman who is posted at the back end of the craft, thus as you float along, you peacefully observe the scenery while passing it, rather than as you approach. While soaking in the experience, you ask Ubertino (as he has introduced himself) just how many palaces there are in Venice. The number he relates (about 450), stuns you more than the occasional intervals of frigid sea spray that mist your face, picked up on the wind. You can see for yourself that there are many, as they are plentifully lining the Grand Canal, but are at a loss to imagine how much money and labor would be required in order to build and outfit hundreds of palaces. Where did all that wealth come from and how much would it cost you to own one of these architectural behemoths for yourself? Querying the latter, Ubertino discloses that it would be hard to find an intact *palazzo* on the market. Today, individual palaces are usually divided into several units. These apartments can cost between one million and four million euros, even more, apiece. As though each building was made of gold, you scan the magnificent coastline with wonderment.

You were previously aware that even to pause for a spell in this city, would be costly. Many of the accommodations that you researched while reviewing hotels prior to your travels, were actually *palazzi* that had been converted. This revealed that it could cost thousands of euros, just for a single hotel room for one week. You were fortunate to find a room that though still costly, was reasonable judging by comparisons to other rates. You were surprised then and now at how steep the cost of living in Venice must be, but owing to the current view, you can also picture just how much money simply keeping such properties in a presentable state would necessitate, thus why living expenses could be so high. In a city of water, the constant damp would inevitably cause havoc to stone, plaster, paint and fabric. That with the general antiquity of most all of these buildings, it would require constant currency and close attention to keep them in basic functioning order, let alone in palatial splendor.

After chatting a little bit more (you chirping various questions between lengths of time spent attending the scenic views), Ubertino mentions that the first floor of many buildings is uninhabitable in the current century due to flooding or the threat moisture and mold pose to inhabitants. Thus, real estate becomes even more valuable due to less physical areas within homes where one can live. Plus, Venice is a small city. If you were in good health, you could walk from one side of this watery metropolis to the other in a morning. The bridges are laborious to climb and descend again and again however, so you may have to stop for an espresso or two along the way, but you can walk the length of the city in a few hours. Thus, homes are more expensive per square foot, much like the congested New York City. Further, as a measurable mass of small islands, you can't just go buy a fresh plot of land and build a new house. The only homes available are the ones that already exist, and have for hundreds of years, homes with exceptional pasts that must be maintained within historic limits. For this you need money, gondolas full of it. According to your guide, inflation due to tourism has also made things more expensive, a factor that hasn't detoured visitors, but is certainly alienating the locals.

Venice has less than 60,000 citizens. The population was three times this much in my great-grandparents' lifetime. Today, the number of sightseers that visit each day exceeds the number of Venetians! Can you believe it? And now, Venice has become very reliant on this tourism and the money it brings to the city. Do you know why?

Our current condition ballooned very quickly. Our city was always a popular destination, but this theme park style of modern tourism progressively began to overtake Venice during the last 50 years. Because of this, many of the ancient vocations Venetians used to master have become secondary to creating business around tourism. Why labor in trades other than those of restaurants, hotels or tours, if you can't profit as much as your neighbor? Why enter occupations that have become irrelevant? Many Venetian traditions are becoming lost, forgotten.

You contemplate this while pondering the fact that your guide too, is a part of this prevailing vise that the tourist trade is squeezing Venice with. Though Ubertino is a trained gondolier, the current business is nothing traditional due to the customer base he must attend. Instead of working to tow around Venetians, he is rowing to accommodate foreign visitors day after day. Gondolas are no longer transportation; they are a joyride into the past. Though he doesn't sound embittered, he does appear saddened by the way the city has changed.

The citizens are all leaving, moving to the mainland. There are more Venetians on the mainland than in Venice! Businesses have inflated the prices on everything from homes to transportation to food. Come to Venice and you can find many Carnevale mask shops, but how easy is it for my elderly mother to find a dentist, post office or a shop where she can purchase affordable clothing? This influx of the tourist-in-mind business seemed necessary so as to accommodate the growing tourism. I understand! We naturally embraced the economic opportunity, but there are repercussions.

Venice

Perhaps we didn't see just how many tourists would flock to Venice. Perhaps the more hospitable we were, the more accommodating, the more that people came. And they do! Each day more tourists visit than the day before it seems. The masses are insatiable! You may think that this is good for me, that I'll earn more money for my family. Yes, well I may earn more, but everything is so much more expensive, being a traditional gondolier is no longer an opportunity for me. And the day-trippers look at our gondolas as though they were amusement park rides. It has even become impossible for common citizens to hail a gondola across the Grand Canal when they need to get their groceries from one side to the other. The prices are too high!

Most of the visitors just come for a single day. They float in on enormous cruise ships and they don't do very much honest sightseeing. Most leave without having learned anything of our history at all! They just eat some gelato and buy souvenirs! The thin lanes choke with tourists! Venetians avoid any street where the masses suffocate the walk; they are like herds of sheep. During the summer, it is impossible for my mamma to get to the Rialto market! These tourist ships, they cause waves that eat at the foundation of our palazzi. Plus the influx of speedboats needed to transport all of the goods to daily restock Venice, as well as the cruise ships, exacerbates this building erosion. Soon, there will be nothing left to see. Certainly, there will no longer be any Venetians in Venice! Already, many caffes are being bought and run by outsiders who want to get in on the opportunity to make money off the tourists. You want to buy a caffe? Sure, go ahead, anyone can run a good caffe. But do you know how to do it the Venetian way?

Do you know how to tell when something is amiss in a city? When 30 percent of the population is elderly and the rate keeps increasing! In other cities, maybe seniors account for 10 percent of citizens, 12 percent? But not here! This is why Venetians love babies! Because we need more of them! But our young citizens continue to flee. Who will take care of all our nonne, our grandmothers? Will the cry from the birth of a Venetian babe fade from Venice forever? Everyone thinks the fate of Venice is that we'll sink into the sea. Perhaps someday! But even before that, Venice will become something worse, a city without its people, which isn't a city at all.

Passing under the architectural feat of the Rialto Bridge, you bite your lip to break a faint quiver, your eyes becoming a little blurry. Observing all of the people crossing over the bridge, like an army of souvenir seeking tourist ants, you sniffle once and then clear your throat of the emotion as quickly as it swept in. Something about the lack of squalling newborns, or imagining the elderly shifting around all quiet and lonesome, makes you wince; a touch of mournfulness, the unease of guilt. You're now a part of the tourist trade that is slowly choking Venice to death.

Signorina, please don't look sad! It is the Carnevale festival! Everyone is welcome to our beautiful city during this celebration! It is a time to forget all troubles and only live for the delights of the world! Just by your handsome, proper costume, I can tell that you spent a great deal of time considering our history and that you genuinely care to learn more about it. You must be a person who can both acknowledge the good anywhere, with the bad. If you love Venice, please do something small to preserve it. That and please, just don't ask me to sing "O Sole Mio"!

Your mind is swimming around the question of how you can help preserve Venice's future. Not quite sure, you commit to researching ways to show your support when you arrive back home. As for now, you will resume the path of the pleasure seeker! You smile languidly and ask Ubertino what "O Sole Mio" is.

The gondolier begins singing with a moving tenor voice; the force and beauty of the sound catches you off guard. You are a little embarrassed all alone in the gondola, as the boatman begins attracting the attention of the crossing people on yet another bridge, which is passing overhead. There are fewer visitors in costume here than in St. Mark's Square, so you likely appear to be something of a rarity. Many begin hurriedly snapping photos and recording footage of the vocal gondolier and you, his costumed company. He pauses in his song and entreats you to go along with the moment.

Pose for them! You are magnificent! Let us show them Venice!

He begins laughing heartily. Very quickly, all shyness aside, you do too. Ubertino is acknowledging the point that all that matters for the tourists is the show, so why not give them one? He begins singing more forcefully and passionately than before while remarkably, still able to direct the gondola with his heavy oar! And you, disguised in your fabulous array, wave proudly to the onlookers. Surprisingly, many begin cheering and waving back! To them, you are a dream. In this moment, you are their desired mirage into the past! From the ever-narrowing sides of the Grand Canal, Venetians and tourists alike, pause to watch the striking, mysteriously masked woman floating by. You make every attempt to appear in the pose of a dignified yet comfortable lounge and you smile pleasantly for them. Repeatedly, you hear the shouts, "*Bella! Bella!*"

At the finish of the song, you question why Ubertino asked that you not request that he sing it. He explains that he did this to joke and lighten the mood. All the tourists ask that the gondoliers sing the same songs. Number one on the list is "O Sole Mio" (the words of which were written by the poet Giovanni Capurro, the music created by composer Eduardo di Capua). Evidently, in an ice cream commercial from the '80s, a male passenger in a gondola in Venice sang the song. The tune was "O Sole Mio" though the words had been altered to communicate how much the singer wanted a frozen treat. Ever since then, many tourists believed this to be one of the traditional songs of Venetian gondoliers. However, it isn't. The song isn't even Venetian but rather a song from southern Italy. However, as with so many recognizable songs that tourists associate with Venice due to the fanciful liberties taken by creative media sources from all over the world, gondoliers like Ubertino are flooded with requests for these songs, each and every day.

It's a tourist thing! How can I tell them no, that I only sing Venetian songs? They're paying for the ride, so I sing to them what they want to hear. Even if I have to do it 10 times a day, what can I do?

And you quite understand. Having sparked your curiosity about his ancient vocation, you ask Ubertino to tell you more about the life of a gondolier.

TURN to page 296.

AT the slower, more observant pace you've adopted, partly owing to the dense crowd with its frenetic merrymakers, it takes you some time to walk the perimeter of the square. You allow each moment to soak in, amused by the masses while lingering beneath the arcades. You then drink in the arresting view of the lagoon while ambling before the bobbing gondolas tied to the shore, next contemplating the stunning architectural feats that are the Doge's Palace and St. Mark's Basilica. You then stroll under the opposite arcade, peeking into the shops and eateries while smiling at the antics of the throng. It is a powerful source of laughter amidst entertainments, friendships, flirtations and fellowship, all accompanied by the pulse of classical music set to electronica. At length, you pass out of the square down an unknown *calle*, in the nature of spontaneous pleasure-seeking elsewhere.

After some minutes of turning down this *calle* and that one, without any specific direction in mind, the roar of St. Mark's Square begins to dull. Continuing to acknowledge each sensation, the coolness of the marble stones that you graze with your gloved hand, the singsong words of a gelato vendor, the warmth and smell of spiced wine wafting from an elderly Venetian woman's wine cart, you find yourself content with the prospect of eventually losing your way. Crossing through other smaller squares called *campo*, you crane your neck with your festively wigged head skyward and consider the living arrangements above all the shops. Venice is notorious for small apartments, unless you own a *palazzo* of course; the city is a cluster of islands after all, which cannot be extended upon (space is precious). You don't necessarily see this as a setback however, considering all of the enchanting experiences one could indulge in, each day. If you had the inclination to do so, you'd take up residence in a cozy Venetian apartment. You'd embrace the undersized living area in exchange for the smell of the sea, fresh fish, healthy walks without cars, chewy delicious pasta, the echo of church bells in the morning mist, the traditional songs of the gondoliers passing under your window each afternoon and nibbling mouth-watering *cicchetti* in the local *bacaro* while sipping on an *ombra* of *vino*. You'd plant a rooftop garden and entertain there on summer nights to the décor of twinkle lights, potted flowers and emptying wine bottles, and of course the view of the city, sea and stars. Lost in your fantasy, you of course overlook the inconveniences of mass tourism, boat traffic with its pollution as well as a plethora of other unforeseen difficulties, just as you'd find in any city.

Entering another *calle*, you file in behind other pedestrians, several who are walking in a cheery costumed cluster. Smiling to yourself you continue to imagine, pondering what it would be like to own a dwelling with a waterside entrance where you could catch a water taxi to transport you all over Venice from right off your home-side canal. Where you'd be privately dropped from out of a gondola after an evening of culinary pleasures. Soon however, you wake from your reverie as you begin to make out the sounds of stringed instruments being tuned, both shrilly and melodiously floating out from a pair of double doors opened wide ahead.

The costumed clan before you enters the venue knowingly; it must have been their planned destination. Approaching the doors, you note a poster encased in glass at eye level next to the entrance, which indicates that you have stumbled upon one of the many concert rooms throughout Venice! It is here that you can enjoy an intimate program in a room that holds no more than say, twenty guests. You had seen tickets for sale online for these lovely, tidy showcases of some of the Baroque period's most remarkable musical pieces. For a reasonable fee, anyone can enjoy a short concert by talented musicians donning period costumes (a reenactment of the delicate musical gatherings that once took place in the private homes of Venetian nobles during the eighteenth century). Some such performances even begin with a sumptuous dinner or the music might be accompanied by ballet. In other words, it can be quite a sensory, cultural experience, not just for the ears but the eyes and taste buds as well!

Today's performance is Vivaldi's *Four Seasons*, which is a four-part piece lasting about 40 minutes. Each segment (respectively 10 minutes in length) is a composition around exactly what the title of the piece denotes, Vivaldi's musical rendition of the four seasons starting with spring. There are several reasons why this particular music is very exciting! The first being that the composer, Antonio Lucio Vivaldi, was not only Venetian, but is now considered one of the most important composers of the Baroque. He prolifically wrote operas, concertos and religious pieces for choir, during the first half of the 1700s. He is also given the rare title of virtuoso, due to the magnificent technical talents he had in playing the violin. Not only did he play and compose, he also taught.

When Vivaldi was 25 he became a priest, his true profession. However, his father Giovanni was a traveling violinist by trade. So while growing up, Vivaldi accompanied Giovanni, seeing a bit of the world and receiving his musical training from him. By the time he was ordained, he was already on his way to becoming a world-famous musician. Sadly for this Catholic priest however, he was asthmatic. As a talented musician, he was probably already disheartened at his lung's inability to play woodwind instruments (passionate musicians often took up more than one instrument), but worse, asthma quickly squashed his ability to fulfill his religious duties as well. Just one year into his vocation, he was given permission to stop giving public Mass because he was too overcome by his chronic illness. He remained a priest for a lifetime, but his daily religious duties shifted to musical ones.

Knowing that this short performance will be worth the hour of time (and the 60 euros), you enter the small concert hall, purchasing a ticket from a woman in a simple period gown at the door. The room is made of marble, as you know much of Venice to be. It is bright and airy and strikes you as the hollowed out, spherical insides of a rock with its vaulted ceilings and easy echoes. Apart from a small stage and several rows of chairs reminiscent of the rickety folding ones meant for the back lawn, there is nothing more for your eyes to explore. Without assigned seating, you choose an aisle seat to ease your heavy, fabric-laden body, and settle in for the performance.

Untying and removing your mask, you lay it gently on your lap, next pulling up some of the folds of your skirt, spreading the plush fabric over the chair next to your own and partially into the aisle, so that it doesn't grow too heavy on your torso for the next hour. Baroque era women must have required doublewide seating, you think, for the spilling out of their pannier-supported gowns. The ticket seller handed you a program upon admission (naming the conductor, musicians and technical assistants), which you peruse. It is written both in Italian and in English and is designed similarly to the pamphlets that you've received on entering a production back home. There are attractive black and white photos of the artists accompanied by text, keeping viewers abreast of their creative credentials. The elegant shots remind you of something you read of theater culture long past, when prima ballerinas, opera divas and instrumental virtuosos, were scouted by wealthy benefactors who would often fund them (occasionally and scandalously keeping them as lovers if an agreement was found mutual). This was not only commonplace during the Baroque era, but also long before and after. A rich man looking to support a gifted and beautiful ballerina for instance, would pay handsomely to make sure her every need was looked after (and her bed held solely for him). Instead of collecting rare objects, the collector desired fine talent. Lesser talent also fell into these traps of prostitution by accepting the advances of paying admirers, likely for survival, as artists were not often paid well. However, patronage did not always spell prostitution; many supporters had only the noblest intentions, to back the arts. Today there is another set of infatuated theatergoers, those who are simply obsessed with the works of talented artists and the premiered pieces of the season. These enthusiasts are always up-to-date of their local artists and performances. Here and there, you may even find a fan so engrossed they will visit a single run, each and every show. They can tell you the nuances, mistakes and triumphs of each one!

Growing bored of the literature, you scan the room and find that the small costumed group that was earlier before you, is settling in after purchasing multiple plastic, bubbly Prosecco filled, flutes from a refreshment vendor, the source of which you are unaware. You assume that they must have secured their tickets, stepped back out and into a frequented *bacaro*, bought their sparkling beverages, and returned. The party, which consists of two men and three women, appear as though they are all dear friends. Perhaps these youthful Venetians have been running around in costume together during the week of Carnevale, sans the bubbly, since they were children. They settle into the seats adjoining your own, as well as several in the row ahead of you. As they chirp rhythmically and cryptically in Italian, your thoughts return to Vivaldi.

Soon after he came to the bitter understanding that he would not be lecturing to a congregation with any frequency, that he would be unable to address his Venetian flock of local supplicants who sought blessings and forgiveness, with any regularity, Vivaldi took a special appointment. He became the *maestro di violino* for the unfortunate girls living in an orphanage, the Ospedale della Pieta. There were a number of orphanages like this one in Venice, which were supported by the local government. Here, girls acquired musical talents and boys learned a profession, so that when they were all old enough, they would have a start to help them adapt to the outside world. Vivaldi taught the girls to sing and to play musical instruments and wrote many of the pieces that they would perform. These bright students at the Ospedale della Pieta became quite popular and performed for affluent audiences regularly, and were celebrated in the city of Venice and abroad. All of this teaching and composing led to Vivaldi creating pieces for royalty. He traveled all around Europe, composing and directing his classical works. During the Baroque, opera was the most desired form of music; nobles were insatiable for each new performance. The bigger the better! This was very lucky for Vivaldi, who was an operatic genius. Even Johann Sebastian Bach (who lived at the same time) found inspiration in Vivaldi, a man who led a full career despite the ups and downs that all great talents face. The *Four Seasons* is his most famous and beloved work. It is considered very special because the music from each season (spring, summer, autumn and winter) are designed to use the sound of instruments to replicate a weave of natural sounds such as storms, animals, running streams and birds, as well as the man-made noises that often accompany these seasons, like crackling fires, dancing merrymakers, the hunt, and more. The Red Priest or *il Prete Rosso* (as he was called due the color of his hair) had accomplished a musical likeness to life itself.

As the ticket seller closes the double doors at the back of the room, the laced, wigged and frocked artists file in from a door stage right and gather on the platform. They take their seats only after a practiced, unanimous bow, authentically dressed much like they would have been 250 years ago. All of the lights in the chamber dim with the exception of a plot of illumination, which masterfully keeps the set in the warm amniotic glow of the anticipated performance. At the commencement of Vivaldi's "Spring", the company of professional violinists force you instantly transported, and with time you are emotionally carried through the realms of all the yearly phases, which the composer so thoughtfully and painstakingly created using the art of the instrument. At length, you recount life at home with family and friends. Though you and your sphere certainly do not spend your time quite the same way that circles of acquaintance during the Baroque did, these four violin concertos are able to draw up memories reminiscent of times past, spent enjoying the seasons: the warm garden and the smell of fresh ripe fruit accompanied by insects buzzing around your face, the unsettling thunder during a summer storm paired with light outages and safe glowing candles, the cool crisp chill and a pot of hot coffee shared, the heat of the fire on blushing cheeks during cherished gatherings of laughter and gift giving. It is all there in the *Four Seasons*, as well as the romance of life, laid out in the glory of perfectly timed, joined and calibrated, harmonies. Your mind envisions what the scene, set to this breathtaking concert, would have been centuries ago. You can see it all; the knowing glances across a room filled with white candles in sconces dripping dreamily, waxy stalactites. A fan covering delicately heaving breasts above a low, tight bodice line. The sensual touch of meeting hands in the dark. The sparkle of gems, the heat of a crowd, the disruptive cough of an old man to the sharp pinnacle of a stringed violin; it is all so close, you can almost reach it.

After the conclusion and several rounds of clapping, bowing and, *"Bravo, bravo!"* the room is abuzz in the exodus. You sit a moment longer; you are in no rush as you ruminate in the musical experience. You wonder why you don't go to the theater more often at home and decide that you'll commit to doing so on your return. As the shadows lift, you begin to shift as you reattach your mask. Unexpectedly, a woman from the small group seated closely, whose friends are now animatedly discussing the performance (or so is your best guess), hands you one of the plastic drams of Prosecco that they had initially smuggled into the room. You've always been taught to be wary of accepting a drink that you didn't see poured yourself, but sense that this beverage is just an extra meant to be shared, in the style that is warmly Italian. She then asks you, first in Italian which you shake your head at with an inquisitive look, and next in English thick with an accent but which you perfectly understand, *"Vivaldi! You like? Beautiful! Bellissimo!"* You grin widely while lifting the unexpectedly gifted refreshment up in a toast-like gesture of affirmation and take a sip, then replying, *"Molto bene!"* or "Very good!" She smiles approvingly and then grasps for, opens and searches around inside a drawstring purse. Clearly a little tipsy, it takes her a minute of searching to produce a business card, which she then hands to you proudly while simultaneously pointing to her friends, who have continued to debate or embrace in their passionate language, you aren't quite sure which. Reading the second card you've been handed today, you see that it is

235

the address for a *pasticceria*, a pastry shop! Reading the word is all it takes for your mouth to begin watering. It is clear that this new acquaintance and her friends (or so it seemed when she pointed to the group when she handed you the card) work in or run this one. Why not repay the kind gesture of a glass of bubbly with a visit and a purchase of a morning pastry? You smile and nod with a, "*Grazie!*"

Soon back out into the *calli*, retracing your steps to St. Mark's Square for reference of general direction, you decide that skirting the crowds and grabbing a quick *tramezzino* on course along the route back to your hotel, will suffice for dinner later this evening. Perhaps owing to a costume that you are not accustomed to wearing, or the initial excitements afforded you during your first full day in this city, you're ready for a rest.

TURN to page 287.

THE aroma of steaming mulled red wine, its draft of cinnamon and sugar, nutmeg and cloves in the coolness of the day, is too enticing to pass up. Its Italian name of burnt wine or *vin brule*, is due to the *vino* being boiled with spices before it is served deliciously hot. It is a very popular beverage on the streets of Venice during Carnevale. You approach the mature woman in her late sixties, who is running her successful business right out of a stable, stainless steel pushcart on four wheels. Half of the cart's top is designed as counter space where she cuts orange slices for her brew, rests patron's cups of wine as she counts out change, or flips through the local newspaper at quieter moments. As needed, she is able to lift up this counter space which also acts as a lid, revealing a cavern of storage area beneath for bottles of wine and spices, cups, a cash box, towels and other serving necessities. The other side of the cart houses a wide and deep stainless steel pot for the festive beverage.

Before you have even asked for a cup, the Venetian wine vendor has lifted the pot lid and neatly hangs it on a useful latch at the side of the vessel. Steam billows off of the exposed surface of a richly dark, eggplant colored liquid. Peering in, you take a deep inhale of the fragrant concoction and imagine yourself drunk off of the scent alone. Floating on the surface, steeping orange slices and cinnamon sticks swirl in a circle as she ladles out a generous, piping hot portion and fills a sturdy plastic cup, setting it on the counter. Quickly lidding the pot again so as not to let too much of the heat escape, she wipes the ladle on her dark apron and hangs it on the side of the cart. She then wraps your cup with a few napkins, likely to both insulate the cup and to keep it from becoming too hot in your hands, perhaps even guarding your pretty gloves from the stain of any wine drips that made their way to the outside of the cup during serving. You proffer the several euros required for the beverage and after carefully taking the heavy cup into your hands, close your eyes briefly as you bring it up to your nose for a healthy whiff before taking a thoughtful sip. It is just hot enough to be tolerable, not quite scalding. The flavors of grape, citrus and spice flood through your mouth, warming your throat as you swallow. You smell the libation a second time, taking a larger gulp; it is truly intoxicating.

Go ahead, drink as much as you like, there is very little or no alcohol in it.

You open your eyes to see the *vino* vendor holding

out a napkin over the counter with one hand, while pointing to her upper lip with the other and then to you. Clearly, you've acquired a purple mustache. Smiling, you accept the napkin, wipe your mouth and then look puzzlingly into your cup. It tastes like wine, a strong one in fact, with the nuances in flavor jazzed up by the spice. Looking back to the vendor with an inquisitive expression, she tells you about her product.

When you make vin brule, it boils for a long time until all of the alcohol burns out of it, it is boiled down into a spiced juice. When you make mulled wine, well then you're drinking! For that recipe, you heat it up with the spices only long enough for it to get warm, but not to the point of a boil for the alcohol to evaporate. Either is wonderful to fight off the cold and warm the heart. Godere! Enjoy!

Alcohol or none makes no difference to you; this drink is festive and delicious! Careful that you do not spill any of the staining liquid on your dress, you walk slowly to a wooden bench for two that is just a few yards from the wine-seller. Carefully setting your cup down on the seat, you plant yourself, adjusting your gown and person until you are comfortable, before picking up your drink again. After a few more sips spent watching other

239

costumed men and women strolling back and forth in front of the shops (several of them also stopping for a *vin brule*), the woman at the stall introduces herself as Nicolosa. You in turn introduce yourself and soon are speaking amicably between the customers to whom she must attend. She is interested in where you come from and what customs you keep in your family during times of celebration, peppering you with questions about how you spend holidays back home. It is a very pleasant conversation as she reveals some of Venice's traditions at Carnevale, as well as a few of her other favorite events. She loves the Festa del Redentore or Feast of the Redeemer, which takes place the third weekend in July and is celebrated with fireworks and an enormous boat regatta down the Grand Canal. Also on April 25, there is the Festa di San Marco or Feast of St. Mark, where there is a regatta for gondolas and her husband buys her roses. You tell her that it is very romantic that he brings her flowers for the holiday and she relates that though he is very generous and brings her gifts sometimes, all men are supposed to give their wives or girlfriends a rose during the Festa di San Marco. Asking her why, she tells you.

In Venice, we also call this the Festa del Bocolo,

the Rosebud Festival. We both celebrate our patron saint, St. Mark, on this day and also romantic love. It is said that sometime in the 700s, so long ago, there was this poor Venetian man. He deeply loved a Venetian noblewoman but of course, her father said they could not be wed. So, he went off to war to show that he was worthy of the nobleman's daughter. Unfortunately, he was injured in the melee and didn't survive to see her again. However, as he crawled around wounded he snatched a rose from a thicket for his lady, which he gave to his friend to bring back to her. It was wilted and bloody when she received it. A detail I'm sure is told to make the story more romantic and tragic.

You ask Nicolosa if she thinks the noble father felt bad after the death of the lowborn suitor, if he didn't regret that he barred the two lovers one from the other in wedlock.

I doubt this. He probably felt this was further confirmation that his daughter should not have married him. After all, he got himself killed in the battle instead of returning valiantly from it. Ha-ha!

The wine seller begins chuckling and so do you. The story is just a legend anyway and perhaps she is right to believe that noblemen didn't have regrets about these matters back then. After all, marriages in the noble class were created for political and monetary gain, not for love. Despite the truth or lack thereof of the story, something nice came out of it, roses given to lovers on that special day.

Chatting further on a mix of interesting topics, you ask her why the marble is stained at a certain height on all of the outer walls of the buildings around this area, and point to marble at the shop entrances across the *calle*.

It's the high waters, the acqua alta. It is a very serious problem in Venice that we have from autumn into the spring, where the tides coming out of the Adriatic Sea rise in the Venetian Lagoon and flood half of our city. Since where we are right now is so close to St. Mark's Square, which is lower than other parts of the city, the floodwaters get the deepest here. During the worst months, November and December, the acqua alta can come for three to four hours a day and the waters pour into this area up to your knees. This is why you see those stains, the seawater flooding in and leaving its mark daily during those months. The acqua alta is caused by the tides, the moon and the sun, and is our punishment for building our city in the sea. It's been happening in Venice for 1,300 years, so we've learned to adapt to the waters during those months, just like we've tailored our lives to the sea in every other way. Did you know that the courtesans in Venice wore tall shoes called chopines from the 1400s to the 1700s, simply to avoid ruining their footwear in the acqua alta?

You wanted to hear more about the *acqua alta* itself and how it affects Venice, but you can always research this periodic flooding later. For now, you're intrigued by what Nicolosa might have to say about Venice's famous courtesans. You get up momentarily from your seat to purchase another cup of hot wine and then reseat and readjust yourself on the bench while she pours for several other patrons. As she finishes, she tells you more.

TURN to page 194.

THE fragrance of spice is in the air as you continue walking along the *calle*. You soon discover that the source is a spice shop too interesting for you to pass up. Entering, you are greeted with a nod by a short, gray haired man who either owns or tends the store. The smell is very powerful and you can't place the scent of any specific seasoning, rather only the combination of many. It is a bit cloying at first and you feel a slight urge to sneeze, though you do not, while taking a look around. Along all three walls, there are glassed-in display areas that only the clerk can reach by walking behind. You are delighted with the presentation of the spices, which is unique compared to what you are accustomed to. At the shopping markets at home, you are used to seeing spices sold in plastic bottles, with holed caps for portioning out a teaspoon or a pinch. But here, there are white ceramic plates laid out on multi-tiered shelving and on them the spices lay freely in neatly heaped piles from where each can be scooped and measured out into whatever portions you like. You can easily identify multicolored peppercorns, several shades of sea salt, lavender, saffron, oregano, bay leaves, cinnamon, nutmeg and cloves. There are also many other piles of spice that you do not recognize; you are in awe of all the variety, it is very colorful! While pondering in what vessel patrons take away their seasoning, you notice different measured sizes of long rectangular, transparent plastic bags that can be filled and knotted off at the top, stacked behind one counter.

Smiling you ask the clerk, hoping he understands English, who buys the most of his spices? With swift comprehension, he briefly chuckles and points to a woman outside. She is vending the mulled wine from a stainless steel cart; the very one you had passed moments ago. He informs you however, that she doesn't pay him with money, just good cooking. She is his wife! You think this is funny and chuckle too. You imagine that she must be a great cook with all of these spices to flavor her meals available to her. You ask him what his preferred dish is that she prepares for him and he replies with resounding conviction that he has two favorites: her saffron risotto with prawns and her breaded and baked artichokes. That sounds delicious to you too!

The store isn't all spice, there are also shelves bearing glass jars of honey and sweet jams, tins of spiced cookies and sealed plastic sleeves of pistachio and candied fruit filled nougat bars. He mentions how good those spiced cookies are with his wife's spiced red wine on a chilly winter's night. You believe it, how cozy! He also has a variety of briny items such as pickled mixed vegetables, stuffed olives, roasted red peppers, artichoke hearts, sun-dried tomatoes, whole clove garlic, pickled asparagus, capers and more. There is a large selection of olive oils as well of course, Italy's butter! You envision happy hours in the kitchen using many of these items to prepare a savory, soul warming meal; most especially the spice.

During the Middle Ages through the Renaissance (and for some time beyond), Venice was one of the richest cities in Europe. It owed its wealth to its greatest asset, the sea from which its people adapted their every way of life. Because Venice was a city built from many small islands in the Adriatic, they had no land to farm to make money from grain and beast. Instead they cultivated marine salt, and traded it by land and sea, which was very lucrative. Salt not only flavored food, it was used to preserve it at a time when refrigerators weren't invented yet, making it a product in high demand. Most importantly, Venetian ships had access to the spice trade routes that had stops all throughout the Mediterranean. There they bought spices that had traveled a great distance from China, India, the Middle

East and Africa, reselling them at higher prices to Europeans. It was a very profitable trade!

In those times, foreign spice was rare and highly desired, thus very expensive. This was because they originated in lands so distant, they might have been imagined; beyond mountains, past deserts, over thousands of miles away. In fact, merchants' stories may have been downright terrifying on revelation; at the very least, tremendously entertaining, inspiring and unique, when relayed to locals upon their return from expedition. Especially if they had returned from travels well beyond seaport trading and actually traveled the Silk Road themselves in the company of a caravan of hired hands. They'd have battled pirates at sea, murderous land bandits, severe illness, mean starvation, ruthless elements, dangerous animals and life-threatening injuries. It could take you many months, years in some cases, to get from Venice to China. You'd then have the return trip. If your husband was a spice merchant making the journey, he may have been gone for a very, very long time on a single pilgrimage for spice...if he returned at all. If he did, goods intact, you'd be very wealthy indeed and your husband would deserve heavy accolades and a good long rest. This type of trade was truly risky business, yet yielded enormous returns. Then perhaps on the next venture, the merchant would stay comfortably in his *palazzo* and hire others to take the journey for him (handsomely paid of course), and watch the profits grow.

Spice was so valuable that nobles counted their stores of it alongside their precious gems! At the time, most Europeans had never, nor would ever taste exotic spice in their food, let alone see or smell it. Perhaps garden grown herbs, maybe some sea salt, but not foreign spice, which is the majority of spice we see in our kitchen cabinets today. It can be said that we now take this luxury for granted, as we are accustomed to having such product within reach at our grocery store. However, during these times of spice trade, some spices were valued at the same price, per weight, as gold.

Your basic diet in medieval times would have been meat if you had the means (or fish in the Venetian's case), vegetables, grains and occasionally fruit, without anything much to season it with. Imagine how bland a charred piece of goat or boiled carrot would daily taste without spice. You may not perish from hunger, but you'd just about die of meal monotony. Spice brought the pleasure to eating, out of what was then simple survival. With spice, dull food became palatable. But that wasn't all. More than a flavoring for flat fare, many spices were valued as a cure for illness and thus sought-after to be administered as medicine. In Venice, doctors wore beaked masks stuffed with herbs and spices that they believed warded off the plague. Sadly it didn't. Though we now know that many spices in fact do hold medicinal properties, most of these devised preventatives and cures procured during the Middle Ages and the Renaissance, were not actually effective. However, as the contrived remedies of the times, spice did create great demand, thus grand expense.

Spice was also used as perfume. Though it is often said that medieval people rarely bathed because water was not always abundantly and conveniently available, or that they believed that bathing did more harm to health than good, historic recordkeeping may support the contrary. It was common for a town to have a bathhouse, or you bathed at home or even out-of-doors in pools and streams when the weather was kind. If you were wealthy, you might even have owned a tub. However, you may not have bathed as often due to lack of conveniences and certainly didn't have modern products that kept you odor free. So, spice and herbs were used to keep offensive body odor in check when applied to your person. It also could perfume a living space or public area (for the wealthy only of course), if sprinkled liberally around.

Spices were also used to effectively dye clothing and decorative textiles, as their varied hues are vibrant and long-lasting. So it was that spice changed a rather dull world by bringing it exotic flavors, pleasing fragrances and glorious colors. Priceless indeed!

You decide against a purchase (though you may come back for some of those spiced cookies before trip's end) but have enjoyed an eyeful (and nose full) of spices and other foodstuff. Heading in the direction of the door while thanking the store clerk politely for your look around, you notice that there is a greenish-black stain at about calf level lining the marble near the door and extending around the perimeter of the room, disappearing out of sight behind the displays. Puzzled, you recognize that it is much like the stains that you saw out in the *calli* before visiting the shops. It isn't outward mold, but rather a coloring that has permeated the marble itself. Pausing and pointing, you ask the spice vendor what this phenomenon is.

Didn't you know that Venice is sinking into the sea? Out of the waters we came, and into them we will return!

Venice

TURN to page 201.

THOUGH you have enjoyed a nice respite in such an inviting little bar, you feel fully rejuvenated and really are ready to settle yourself into your hotel room and get some rest. You aren't going to worry yourself over the man outside since you figure it is only because you are fatigued and a stranger in this city to have felt any anxiety in the first place. In any case, it is better to be off now while other pedestrians are out and able to give you directions should the bartender's verbal map get lost on you. You rebutton your coat and wrap your scarf securely around your neck supposing the temperature outside is a little cooler than before with the sun having set. Pulling your luggage behind you, you are momentarily, if not a little clumsily, out on the street again (it is never easy to tow rolling luggage over doorways and cobblestones).

TURN to page 66.

FLOATING along the Grand Canal, you continue to take in the scenery while reclining comfortably on your watery transport. The stranger riding beside you introduces himself, and apologetically for not having done so sooner, as Biasio. He too seems more relaxed in his seat across from you after having shared a few stories to ease the awkwardness of having made his way into your boat. A questionable smile creeps onto his face as he states that the reason he did so, was not to save money by splitting the fee, but rather for a very different reason. He claims that though boating is a way of life in his birthplace, even since childhood he has maintained a sad secret; he's afraid of deep water and never learned how to swim! He walks wherever he needs to go. He does enjoy a gondola ride from time to time during days of festivity, leisurely taking in Venice from its waterways in the same way his ancestors did during the Carnevale, but didn't have a friend to share a trip with him today and doesn't like to ride alone. In case there was an accident and he was thrown into the lagoon, he feels safer not riding just him and the gondolier. If the boat were to overturn, he would need for you to promptly save his life. He would then be fully indebted to you for your lifetime like a genie rubbed out of an oil lamp, granting wishes, or something like that. Because he is grinning oddly, you are certain that he is telling a falsehood. You laugh outright and search his face, trying to find some other expression in his masked demeanor, which will give him away as an affirmed liar. In response to your reaction, his quirky smile turns down into a frown. As if miming disappointment, he tells you that it has hurt his feelings that you are laughing at his grand misfortune! After all, who ever heard of a Venetian that was afraid of water? Can't you see how tragic his plight?

This makes you laugh even more merrily of course, as his act is not only unexpected, but clever too. Quite the comedic storyteller, he is soon laughing with you as he is unable to keep up the frowning farce of the insulted and before long, is telling you some of the most delightful, if not random, facts about Venice of which you were not yet apprised.

Did you know that it is illegal to ride a bicycle in Venice?

No, you did not know this. Still amused, you chuckle. The mention feels silly and the look on Biasio's face appears grave, as though this knowledge was rather serious to relay. Perhaps because he wasn't afforded the youthful memories of riding a bicycle as a child and takes this affront very seriously. Upon consideration, it seems common sense that bicycles in Venice would be annoying to pedestrians and difficult to use with all of the bridges. You wouldn't be able to ride very far, either because the *calli* are too narrow and crammed with people, or because you'd need to pick up the bike and carry it over a bridge every 30 seconds.

Next he informs you that the first newspaper was published in Venice, adding that it was released once a month and that each copy was written out by hand! Such papers called *avvisi*, or announcements, would be located at an advertised place for purchase (you'd have to walk the distance to buy one as an *avvisi* would not be delivered to your home or readily available in your neighborhood). The first of its kind was the *Notizie Scritte* published in Venice beginning in the year 1556. As a recognizable historic compass, this was the time of the Tudors in England. Elizabeth I was 23 years old and would become queen of England two years later in 1558.

You could buy this informative paper for a single *gazetta*, which was a coin then used in Venice and there were two versions of the paper: one for the public and one for a select clientele, which contained more sensitive information not widely shared. The *avvisi* would carve up news of the economy, information of other Italian cities, discuss current political happenings and let you know what military conflicts were brewing. Soon, this natal version of today's newspaper took root in other cities and became more like the versions we are accustomed to digesting today. After a time in the city of Venice it began being called a gazzette (due to its original coin payment) and increasingly traded serious news for gossip (some of the best around town) and progressively became more readily available for purchase.

Did you know that the first eyeglasses, or spectacles as they were then called, were produced in Venice?

You were unaware of this fact as well, how interesting! It would seem that eyeglasses were invented in Pisa, Italy in the mid-1280s. Though there were other ancient methods for amplifying sight all throughout history up until then (such as viewing a letter from behind a glass of water or peering through a semiprecious gem for its magnifying properties) it took a while for eyeglasses to be invented. Once they were, it took no time at all for Venice, already beginning to be known for what would soon be unparalleled glassmaking, to yield them in quantity.

The first fork used for eating in Europe, was in Venice! Excellent for pasta!

This you can hardly believe! What is known to be true is that Venice is the first place in Western Europe that a fork is documented being used as a tool to aid in gobbling down one's repast. In the ancient world, there were tools described in text that sound something like a fork, but without the paintings to prove what the writings were recounting. There are several competing Venetian stories. First there was a beautiful royal woman from the Byzantine Empire who was wed to the Holy Roman Emperor Otto II in AD 972, officiated by Pope John XIII. Her name was Theophanu Skleraina. After becoming empress, she traveled with her husband a great deal. Though she loved luxury and beautiful things, she was also very intelligent and involved with her husband's business as ruler, learning the skills it took to guide her young son as emperor at her husband's passing. In the year of her marriage, she is said to have been at a royal banquet twirling around a fork. The other guests were quite shocked, possibly disgusted, by how she stabbed her food and brought it to her mouth with it. This feast took place in Italy (some say Venice). Then there was Maria Argyropoulaina, whose grandfather and two uncles were all Byzantine emperors (Romanos II, Basil II and Constantine VIII, respectively). In AD 1004, she went to Venice to marry a son of the then doge, and is said to have packed forks, golden ones that she wielded at her wedding dinner. Considered narcissistic, at her death from the plague in AD 1007, it was written that perhaps her use of forks was part of the reason she was struck down. Whichever fashionable lady provoked the trend first, Venetians were soon packing forks of their own, even carrying them around in little boxes when they went to eat elsewhere from home. And so it is that though it is widely circulated that Venice gets all the credit on the fork, at most it is likely that Venice is the first city in Western Europe to embrace the instrument.

Next, Biasio informs you that Venice opened the first casino in Western Europe as well. The news is definitely interesting, but not all that surprising to you considering the city's vibrant history. This gambling house was called Il Ridotto and opened in the San Moise Palace in 1638. Of course, betting on game in the world was nothing new and had been around for more than a few thousand years. Unlike today however, governments weren't always closely monitoring gambling. In Venice, people were gaming on the streets, which the Venetian government frowned upon, hence making it unlawful. It wasn't long before citizens were hosting illegal gambling in secret places for private admittance only, perhaps in a home or business. These illicit gaming dens were actually what Il Ridotto was named after; the word *ridotto* meaning private or closed, this first casino took its title from the secret places that it was looking to extinguish. Il Ridotto was a legal, public casino, thus the government of Venice took a cut of the income. This could be a clue to why the authorities didn't like the street gambling and secret gaming; they weren't able to tax it and take their portion of the money to be made.

Though Il Ridotto was open to the public, it wasn't as unrestricted as you'd imagine, such as the highly accessible casinos you may find today. There were strict rules about one's attire and the gambling was for high stakes. This meant it was mostly nobles and the very rich that were participating. Il Ridotto had a long run, 136 years, finally closing in 1774. Officials felt the place was getting too out of hand at that time and wanted to rein in the intemperance.

Floating placidly, the gondola soon turns off down a lesser waterway from the Grand Canal. You ponder how interesting it is that there is a first for everything and wonder what distinctive inventions came out of your own home city. You consider where you would be spending this moment with this man Biasio, had your chance encounter happened there. What unique facts would you have to share with him if the coin was overturned? The momentary quiet is serene; gentle waves lapping at the boat, a distant gondolier's cries echoing between the marble *palazzi*, muffled voices from pedestrians walking over bridges as you pass under. Though more shadowy here due to the height of the buildings which are hugging far more closely than on the larger canal, lengths of the sun's beams make their way into the water, casting it a rich emerald green. Removing a glove, you let your arm hang over the side of the boat lazily while dipping your fingers and allow them to skim the top of the cold water as you glide along. You wonder giddily if there are any fish down there and whether they nibble.

Just as Biasio begins anew by starting to tell you that like the first casino, Venice also opened the first opera house, your attention is interrupted as a joyously shrill greeting descends from overhead.

CIAO, CIAO, BIASIO!

It is a female's voice and as you strain your head upwards to look around, you see a window with double shutters open wide and a beautiful woman leaning out of it, waving her hands frantically with a beaming smile on her face. She is dressed in a simple burnt-orange gown, waves of thick curly black hair piled high on a head neither powdered nor wigged and a natural, unmade face. Appearing familiar with the lady, Biasio returns her happy greeting.

Ciao Nezetta! Scendi e soddisfare con me!

He begins gesturing with his hand in a way that suggests that he is asking her to come down. Not understanding Italian, your read on his nonverbal motions are quickly confirmed when the gondolier asks if Biasio would like for him to pull up to the water entrance below what you now acknowledge to be an especially breathtaking *palazzo*. Your companion confirms and you are soon floating into a water garage beneath the building. As your masked eyes adjust to the darkness, it is as though you've entered a hollowed out cave within a giant rock on an exotic island, only it is a reflective room of water beneath an Istrian marble palace. It is cooler than out on the lesser canal and engulfed in complete still devoid of any breeze. As the gondolier pulls up to a set of narrow stairs leading to an elevated stone platform, you peer over the side of the boat. The water is aglow, you aren't sure how, appearing as tropical waters do, turquoise and transparent. In the depths, you indeed see fish swimming frantically to-and-fro, some of them quite large. You replace the glove on your hand and search out the source of light. You spy along the edges of the deep, floodlights beneath the water, likely drilled into the marble pillars that are part of the foundation of the behemoth dwelling overhead. It is much like a driveway you think, with lights to guide your boat safely in after dark. Instead of a parking lot however, you think of it as a parking pool!

The gondolier gently guides the side of the vessel alongside the water stairs. Within moments, from an aged timber door that reminds you of a medieval dungeon entrance, the woman from above pushes happily through yelling for Biasio, a cumbersome set of brass keys clanking loudly in one hand. Distracted by her enthusiastic arrival, you hadn't noticed Biasio's absence before feeling a terrible tipping sensation and a bone-chilling splash like a bucket to the face. Unable to see with much water in your eyes, you hurriedly pull at your gloves and then with bare hands, try to untie your mask. Accomplishing this, you wipe at your eyes and are momentarily anxious and confused; hearing a scream, muffled cries and splashing while your eyes are shut tight. Though still blurry with spoiled makeup dripping into your eyes, you manage to make out the situation. Your boat is tipping dramatically to the waterside due to the gondolier leaning all his weight in the direction of the aquatic depths, his oar outstretched to a frenetically struggling Biasio who is splashing around in the frigid waters. It is immediately evident that he indeed, cannot swim and with wild eyes, appears very afraid. He isn't grabbing for the outstretched oar, possibly unaware of it in these stressful moments. From overhead you hear shrieking from the maiden and a lot of noise coming from the keys that she is hysterically jostling. You can't understand a single word she or the gondolier is saying. With what you see before you, you guess that having slipped on a pool of water in the bottom of the gondola as he tried to mount the staircase, Biasio has fallen into a serious situation.

Though you are becoming very stressed from all of the commotion and the terrible state of affairs, there is only one thing to be done, and clearly you are the one to do it. Running your fingers between your wig and your head, you firmly pull it and cap off despite the smarting sensation from several securely placed hairpins pulling at your roots. As they fall to your feet, you quickly untie the mantle over you shoulders and let it slide down your back, simultaneously unhooking your bodice and overskirt. They too fall to the bottom of the boat. With still more layers that there isn't enough time to remove, you hope that the weight of the garments still intact will not drown you. You are not for reckless gestures, but smart ones, so rather than diving into the blue without a way of knowing the exact depth, you quickly push your feet over the side of the gondola and plunge into the cold. The air in your lungs ceases short in your throat while you pull up from submerged to the surface; you have never swam, let alone bathed, in waters so icy. The top of your head feels numb and shocked, clearly the most sensitive part of your body. Breaking the surface, you wipe the water from your face and swim hesitantly toward the struggling victim, who without such masculine strength and strive, may have sunk by now. You try to focus your swim in your arms, fearing that constant kicking may entangle your feet in your skirts, rendering you unable to help.

You know full well that saving a drowning victim is

dangerous business. In their fear and flailing, they can pull you under, drowning you both. Calmly approaching, you tread water just before Biasio and call his name firmly, telling him to focus on you and to relax, that you will help him. With this first attempt, he continues to splash too harshly for a save. You call his name a second time and strongly tread, raising your body up just out of the water enough as to be his main focus and beg him to be still. Despite looking at you like a wild animal ready to pounce and force you under with him into the watery depths, something registers. He stops moving his arms and looking directly into your eyes, begins to sink without the aid of any movement to keep him above water. In that moment, you dart in to swim behind him, sliding each of your arms under his armpits and pull him forcefully to the surface until he is floating, head raised into the cold, salty air. With all the muscle you have, knowing your feet could ensnare at any moment leaving you incapable of pulling him to safety, you swim with all your might. Swimming backwards and tugging his heavy body to the boat, you feel a wrenching hand grab your shoulder, pulling you closer to the gondola. Your head sinks below water for a moment, but on surfacing, you recognize the gondolier's masculine hands pulling

Biasio out of the water and into the boat. With the release of cargo, you turn over and breaststroke around the boat to the marble stairs, hauling yourself up until you are half sitting, half laying, frozen on its cruel hardness.

Time seems to stand still as you rest your head on your arms, working to catch your breath. When you lift your head up, you see the woman at the top of the stairs watching you as though you are an alien from another planet; she drops her keys with a noisy clatter to the brick at her feet. Biasio is heaving in the boat while the gondolier claps him harshly on the back repeatedly, evidently aiding the poor victim to repulse any water he may have inhaled during his desperate moments. Peering back up, the lady seems to have snapped out of her surprise. In an instant, she has assisted you up off the stone and is guiding you arm in arm through the massive door. Looking back wearily, you see that the gondolier is following in tow with his ward, of which with sheer force, he must have manhandled out of the boat and up the stairs. They enter into the *palazzo* not far behind.

TURN to page 332.

AFTER some time sitting under a man-made heaven, observing an abundance of beautiful mosaics detailed with exhaustive dedication, exemplifying both stories from the Bible, as well as those histories of St. Mark which brought him to rest in Venice, you feel a little ashamed that you've been taking respite for so long. However, your gown does require quite a bit of posture and is heavy in the fabric. Adding that you are not entirely used to wearing a wig, mask, gloves and mantle, it truly is a bit easier sitting still just now as you observe, which in any case, feels more reverent than walking about from this scene to that as though you were in a museum. Furthermore, your silence amongst the pews where so many Venetians have fervently worshiped, head's bent in hope and appeal to their Lord to the sounds of complex, breathtaking hymn, you feel some connection to their experience. Crediting the view, it's hard not to.

At length, a woman sits the distance of several arms of you. She too is wearing a rather fine dress, though hers is of black silk. Her side panniers spreading outwards of a foot on either side of her hips, they accentuate a slender waist. Her gown is completely studded with sparkling crimson crystals that reflect as she shifts around while finding a comfortable position on the wooden pew. Her bodice is modestly high necked. Over long brunette tresses, she is veiled in scarlet lace that falls to her bosom and the middle of her back respectively, her locks cascading much further. The stitch of the veil is so fine that you can easily make out her pretty face, eyes of which are masked with a wide black velvet ribbon, scored with eye slits. Around her neck hangs a thick chain, adorned with a gold crucifix. Four large rubies ornament each point of the cross. She appears to be about your age, perhaps just a few years older. Despite not being the perfect judge of historic attire, you do experience a momentary surge of excitement out of the admiration due the authenticity of this lady's costume. She is the vision of a true noblewoman coming to worship in St. Mark's Basilica during the Baroque. You have always found it fun to regard other women's choice of fashion, even replicating an attractive clothing trend or hairstyle now and again. How much more amusing at this moment to imagine that you are in the eighteenth century noting the fashion of this lady, who appears both devout and mode simultaneously; perhaps on another outing, you'll purchase and don an elegant lace veil too!

Venice

Your focus turns to other awed guests, shuffling quietly, communicating in indecipherable whispers one to another. You hear a forceful sneeze somewhere in a distant corner of the church, the sound of it echoes. There are a smattering of visitors peppered throughout the pews. Some crooking their necks to get a better view of the glorious bullion vaults while others have their eyes closed, heads bowed in quiet reverie complimented by silent prayer. In the midst of the wide aisle between your park of pews and another set, there is a simple timber box supported by a marble pedestal. It is crafted with a heavy wooden lid that is kept sealed by a padlock, chiseled with a thick slit on the top for donations. A mature man, perhaps in his late sixties, dressed in a brown leather jacket, plaid button-up shirt and tan cotton dress pants, pushes some loose change into the slot. Owing to the dull clanking sounds, you assume that the coins have fallen into a full nest of monies rather than into a vacant abyss at the bottom of the tithe box. You could imagine how easily charitable sentiments can surface in a place such as this, not only due to the natural human remembrance of those less fortunate or for the good of the administration of the church, but also in the certain understanding that some of the offerings will be

269

used to keep this profoundly moving, glorious monument, in pristine upkeep. A dedication to the generations of architects, craftsmen, artists, generous sponsors and fanatic storytellers that burned to keep Venice's history alive; each coin is assuredly worth every euro.

Unexpectedly, the woman aside you asks you a direct, perhaps rhetorical question. In English, accompanied by a distinctly Italian accent, she asks if this basilica isn't the most beautiful in the world? You smile kindly and turning in her direction, softly answer that while you have not seen all that many churches that can claim a history half so impressive as that of St. Mark's Basilica, you can truthfully say that you have never encountered a house of worship as beautiful as this one! Within a few moments, you both have exchanged names and are chatting amicably and animatedly, while still keeping to a hushed and proper tone.

You soon discover that Carmela, as she is called, is Venetian and can trace her ancestry to a noble house in Venice from centuries ago. You find this tremendously impressive! She rebukes this sentiment however by owning that if only one's family commits to collectively keeping track over the years, it isn't hard to trace ancestry. In fact, she asserts, you yourself could also be of a grand line or a historically interesting lineage, despite your ignorance due to poor recordkeeping on your family's behalf. After a few minutes of introductory mentions, including how you planned for and found yourself in Venice, she shares some unique context to her veiled visit to St. Mark's Church.

My family is of noble descent and has lived in Venice for centuries. The luxury of this heritage doesn't translate privilege to my life now, but it certainly would have been interesting to experience living amongst the generations of my family in times past. I visit the Church of Saint Mark simply because it's beautiful, regardless that this particular basilica doesn't have any specific connections to my family. Coming to the church veiled is rather a matter of contemplation for me. You see there was a certain practice amongst nobles in Venice to send their unmarried women to nunneries, where they lived out their lives, absolutely cut off from a normal life. My family is able to trace several such female relatives who took the veil and were given up to this fate. When I consider this, I am very thankful for the liberties that I enjoy today.

You are both intrigued and a little confused. It's

amazing that your new acquaintance can trace such a history and that she shows a sensitive regard for the women's experiences in her lineage, but wonder what she means by sending women to nunneries. Wasn't entry into a nunnery a choice where women who desired to devote their lives to worship, could? You ask her as much and her answer is both fascinating and alarming.

From even before the Renaissance, women have been sent, demanded, to the nunneries. There were once laws in Venice that no woman was to be made to, or tricked into, going to a nunnery against her free will. But it is likely that the majority of women, who committed their lives in those days, were in fact forced or tricked into giving their vows. There were nunneries all around Venice, filled entirely with noble women! This is sadly due to one reason, inflation of dowries. When a family wanted to betroth their noble born daughters to men of other noble houses, they needed to have very large dowries in order to attract the most profitable grooms. A dowry was essentially a wedding gift, or payment rather, that a groom received for marrying the bride of his family's choosing. The dowry could be considered forced conciliation for taking a bride not of his choosing, because it benefited the groom's family;

dowries were bloated with money, land and titles and the bride's family was usually of some useful connection to their own. These transactions had nothing to do with love; marriages were about making bonds that would benefit the fortunes of both families involved. Now, let us say you came from a home where there were five daughters. Even if your family was very rich, inflated dowries made it so that only one or two of your girls could be married. You just couldn't afford to wed them all.

An irritating hushing noise is heard from two pews behind the one that you are sitting in. Clearly, the chat between you and Carmela has unsettled someone desiring a more observant experience. Peering over your shoulder, you find that it is an elderly Italian woman with a square of lace upon her head, pinned and resting lightly upon cottony, silver hair. Her brows are furrowed amidst wrinkles; she is golden in years and despite a hint of frailty, there is a beautiful, proud strength to be regarded in her features. Despite the immoderate censure and the fact that it is visiting hours for tourists rather than during a religious service, you honor her request for quiet; you've traditionally always respected your elders. Scooting closer to your friend, Carmela restrains a laugh as you lean in to hear her continue her dialogue in whisper.

You may be asking yourself, why couldn't unmarried daughters simply stay at home? There could be several reasons why their families would not allow this. Perhaps they felt their daughters would grow to be a financial burden that they could not support for a lifetime. Nunneries were a safe place to send their female children, where their living expenses were a fraction of the cost of their lives out in the world. Or, perhaps their reason was to safeguard their daughters from the temptations of eloping! For your daughter to marry outside of noble blood or conceive out of wedlock by a fortuneless lover would endanger the family's name and finances. Noble blood and monies must stay pure and within the family after all! Therefore, some noble daughters were selected for fine marriages and for others, it was decided they would live their lives enclosed in a living tomb!

Your eyes wide with this new information, you must certainly be giving away the fact that you are hanging on to her every word. Though you previously understood the history behind marriage politics, this aspect of a nunnery is rather shocking as well as terribly intriguing. Keeping your voice respectably low, you ask how it was that women were forced or tricked into a nunnery and why she called it a living tomb. Continuing, she informs you.

As with any young woman of that time, you were without money of your own and unlikely to be able to earn it for a living. Therefore, you were not of the liberated mind of women today; that you could just walk away from a situation that didn't agree with you. And as a noblewoman, you would also have been imposed upon to believe in adhering to the duty of your family. You would have been raised from birth to deem that doing anything in disobedience to your parents would jeopardize your family's honor, thus making you the most ungrateful, shameful of criminals. So, as a youthful girl in your bloom, your parents may have tricked you into believing that the nunnery was a heavenly place where you would be well looked after while fulfilling your worldly, familial duty. You'd have likely been directed to an establishment that housed those of your aunts, cousins and sisters who had also been assigned the same fate. They too, despite any unhappiness to their own lot, may have elaborated on the golden glory of the nunnery, to fish you in without much trouble. You would have been young and naive, trusting in your parents and family who you ever believed, loved you. Truly, most of these families may have indeed loved these daughters as much as the ones they would send into marriage. Sadly, they assuredly prized their wealth and rank in society, more.

Once inside, these girls would have quickly found, all that which their noble parents had described to them, was false. As women who had not truly desired a life of prayer and solitude, without the prospect of a husband, love, children and the joys of simple liberty, they would have suffered hell. Could you imagine living 30, 50, 70 years in an enclosed nunnery?

You quickly ask what this meant, an enclosed nunnery. She explains.

Because a nunnery is of course, a religious institution dedicated to a life given up to religious devotion and purity, relations with the outside world would have been strictly prohibited. In fact, there were many years at the height of strict rule in convents where even windows overlooking public streets and waterways were bricked off. Where only a few older, devout nuns were allowed to purchase supplies for the convent or interact with tradespeople of any sort. You could go years without seeing anyone but the other nuns that you were locked in with, and perhaps a few male clergy meant to speak service and hear your confession. Depending on the management of the establishment, life could be even direr. Some were so mismanaged that nuns starved and froze in their sparse, drafty sleeping cells.

You find yourself asking aloud if every nunnery was as bad as that.

Surely not, many convents allowed visitors though visitation was only permitted for the closest, proven relatives and you would have met with them in a room divided by a grate or bars, nuns on one side, family on the other. As for common stricture, in many nunneries, rules were broken for years without strict governance and noblewomen there might hoard allowances from their families to purchase private stores of wine, fabric and food to stock in their rooms. They may have decorated their cells or kept small pets. No matter what the bend in rules however, your world would have been strictly guided by regulation and enclosure. Thus, any overlooking of regulation in a nunnery could never have compensated for a life of imprisonment. Unless of course you had truly wanted to be a nun; if that was the case, convent life would still have been difficult and you'd have regularly experienced mean disagreements with all the women within who were not following the laws and schedules as they should. You would have felt that they were disgracing the very place dedicated to, and the purpose for, having taken vows.

So it can be said that convents were holy safe places for a life's devotion for some and a place of captivity for the majority. Those who felt they were prisoners tried to create relationships with the outside world or recreate the world outside, within. For instance, many would attempt incorporating fine fabric, embroidery and lace into their plain, convent-wide uniforms, which was prohibited. They might expose their hairstyles from beneath their habits or wear decorative pieces to set themselves apart, which was not allowed. They would have found a way to own, hide and covet personal artifacts, which was shunned. They would develop cliques, usually containing the members of their family residing within the nunnery, and would have gathered together for late nights of games and singing, within their cells, often breaking curfews and skipping devotional meetings, regardless of the constant threat of punishment. They would have assembled in their rooms

*for meals and avoided eating with the other nuns,
pretending they lived separate lives from their realities.
Many would have used the food sources of the convent
kitchen to bake and cook special food items, to share
with their visitors or send with lay nuns who could run
convent errands, out into the community of their past; an
effort to keep friendships alive. They would have even
deprived themselves of their own rations to do this if it
meant they could have gifts to give to the world to
attract love and attention. Perhaps they would plot out
individual feet of soil to tend and call their own, in the
confined garden that should have been shared amongst
all the nuns; the fruits of their labor they may have kept
for themselves or used to cook for those outside whom
them hoped to receive a visit from, or even just a letter.
They would have spent months embroidering special
pieces for family and friends, again so as not to be
forgotten. Even stitching endlessly for their betrothed
sisters on the outside with whom they so bitterly wished
they could trade places. Some even attempted to run
away. Those who helped them risked severe punishment,
perhaps even death depending on the nature of the
relationship that they forged with the fugitive nun.*

When it is Carnevale and I put on this veil, I

sometimes think about the freedom wrenched from so many women, justified as honorable sacrifice for the longevity of their families. And though I am awed by the humility of women who made the choice to live in a nunnery out of true religious piety, I am equally saddened for those who unwillingly were led, never again to leave their confinement, while life continued outside. You must imagine the wailing of young girls in their homes when their parents told them where they would commit the rest of their years. Some would have rather died than be separated from their current lives and the potential futures they might have had. And indeed, many did die, in spirit at least, the moment they entered the nunnery. What a cliché. To lose your spirit rather than be filled with it, in a place meant to foster it in its purest form.

However, there is another side to this story as well. Noble Venetian women destined for marriage unions may not have had better outcomes in their lives outside either. It was a gamble. Perhaps your betrothed was a drunken, money hungry, prostitute-seeking lout, old enough to be your grandfather. You could have been destined for the type of man who made you ill whenever he entered the room, someone who was unkind, even abusive. Certainly, many young brides may have walked away elated and relieved with their parents' choice once their groom's identity was revealed. Sadly, if a handsome face initially mesmerized them or it was the fortune held by their betrothed, they would have quickly seen just how disillusioned they were once their wedding vows were sanctified. So, for many a noble Venetian bride, there was a wish that they could as well, switch places with their convent sisters. The cry was heard both ways.

For a pass of time, you both sit in silence contemplating the vast, elaborate beauty within the church as well as the plight of many of history's Venetian noblewomen. It is so open and airy that you find it impossible that you could be at all claustrophobic, but sense yourself increasingly becoming so. Perhaps it is the constricting nature of your costume, of which you are not accustomed. Or perhaps, you are ready to revisit your freedom out in the open air beyond the walls of this breathtaking church, which freshly reminds you of how so many religiously exhausted their lives; it was beautifully sacrificial or sacrificially tormenting, as individual stories from convents would have exposed.

After a few more minutes elapse, Carmela extends

an invitation to visit her home tomorrow evening, as her family will be hosting a dinner to celebrate the Carnevale! An intimate group of friends and family will be gathering and there will be delicious food! Will you come?

IF you accept the invitation, turn to page 358.
IF you decide that you would prefer to wait and see where tomorrow takes you, turn to page 318.

WITH great haste, you enter the courtyard at Hotel
Fato and peering up at the building, find that it looks
newer than you remember, the marble sparkling white
and clean. At the back of the yard's enclosure, you
observe a massive wooden door open wide to expose a
marble dock under the structure that leads to a canal.
Though you are inclined to get into the hotel, you feel
drawn to the dock. Walking warily toward it, your eyes
strain to assess what it is that you are seeing floating past
on the water and then chillingly it registers. It is a black
gondola with a roofed compartment in the middle. The
man steering the boat paces the oaring slowly and is
dressed all in black: tights, knee-length breeches, a
doublet with long fitted sleeves and a black mask. It is a
funerary vessel and as surely as you live, there is death
within that compartment. You stop short in your tracks
as it passes out of view and feel a tremble within you as
a second gondola floats past. The gondolier guiding it is
dressed much like the first, standing on the deck at the
back. On a bench in the middle of this boat, sits a
woman veiled in grief and dressed in a tight ebony
bodice with ample lush black satin skirts, shiny even in
the shadows. There is a diamond choker around her neck
and chandelier earrings of the same dripping from her

ears; they sparkle from beneath her cover. Not a muscle in your body moves as you observe her passing. You feel like an alarmed cat that arches its back, fur sticking up on end and eyes open wide. In that moment, she bursts out into an extraordinary wail the likes of which you have never heard, exposing you to the depths of her sadness, her mouth gaping with her cries. An icy breeze gives you the shivers to the sound of nearing thunder. In an instant her boat too is out of sight. You stand petrified as you listen to the echo of her howls, whimpering and weeping. When you can hear them no more, you seem to break out of a trance and turn to the entrance of the hotel, eyes still wide and hands trembling.

Entering, reception looks much the same but with several alterations. In place of a telephone and fax machine, there rest several leather-bound books, perhaps one for guest sign-in and the other, a ledger. Between them, a glass inkpot and an upright feather quill. You nearly cackle with insanity as you eye the room suspiciously in a game to find what all is out of place. A set of elegant mahogany chairs with ornately stitched fabric cushions are arranged in place of a modern couch, unlit candelabra standing on marble tables in place of electric lamps, velvet window treatments too rich to imagine are certainly not your average hotel lobby curtains. You take advantage of there not being a soul around (should you be calamitously prohibited from ascending to your room), and bolt up the steep stairs, pulling your skirts up to your knees in a frantic hike. Before your room you search out your key and fumble to use it, but find no need when skimming the door, it opens from the slight pressure.

As you enter the chamber and shut the door behind you, it is clear that it is the same one you slept in last night, but again, without any up-to-date amenities. To your surprise, a young lady dressed modestly in a tan bodice and full straight skirt, her dark hair bound in a pretty weave of braids at the top of her head, is sitting in a wooden chair placed next to the partially open shuttered window. A writing desk is still where one was, but it is more finely crafted and arranged with a metal inkwell, a writing pen made of glass and two candles set in brass holders, unlit. The woman sets the stitchwork that she was attending to beside her on the desk and in the Italian language (which you had previously no lessons in before) speaks and is understood by you.

Mistress! Where have you been? What are you wearing? My goodness, what is wrong? You look as pale as if you'd seen a spirit! Where did you get these clothes? What is this on your head? Madame? Madame!

It is in that moment that you begin to see hazily and as though the sparks off a hot iron, are blindingly shooting before your eyes. You identify the cold tingle of a faint coming on but are powerless to stop your body from being taken by it. The woman too seems to recognize your plight, and jumping up, rushes forward to catch you as you slump to the floor. You feel your head and back restrained by the lady's swift save and are relieved not to experience the painful crack of your body hitting the rug covered stone floor as it fell. You sense the stranger guide your torso softly to lying flat on the ground as she shrieks, "Contessa! Contessa!" Her pleas are so close, yet echoing away. You then succumb to the darkness.

TURN to page 307.

YOUR eyes slowly flit open as you awake to the sound of happily chirping birds, several of which must be sitting on your window ledge as they are having a very close and loud conversation; it sounds important. You are nestled quite snuggly under your wool blanket and lay quietly for a time listening to the chatty larks. You giggle softly to yourself imagining what they are saying to one another.

Today, today! It's the day! The day for the ball! To the ball, to the ball! Let's get ready for the ball!

Perhaps they are only singing about seeds, berries and twigs, but you are so wildly excited for tonight, you can't help pretending that their twittering is in anticipation as well. You are so comfortable that you could doze off for a time longer. However, you've had a luxuriously long and sound sleep already and don't want to waste time unnecessarily when there are so many memories of Venice yet to be made.

Rising from bed to open your shuttered window wide, you find that the gossipy birds are balancing delicately on a clothesline not far off, tweeting to one another incessantly like best friends catching up on all their latest news. It is another lovely, sunny day and already feels a bit warmer than the day before, despite still being a rather early hour. Down below, several couples are breakfasting on cups of creamy coffee, crispy bread, cheese, cold sliced meat and fruit salad; it looks delicious and reminds you of the date you've set with a sugary pastry (or two)!

After bathing, you feel quite refreshed and alert. Dressing simply in street clothing and applying only a bit of natural looking makeup, you are ready to eat and walk out of the hotel eagerly looking forward to the delicious treats you'll try. As you exit out of the courtyard, you hug yourself in your warm sweater and take in a deep breath of cool salty air, feeling happy as you look to the endless blue sky provided in this new day. Still early, there are only a few people out and the walk to the *pasticceria* takes no time at all. Of course, you have to stop several times for directions. Once, inquiring with a vendor readying his yet unopened shop with a sweep to the cobblestones before his door and a second time with a local woman walking a scruffy brown dog. Both were helpful in pointing you in the correct direction after showing them the address card given to you at the Vivaldi concert.

Standing before the *pasticceria*, the display seen from outside is a confectionary dreamland. Darting from one tray to the next, your eyes are delighted by the vision of cream filled pastry puffs, nut and raisin biscotti, strawberry tarts, cookies topped with jam, almond nougat, lemon cake, tiramisu, crescent almond cookies, cheesecake, jelly filled donuts, lemon cookies and pound cake. Absolutely heavenly!

The warmth of the shop envelops you as you enter and the intoxicating aroma of baked goods, doughy, sugary, comforting, and delightful, greets you. It is a tiny yet highly trafficked spot, thus only a glass counter is provided for eating (standing room only with no seats). It is crowded, which isn't surprising as the room is no bigger than a small studio apartment, the kitchen hidden from view behind a curtained doorway. Behind the long serving counter, there are several baristas making aromatic black beverages with the aid of two shiny gold espresso machines. Standing in a corner out of the way to observe the pulse of the scene for a moment, it is evident that Venetians stopping into the *pasticceria* on their way to work each morning are in-and-out quite efficiently. One enters, requests a baked good and an espresso, stands and consumes. The order is served up with one tiny napkin and after pleasantly inhaling a delicious breakfast treat, perhaps fitting in a few words of greeting to any familiar faces, one makes a swift wipe to their mouth to remove any errant breakfast crumbs, takes a last sip out of their coffee cup and, "*Ciao!*"

Making your way to the counter, you pleasantly wait until a barista becomes available and then point out three small delights from a selection under the counter (who could choose just one) and ask for a coffee with cream. When you are served, you can't help but smile. The white ceramic plate of pastries is so pretty it deserves a photo; you are disappointed that you forgot your camera on this outing. You are especially pleased when you realize that they do not serve your selections in disposable pastry bags or your coffee in a to go cup, neither do they hand out paper napkins in excess. Back home you can't remember how many times you went through the drive-through at your local coffee shop, or walking past grabbed it to go, always being served with disposables. You imagine that not doing so strains the dishwasher here, but sure saves the environment a lot of unnecessary waste.

You stir a few packets of sugar into your beverage, letting it cool a moment before venturing a sip. When proceeding, you alternate soft and chewy bites with a fortifying swallow of delicious coffee. It tastes as good as it looks, even better. You could definitely do this every morning! Even more certainly, your breakfast tastes fresh and is clearly handmade using excellent ingredients. You try to eat healthy food at home, but are definitely guilty of indulging in the occasional processed breakfast pastry, which tastes overly sweet and dissatisfying compared to the delectable selection you're enjoying now.

Into your second pastry, you survey the room again and find that though small, it is cozy rather than claustrophobic and the lighting is bright and cheery. If you'd set off from home having woken up on the wrong side of the bed, this place could turn your mood around. You wonder to yourself where any of the patrons from the Vivaldi performance are, as you don't recognize any of them as the employees behind the counter. Despite the group at the concert being masked and in costume, you're sure you don't see any of their features on the faces of those around you. Perhaps one or two of them are making the pastries in the kitchen. However, it doesn't matter to you. You made a polite visit as a means of reciprocating a kind gesture, spending in this shop in exchange for the unexpected Prosecco given. However, owing to the delicious bite you've just popped in your mouth, you don't feel like the stop was an exchange of kindnesses, it is *you* who has been treated once again!

Nearly finished, you ruminate in the last sips of your coffee and dream of the pending event you'll attend this very evening. Distractingly however, a middle-aged woman with shoulder length blond hair and a smart tan coat who was a moment ago chatting amicably with another female acquaintance, begins to cough. What begins by sounding like a tickle in the throat or a harmless few crumbs that have gone down the windpipe, quickly becomes a dire need to expel something fully inhaled. The woman is facing away from you in the direction of her companion so it's hard to see her face or gestures, which would give you a clearer indication of the situation. However, there is no mistaking an honest choke the moment the woman begins grabbing at her throat and her friend, calling her name, tries reaching around to hit the victim forcefully in the middle of her back. You hear some shuffling and concerned voices in the room, but can't take your eyes off the struggle happening just before you. You feel suddenly compelled to help. Though you are not sure of exactly what to do, you're hoping that what you vaguely remember of lifesaving skills will be the answer.

Seeing that her back slaps are not helping the situation, her friend stops the useless action and placing her hands up to her face, yells out beseechingly, though you do not understand the words. You quickly approach the choking woman from behind and tell her that you are going to help her, unsure if she even hears you, or understands English if she could. Not expecting a response, you can only imagine as she continues grasping at her throat and making unnaturally raspy noises, that her very being must be filled with terror in this moment. You wrap your arms around her and holding your hands together in a tight fist with tucked thumbs, place them under where you expect her rib cage to be, yet above where you'd find her belly button. You then pause a single moment to spiritually prepare and mentally focus on performing the Heimlich maneuver. You hope this is the right position on her body, as you can't be quite sure with her being dressed in her winter garments. In an instant, you commence with five quick and firm inward and upward thrusts (the motion best used in helping a choking victim to repel what is trapped in an airway). Nothing happens. You notice that the skin of her hands, which continue to claw desperately at her throat, are beginning to appear an eerie blue indicative of a lack of oxygen.

Taking a deep breath and calling on all your strength, hoping that your efforts will not injure her, you repeat another five thrusts with even greater force than the first time. Miraculously the woman expels a damp piece of bread on the final thrust and then quickly inhales what may be the deepest breath she's taken in a lifetime. Within moments, her color returns to her, turning even a bright red, as her blood vessels respond to life giving air. She releases an unprecedented stress with every exhalation.

In this moment, you consider taking a vacation from your vacation (Verona is just a short train ride away). Did you just save a woman's life? As her companion swoops in to hug and console her, you stare blankly at the last of your pastry selections, half-eaten and lying on the floor where you must have dropped it. You consider how strange life can be, how much can happen before even finishing one's breakfast, how everything can change in an instant. You hardly notice the commotion around you as you pick up your dropped delicacy, placing it on the counter, and then attempt paying for your breakfast. The barista, who you try to give the euros to, flatly refuses payment (clearly a gesture of thanks). You can't know exactly what everyone is saying, but it sounds like a mix of shock and relief. The woman is going to recover just fine, judging by her copious tears intermixed with smiles, clinging dazedly to her friend. As for you, you are going to return to your hotel and take a deserved nap. You want to be well rested for the evening ahead and a doze to ease your newly frazzled nerves won't seem like a waste of time, but rather a pleasure. Exiting the shop, you encounter several warm and genuine smiles. You don't look back but are certain that a few of the patrons are watching you trail away through the window of the *pasticceria.*

Soon back in your room, you return to the state whence you first rose some time before, closing the shutters and crawling back into bed wearing the most comfortable nightclothes that you packed. For at least a few hours more, the world and all its frivolities can wait. For now, you will revel in a life saved and be thankful that fate took you just where you needed to be and when. When you wake, the revelry will begin.

TURN to page 397.

SOON your guide turns the gondola down a lesser waterway off of the Grand Canal. This signifies the second half of the boating excursion on a route that will eventually return you to the place whence you embarked. These narrower waterways also afford you a closer view of the *palazzi* and their waterfront entrances. You scan the ancient buildings and their ornate casements; windows surrounded by marble engravings, the twisting beauty of vines and exotic Byzantine patterns. From one especially stunning balcony, you imagine a medieval maiden (perhaps a rich merchant's daughter) leaning out with anticipation for her noble betrothed who approaching by gondola in the moonlight, serenades her with a sweet ballad. You smile to yourself at your romantic (if not a little cliché) ponderings. Considering the short life expectancy in those days however, a maiden deserved all the moonlit meetings she could get! Your reverie is broken when Ubertino asks an unexpected question, which you acknowledge is his introduction to telling you more about the professional life of a gondolier.

Are you familiar with Venetian blinds?

You tell him that not only do you know what they are but you also have them in your home. They are window treatments built out of horizontal slats that can be manually shifted up or down by string or stick to either let the light into a room, or block it out. He nods approvingly.

Did you know that Venetian blinds were used for the gondola?

You shake your head "no". As a matter of fact, you had never even processed that the name Venetian blinds was associated with this city. It might seem like common sense, but it never crossed your mind. Knowingly in for a story, you ask Ubertino what these blinds have to do with his boat.

I will tell you, but first answer this. How many gondolas are within view to you now?

Taking a moment to look behind and before your own boat, you count only two. He then asks how many you recall seeing at any given length along the wider Grand Canal. You suppose about ten others and tell him so. This seems to be the leading answer he was looking for as he delivers more information.

There are around 500 gondolas in all of Venice today, perhaps less. Most of them are public gondolas, catering to the tourists while a very small number are privately maintained, the owners sometimes renting them out to citizens for their remarkable occasions, such as a wedding. Legally, there are only 425 gondolier licenses, perhaps a few more, issued through Venice's Gondolier's Guild. These licenses are highly coveted and very difficult to earn.

To pursue this profession, you must first find a veteran gondolier who is willing to keep an eye on your studies and monitor your arduously earned progression. He is there to give you guidance when it is required. Next, you must document 400 hours of learning time and practical practice, 400! Once that is accomplished, there is a very difficult test before you. This exam will judge many things. First, you have to show determined strength and the ability to manage a gondola all on your own. However, this isn't enough. You must prove yourself not just a driver, but also a master of your vessel as it navigates the tumultuous sea. You must also have a deep understanding of the geography of Venice, have it memorized even, every mysterious and hidden waterway. An aspiring gondolier must also be able to demonstrate a passionate knowledge for the history of Venice's architecture and the city's culture. After all, half the pleasure of taking a gondola ride is the scenery while the other is the interesting information you acquire from your tour guide along the way.

Trainees are also tested on their safety skills. If you ask me, they should also be a strong swimmer, just in case! HA-HA! But in general, they need to be able to drive a gondola very well, protect their riders from harm, and also be entertaining! A singing voice doesn't hurt! And an endless supply of striped shirts, HA-HA! Ok, I jest!

The Gondolier's Guild has been in place for 1,000 years and monitors the gondola profession of Venice very closely. It used to be that a man would bequeath his gondolier's license to another male relative, usually his heir, at the point of retirement or write it into his will ahead of time out of precaution in case of his unexpected death. Today, though it is difficult to do, one earns their gondolier's license and certainly does not have to be born into this lineage to be granted one. I have heard however, that on the sudden death of a Venetian gondolier, his wife if he is blessed with one, receives his license as a sign of respect. I'm not certain of the truth in this, as the Gondolier's Guild does not advertise this policy. But I believe that it is correct. Gondoliers are of a small set who with all their passion, perpetuate an all but forgotten tradition and deserve to be honored after a life's commitment to it. Of course this wouldn't stop the lot from being 425 or so licenses in rotation. The offering of this cherished document is simply a symbol of honor to the gondolier's widow.

I apologize, my tongue paddles off the canal we're on. As I said, there are only about 425 papers assigned, strictly allotted and no more. If they are all held at the time of your application, you may be waiting a long time until the stars align and one becomes newly available. But having come that far, it is worth the wait.

You can see the satisfaction in Ubertino's face as he says this. Perhaps he was one such apprentice that having achieved the required training, had to wait for a license to become available before being granted the title of a Venetian gondolier. However, there is one question that remains in your mind. Not long before, he claimed that with all the hardships brought on by the tourist trade (such as economic inflation and a theme park mentality toward his boat), it made it questionable as to whether becoming a traditional gondolier still seemed worth it. You are tempted to ask him. But after a pause, you yield when judging by his expression, it is clear that he couldn't be happier in his chosen profession, no matter what frustrations he must face.

Now imagine these waters in the years between the 1600s and the 1700s, brimming over with gondolas. Today there are less than 500, but then, there were anywhere between eight and ten thousand of these vessels! And that was not all! Though gondolas were very popular, there were a variety of other vessels mastering these waters as well. Can you even imagine how many boats there would have been?

In those days, to the usually open-air gondola, there was a popular addition made to the body of the craft. It was a little enclosed cabin where you are sitting now, called a felze. Because Venetians were driving all around town in their gondolas, much like people do in their cars in other cities today, there was a lot of traffic and as a passenger, you would have been exposed to the hot sun and rain. So, the felze was useful in protecting the rider. But that's not all. You'd have been riding alongside so many people out in the canals that you may have felt too exposed, too closely watched, too often addressed. So, the felze also worked to hide your identity on your travels and protect you from the gossipy gawking passengers in the next boat over. However, if you wanted to secretly check out the scene you could reposition the slated shutters along the sides of the felze.

Venetian blinds, your very own adjustable windows! Venetians did not invent these shutters however; the idea came from the East I believe. But we made good use of the creation!

You look around this narrower canal as you float along and try to imagine the scene during the Renaissance and early Baroque, when gondolas were as thick as jungle mosquitoes. The sides of the vessels probably skimmed one another during the more highly trafficked hours of the day like cars gridlocked side by side in a Los Angeles rush hour. That would have been trying if you really had to get somewhere in haste, but perhaps a remarkable time to people watch during the eccentric days of the Carnevale.

The felze were removed, it is believed, when gondolas became more widely used for touring rather than for transportation. Tourists don't want to be inside of a cabin when they ride in a gondola. They want to be out in the open so that they can see the view and take photographs.

Did you know that gondolas used to be painted in a variety of colors? Now they are only painted black. This is due to a sumptuary law being applied to gondola embellishments some centuries ago. Sumptuary laws were very common in history. They limited people from extravagance. They were restrictions set on what citizens could wear or eat, even what color they were allowed to paint their boat, dependent on their rank in society. If you broke a sumptuary law, you had to pay a fine and the government took the profit. Even at the risk of this fee, people broke sumptuary laws all of the time just to flaunt how grand they were and what risks they were willing to take to show off their wealth. Very often, these laws were meant to keep those with lower social status, despite their financial success in life, from behaving above their rank. Imagine a noble born Venetian riding around in a gondola carefully painted with an expensive colored lacquer. Moments later, a middle class merchant who has earned his wealth through trade, comes floating by in a boat with the same expensive lacquer, perhaps even more decadently adorned, a stunner of a boat! Well, that would have made a noble fume! HA-HA! Can you believe it? How dare that rich merchant get above his status! What was he thinking painting his boat so exquisitely? HA-HA! History is crazy! Imagine today if someone told you that you would receive a fine if you toted around a Fendi or a Prada bag because you weren't born a noble, even if you could afford to purchase one! Ah well, times are different now. Except, we still paint our boats black as I guess everyone got tired of receiving those fines!

Did you know that even the stripes on a gondolier's shirt must be of a precise width per the Gondolier's Guild? I would tell you more but as you see, we are soon to pass under the Ponte dei Sospiri and come to the end of our journey. I will give you a moment of silence and not distract from the view. In a minute, we shall dock.

Floating under the Bridge of Sighs, you recall a line that you recently read by Lord Byron, a revered British poet from the early nineteenth century. He was an avid traveler and spent seven years of his life in Italy. During one spell in Venice, he lived with a married lover (he was not her husband). The couple frequently argued, causing Byron to leave his house and fall asleep in his gondola for the evening. His paramour, who had left her own house and husband to live with him, had quite the passionate flare. It is written that at one point, Byron had enough of their crumbling relationship and asked (or perhaps demanded) that she move on and to vacate his dwelling. She threw herself into a canal. You aren't sure whether she drowned or if she swam to safety. But, you'd like to believe that her heritage as a Venetian made her not only passionate, but a strong swimmer! This unique occurrence was only one of many in this poet's rich life. And in his poem "Venice", of the Bridge of Sighs he wrote, "I stood in Venice, on the Bridge of Sighs, a palace and a prison on each hand."

And it is so that to your right, there is the Doge's Palace. To the left, the Piombi prison. And above, a limestone bridge with carvings out of the rock creating ornately grated windows. The convicted, having been sentenced in rooms of the palace meant for interrogation, would walk over the bridge and into their enclosure. It is said that the bridge was not thusly named until Byron titled it so. What influence is in the pen of a poet!

The last glorious moments of your gondola ride are spent in silence and though you would gladly float along the canals in this manner for hours more, you do feel as though this passing hour of sights and stories was even richer than what you expected. The fee paid was nothing to the experience gained. After the vessel is securely docked, Ubertino offers his hand and steadily assists you back onto the marble edge of St. Mark's Square. You sincerely thank him for the safe excursion and all the insight into Venice that he shared; it was very much appreciated. After shaking hands, you depart the waterside happily, as you'll cherish your gondola ride always. Walking back toward the inner square, you have a mind to further embrace Venice's history. As you are just a short distance away and there is still time to do so, you shall visit St. Mark's Basilica!

TURN to page 187.

PREPARE your mistress! I must bleed her. It is the necessary course of action to relieve the illness from her body. Judging by her fast fainting and the onslaught of this fever, as well as those devilish words of strange machines, we must work quickly to restore her humors.

Even before your eyes begin to flutter open, slowly exposing you to the soft candlelight in the room, you can hear a man's voice. His confusing words repeat several times in your mind as you begin willing yourself to come to. The room is warm, your body damp and there is a pressing thirst in your mouth, but you are not terribly uncomfortable. As you open your eyes, you start to recognize the situation which continues to be ever more bizarre. You are lying in the bed of your hotel room and it is immediately clear that you have not woken from this inexplicable situation; you appear to be living and breathing in another century. Asking for water at a whisper, you snatch the notice of the lady who caught you in a faint after having assailed you with questions. Startlingly, she is standing close to the door next to the figure of a tall man with the face of a white beaked bird! If you hadn't recognized this beastly vision, you may have been worse frightened indeed, but it quickly registers. It is only the unmistakable mask of a Venetian

307

doctor, who afraid of contracting a deadly pathogen wore a long beaked mask stuffed with spices and herbs in the hopes that it would prevent contagion.

Promptly approaching your side, the woman grabs for a dainty glass set on a silver tray from your bedside table and fills it with water from a crystal decanter. She hands it to you gingerly and with concern in her eyes. You ask her how long you have been sleeping, warily watching her every move. Until you fully understand the complex situation you've fallen into, it is best to be careful of everyone. Perhaps she would have allowed this masked being to cut your arm open to bleed you while you were out cold! This was a procedure very commonly applied by physicians from ancient times on through the 1800s, meant to alleviate dozens of illnesses by allowing the blood to escape the body along with any alleged impurities within it. The practice was thought to rebalance one's health but usually carried the ill victim closer to death rather than safely away from it. Before modern medicine, an understanding of the transmission of germs was unknown and a doctor's implements, very unsanitary. Having made an incision with a rusty (even if undetectable to the naked eye), contaminated knife into a vein in your arm or leg, a variety of unsavory things could have happened. You could get metal poisoning, contract a *worse* illness than the one you are already suffering with from the past patient whose blood still clung to the tool, or inadvertently make way for bacteria in the vicinity to enter your body through the open wound. Or perhaps, your doctor would bleed you and finding you weaker after the procedure, would do it again thinking he had yet to cure you and you would simply waste away and perish after a few days or week of agony. Or, the first cut might simply be taken in a most copious vein, causing your death readily if the bleeding could not be stopped. Many people of course lived after being bled, which may be why doctors continued to apply this medical tactic. However, it could certainly exacerbate the length of healing time of the original ailment and even damage the patient's vitality for a lifetime.

My lady, it is nearly dawn. You returned quite before the evening and after collapsing, remained unconscious through the night! And what a night it has been! A terrible storm arose that would make the dead walk! But not you mistress! Such a continual cracking and trembling of thunder and blazing lightening that made me shudder so!

You ask her what her name is just as you sense the bird creeping in more closely. He is dressed in a long black robe that covers all of his body; his black-gloved hands peek out from the ends of his billowy sleeves. You can't keep your eyes from darting to the lady and back anxiously to him several times. You are nervous that he will pull a knife from those ebony cuffs, or something worse: vials of poison, viperous snakes and irrevocable curses. Appearing nearly faint herself, the woman sweeps her worried hands over her face and cries aloud.

Oh angels in the heavens! Guide my lady back! What will become of me, of all of us, if her life is to slip from this world? Contessa, it is I, your lady's maid Belloza!

Having clenched the distance, the ghoulish surgeon reaches out with one hand and places it tenaciously on her arm. Though he appears to be looking directly at you from beneath his disguise, he addresses the maid by entreating her to waste no more time! The release of blood will be the only way to reverse such a slipping from the world, as she so fears. In that moment, you sense that he would bleed you for his evil pleasure rather than as an honest cure. You shake off the slightest tremble.

Regardless that the powers that control the world's rightful reality seem to have shaken yours up most unexpectedly and violently, there is one thing you are very certain of right now. You must be clever in this moment, as it may be your only way to gain precious time while figuring out this situation and deciding what to do in it. Perhaps you can fix it, if there is a way. You slowly take a few more sips of water, using the mere seconds to think. Then, handing the glass back to Belloza, you push yourself up a little higher on the plush pillows behind your head in an attempt to appear stronger and more alert since you can't pull off the image of complete confidence. Turning your head in the direction of the pair, you first address the morbid vulture and then your maid.

Good doctor, is this the way that you speak before a countess? As you can see, unless your vision is marred by your physician's mask, I am no longer unconscious and am certainly not in any danger of leaving this earth anytime soon! Should you have a recommended cure, it is I, not my maid, that you should direct your proposed course of action. Belloza, of course I know your name! It was a farcical question. Have you forgotten how I jest with you to make you laugh when you are heavy-hearted? It is clear that my sudden behavior has stressed you, but all is well! It was just a foolish joke dear friend.

Bowing deeply, the doctor retreats back to the edge of the room and into the shadows where only a bit of candlelight's glow flickers from off of his white beak. In deference he apologizes for his rudeness (it is clear that he knows who holds the gold for his payment in the room and certainly would not wish to offend that source). Smiling meekly, Belloza states that you have not japed with her any time lately due to your recent loss and that your joke is unkind after such a treacherous night! You wave her words away dismissively and ask her what it was that you said in the night that sounded so bizarre? Standing closely, she whispers to you.

My lady, you were sometimes half-awake though unconscious and speaking of strange things! First, you pleaded for me to call your family. I tried to calm you and cool your brow. I tried to convince you that calling out to them would be fruitless as they would never hear you all that way away in Padua! But you were very stern and insistent. You repeated that all that was needed was the 'fone'. Contessa, a fone? I asked you what this was and you repeated, 'Fone, fone, a technology'! When I still didn't understand you, you called me an ignorant goose!

Then, you told me that you wished to go home instantly! But, I told you that you must first get well and then we would have to prepare a carriage on land to greet us from off the boat out of Venice to take us to your estate. Again you called me a fool and said that you would take a 'playne' to get you there because it was faster! I was so confused! When I asked you if a playne was a technology too, you cursed at me and said that it was a machine!

It is instantly clear to you that in your sleep, you entreated Belloza to use a phone to call your family. If the situation were not so dire, you'd probably laugh aloud at this calamity! Of course she thought you were nonsensical! Phones haven't been invented yet, or airplanes or modern technology! She was at a loss as to how to fulfill your request. You must now counteract the things that you said in your sleep.

Oh, my faithful servant! Forgive me for scolding you so in my fretful state! I have indeed been ill it seems. I fear that during yesterday's Carnevale festivities, I was rather overindulgent! The dancing in the squares, the wine and perhaps, one too many oysters! I assure you that I was filled with exhaustion and enjoyed too many of the richer delicacies. Those things I spoke of, ha-ha! They were only odd contraptions devised by Leonardo da Vinci! I had read about his inventions recently and these remembrances must have befuddled my mind during my restlessness! It is nothing, I assure you! I need only a little repose and then I will be quite myself again!

Skeptical, Belloza questions how you came to be in the clothing that you were wearing as it was not the attire that you left the hotel in. Ugh, so many questions! How can you circumvent them all?

Oh that! A merchant's daughter sold these items to me from her family's shop, foreign fashions of course, and I gave my original clothing to a mendicant woman on a bridge. Do not scold me! I am sure that you will say that yesterday morning's attire was grander and that I should not have given those items away. Simply call it charity and the unpredictability of the Carnevale!

Nodding, Belloza appears more at ease after hearing your liar's tale. This will at least give you time! However, you must glean more information about who you are from her without raising suspicion in order to assess what is next best to do. At the moment, you can't do this easily. The doctor seems to be growing impatient judging by his shifting figure, ominous in the background. Thinking quickly, you review what you know right now. First, you are a countess as Belloza called you so. From what you understand of history, this means you are probably wealthy, perhaps even noble. From the conversation, it seems that you own an estate in Padua and have family connections. You have recently experienced some loss, though you know not what and due to the fact that you are traveling alone with your maidservant, you are either visiting Venice for the Carnevale for pleasure, or for some other mission, or both. As you note the beginnings of the rising sun through the cracks in the shuttered window and one lone peep coming from a restless bird somewhere in the courtyard, it is nearly morning. You cannot hear any rain; the storm must have passed completely. Quietly, you ask the maiden one additional question.

Belloza, remind me what our agenda is this day. I have quite forgotten it in this state of fatigue.

She does so promptly.

Madame, tonight is the grand ball held at your cousin Amedea's palazzo. I know I haven't been quite honest with you, but I now admit that it was a shock that

Your Ladyship decided to bring yourself out of mourning from your estate in Padua, having hardly spoken a word to anyone after the untimely death of your beloved husband, the count, six months ago! But, I know that you said that you would not miss this merriment and that it was time to begin to live again. And I agree! I know that your mood has grown less sullen and more cheerful since we arrived a few days ago, but yesterday when you told me that you would walk out alone for fresh air and did not return for hours, I feared that you had drowned yourself out in a canal from grief and that I had been a fool to think that you were on the mend after all. As you were gone so long, I was so worried! This turned into complete bewilderment when you returned, wearing this colorful fabric, as you and I both know that you have not been out of a black gown for all of these long months! I now see that yesterday, your grief broke! I'm glad that it was not in madness that you lingered out so long, but rather with pleasure! It pleases me that my mistress has returned some of her cheer though I fear that you have quite worn yourself out! If you do not wish to go to the ball this evening and prefer to attend the evening Mass as has been your regular habit since the count's passing, we shall go and pray for his soul as is usual my lady. Or, we can return home, as you had so fervidly demanded in the night. Shall I begin to prepare the journey as you rest?

If only Belloza knew which home you had meant to return to.

IF you decide to travel to your estate in Padua until you figure out what to do next, turn to page 348.

IF you will attend your cousin's majestic ball in hopes of securing a solution, turn to page 496.

IF you wish to attend Mass, as was the countess's tradition while in mourning, turn to page 369.

WAKING early and refreshed after a deliciously sound sleep, you are quite content with the way you ended your previous day. After thanking Carmela for sharing some of the history of convent life and for the special invitation (which you politely declined on account of having so much touring yet to do), you left St. Mark's Church and took a long and gratifying walk through the maze that are the *calli*, savoring all there was to see and surprisingly without any anxieties in the possibility of getting lost. As the day grew late, you stopped into a *bacaro*, sitting to devour a bowl of delectable *gnocchi*, also purchasing a slice of fluffy tiramisu to go. Having asked for directions from the keeper who seemed very used to assisting tourists, you easily found your way back to the hotel. It took a bit of time to remove the day's costume, accessories and makeup, but once accomplished, you took your dessert to the courtyard, lit with the strings of twinkle lights glowing in the dusk. Cocooned in a thick sweater, you enjoyed your delicate treat with a hot cup of tea. Before long, you were sleeping with a luxurious heaviness in your room.

In the brand-new day, you are prepared to walk out for breakfast, dressing warmly in comfortable street clothing. Despite the appetizing tray you enjoyed the morning before in your room, a second daybreak filled with sunlight and fresh air greeted you and you wanted to soak it in with a stroll. You were sure that a simple yet appealing meal would not be hard to find and you were right. You hadn't noticed before, as you were concentrating more particularly on the shopfronts and costumed populace, but there are many *pasticcerie* or pastry shops offering coffee and doughy delights, throughout Venice. After passing a few with sparse window displays and scattered with hurried locals, you stop at one exhibit colorfully stuffed with baked decadence: cream puffs, cookies, cakes, breads and various desserts covered in sweet glaze and fresh ripe fruit. Though most *pasticcerie* limit their accommodations inside the cafe to standing room only along an elevated counter for guests to consume their espresso and pastry, this one also has a smattering of tables and chairs outside the shop along a scenic canal. Perfect!

After ordering a coffee with cream and a selection of mini pastries, you take a seat outside. You couldn't have found a better place to enjoy your morning meal; it is peaceful and enchanting. Not at all in a hurry, you enjoy every soft bite and then gather the escaped crumbs, seeking them out on your plate with a dampened finger and bringing the last grains of sugar and crusty bits to your mouth. The coffee is strong yet without any harsh bitterness, completely smooth and fragrant with a splash of creaminess. Satisfied, you sit back relaxed in your seat and nonchalantly observe the passersby walking to their morning destinations, as well as several motorboats traveling with small loads in one direction or the other. Their engines set to the lowest speeds, the revolutions of their motor fans hardly make more than sputtered, gurgling reverberations beneath the water's surface. No one seems in a desperate rush, which you find pleasant. If only the beginning of each of your days could start out this way, rested and lacking your usual predictable and frenetic routine.

Despite the crispness of the temperature you are quite comfortable as you recline contentedly in your seat, taking pleasure in the serenity of the Venetian cityscape and the local sounds. Soon, several ladies take a table not far from your own and begin chatting amicably while eating. You unintentionally overhear their conversation due to their closeness in the vicinity and the lack of other noises to distract. Speaking

English, it is soon evident that they are tourists much the same as you and are sharing a cheery review of their previous day's excursion. Unanimously, they seem to have enjoyed a glass museum on the island of Murano called the Museo del Vetro.

Glass is to the island of Murano what lace is to the island of Burano. These islands are about two miles and six miles away from Venice, respectively, within the lagoon. They are two locales where singular crafts were woven into their histories so intimately, that the very name of the islands gained celebrity status throughout Europe during earlier periods. To an extent, it remains so today. Being such a clear and beautiful day, why not take a half-day excursion to Murano and see the glass island for yourself? As a matter of fact, though you could easily take a public *vaporetto* to the island, wouldn't it be a treat to take a private water taxi instead? You could easily arrange to be picked up at your hotel's waterside dock!

Having devised your plan, you walk back to your hotel and ask the concierge to assist you in securing a service. You ask that the pick up time be delayed for half an hour. In that time, you grab a knitted scarf, hat, gloves and sunglasses from your room, for extra warmth and eye protection out in a speedboat on the open waters. Then (having also inquired at the same time about the taxi as to a good shop nearby), quickly grab a few items to picnic with in Murano. There you are able to secure a sizeable portion of fresh caprese salad carefully packed into a transparent plastic container. The combination of ripe tomatoes, fresh mozzarella cheese, bright basil leaves and flavorful olive oil, sprinkled with sea salt and freshly ground black pepper, will be a delicious midday meal. You also grab a container of sliced ripe cantaloupe, a small bag of shelled pistachios, two chocolate-dipped almond biscotti and several bottles of mineral water. After paying, the clerk places all of your items into a handled paper bag, throwing in a few napkins and some plastic cutlery. You couldn't be more ready for an island excursion!

Returning to the hotel, you find that your water taxi driver has arrived and is chatting with the concierge. Breaking conversation, he leads you through a back door in the courtyard that leads to the water dock of the hotel, where you both hop into his speedboat. Backing out into the canal, you sit back easily in the sharp little craft, wrap up snuggly and prepare to enjoy the ride!

While on the canals within the city, the driver takes

you at a respectable speed mandated for all traffic so as to avoid as much wave damage to buildings as possible. But, once out on the lagoon, you are speeding away from Venice like an escaped bank robber! Wearing large dark sunglasses, your scarf flitting behind you in the salty wind, the sun in the sky, alone in your own rented speedboat, you can't help feeling like a celebrity. As Murano is just over two miles away and you are not traveling in a water-bus which must make multiple stops along the route to drop off and pick up passengers, it takes you no time at all to get there, a little to your disappointment. However, the driver states that he will pick you up four hours hence at this same boat dock and if at that time, you aren't expired from touring, he'll be glad to extend the duration of the ride back for your viewing pleasure. Watching a *vaparetto* approach from a distance, you affirm the name of this dock (water-bus stop Murano Museo), thank him and then are off to learn the history of glass.

Not far from the Museo stop you find the Palazzo Giustinian, the palace that houses the glass museum. After paying for entry, you kindly ask the ticket clerk who is also acting as a coat checker, if it would be permissible for you to stash your lunch, which she kindly stows away on your behalf. Walking in, you grab a pamphlet offering a bit of the building's history and explaining some of the exhibits within, here for your discovery. First you learn that the Palazzo Giustinian (though it does not state the date it was originally built) once housed a line of Torcello's bishops.

Torcello is another island near Venice with a very rich history. Just over six miles away within the lagoon, it was populated even before Venice and was the first of the local islands to protect those peoples fleeing the mainland from invaders. Though today there are very few who live there (perhaps less than 20), it once had the densest population in the lagoon, built up with ornate *palazzi* and medieval churches. The island became a trade location predominately selling local sea salt (which was an important commodity for land dwellers). Unfortunately during the 1100s, the water around the island became too swampy as rivers from the mainland forced watery debris out into the lagoon in the direction of Torcello. This made for mosquitoes, a veritable breeding ground. Thus, trade was difficult as ships found they were cutoff from an island surrounded by silt. Simultaneously, Torcello's population became greatly diminished by its very own plague of malaria, transmitted by clouds of vampiric mosquitoes. Those who didn't succumb to the virus relocated to the other lagoon islands and started anew. It didn't take long for Venice to take advantage of what quickly became a ghost city. Venetians took a float on over, pulling down abandoned buildings so that they could use the materials to further build up their own city. Thus today, Torcello is a quiet grassy island with only a few buildings remaining and a population that you can count on your fingers and toes. How it came to be that Torcello's bishops took up residence in Murano at this palace for a spell in history, you aren't sure. However, upon entering the gothic landmark it shows itself superb. For you, that's reason enough.

The glass collection found a home here in the mid-1800s while the *palazzo* served as Murano's city hall. It only took up one room on the first floor, but as the collection grew, it ended up spreading throughout the entire building! You happily discover that this compilation has gathered more than just Murano's historic pieces, but also ancient glass artifacts and precious works from worldwide as well. You find that the entire collection, whether found pieces globally or locally, come together fittingly to tell the story of glassmaking.

First, you peruse the archeological collection and are delighted in the delicacy of some of the world's oldest intact pieces. You find it almost incomprehensible that any remain uninjured considering glass's fragility! Using blowpipes as early as 2,000 years ago, glassmakers pushed air from their lungs through tubes and into molten glass, which took shape within clay molds. The bubble formed within these objects created miniature vessels that could hold precious treasures such as expensive medicines or rare perfumes. Using similar techniques, bottles, vases and shallow bowls were made and then decorated with engravings or by attaching other smaller pieces of handmade glass.

As you pass through the centuries by collection beginning in the 1400s, you are able to note a progression away from predominately utilitarian items toward ornate display pieces as well. The decorative abilities quickly expand, and begin to perfect the use of powdered minerals to create color, filigree (which appears as decorative threads within glass) and gold leaf applications. There are elaborate pieces of etched crystal, enameled glassware of exquisite design, intricately constructed chandeliers and elegantly crafted glass mirrors. Reading each plaque posted before the pieces that most catch your eye, you are educated to excess about glassmaking history; everything from ancient technique to the exhaustive expansion of decorative application. The progression and variances are so numerous that it clutters your brain. Glassmaking is a rich study all its own!

From your pamphlet and various readings throughout the museum, you begin to understand why Murano was so important to the world's glassmaking industry. As it happened, the craft had already taken hold in Venice and was going strong in the late 1200s. However, this production required very hot ovens to heat minerals (mainly seaside sand) into a molten state. With Venice's buildings being mostly constructed of wood before those later marble giants standing today, citizens were worried these glassworks would loose flames on their dwellings and burn them all down. So, in 1291, Venice sent the glassmakers packing off to the island of Murano. Soon thereafter Murano's glass became renowned and the city, Europe's largest exporter of it! Over the coming centuries, nobles abroad went wild for Murano's intricate and colorful beads, shiny mirrors and enchanting chandeliers. Those island artisans became so coveted that there was enforced a law that glassmakers could not move away from the Venetian Republic. If they did and were caught, they would be sentenced to death. While remaining however, they lived an advantageous life, becoming wealthy and celebrated citizens with noble privileges. Examples of this from the 1300s were dismissal of legal troubles (overlooked and forgotten by the government), the ability to flaunt swords on their belts (which were very expensive and usually reserved for medieval knights) and permission to profitably align with noble families (though marriage connections).

Glassmaker's daughters were married as if they were noble born while their birth sons were passed their highly secretive trade (thus having an income for life) and the blowers themselves were rich and influential. There of course was good cause for all of this. These tradesmen labored fiercely to perfect and beautify glassmaking, a very complicated art form. These pieces were glorious in what was often an insipid world; most common people would never have seen such delicate beauty before. Without the glassmaker's secrets, these exports were near impossible to reproduce. Even today, fine glass from Murano is trademarked so that other makers worldwide cannot pretend to replicate it and sell it in the same class or with the same profits. Just like a counterfeit purse, a discerning eye would know the difference in quality. Regardless, imitation products are always in demand despite the fact that buying these items greatly hurts the industries that provide fine artisan work, no matter how protected.

After several hours admiring the *palazzo* and its many rooms of glass, arranged in the timeline of all its triumphant discoveries and refinements, beautifications and glories, you gather your cold weather wear and packed lunch and head out into the streets of Murano. Walking for a time, you enter several shops to appreciate some of the locally made items on display. You are met with an unexpected variety of glasswares to be sold: tiny creatures of every sort, crystal flowers, elegant pendants, long beaded necklaces, serving ware of every kind, perfume bottles, lampshades, chandeliers and statuettes. The colors and decorative styles are so vast that you are amazed. After enjoying a full viewing of what is offered, you carefully pick out three glass bead bracelets in your favorite colors as a reminder of your visit, selecting several more as gifts to share when back at home. You can't help but clasp one of yours onto a wrist as you walk out of the shop, wanting to wear your purchase right away.

Strolling around Murano, you find that its architecture appears much the same as Venice, only more sparing of the marble. It too is made of a marrying of small islands connected by bridges. However, it is less than a mile wide and there are only seven little islands, whereas Venice has 118 (though some are rather tiny indeed). Compared with the 60,000 or so citizens of Venice, Murano has only around 5,000. But it is just this that makes the place feel intimate and calm. Despite the tourists who pause here daily to view some of the best glassware Italy has to offer, you imagine that it is quiet and serene each evening. You could see yourself owning an apartment above any one of the local glass vendors, perhaps commuting by *vaperetto* to Venice to work during the weekdays, such as many in the world take a train into a city for their employment. It would be a different life, certainly a lovely one. Finding a bench along a peaceful canal, you pull out your lunch (simultaneously admiring your bracelet) and enjoy the simple yet tasty items that you selected. Watching the world go by with each bite, you are very pleased with the day and reminisce over several of the things you've seen so far in Venezia as well as imagine what more is yet to come. It makes you think about the countless other places in the world that you'd also like to see, and how rich just a slice of any city with its unique culture, can be.

Finishing your picnic, you put your empty containers back into your lunch bag and checking your watch, find that affording yourself a slow walk, you'll be back at the Murano Museo station just at the right time for your pick up. With your bags in hand, snug in your warm clothing, you stroll contentedly to the dock, confidently enjoying each moment alone while anticipating what Venice and the world, have next to offer.

THE End.

ONCE through the door coming from the dock, you enter an open-air courtyard surrounded by a gothic style portico built out of reddish-orange marble. The floor of the courtyard is designed with a checkered pattern using squares of cream, red and orange stone, which has been painstakingly polished to perfection. The sunlight above floods directly into the courtyard and in one corner of the exposed square, there are set several massive stone pots planted with leafy trees. Under the portico on all sides is a promenade much like the elevated one crafted on three sides of St. Mark's Square. You could take a walk around the perimeter of the courtyard on the rainiest of days and still remain dry. Being guided across by the lady, you look up to see that the *palazzo* is built up on all four sides around the courtyard. There are second and third story windows and balconies above the portico looking over this place, an open space, which in the warmest months would be treated like one's private yard, protected from the canals and *calli*.

Once on the other side, you are led through another large wooden monster (this time with double doors), and then swiftly directed up a wide set of marble stairs. Ascending two flights, the first in the direction opposite of the courtyard (you got a peek of an alternate canal out a window on this side) and the second back into the direction of it, you find yourself on what must be the uppermost floor. The staircase and the open hallway you are now treading down are constructed of hundreds of tons of marble. It's open and drafty and you wonder how anyone could heat this place. Some yards down the hall, the lady in her orange gown and with warm concern in her eyes, shows you into one of what must be many rooms in the *palazzo*. She closes the door behind you both. You are relieved to find that this room is of a higher temperature; there is a toasty radiator working its magic along one wall.

Though you can't make out just what she tells you as she quickly points here and there in the room, you feel that she is trying to give you some direction. At a point, she pauses to make a call to someone using an old-fashioned circular dial phone set on a round wooden table next to a plushy upholstered chair. Blurting out a few words that sound like frantic asks, she hangs up almost as quickly as the call was made. The room is a bit dim, a bedroom. Moments later a very motherly looking middle-aged woman wearing a simple grey, knee-length dress and stockings, covered up with a warm knitted sweater, bursts into the room. She waves her hands around in the air with a large fluffy white towel in each. Hardly taking five steps to get to you from the door to where you've been standing like a frozen statue for the last four minutes, she kindly leads you into the direction of a warm bathroom. It feels bright and cheery as she flips on the lights. It is equipped with a modern shower and the air smells clean like soft and sudsy soap. She sets the towels on the edge of a sink and points to a clean white robe folded neatly on a shelf which also houses a number of other essential items: creamy bars of soap, stacked washcloths and bottled shampoo.

Despite how bizarre your day has become, you aren't overly stressed and are going along with the turn of events as best you can. In fact, you are curious as to what will happen next. You are educated in the fact that leaving freezing wet clothing on is bad for the health and are quick to understand that the young woman had called a house attendant to see that you had what was necessary to get clean and dry, as swiftly as possible. Dramatically speaking, these were the kinds of situations in history, which caused unfortunate souls to perish from high fevers and pneumonia. This certainly wouldn't be a concern for you today with the advantages of modern medicine (you hope), but you can't wait to get warm and dry again nonetheless. Finally left alone in the bathroom, you go about doing just this. The hot shower feels amazing after your icy plunge!

After toweling off in the luxuriously steamy room, you are happy to find a blow-dryer to dry your clean head and some face cream too, which you apply to your makeup free face; it smells faintly of cucumber. It dawns on you that your features must have been quite a sight to all who looked on you after rubbing the canal water out of your mascara laden eyes. You must have appeared as though you were crying tears of black. Oh well! A hero can't always have perfect makeup you think, shrugging with a smile. Soon finished, you wrap up in the earlier proffered bathrobe and walk back out into the bedroom, which is now brighter than before with several windows' shutters open outwardly for the sunlight to enter in. The glass is still shut however, to keep the cold out. On the round table next to the phone is a polished gold tray with a bowl of hot broth, some crusty bread and a steaming cup of tea. Of course, don't mind if you do, but this is really getting to be too gracious. You sit to take advantage of the offering, not quite sure in any case that it would be prudent to wave anyone down in the grand hallway while only wearing a bathrobe. You're sure the ladies will return shortly.

Your mind wanders to Biasio as you take a spoonful of broth; it is absolutely delicious and light. You dip a few bits of bread right in and are eager to eat them. Not quite a meal, just a bit of sustenance after a swim. Oh yes, Biasio! You're sure he'll be just fine but can't believe he was telling the truth when he said he could not swim! How dare he go slipping out of the gondola into the water like that! Perhaps because you were able to help him the event no longer seems as serious, but during those unpredictable moments it was scarier than you'd like to admit. Especially the fearful look in Biasio's eyes as you swam to him. And who is that woman anyway? You didn't think too much of it, but it seems as though *he* might have asked whether you were willing to pull up to the dock or not, both having paid your share to the gondolier. Perhaps you didn't have the time to spare while he made a pit stop to visit his girlfriend! Of course, you didn't really mind, as you'd never seen a water garage under a Venetian palace before, but that is despite the point.

Looking around, you dreamily regard a grand four-poster bed; its wooden pillars ornately carved and topped off with a satiny canopy. The bedding looks so soft and there are more pillows than any one person could ever need, what a luxury! There is a knock on the door just as you are sipping the last of the broth with the bowl brought up to your face in a most unladylike fashion. Setting it down and patting your mouth with a napkin, you see that the older woman has reentered. She seems to be satisfied as she gets a look at you, you clearly appear less washed up than before. She brings you a pile of clothes, which you promptly put on in the bathroom: a pair of loose fitting yoga pants, a t-shirt and an oversized knitted sweater. When again in the bedroom, she holds up a pair of running shoes, which you slip on. They are a little snug, but will work just fine to get you back to your hotel.

Leading you out of the bedroom and back down the same stairs that you first ascended, the woman hands you a thick wool coat and scarf when at the door entering the courtyard and then leads you back out to the dock. There you find the young woman, now out of her costume and wearing jeans and a jacket, handing your gondolier several bottles of unopened wine. By the looks of it, the boatman was probably also invited inside during the time it took you to bathe and eat, as he appears warm and cheery as he accepts the gifts. On seeing you, the lady draws near and hugs you, blurting out a few words that sound grateful. You smile and wave kindly once safely in the gondola, which appears completely tidy. You aren't sure where any of your things have gone to, and oh, you've left those damp clothes in the bathroom! However, you've had enough excitement for today and can retrieve your possessions later. Soon back out onto the local canal, you ask the gondolier what had happened.

As you suspected, Biasio slipped into the water. After you both were brought into the dwelling, the gondolier was politely asked to warm up and wait a spell in a sitting room. There, he took some coffee and a toasted *panino* while he shook off the uncomfortable experience. The young lady, Biasio's sister, who mentioned that she had just arrived on holiday for the festival, soon assured him that the victim was quite recovered and that you, the good luck charm in all of this, would be down again soon. She paid him a bit extra to take you wherever you wanted to go.

His sister! As familiar as she was with the residence, you wondered how she was connected to it…could this *palazzo* be their family home? Why wouldn't he have pointed it out to you along the journey? If it hadn't been for her, you and Biasio would have floated right past!

Your thoughts can't help but drift to the conversation and laughs that you had with Biasio and you wonder if you might see him again. It is unlikely, you only told him your first name and he doesn't even know where you are lodging. Even when you come back to retrieve your costume and accessories and to return these borrowed items, what are the chances that he'd be home and available for conversation? Suddenly a bit tired, you ask the gondolier the name of the *palazzo* so that you can find it again, and then request that he take you to the dock nearest to your hotel. Contemplatively, you enjoy the rest of the ride in silence while taking in the passing scenery.

After arriving back at Hotel Fato, you quickly find that you have overlooked a very important detail. In all the commotion, you had quite forgotten your passport, money and room key (waterlogged or no) when you left your clothes behind. Fortunately however, a capable woman from the front desk is able to locate the phone number of the residence with the name you had (thankfully) retrieved from the gondolier. Speaking to someone at the home, the helpful staffer works to console you. After sharing the hotel information, she is told that someone from the residence will be able to deliver all of your left possessions, sometime tomorrow morning.

Resting easier, you were lent a second key and spent the later hours of the day in your room, writing out a few letters using the complimentary stationary provided by reception. As night falls, you are sleeping soundly.

You jerk awake and sit up in your bed, your eyes adjusting to the soft light of dawn coming from your shuttered window. There is singing, a masculine voice, which has woken you. You groggily surmise that while being in Venice, a bellowing gondolier isn't all that unusual. Blinking your eyes sleepily, you ponder why the song seems so loud as the nearest canal isn't just below. A gondolier's solo would sound muffled from your room. You wonder if it could be coming from the courtyard.

Wrapping your wool blanket around you, your hair an uncombed mess and your mouth a bit dry, you get out of bed and shuffle over to your window, opening it inwardly and then pushing the shutters out. You lean out of the casement to see who is making all that…oh! Oh no! Oh, that's *Biasio*! Even without the half mask that you'd previously seen him in, you recognize him immediately. What a handsome man! You instantly pull back out of the window and retreat a step into your room. You scrunch your nose and with an awkward face, ask yourself if this is really happening. Did *you* fish that good-looking man out of a canal yesterday? Has he just woken you from your heavy sleep with a serenade? Your stomach begins to turn a pleasant, unstoppable flutter as you consider how embarrassing a movie style act of chivalry can be. What will all the other guests think? As he continues to warble, you devise how best to get him to stop. Leaning out again, you can only imagine what a freshly woken ogre you must appear. Turning your head to the left and to the right, other sleepy faces are witness to the act; a few heads poking out of random windows.

You try putting your fingers up to your lips to hush the man, but his singing (which you are surprised to acknowledge is very good) continues. You're awake now! Trying to keep the chill out by clasping the wool blanket to your front with one hand, you use the other to wave awkwardly while shaking your head "no". It is to no avail. As you believe the song must nearly be finished, you give up and listen patiently. Though you

341

try hard not to, you can't help but grin. Feeling a blush coming on, you place your free hand over your eyes and shake your head. At the conclusion of the serenade, a few of your neighbors clap approvingly as you stand unmoving, biting your lip and holding back a huge smile. Calling up, he wishes you a, "*Buongiorno*!" After you return the greeting, he states that though he cannot stay longer, he's left you a package at the front desk. The staff was so kind as to point your window out to him as well, he tells you, winking. And then with an irresistible smile meant just for you, he waves and exits out onto the *calle*.

Alert and bemazed, you hastily dress and descend to the lobby. There await two boxes wrapped in brown paper: one large and one small. There is also a small paper sack and an envelope. Carrying it all back to your room, you first open the envelope. Enclosed is a letter.

TURN to page 493.

Venice

SCARF snuggly wrapped around your neck and coat buttoned, luggage in tow, you make to head toward the ladies' room at the back of the bar. Pausing to look behind you, you find that all the gathered company in the *bacaro* is busy about their business; no one will see you slip out of what you presume to be an employees only exit.

The air outside is crisp enough to see your breath as you assess your surroundings. Before you, there is a thin lane that stretches behind the buildings at a width of about eight feet, running parallel to a canal. To your left at some distance, the path looks to lead to a small bridge. Negotiating past back door refuse and clutter, you are dismayed to find that there is a locked gate, which will not allow your admittance onto the path that goes over the bridge. Common sense tells you that the lock is in place to keep thieves and vandals from breaking into, or spray-painting graffiti on, these buildings after dark. Your assumption seems correct, when hobbling with your suitcases back in the direction that you came, you find another gate closed and padlocked at the other end. Not only a little chilly and increasingly exhausted after all your travels, you are now feeling a little nervous in your situation. You could wait for one of the staffers from the *bacaro* to take out the trash and let you back into the building. Or, you could knock on the door, though you aren't sure with the noise inside that anyone will hear you. You could wait at one of the barred gates for another pedestrian to go by and then entreat them to assist you. Or, perhaps a boat will float past; you could flag it down and ask for safe passage across the canal. However, you aren't so sure how comfortable you are with getting into a stranger's boat when you were trying to put distance between you and another unfamiliar person in the first place. No matter the solution, the person who comes to your rescue is going to wonder how you found yourself trapped here.

Walking back to the exit of the bar, you stand anxiously eyeing the initial bridge looking for an alternate solution while twisting the airline tags still attached to the handle on one of your suitcases. This is when you hear a voice behind you. Despite a little jump in your nerves, you are glad that you are so soon to receive help. That is until you turn around and your relief turns to dread.

Buonasera, Signorina!

It is the man from without the bar, though you are shocked to imagine how he could have gotten past the gate behind you without some commotion and notice!

Hello...how, how did you get back here?

You question the man while puzzling at his pale complexion and stunningly authentic costume. From more closely, only about six feet away, you can see no lack of fine detail and sparkling studs; are those real gems? He smiles warmly, but it doesn't do much to relieve a deep and growing sense of fear. He seems to notice your discomfort.

Please do not be alarmed mistress. I cannot harm you.

Yea, right! Don't predators say things like that to lull unsuspecting fools into getting a little closer? You wonder why he said cannot rather than would not.

What is it that you want? I will scream if you come any closer!

You squint as your eyes take notice of one of his hands, which is stretched from without his cape and balancing on top of the ebony knob of his cane. It looks ashy and, smoky even, almost *transparent*. Your eyes dart back to his face as he speaks.

Forgive me, please forgive me.

Inspecting his face, you find that he has a younger visage than you were initially sure about. Perplexing is a far off sounding echo in the reverberations of his voice, almost as though you are hearing him speak on the radio but you're having trouble tuning in to the station. His words don't seem like a fake response to your being scared, but rather desperation for his own condition. You feel sorry for the man, though you aren't yet sure why. Despite this, his presence terrifies you.

Sir, you don't seem well. I'll just knock on this door and we'll make sure to get you some help.

Just as you turn to pound at the exit of the *bacaro*, the man bids you to wait.

Please…oh please! Only a few minutes…it has been so long since I have spoken to anyone. You are the first person in a century to have been able to see me. Please, just a moment?

Some feeling of pity piques within you and your fist falls short of the door. What does he mean a *century*? Turning your gaze in his direction, you inspect his face, which is eerily pale and filled with a genuine sadness. He looks down to the ground.

You see, you look like my beloved. That is why I noticed you in the window. I never thought that you would actually see me too, no one usually does.

Beginning to tremble, you tell him that you don't

understand what he means, he is clearly in distress; wouldn't it be best to get help? But you know deep down that help won't matter; the man before you isn't real. He is a ghost.

TURN to page 513.

GOOD doctor, I will no longer require your services. It is only excessive merrymaking that brought on this state, of which after my long months of mourning, I was not prepared. Today, I shall return to my home in Padua where fresh air and rest shall restore my health. The local physician there will see to any of my forthcoming needs. Belloza, I shall take respite as you prepare for our journey. Please pay the doctor from our purse and request a good meal for me to break my fast.

You are shocked by the words coming out of your mouth as you test your acting skills like never before now. You are careful not to make any assumptions about the life of the lady who you are pretending to be. Eventually Belloza and anyone else in the countess's circle that you may encounter, will reveal enough that you can start playing off of what you learn to keep the act going. You just hope it doesn't take that long to find a way to return home, your real home. You can't even comprehend why you have chosen to go away from Venice to this estate in Padua except that there must be some reason why you've been selected to take the countess's place for a spell. You hope that it is just a spell. How very strange that her hotel room during this Carnevale, the year of which you are uncertain, is the very same room that you took in the modern day. What if you had stumbled into the past only to find that the building that housed your hotel didn't even exist? You are at the very least content with having had a warm place to sleep last night and satisfied with not traveling in time to find yourself without any resources for survival.

Belloza, immediately moving to fulfill your requests, pays the doctor who humbly nods without a word and then slips away to vulture on other prey. After opening the window and spreading wide the shutters to let in the light of dawn, the maiden closes the glass snuggly to keep out the chill. With a trained determination while the soft glow of the world becomes a full and bright sunny morning, she comes and goes in preparation. You can see that she has a private room across the hall from your own, not surprisingly as there was not another bed for her here, or the clutter that you would expect to surround a noble lady: luggage, expensive clothing, general items of elegance and pomp.

Within half an hour she has filled a standing washbasin in a small anteroom, the one that used to be (or rather isn't yet) a modern bathroom. As you enter it now, you find that it is a private powder room arranged

349

with a vanity table supporting a mirror and a bench adorned with an embroidered cushion, as well as a potty chair of carved wood with a secreted porcelain basin below a hole in the seat. There are a variety of pretty items spread upon the vanity counter, all of which are presumably the countess's: hairpins, powder, rouge, decorative feathers, a pink fabric box filled with faux beauty marks and a vial of delicate smelling perfume. As Belloza sets about to order breakfast and make the travel arrangements, you pull back your hair with a found ribbon and wash up. You aren't quite sure where your dress went, or any of the accessories that you were wearing for that matter, as you are only clothed in your shift. Belloza must have assisted you out of those more cumbersome pieces before dragging you off of the floor and into the bed. You wonder where your passport and euros are. Perhaps they've disappeared along with your past life, your inner voice murmurs. You momentarily despair but then remind yourself that only a positive attitude is a helpful one while you scrub your face, neck and arms from the steamy water using a soft cloth and a scented round of soap.

After freshening up, you find a hot breakfast waiting on a tray on the desk aside the chair where you first saw Belloza stitching in the room. Sitting down, you curiously review it like a food historian might, and find that it looks very appetizing. Crusty toasted bread, sweet fresh figs, a haphazardly cut wedge of creamy cheese, honey, hot drinking chocolate and strong black tea. As you eat breakfast, you unexpectedly delight in every bite, feeling quite the lady to be served with polished silver and pressed napkins. There is even a spray of fresh lavender sprigs tied with a dark purple ribbon resting on the tray; you smell it and it is intoxicating.

As you are on the brink of finishing your meal, Belloza enters the room to notify you that your trunks are mostly packed. All that is left are your toiletries and traveling clothes; it is time to dress. Fortunately, her selections are quite simple and more comfortable than you would have expected in the eighteenth century. All except for the corset of course! Though it creates a lovely silhouette beneath your gown and a healthy dose of feminine bosom for display, the cinching is almost unbearable (this is a sensation that you are not accustomed to at all). The maid entreats you to stop fidgeting as she works the laces at your back, pulling them tighter and tighter. You make a quick excuse that you are still feeling slightly weak after such a fitful night. Taking pity on you, she ties the strings at the intensity of what will only give you a throbbing ribcage rather than agonizing bone disfigurement. You wonder what longtime corset wear would do to the arrangement of your internal organs.

With Belloza's assistance, you are soon wearing a white cotton dress with only moderately extended hip panniers. Around your waist is tied a wide lavender ribbon and white lace falls elegantly around your elbows from your half sleeves, also framing your décolleté. Next sitting at the vanity, she works to brush and arrange your hair in a lovely way. Piling it in an elaborate mound on the top of your head, it appears as a charming happenstance rather than a planned creation. It is a wild windblown updo. Fetching, not unkempt. She delicately tucks a few of the lavender sprigs into it. You had snatched them from your breakfast tray and were idly sniffing them as you patiently accepted her attendance. As a muffled knock comes from the outer bedroom door, you try to appear familiar with the makeup items on the vanity and apply a light layer of powder and a touch of rouge on each cheek while the maid answers the interruption. Examining yourself in the mirror, you smile; the effect is very pretty. As she reenters the anteroom, you note that Belloza is carrying a small package wrapped in tan linen and bound with twine.

Madame, the miniature that you commissioned in Padua has arrived. As you will no longer be attending the ball tonight to hand-deliver your portrait to your cousin Amedea, shall I order a man to carry it with a missive of departure? As she will not see you in person, I am sure that she will cherish this! Though I have not looked upon the outcome, I well remember that you made a fine model for the sitting my lady, even in your sorrow.

You sit up a little straighter and more uncertainly at the vanity. Your smile slowly melts away as you consider what is in her hands. A portrait of the countess! As you look at your reflection, it is certainly you that sits before it. You had wondered how it was that Belloza had believed that you were the countess when you look just the same now as in modern times; nothing of you ever changed. You shiver, imperceptible to the maid, as you consider what lies here to be seen in the painting. Looking to her you extend one hand.

Let me see it please. Meanwhile, be kind enough to bring me the gown that I purchased from the merchant's

daughter yesterday. I want to reexamine its make before
you close the luggage for the journey.

Complying, she hands the package over to you and exits to the other room. You can hear clanking from your breakfast tray being carried away. Laying the parcel in your lap, your hands begin to shake and your mouth feels dry. Pulling at the twine it is easy to open the parcel to the contents, which first exposes the back of the frame. There, freshly written in black ink is the signature of the artist, the year, and *her* name.

The year is 1779 and the woman who sat for the portrait is Contessa Ciossa Fortunato. Sucking a slow yet calming breath into your lungs, you turn the miniature over, the frame no bigger than the palm of your hand. Your eyes grow wide and you blink several times in amazement. Unable to control yourself, you let out an emotional cackle and then instantly frown. The woman in the painting looks just like you! How could this be? Have you slipped into a past life? You'd never really considered that sort of thing before. If it were even possible to live more than one life, would you look the same each time? Would that go unnoticed to historians? Wouldn't someone see an ancient painting in a gallery at some point and find *their* face hanging on a wall?

Perhaps one relives their life only once or twice; you guess that this could easily go unnoticed during the thousands of years of humanity. If any of this is true, what is fate's reason for returning you to *this* past life? You consider how eerily ironic it is that your future self has visited the very same city and even the very same hotel as your past self once did so long ago.

Belloza returns to the room to collect the loose items from the vanity for packing, as well as the portrait, which you have rewrapped. A few minutes later, she brings your modern made costume. After peering at it quizzically, she exits. Though certainly not as authentic as your present uniform, it does pass for eighteenth century clothing, however inexactly. You are thankful that you hadn't been transported wearing blue jeans and sunglasses! As the maid busies herself with the last of the packing, you reach into the hidden pocket of the gown. There as they were, are your passport and currency. Finding a spare linen wash square, you wrap the items in it momentarily. Bringing the gown out to Belloza, you ask that she repack it.

As she returns to her chamber, you look around frenetically trying to remember exactly how your modern day hotel room appears and what has changed over the centuries. Though it looks much the same, upkeep would have been applied everywhere, except perhaps to the marble block flooring. Your best guess is that at most, it has only had to endure years of polishing. You scurry around the room like a dog on the hunt for table scraps, looking for some flaw in its surface large enough to hide your passport. You are rewarded when you discover one stone shifting ever so slightly away from the wall at a corner of the apartment near its entrance. You quickly remove the document from the linen and fold your paper euros into it along with a few spare coins. At the last minute, you grab a sprig of lavender out of your hair, hiding it within the pages as well.

Squatting and bending to the floor is more difficult than you imagined while wearing a corset. Your soft billowy skirts make things even more inconvenient. Pushing them out of the way, you are able to slide the passport down into the space between the stone and the wall with a little force. Inspecting, the hidden items are undetectable. Standing up, you deposit the rag in the powder room just as Belloza returns.

My lady, all preparations are made. What shall I do with the portrait?

Looking confident and collected, you reply.

Oh yes, please have it sent with my regards and of course, regrets for my sudden departure. I will post correspondence to my cousin once I return to Padua. I am quite ready for the journey, let us away.

TURN to page 378.

YOU were delighted to be invited into a Venetian home for a celebratory meal! Having accepted the invitation, Carmela stated that though dinner was to be served at 7 p.m. the following day, you were more than welcome to arrive at her home an hour earlier if you'd like to see some real Venetian cooking in action. Her *nonna* (grandmother) will be making several extra special dishes and is quite the storyteller. Thinking that that sounded delightful, you told her that you'd come by around 6 p.m.! Before leaving St. Mark's Church she gave you an address card, proffered after pulling it out of an elegant drawstring purse, a formal yet stylish gesture. You would have had to have written your own address on a scrap of paper had it been the other way around; you like the printed card. After thanking her and making your way back out into the crowd, you found yourself taking a long walk all throughout the San Marco district. Having enjoyed all that the day had brought your way up until then, it felt wonderful to simply be, using your senses to embrace all that the festive streets had to offer. You weren't even nervous about losing your way, and as it turned out, you easily found yourself back at your hotel after a thoroughly long viewing of the *calli*, shops and costumed revelers.

Upon your return, you considered changing into street clothing and grabbing a few *cicchetti* at a local *bacaro* to end the evening in good taste. However on entering the courtyard at dusk, adorned beautifully with white twinkle lights, you found that the hotel was serving a buffet dinner. Spread out on a long linen covered table was a delectable selection of small bites and delicious wines, all local favorites, arranged specifically as a special celebratory treat for the Carnevale. With candles on the tables and ambient Italian music flowing in from a few well-placed speakers, you couldn't resist. But what really drew you in were several outdoor wood burners, already aglow with toasty red-orange fires. Paying the buffet fee with the front desk, you reserved a seat and then went up to your room to change out of costume and into warm clothing. You spent the evening quite pleasantly at table soaking in the fresh air, cozy atmosphere and delicious food and had no trouble achieving a sound sleep once snug in your bed.

The new day being just as beautiful as the last, you woke refreshed and enjoyed breakfast in a local *pastecceria* with a plate full of doughy pastries and coffee. You spent the next hours pleasantly with a visit to the Venetian Arsenal. The Arsenale di Venezia was the location in the city where shipbuilding took place starting in the early twelfth century. What made it very unique was that it was one of the first sizeable manufacturing operations in Europe. From the early 1100s on through the late 1700s, the Arsenal constructed most of the Venetian merchant ships that were sailing the trade routes. Located in the *sestiere* of Castello, workers throughout the Arsenal made individual parts that were then married to make a single ship. The operation was very efficient and produced new vessels in remarkable time. It was also unique in that everything necessary to outfit a ship was made there, all in one place. The Arsenal also acted as a service station for boat repairs. Such an amazing operation yielded many improvements to the art of shipbuilding over the centuries, employed thousands of Venetians and was the key to what made Venice's naval presence extraordinarily powerful.

After touring the Naval History Museum and the architecture within and around the Arsenal, you enjoyed a few slices of pizza in Castello and then wandered back to the San Marco district. It was quite a pleasant, as well as educational, way to spend the day. Once returning to your hotel, you took a short nap before freshening up to walk to Carmela's, dressing in a cashmere sweater, sleek pants and stylish flats, garnishing your neck with a sparkly necklace. This was one of several outfits that you had brought along should you not wish to wear a costume (or blue jeans) on any special outing during your holiday. After securing proper directions at the front desk, you walked to the home of your new friend, stopping to pick out a variety of delectable cookies which you requested be boxed especially to present to your hostess.

Just now arriving at the address, you find that it is a historic *palazzo*. You assume that it has been divided into separate units judging by the fact that Carmela mentioned that she lived on the second floor. You are immediately impressed when entering through an iron gate from off the *calle*, you find a most grand colonnade open to the air and constructed with ancient marble flooring and covered with a high ceiling. Within, there is a commanding arched doorway, leading one to ascend a stone stairway to the apartments. It is quiet and bare of outdoor furniture, excepting six or so hearty potted trees, each no taller than your person and spread around the gated perimeter. Walking up one story of stairs, you locate what must be the first floor unit, although there isn't an apartment number posted on the door. Climbing a second set of stairs, you find another dwelling and knock politely at the entry.

You can hear muffled laughter coming from within. As the door swings open, you are greeted by a gust of floral perfume and an attractive middle-aged woman dressed sophisticatedly in a knee-length chestnut colored skirt and a cream blouse. Her neck and ears are ornamented with pearls and her dark hair is bound in a low bun. High heels swathed in Italian leather click on the marble floor as she welcomes you into her home. She introduces herself as Maria, Carmela's mother. You find that she already knows your name, as Carmela had informed her that you would be amongst the guests. She kindly ushers you into a hallway where she hangs your coat in a closet stuffed with fur and wool. As she directs you into a large living room, richly furnished yet easeful, you see that there are already a number of guests lounging comfortably on plush couches. You wave and everyone greets you warmly, chirping a variety acknowledgments in Italian. Maria next leads you to the kitchen where you find Carmela delicately arranging appetizers on white ceramic serving platters while her *nonna* (Fiametta as she is introduced) prepares a dish on the stove. The cooking smells are enticing and the kitchen cozy and warm. Fiametta is also a lovely woman, her features very similar to both those of Maria and Carmela. Only a few pronounced lines about her face (likely from all her smiles and laughter through the years) as well as a few errant silver strands of hair, give away her age difference. The ladies in Carmela's family have good genes as they say! Furthermore and lucky for you, everyone speaks English fluently, making for easy and pleasant conversation.

After giving Carmela the box of cookies and washing your hands, you offer to assist with the preparations. Given the simplest tasks, you are asked to arrange the treats that you brought onto a three tiered silver tray for the guests to nibble on after dinner and also to slice a few lemons and limes to flavor several pitchers of icy sparkling water. As Carmela and Maria flit in and out of the kitchen in that focused way that hostesses often do, Fiametta takes her time lovingly stirring a pot full of simmering yellow cornmeal. She informs you that she's just started the stirring process for polenta! It takes a lot of water to saturate the cornmeal as well as up to 45 minutes of continual stirring in order to get the right results. Once complete the thick and creamy polenta can be eaten as is, or fried until crispy. It is a rich and delicious dish no matter how it is served. As she stirs, you chat amicably about where you are from and what you've liked so far about Venice. She asks you whether you've enjoyed any delightful dishes yet and what you like to eat back home. You tell her about your family and she tells you a little about theirs. It's a pleasant conversation, though it does make you miss having quality time with your own grandmother. You tell Fiametta that Carmela mentioned her having a lot of great stories. Wouldn't she tell you one or two? Continuing to swirl the cornmeal dutifully, she shares several true tales from her youth.

There was the time her dog jumped out of her family's boat while she was on an errand with her parents. It swam around in the canal and wouldn't come back to the boat. It was having a great time splashing about and barking at everyone. This held up traffic and other boaters were beginning to get impatient. Being yet a girl, Fiametta screamed fiercely, drawing even more attention, until her father felt forced to dive in and collect the mischievous dog. The gondoliers shamefully laughed at him as he struggled to contain the rebellious animal. She is now certain that this must have embarrassed him (the act was chivalrous but not exactly heroic). However, not being able to help it, Fiametta and her mother were soon laughing as well. As her father pushed the frenetic dog up into the boat and tried to climb back in himself, the animal jumped right over his head back into the canal, making a merry splash. The save had to be repeated, much to the gondoliers' amusement. Despite his struggles, her father was eventually laughing too, though it wasn't until they got home much later. After that, her pet had to be tied in the boat any time they went out for a ride.

Then there was the time she was shopping with her mother at the *pescheria*. She was young then too and stood only tall enough to see all of the marine life on display at table height. As her *mamma* negotiated the price of shellfish with a vendor a short distance away, a fish began to speak to her! She was very startled and watched the fish closely with big eyes. Though the creature (an ugly red monster with gooey black eyeballs and a gaping mouth with little jagged teeth) never moved its lips, it jiggled as she heard it speak. It asked her if she could free it! Looking around, she was in awe that a talking fish at the Rialto market was speaking to *her*. It felt like a secret. She became proud that it had chosen her to assist it with its great escape. Determined, she snatched the hideous beast from its bed of ice and ran with it to the canal a short distance away. There she tossed it into the water with a big grin on her face and wiped the fish slime off of her hands onto her fine, cream colored wool coat. She was very happy with herself until the submerged animal floated back up to the surface and was carried away in the drift. It couldn't swim. It was clearly dead. With this, she started crying hysterically. To make matters worse, two elderly ladies had seen what she had done and scolded her for wasting such an expensive, delicious fish. When she tried to tell them through her hot tears that the fish had told her to free it, well, this caused quite a scene. The ladies cackled and snickered, calling her a naughty little girl and a liar too! Her mother soon came and snatched her away from the harpies. Telling her *mamma* what she had done, they returned to the vendor whose fish she stole. It turned out that he was guilty of a mean trick. Having squatted down behind his table, he had reached over the top and shook the fish about, asking Fiametta to free it in a funny fishy voice. He apparently played this little game a dozen times before with other children, only, they figured out the trickster without hesitation. Fiametta was the first child to snatch a fish and run with it. After apologizing to them both, he gave Fiametta a plastic bag filled with water and knotted at the top with a small, live fish in it. She freed that one too.

You are charmed by her recollections, ones only a Venetian could have. She breaks the storytelling to say that the polenta is done and that dinner will soon be served. Looking at the creamy golden dish, your mouth begins to water. You move out of the way to allow room as she pulls out from the oven, several serving platters that were keeping warm. Tonight's feast will consist of polenta topped with buttery mushrooms and minced parsley, chilled melon and prosciutto salad, cheesy buckwheat *bigoli* pasta and sautéed Venetian shrimp and scallops. For dessert the party will be treated to Fiametta's ultra rich tiramisu (and your cookies of course). You wonder if you will ever eat so well again once you leave Venice!

Helping the ladies to set the dining table in the next room, which is decorated with Murano glass handcrafted candelabra and crystal vases bursting with fragrant bouquets, there looks to be room to seat 20 guests! You wonder if all the dining tables in Italy are designed to accommodate large gatherings, or if that is just a stereotype that you heard somewhere. As Maria calls everyone to be seated, the exodus of friends and family from the living room into the dining room brings with it laughter, the clinking of wine glasses and the warmth of Italian conversation. Once seated to the repast, Carmela's father (who you easily pick out by the facial resemblance and prominent seat at the head of the table) heartily toasts to the company, the Carnevale and to La Serenissima, the Most Serene Republic of Venice! With that, the meal begins. As the jovial guests share food and amity, you can't stop smiling over the perfection of the moment. Some of the conversation you understand and some you do not, but it makes no difference. The harmonious sounds of fellowship need no translation.

THE End.

WITH the black ghoul still standing close to the door as the light of morning begins to flood through the cracks of the shuttered window, you give directions to your lady's maid in a hushed but direct tone.

Please send away this good doctor and pay him from our purse. I am no longer in need of his assistance. We shall attend Mass this evening as per my regular routine and then you may have the night off to join in the masked revelry of the Carnevale. Only, as you are about the merrymaking, I'll wish for you to make a brief stop at my dear cousin's palazzo and make excuse for my not attending her grand ball. For now I would like for you to prepare my toilette and arrange a filling breakfast for us both, I am famished! After I am dressed you may take a nap if you wish, as I am sure that you are very tired from such a sleepless and stormy night. I will take a walk and get some fresh air as you rest.

Moving to dismiss the doctor Belloza exits out of the room leaving the door open halfway, the doctor trailing behind her into the hall. Leaning forward in the bed for a better view, you see that she has a room opposite of yours where she enters at present while the doctor waits. He turns his beak back in the direction of your door and cranes his neck, making some last observation of the prey that got away. Leaning back against your pillows, you busy yourself taking another sip of water from the half filled glass on your bedside table. You believe that just the sight of a doctor dressed in this way would be poor for anyone's health! The vulture looks to bring death with him rather than hope for one's recovery.

Reentering the hall from her chamber, the maid asks the doctor into her room to pay his fee. You take the opportunity to get out of bed and find that in an anteroom (previously where your modern bathroom had been) there is a dressing room. Within, there is an ornately embroidered screen taller than you and designed for dressing privacy, a porcelain potty-chair, a washbasin and a vanity table complete with a cushioned bench. There displayed are a number of delicate items that presumably belong to the countess: an exquisitely painted hand-held fan, ribbons, powder, rouge, velvet beauty marks in a little box, a hairbrush and vials of perfume.

Sitting down to the vanity, you review your reflection in the mirror. Though a little tired in appearance, it is with great relief that you find your own face staring back at you. As you were lying in bed a constant question invaded your thoughts. How can it be that Belloza believed that you were her mistress? It doesn't take long for your question to be answered.

Madame, would you like for me to deliver your commissioned portrait to your lady cousin when I go to make regrets?

Entering the powder room she holds something in her hands, which appears to be a small framed painting. Unfortunately you cannot see the image as it is turned over in her hands. You can only glimpse the canvas exposed at its back. As you should already recognize the item that she holds, she does not mean to display it to you. Considering how to respond, you skip only a breath before praising her for reminding you of the painting! She should deliver it and wrap it nicely too (as it is clearly a gift that the countess meant for her cousin). Extending a palm expectantly, you tell her that you'd like to regard it once more before she does so. Obeying, she hands it to you and exits the room.

Hesitating to turn it over, you note from the back that it is a canvas painting tacked to a polished wood frame. In all, it is a rectangle no bigger than your hand. In several lines of a fine ink flourish, there is a signature (presumably the artist's), a year and the name of who you are sure is the sitter; Contessa Ciossa Fortunato, 1779. Your hands begin to tremble ever so slightly as an anxiety creeps into your chest. Without even turning it over in your hands you are certain that it is a portrait of the lady, the very woman you are playing to be at this disquieting moment. Rotating it over, the frame nearly fumbles out of your unsure grasp and you get your first glimpse of the image. Trying to remain composed, you are shocked to find that the lady within the portrait appears to be *you*. How could this be?

As Belloza reenters the room to fill the standing washbasin with steamy water, you set the frame on your lap and pretend to be inspecting one perceived flaw or other on your face, your fingers quivering as you smooth them under your eyes and over your forehead. As she leaves, you pick up the likeness once more. There is only a single explanation that is feasible to you. You've had a past life and have switched places with your past self. Has your past self been transported into your future life? You wonder how she's getting along, dreading to imagine. Perhaps she too was shocked into a faint and will soon wake only to ramble like a madwoman, disturbed by her misplaced existence in the eighteenth century.

Many questions run through your mind as you view the beautiful painting before you. There is the image of an elaborately dressed noblewoman in a fine ebony gown, the artist even capturing the sheen of the silk. Her towering powdered bouffant is adorned with white roses. It looks everything to be you though in another period in time. Only, the eyes are not yours. You see in them another life lived in another time. Do you share a soul with this repeated life? You share a physical exactitude for certain! Though lovely, she appears somewhat dark in spirit. You assume that it must be grief. This isn't surprising having lost her husband. She must have loved him very much. Becoming emotional, you feel tears beginning to pool in your eyes. You feel sorry for you both; her with her heartache, trying to acclimate in a frightening future and you terrified that you'll never return home. Wiping a tear that has dripped from your lashes, you sniffle and grab for an embroidered handkerchief too pretty to wipe your face with though you do so anyway. You are supposed to be a countess after all! Lost in wondering how you will manage to return to where you belong, you hardly notice Belloza reenter the room.

Now mistress! Gone and gotten yourself down

again? Madame, you're just overrun and can't help but grieve, but the sun will soon be shining! I know you miss your husband my lady, he was a good man and we all loved him. Go on and have your cry now while I dress your hair, but then you must cheer up and eat some breakfast. I've ordered your favorites. You must also try to enjoy that promenade in the fresh air! My lady, even after tragedy, we must live!

Lifting your head, you force a smile for Belloza in the reflection of the vanity mirror. While wiping your eyes and nose, you tell her that she is right. As you sit in silence she attends to your hair, weaving it into a simple yet lovely style, all pinned and powdered. You play with the ribbons on one sleeve of the shift you are wearing; all that is left from the costume you wore into the room the day before. Clearly the maid helped you out of the cumbersome gown before dragging you unconscious into bed. You wonder if your passport and euros, a not yet created currency, are still within your secreted pocket. You guess it doesn't matter, what good would these items do for you here? At most, if discovered they'll confuse Belloza, who will believe you picked up some very strange souvenirs on your outing yesterday! Finishing, she leaves you in privacy to bathe, washing your body out of the warm water at the standing basin with a soft cotton cloth and tea rose scented soap.

Dressing in fresh underpinnings and a pretty pink morning robe which you find lying over the dressing screen, you reenter the bedroom to discover a delicious breakfast set out at the little table where Belloza had set her sewing the evening before when you had entered the room. Sitting in the comfortable chair next to it, your eyes feast. You are absolutely ravenous; this meal is certain to fix that *and* raise your spirits! A bronze tray is laid out for your pleasure and fit for a queen. There you review a cup of piping hot black tea and cream, a juicy segmented orange, crispy toast with butter and dark berry jam, two boiled eggs with a miniature silver salt bowl and spoon, and a cut of cold succulent ham. There is also a delicate linen napkin, ironed and folded neatly, as well as a few sprigs of aromatic rosemary bound with a red ribbon; you snatch up the nosegay and sniff it eagerly. You call out to the maid who enters from the hall a few moments later holding something like a newspaper, as well as a sealed letter. Asking her whether she isn't joining you for this breakfast, she asks if she might not sit with the other ladies' maids downstairs to eat while you read your correspondence and the daily gazette, your normal routine. You've only received one letter this morning, she regrets.

Acknowledging her want to chatter and gossip with the other ladies, perhaps to see who else may have the evening free to gallivant (a rare pleasure), you consent easily. Handing you the papers, she is off, closing your room door behind her. Setting aside the items, you take your time to enjoy the tray; there is nothing like a good breakfast to ease one back into life on the roughest of days. With every buttery bite, salty nibble and sweet peck, you are amazed at how easily good food can restore one's positive outlook! Peering at the gazette lying on the table, you are certain once scanning its pages, you'll get an interesting snapshot of the culture and concerns of today's waking city. More interesting is the letter, which is sure to give you a better understanding of the woman you embody, at least from the pen of an acquaintance. After finishing your last bite, you take a relaxing sip of tea and wipe your hands on the pristine napkin, soon picking up the missive.

The paper is yellowish in tint and on the front is written the name of the countess. You feel like an imposter as you break a golden wax seal that holds the letter neatly closed. The stamp in the wax looks to be some sort of official symbol, and as you open the correspondence, you find that there is only a single sheet.

To The Esteemed Contessa Ciossa Fortunato,

Your presence is demanded at the Palace of the Doge for immediate questioning by the Venetian Council of Ten. This is an urgent matter forwarded from the city of Padua, relating to the death of your husband Conte Fortunato, some six months gone. Recent revelations following your leave to Venice from your estate have elicited a need to review the circumstances surrounding his tragic end. With the honor that is due your ladyship's status, we allow you to come unaided by our guard at the appointed hour of noon. If you fail to be seen at this exact time, appointees will come to pursue and guide you to this destination.

Humble Servant of Justice to the Serene Republic,
Signore Giudizio

TURN to page 427.

IT isn't long before you are drifting along the canals by gondola on your way to your cousin's *palazzo*. Belloza suggested that she hand-deliver the item herself since your journey out of the city would carry you past Amedia's grand palace. You agreed with the understanding that she would hurry her task and that you would remain in the boat.

This is officially your first gondola ride and no matter the present circumstances, you try to enjoy it. Having layered up with a warm mantle, you feel perfectly comfortable except for the occasional shortness of breath caused by the tight corset. Dressed more simply but similarly, Belloza appears to enjoy the ride, watching the bridges pass overhead while attentive to the sounds of a waking Venice. You are both wearing a half mask, as is the boatman. In fact, everyone you see is outfitted thusly as during the Carnevale, no one goes about unmasked. Though there is a *felze* built onto the boat (an enclosed cabin for two that would give your ride privacy), you and your handmaiden have chosen to sit in the open air. The waterways are far more crowded than they were in the modern day, stuffed with a variety of vessels, not just gondola. It was in fact another type of craft, liken to a sturdy and elaborate rowboat, which picked up your luggage at the hotel dock to deliver it to your carriage in anticipation of your pending travel to Padua.

Belloza? Yesterday just before arriving at the hotel I saw something gruesome. There was a very sickly man struck down with open wounds being pushed around in a wooden barrow. Have you ever seen this before? I was surprised by it and frightened too. How sorry I was for him.

Smiling warmly, she pats your hand before replying.

You are such a softhearted one madame. During the Carnevale, you may occasionally find a poor wretch succumbing to syphilis. What you saw were sores brought on by the disease of which as you know, there is no cure. It is gruesome indeed, but the syphilitic are exhibited as a reminder to the frivolous during the festival, that life is fragile. Perhaps it is a warning against excess. I am not exactly sure.

You are shocked and saddened, especially because you know that modern medicine can cure the affliction with the proper diagnosis and medication.

There was also a woman floating behind a funerary gondola. She seemed to greatly grieve her loss, much like I do, of course. Where are Venice's dead buried? There can't possibly be a plot of earth large enough amongst all these palazzi to properly attend to the city's departed citizens.

You found yourself curious, as you knew that Venetians in your time are buried on the Isola di San Michele or cemetery island of St. Michele. It is a small island not far from the Cannaregio neighborhood of Venice and which hosts an ancient church. However, it wasn't until the early 1800s that it became a place for the dead to sleep when it was established that the burial practices previously used on the main island, placed Venetians at risk for foul disease.

You are right that Venetians do not have the same open land that we do in Padua, my lady. But the dead are buried right here under the stones. If you own a palazzo, you'll have your family laid to rest beneath your courtyard, or in your garden such as are Amedia's parents. Don't you remember your aunt and uncle? Madame, wouldn't it be delicious to live in Venice? Don't you like it here?

No wonder a cemetery away from Venice needed to be created. You imagine that decomposing bodies, beneath these stones and in the gardens, would contaminate the local wells or infect rooting dogs and rats with pestilence if a body was unearthed. You shudder briefly and then try to smile for Belloza.

Yes, I do like it here very much. Though, I feel I have a whole world to become newly acquainted with. I mean, because of my husband's death of course. I feel like I am starting over again.

The maid provides a consoling nod. If only she knew that it wasn't a husband you were grieving, you didn't even know the count.

Belloza, do you ever feel that your whole world has turned strange and will never be right again? That you aren't sure how to find your way? I feel a constant unease and am not certain how to go back to how things were.

Appearing to think on it for a moment, she reaches into a basket at her feet and pulls out a stuffed handkerchief embroidered with cheery sunflowers along its perimeter. Unfolding it delicately in her palm, she reveals a handful of crisp round cookies and extends them to you. You select one and soon you are both nibbling.

It has been a while since you were this open with me contessa. If I were to guess, Venice has done you some good and that you'll soon find yourself again. But speaking frankly, sometimes I do feel this unease even when I am unsure exactly why. The feeling can nag at me for quite a while. But eventually I find that my unsettled humor is due to something left undone. Perhaps I owed someone an apology or needed to take care of something important. Once righted however, things seem to fall back into place. Perhaps my lady, it simply feels this way for you right now because you are sad that you will not see your husband again in this life and there are more things that you wish that you could say to your beloved. Everyone who has lost someone has felt this way. You will have to learn to carry on despite your inability to make things perfect.

You consider Belloza's wise words and imagine that she has been a very good friend and companion to the countess. Opposing her last remark however, you hope that you will not have to reconcile yourself with having to leave behind a life and loved ones. There must be a way back. Taking another bite of your cookie, which tastes like sweet almonds, you think back to what could have been left undone, as she suggests, in your modern life. The last thing you remember was making the decision to retract from the water's edge once that strange man asked to share a gondola ride with you and to split the cost. You felt a little uncomfortable with the offer and declined it. Were you supposed to enter the boat with that man? Perhaps there was some purpose. But this is nonsense! You can't imagine that that situation had anything to do with the strange circumstance you now find yourself in.

You compliment the delicious cookies. Belloza tells you that they are traditionally Venetian and that she secured these from a local *pasticceria* while you were out the day before. You suggest that she saves one for the cook in Padua so that they might replicate the recipe and she agrees. Sitting in silence, you both observe the passing scenery, which comes further alive with every passing minute. Each bridge you pass under seems to display more celebratory pedestrians than the last. Floating beneath one such bridge, you are showered with yellow, white, pink and red rose petals; even your gondolier smiles. Approaching another, you enjoy the playful music of a mandolin and lute, a dancing fool hopping about to the festive tune as others clap merrily along with the beat.

Before long, you are docking at the waterside entrance of the destination Belloza directed the boatman, your cousin's home, nestled on a lesser canal between two highly trafficked ones. The waterway is peaceful with hardly a boat traversing it aside from a few vendors making deliveries to the *palazzo*, likely in preparation for the grand ball this evening. As the maid carries out your wishes by entering to deliver the portrait with your regrets, you decide to exit the boat and take a quick stroll along the *calli* surrounding the property, as you may be traveling at great length and you think it best to get a moment's stretch. You would of course have delivered your regrets yourself, but feared that the countess's cousin would have asked you direct questions or drove you into deep conversation. You would have been at a loss to address anything substantial, as you are not the countess and it would appear that you were very ill. You can't risk being thrown into a madhouse if it soon becomes apparent that you have no recollection of a life lived in the eighteenth century. Leaving the gondolier behind, you assure him that the business within will last no longer than a quarter of an hour. You'll return by then.

Alighting from the boat you follow a stone path along the palace walls, which you find barren of anyone else. You soon find yourself at the entrance of a charming high walled garden. Entering, the path circles a square of winter greenery, stone benches and marble statues overgrown with ivy. The walls protect any noise from encroaching and all you can hear are a few birds chirping around you. There is another entryway at the far opposite side of the garden some distance away. You decide to walk the length of this hidden Eden and back again before returning whence you came. What a serene treasure amidst these marble behemoths!

You walk slowly along the stone path, taking in the sea air mixed with the scent of pine and dirt. A terrible thought flits into your head at wondering whether there is anyone buried here. Well, if they are, it is a peaceful place and certainly better than beneath the stones in a highly trafficked courtyard.

From amidst the natural sounds of the garden you suddenly hear a muffled whine. The noise is very unexpected. You stop and stand as still as stone listening for where the sound is coming from. In the year that you belong, despite the fact that crime exists, you would have felt comfortable seeking out the source of the noise quickly, even out of simple curiosity. As a good citizen, you would have wanted to help if there was someone in need. However in *this* day, you are very unsure of your surroundings. What if there is a violent street thug with a knife? Perhaps even a pirate with a sword waiting in the bushes to steal you away on his ship! Or a plague inflicted street dog ready to bite your leg! Or, or, or what? You can't think of any other dangers at the moment.

You hear further sounds, struggling masculine breaths and some choked, hushed sobs. Moving again, you take delicate steps in the direction of the noise, soon pinpointing that it is coming from along the wall of the garden behind a cluster of tall fir trees jutting out in a semicircle. Of course, your half mask gives you absolutely no protection. For some reason however, it makes you feel more secure like a child huddled beneath a beloved blanket which keeps them safe from their imaginary ghosts. Moving closer, it sounds to be a weeping man. There is an entrance to slip through between two of the pine trees along the wall, where clearly is a secreted place, but you are afraid to peek within. Whoever is behind may have wished for privacy. Or, something more fearful could be within. What if someone is hurt and in need of help? Braving your fears, you approach the trees and peer inside.

Your eyes grow wide and your heart begins beating

very fast at the revelation of who is before you. There nestled behind the trees are a marble bench and a sitting man. *He* is finely dressed and very attractive in spite of the plentiful tears streaming down his face from beneath a half mask, his head of dark hair hanging heavily in sorrow. Even from this angle, you can see that it is the stranger from the gondola station, the very one who offered to split the price of a ride with you. Or at least, it is the exact image of him. Eerily, you sense there is a purpose for your happening upon this being right here and right now. This is the moment Belloza spoke of, something fixing, perhaps righting an unaccomplished task that never happened when it was meant to.

Lost in grief, he doesn't appear to notice your presence. There beside him is a circular black basket. It is lidded and one of the man's velvet clad arms rests heavily upon it. You hadn't noticed before, but now can clearly hear a close and dull hissing. It is coming from within the basket. Is that a snake? It is for certain the sound of a creature trapped within and eager to get out. The sound becoming louder, you imagine that the animal is maddened and perhaps afraid. For certain, it is a viper, you are sure of it.

Being one of the stranger moments you've ever

387

found yourself, you gather your courage and address the man who you remember so clearly as being one of the last people that you saw in your true life.

Sir?

He looks up at you with complete astonishment, his gasps halting in your presence. He had clearly not expected to see anyone else here. Furthermore, he doesn't recognize you at all. Perhaps because this man has never met you before, only his future self has.

What are you doing in my garden?

You are surprised at his strong tone considering his earnest grieving from just a moment ago. He is perhaps angry to have been found in this manner by a stranger and accustomed to speaking frankly to anyone he wishes. Having shaken the basket with the slightest movement, the hissing within grows agitated. The hairs on your neck prickle with discomfort and in that moment, you realize his tone isn't out of irritation that someone has happened upon his garden or even that he was found lamenting. Your presence upsets him for quite another reason.

I was taking a walk and didn't know that this was a private path.

He makes to enlighten you, his face grimaced and

red with emotion.

Well it is. Do you see there? My estate the Palazzo Forza and this is the garden belonging to it. My lady, I can see that you are of elegant rank so I kindly ask that you to exit my property, rather than demand it.

You note that he is a close neighbor of the contessa's cousin and wonder if the countess and this man (clearly of noble breeding) had ever brushed shoulders. Without moving to leave, you regard him carefully. Guilt shines upon his face, as well as surprise, irritation and sorrow.

How very lucky you are, what a beautiful garden! I am Countess Fortunato and my cousin owns that estate just there. I am sure that you must be acquainted with her?

Looking slightly dazed, he becomes quiet for a moment before telling you that his wife once was. Ah, there it is, a wife that once was and now isn't, you presume. A slight shift in his arm shakes the basket enough to bring on a sizzling hiss of warning. Looking into your eyes, his pained stare entreats you to leave him to his grim plans. You cannot however, no matter how displeased, angry even, he may become.

I can hear that you have within your basket a

snake? Ah, these creatures can be so very useful if they are not venomous to people, to let loose in your garden to control the mice and rats.

He looks at you defiantly and with shame. Of course, he had no intention of freeing the viper into the garden to hunt vermin. Unless of course after receiving the fatal bite he was seeking, the animal escaped on its own. But being already dead, he would no longer be concerned with the snake's whereabouts.

I have found however that cats make just as effective hunters and far better company. Wouldn't you agree? But these matters are better left to the gardener I find. If I am correct, then it isn't a local snake as there cannot be many slithering about this marble city on the water, but rather one you purchased off a merchant of exotic goods, which I hear are everywhere in Venice. I wouldn't know firsthand however, as I am from Padua. Ah well, I've always wondered what it would be like to keep a pet monkey. You can buy these in Venezia as well I am told. But I hear they are wild to the utmost and like to bite and screech, how unpleasant!

You know what animal is a good hunter of vermin? Owls! Once when I was a child, I witnessed my mother walk out onto the balcony of her room at night holding a candle. Besides the tiny flame, she was shrouded in darkness. I cannot remember why she went outside...perhaps she had forgotten something there. Believing the light was the glowing eyes of a little animal, an enormous owl swept out of the shadows to snatch it. Its wings beat against my mother's face before it flew away without its perceived prey. My mother was stunned. It was quite exciting! But, I dare say an owl wouldn't work for you here.

You recognize the faintest hint of a smile touch the man's lips. You must look very eccentric chatting on, but the distraction seems to be working. You briefly turn to a more serious mention.

You know, I recently lost my husband, eternal blessings on his soul. I came to visit Venice and my cousin to try to cast off my terrible mourning. I will never forget my beloved of course but it is now time for me to remember the joys in life. I know as well as anyone in what a cruel and strange circumstance we may find ourselves from time to time. Life is very bizarre; you can take my word for it. However, no matter what we lose, the journey is always worth continuing until it is truly and naturally our time. I hope that I am not too forward sir to speak bluntly, but I am certain I came upon you in a woeful state. I would not overstep and press why. But I can assure you that all great pain dulls with time and happiness renews. A weasel! That is what you need! They are excellent predators! Loose one of these in your garden instead!

A smile breaks on his face. He must think you a strange woman but at least he is momentarily amused. Momentarily is all that is necessary to change one's course.

I am glad to see you smile! We should all make a practice of smiling more. Perhaps it is a bold request sir, but might you accompany me to my cousin's masquerade this evening? You are our neighbor of course and I could use a learned companion to teach me something about your wonderful city. I am quite ignorant of the ways of Venice, you see. In any case, there is nothing like the seething humanity of a ball during the Carnevale season to keep your thoughts merry? I see that you are of elegant rank as well sir, so I kindly ask you to do this, rather than demand it.

Slowly standing, he removes his mask, his features appearing astonished by your candid request. Seeing his full visage for the first time, you find that he is remarkably handsome. First telling you his name, he gives assent to your request and then bows nobly before you. With a soft curtsey, you leave him to collect himself and make to exit the garden. You are certain that you will see Signore Sognare at the ball as he has given his word. You must hastily relay to Belloza the change in plans. As you walk out of the green, you are unsure how you'll play the part of the countess before your cousin and much of Venice's elite. However, that is the price you'll have to pay in order to detour a life on the brink of extinguishing from grief. Hopefully, no-you're certain, Sognare will soon remember how much life is worth living.

This is your last thought when, though walking in the same place you find yourself halting as you approach the canal; a speedboat whizzes by. Still dressed in the white gown that Belloza had laid out for you back in time, it takes a moment for reality to register. You are back again in the modern day! Both relieved and elated, you rush on foot to find the Hotel Fato, asking random people for directions on your way with a huge grin on your face. Returning, you claim a lost key with the staff at the front desk; they lend you a spare.

Entering, you are unsure just what to expect and so remain still as you scan the room. Clearly, someone else has been here and you're certain you know who it was. The countess having briefly switched places with you, entered the room after a day of festivity only to find your modern luggage, her lady's maid nowhere in sight and a mythical modern bathroom. You find the contents of your luggage lying around the room. She must have dismantled everything that you still had neatly packed in your cases. But, as you do not see any genuine eighteenth century clothing anywhere, you assume that she remained in the clothes that she was wearing when she arrived, likely sleeping in them throughout the night. Calling the front desk, you receive confirmation that *you* had ordered dinner last night and breakfast this morning. In fact, the maid service picked your breakfast tray up from your room before you went out in costume just this last hour. Though nothing was said when you came back asking for a new key, it was a surprise that you returned so soon and in a different costume. Hopefully there was nothing wrong with your food? Is that why you are inquiring?

You hang up the phone with a smile and let out a great sigh of release. Seeing your open wallet laying on the writing desk, your ID card pulled from its place, you are certain that Contessa Fortunato learned of your existence. You are soon rooting up your passport and its contents from the crack in the floor, worn and stained after a few hundred years, but still there! It is all too baffling. You wonder what Belloza will think when she finds her mistress dressed again in the outfit that you said had been given away to a beggar!

Without wasting any time to change out of the countess's gown (you are sure to be the best dressed visitor in the *calli*) you make to leave the hotel, your sights set on the library. As you exit out of the lobby, the front desk attendant praises your elegant costumes. Two outfits in one morning! What a true lover of history!

Once entering the Biblioteca Nazionale Marciana just steps from where you originally fell back in time, you have many historic documents available for review; you are certain you'll find something. It doesn't take long for you to locate both the names of Contessa Ciossa Fortunato and Signore Sognare. There are some general life mentions including important dates in their lives and properties owned, as well as copies of portraits made of them by talented artists. This is at the very least some proof of her resemblance to you, though you'd never show anyone; they would only think it an odd coincidence. However, the most interesting tidbit you find is that the two were married in the year 1781. Two years after your snapshot into their lives! You wonder what the countess must have thought when she found herself instantaneously walking alongside her cousin's *palazzo* after her bizarre journey, just where you left off. Or to how she reacted to Lord Sognare's attendance when he met her at the ball that evening. She of course would have remained with her cousin on her return out of the garden, being too overwrought by her strange time travel. She would have been just as euphoric as you to feel her usual reality once more. More questions enter your thoughts, but you guess the rest *is* history.

There is one nagging question that you cannot escape however. Was there something that you missed when you decided not to accept the ride along from the stranger, the man with a past self who appears to be Sognare? In missing that trip, was there something that went undone? Perhaps not able to do so in this life after you missed the moment, were you sent back in time to make things right? You guess you'll never know. For now, you are ready to rekindle your Venetian adventure!

THE End.

HAVING had a morning adventure to the local *pasticceria* for breakfast and some fresh air, as well as an afternoon of sublime rest to fortify you for the pleasures ahead of you this evening, it is now time to prepare for the ball! After slipping into a white deep necked under gown, you wash your face and then sit to the mirror at the desk, observing your visage with a cup of hot mint tea in hand. You nibble on a crispy caprese panino which you had delivered to your room as you decide what look you wish to achieve; best to go to an evening soiree with something in your stomach!

First, you brush your hair until smooth and then secure it neatly under a nylon cap, using a few well-placed pins to hold it in place. Softly applying lightly scented white powder to your face, you carefully pat and blend until you achieve an even coverage of talc, as was the fashion in the eighteenth century. Brushing your eyebrows into fine arches, you pencil them in full and dark. Next, you crimp each set of lashes with an eyelash curler and apply dark mascara liberally. For added lush, you use a set of tweezers and clear lash glue to apply a few extra faux outer lashes. After the adhesive is dry, you blink several times in the mirror; you've achieved the right flutter! With a soft brush, you swipe a gorgeous wine colored blush up along your cheekbone and also a tap to the chin, nose and forehead to add a whisper of color to balance the tint of your features. Lifting a dark circular, navy fabric beauty mark (tiny and sweet) from off a sheet with other shapes and sizes, you attach it just above your upper lip to the left. The back of it is tacky and sticks easily in place. With a rich wine colored lip pencil, you outline your lips so that when applying your lipstick and gloss, the color does not feather out and bleed around your mouth. After filling in with lipstick and shiny gloss, you pucker in the mirror and fancy that you could be a lip model.

You select a pair of crystal earrings that drip aside your neck like lustrous chandeliers and hook them into place on your elegant ears. Next, you slip on one of the wigs that you had carefully chosen for this special trip. It is a grand white wig crafted delicately with puffy white curls, which towers only six inches higher than your forehead but gives you an elegant height and lovely playfulness. You spend a bit of time once it is securely in place, pinning its abundant white coils into the most attractive and feminine style. The bounty of white curls look sporadic yet coiffed. Though it may ruin the synthetic hair permanently, you mist the wig liberally with hair spray. This is your first (and may be your only) Venetian ball and you'll chance ruining one wig if it means your bouffant will remain in place just where you want it. For added sparkle, you brought along an aerosol can of hair glitter. Entering the bathroom, you hold your head carefully above the bathtub and gently spray a little cloud over your wig, allowing it a moment to settle. Eventually reviewing the outcome in the bathroom mirror, you are satisfied with the misting of gold and silver sparkles, which are now throughout your hair. You're positively the most glamorous, fabulous, beautiful creation and without even a hint of gaudiness.

With at least a half hour of struggle, you place a corset on and then lace it up the back, looking over your shoulder and into the bathroom mirror to guide your success in the laborious task. When complete, your laces are not half so tight as they would be if someone else had pulled them for you. However, the corset is still cinched enough to create a gorgeous silhouette for your frame and give a sumptuous push to your bosom, without your feeling unable to breath or eat throughout the evening. Stepping into a set of panniers constructed wider than the pair you wore beneath your day dress, you wonder if you'll have to walk sideways through the thin *calli* all the way to the ball. They extend several feet out from either hip, and you love it! Next, you choose between the two evening gowns, one wine colored and one a midnight blue. As they are constructed of silk taffeta, their sheen is gorgeous in the light. You select the blue gown, as its fabric appears like a reflection off moonlit waves on the lagoon. Constructed into two parts (both easy to put on all by yourself), you first pull an elaborate underskirt decorated with ornamental black brocade over your head and pin it into place at your waist over the panniers. Next, you pull the bodice (which is attached to the overskirt) on like a jacket and latch it with its fastenings at the front of your torso. Smoothing out the overskirt, which spreads open wide for the underskirt's brocade to display through, you then adjust the sleeves, which end at the elbows with layers of bunched black silk. Stepping before a full-length mirror attached to the inner door within the armoire, you find that you are absolutely gorgeous! Stunning! You are a beauty in blue, like midnight waves rushing at a pirate ship in the moonlight, the queen of the Adriatic! The becoming ensemble could hardly be more complete, except for a half mask especially made with the same taffeta as the gown, which disguises your identity.

Over the course of the next 40 minutes, you first carefully pull on a pair of thigh-high black stockings. Convenient to the modern day, they make use of a unique tack (which does not damage tender skin) to keep them in place without the use of a garter belt. You find this convenient; what if you have to use the ladies' room? You don't want to have to fuss with waist-high nylons with all these layers! Your hosiery is topped most attractively with black lace, which makes you feel secretly more elegant. Perhaps women should wear pretty under lace more often, as eighteenth century noblewomen did. No one need see the garments but the lady herself in order to feel more special and feminine!

Difficult as it is to bend over, you lace up a pair of knee-high black heeled boots, which you find sturdier than any other sort of heel. With the length of your skirts being what they are, the boots will mainly go unseen but will still give you a lofty height from which all of your blue waves of fabric will flow. Like your day dresses, the skirt of this evening gown secrets a pocket on each side between lush folds. Anything stored there will go unnoticed, safe and secure. You place a few cosmetic essentials, a white cotton handkerchief, and your passport (which you feel more at ease to keep with you), within one such pocket.

Finally, you pin several crystal pendants into your towering tresses and a single broach onto your breast just below your décolleté, next slipping on a pair of elbow length black lace gloves and an ebony mantle. With just a hint of womanly perfume applied to your neck, breast and hair, you feel ready to depart. Grabbing the address card given to you by the mysterious man on the promenade around St. Mark's Square, along with your room key (both carefully placed into your skirt's second pocket), you take leave.

Before leaving the hotel, you spontaneously stop at the front desk and ask the concierge to hail you a gondola. You'll be able to embark at the waterside entrance just steps away. This will afford you a relaxed ride to the *palazzo* without the stress of trying to find the correct address. Giving you a wait time of about 15 minutes, you inquire after a banking machine and walk just around the corner to pull the necessary amount of euros for the gondola ride to your destination and more in case you decide to take one on the return trip as well, as well as the entrance fee required for the ball. For good measure, you take out extra besides for any unforeseen expenses. You find it amusing to be using such a modern machine while wearing eighteenth century style clothing, what a contrast!

The sun has set and it is now fully evening. This night will be what dreams are made of, you are certain. The salty sea air fills your lungs and your breast heaves with the sporadic pulsing of excitement. Your heart beats quickly while smiles and cheer permeate your face. Returning to the hotel, a staffer guides you safely through a large wooden door set at the back of the courtyard. It leads to a canal where a gondola awaits. You step gingerly down a set of marble stairs and board the boat. In this moment, anticipation builds within your chest and looking around you, you feel as though you have quite literally stepped back in time. The excitement within you begins to build exponentially over the forthcoming ball, an event that you've dreamed about for months. It is an occasion of the past that is repeated rarely in the world in these modern days, an authentic masked ball of the Carnevale, and you are heading there now! You're not simply attending a public fete, but have been invited specifically to a private one!

Seated comfortably in the open air of the night in this famous vessel upon a velvet-upholstered settee, you shrug warmly beneath your mantle and prepare to stamp each moment of this precious ride into your memory. As you float along the canal on your way to your destination, you solidly believe that life is what we devise. We cannot expect for any place or anyone to make it pleasurable and beautiful on our behalf. We must seek happiness, create it from our own imaginations and make it a reality, for ourselves. Having planned this special trip over a long course, *you* made your dreams become reality. You truly are the painter in your own tableau of joy!

Floating between the dark and ancient *palazzi*, every moment brings you nearer and nearer to this historic, mysterious and thrilling occasion of a lifetime.

TURN to page 439.

THOUGH the time spent with Biasio was adventurous indeed (the gondola ride, watery rescue and morning entertainment), you've decided to fold the memories away as a chapter of your trip and create a new chapter for today! As with all cities, Venice is filled with so many wonderful things to see and to do, and of course, to eat! Therefore, as exciting as dinner in Biasio's *palazzo* sounds, you are going to decline the invitation for other pleasures that you make all on your own.

On account of Biasio, you enjoy several delectable pastries, but also order some fragrant hot coffee and fresh sliced fruit from the hotel kitchen. You dress comfortably in a favorite pair of jeans and a sweater, layer up in a jacket and scarf and are soon on your way. You had found wonderful reviews of an art museum called the Gallerie dell'Accademia. Being a rather small venue it won't take much time at all to tour the art, all of which was painted before the 1700s. You'll have walked the galleries by lunchtime and then can enjoy an alfresco lunch. How lovely!

Setting out on foot, it doesn't take long at all to reach the museum, which is located in the *sestiere* of Dorsoduro. You find the museum devoid of many visitors, its echoing chambers hung with antiquated art and halls filled with silence and contemplation. While strolling in solitude you are able to take the time to admire or pass up whichever piece moves you or doesn't. There are so many enormous works of skill! The themes of life, love, birth, death, rebirth and of course Venice, are displayed all around you.

You are intrigued by many of the pieces but stop to admire some in greater detail, such as *La Creazione Degli Animali* (*The Creation of the Animals*) by Jacopo Robusti, or Tintoretto. Within, God is portrayed as a wise man floating over land and sea, with silver hair and a wavy beard. There is a luminous glow around his robed body and one of his hands is outstretched in the making of worldly creatures; this is Tintoretto's vision of the creation story from the chapter of Genesis in the Bible. You are taken with the unique appearance of the various animals. Though they are easily recognizable, the fish look awesomely prehistoric! You wouldn't want to dangle your toes in the waters of this painting with those scaly, bulgy eyed, gaping mouthed creatures swimming in the murk. In the sky, there are many kinds of fowl flying in pairs: swans, vultures, egrets, duck and pheasant. You wonder why the fish aren't swimming in partners like the birds. Perhaps their ugliness scared away their mates! On land there are deer, wild hares, a tortoise, a wild boar and horse, and you are pretty certain, an anteater poking its head out from behind a tree; perhaps he's shy. It is simply, a wonderful rendition of the first animals waking up to a new world and meeting one another.

As you tour the Accademia, you are greeted with much Christian art and are awed by the dates of the paintings, some of which are from the fourteenth century! You assume that these pieces were mainly made for ancient churches. You are always amazed to see such antiques and wonder how they kept from marring for so long. You are certain that most art of this age in fact didn't keep and is lost forever. Within these pieces, you are entranced by the use of bright colors and gold leaf. You can only imagine that worshipers in the medieval times were completely in awe to see such paintings, as they were very rare and expensive additions to any house of worship. The very glow of the gold leaf by candlelight on this religious artwork would have proved dazzling and emotionally stirring for visitors, many of which would never have seen a painting before!

One such painting would definitely have had such

an effect. The *Storie della Passione di Cristo e Giudizio Unversale* (*Stories of the Passion of Christ and the Last Judgment*) by Giovanni Baronzio. Painted in the 1300s, this medieval piece is comprised of six paintings, which in sequence show Jesus of the Bible during his insufferable torture on a wooden cross. In the final scene, he is seen sitting in Heaven following his death and resurrection, surrounded by saints. Even without the religious connotations, the very act of crucifixion (which was one form of execution in ancient days) is horrible to consider. Painted with gold leaf, vibrant reds and ominous black paint, the row of paintings explicitly captures a cruel and somber affair; any modern viewer would have no doubt of the absolute suffering a crucified individual would have experienced on a cross, after observing such a work. For those people in the fourteenth century who rarely, if ever, saw works such as these, they would have been doubly affected.

Moving into the fifteenth and sixteenth centuries, such religious themes in painting seem to remain the same, only the large landscapes filled with vibrant blues, greens, oranges and white become magnificent. You note such beautiful scenes and use of color in the *Compianto sul Cristo morto* (*Lamentation over the Dead*

Christ) by Giovanni Bellini and a helper, as well as the *Madonna dell'Arancio* (*Madonna of the Orange Tree*) by Cima da Conegliano. Walking through the gallery, you find some rather enormous paintings, individually covering full-length walls! You wonder if many of these giant pieces exist today because they are harder to lose or change hands. You also ponder at how long it would take a painter to complete such a colossal work. You assume *years*.

One after the other, you are met with exceptional works of infinite detail: Biblical renderings, complicated battle scenes, noble portraits, mythical characters, carnal nudes and festive gatherings. They are all powerful, sensual, beautiful and grand in their own individual and splendid way. The scenes of Venice are currently of your particular interest. There is the *Miracolo della reliquia della Croce al ponte di Rialto* (*Miracle of the Relic of the Cross at the Rialto Bridge*) by Vittore Carpaccio which shows a Venetian architecture different from the one you can see today. Medieval Venice with its wooden Rialto Bridge (instead of marble), soaring chimneys high above the homes (all gone), and gondolas with canopied sitting arrangements whose drivers look as though they could join a band and take up their swords against the

Montagues and Capulets! Is that a fluffy white dog riding at the anterior of that gondola, front and center among all in this grand portrait of Venetian wealth and religious observation? He's got a good seat! The *Processione in piazza San Marco* by Gentile Bellini from the late fifteenth century is amazing! It doesn't appear that much at all has changed in St. Mark's Square, or to the Basilica, in 500 years! The figures filed in the religious procession are impressive, yet you imagine them a little bored, their muscles aching as they stand in such a long ceremonial line.

After some hours of browsing the halls in contemplation of all that it is to be human, which seems to be the very core of art, you find yourself in a long passageway surely not far from the exit of the museum. It is there that the artist Pietro Longhi treats you with a sampling of his miniature scenes. You are delighted! There hang before you a small selection of the real-life Venetian pictures that he painted during the eighteenth century. *The Tailor*, *The Concert*, *The Dance Lesson*, *The Apothecary*, *The Venetian Lady's Morning* and *The Soothsayer* hang delicately side by side. These are just a few of the many capturings of daily life that Longhi painted, others being in alternate galleries around the

410

world while some are in the possession of private collectors. Of these, you get a true taste for local life in the 1700s, the very time period that you wished to emulate on your trip with your costumes during this Carnevale.

You are sorry for the young lady in *Il Farmacista*, wondering if she ever got better. You try to imagine what was within the medicinal jars the man of cures had stowed away upon the shelves of his walls and if the lady, as she gazed to the ceiling while the doctor peered down her throat (suppressing her tongue with a stick) was feeling anxious. In *Il Sarto*, a wealthy lady sits to viewing the fine work of a tailor's black silken gown while a little girl teases a white puppy with a ring toy and a maid with tea tray in hand, looks patiently on in the background. The Venetian lady in the artist's captured morning is being attended to by not one, but three servants: the lady's maid who adjusts the laces on the noble woman's sleeve, another who holds up a mirror so that she may view herself and yet another serving coffee from a tray. The smiles, taunts, gestures, flirtation, admiration, courtly manners, artifacts and people from Longhi's depictions are worth a long and thoughtful viewing. For a moment, you wish that you could transport yourself into one of them and see the scene for yourself. Though not in the Accademia, others of Longhi's pieces, such as *Painter in his Studio*, *A Theatrical Scene*, *Reception before a Wedding*, *Peasants Dancing the Furlana*, *Il Ridotto* (gambling house), *A Fortune Teller at Venice*, *The Dancing Lesson* and many others, show the intimate moments and details of daily Venetian life in the eighteenth century. It is as though someone had taken a photo of the streets or from within one's home, immortalizing those glimpses: the powdered faces, the wigs, the gowns and masks. The pieces are simultaneously cheerful and mysterious, very special works indeed!

Exiting the museum into the sunny day, you consider what next you should see. Perhaps you'll grab a gelato first, and then decide!

THE End.

YOU are intrigued by the special invitation and decide to join Biasio at his *palazzo* for dinner this evening. You spend the day gloriously with some shopping, a delicious pizza and salad lunch in a cozy eatery, and a visit to the top of the Campanile in St. Mark's Square. Towering over all of the other architecture throughout Venice, you are granted an amazing view of a city nesting in a lagoon, from the heights of the bell tower. While shopping you picked up a vintage perfume atomizer filled with an ambrosial fragrance of your choice, and an attractive stationery set carrying your initials stamped in gold foil. You may decide to send a letter using your purchase this very week. You also made a few other select purchases, simply enjoying a tour of all the luxurious and creative shops around the city. It was a charming and full day; you most especially enjoyed watching the various costumed merrymakers mingling in the square, which was as full as ever with festive personalities and their bright creations.

Finally returning to your hotel, you take a little rest, enjoy a hot shower and sip on an espresso to prepare you for an evening out. You decide to wear one of several elegant sets that you brought along on your trip just in case donning a costume was not on your agenda on any given evening. Tonight, you are happy to dress comfortably and as yourself in a sleek pair of black dress pants, a cream cashmere sweater and black high heels. Carefully applying your makeup and setting your hair in your favored feminine fashion, you then flourish a misting of the new perfume you purchased about your person; a scent which is both floral and spicy. You apply a gorgeous red lipstick to your already classy visage and then hang Biasio's gifted pendant around your neck, the delicate piece sparkling in the glow of the setting sun that is filtering into your room. Observing your appearance in the warm orange and red hues of the setting star that cover your image as you sit before the mirror at the writing desk, you are filled with an unexpected anticipation.

You are excited to wrap up in your warm coat, scarf and gloves, and to walk out and be whisked away in a gondola. The ride will be memorable in the dusky light, just as all of Venice is setting out in costume on their journey to their festive destinations for dining, dancing and masquerading. You are also feeling a flutter when thinking about this new acquaintance. Of course, you know nothing about Biasio and honest to yourself, only expect from tonight's dinner, some further education about Venice and its local culture, and perhaps also a delectable meal and some fine wine. That would be perfectly enough for you, a warm and pleasurable way to spend any evening, without needing even a hint of romance. However, there is some spark within you each time you remember that handsome, unmasked face peering up at you from below your window this morning.

Within half an hour, you are floating along the canal on the way to Biasio's estate and the ride is every bit as special as you imagined it would be. Venice's splendid and mysterious inner maze of waterways and ancient buildings are deeply stirring at sunset. Gliding along amidst the shadows, you feel exhilarated by the echoes from distant squares; bubbly, delightful laughter peals from some length away. As it becomes fully dark, you watch one masked couple enter the dim opening to a narrow side street from off of the waterside. You wonder if they aren't stealing a moment together to embrace in secret. Ahead, a woman in a lustrous dark gown and a black veil covered in gold shimmer walks alone and hastily over a bridge before you. You wonder where she is making her way to: a masked ball, a gathering of friends or an intimate dinner for two? Passing alongside one marble palace, you are pleased to see a festive illumination glowing warmly from several windows above, which are wide open. Hearing clinking glasses and music floating out from within, you soon observe shadows cast onto the dark building on the other side of the canal as though it were a merry puppet show. The figures flit around quickly and buoyantly, surely greeting one another happily at the start of a party.

Before long, the gondolier is smoothly pulling the vessel into the watery parking spot that you remember vividly; the pleasant ride has ended all too soon. The lights below the water, like shimmery orbs, guide the parking and you alight. The gondolier ties up the boat and climbs the stone stairs. Standing off to the side, he lights a cigarette and gazes contemplatively out into the night. Perhaps he'd rather be at home with his wife, some home cooking and their own happy celebration. As you approach the large wooden door that leads out from the waterside and into the courtyard, you note a rope hanging from a bell attached to the wall. Pulling it just twice, you are surprised at how loud the clanging is. In moments, the door opens and there before you is Biasio's sister and two other ladies beside. They are all dressed in costume and make an absolutely gorgeous bunch; you believe they should be photographed for *Vogue* magazine right here in the courtyard ahead, as they are insanely fashionable, at least for the eighteenth century! Biasio's sister greets you with an amiable smile, a double "*Grazie!*" a kiss on each cheek and a "*Buonasera!*" Her face is unmasked but you note that she is carrying one in her hand as she follows the other ladies out to the parked gondola from which you just hopped out. Putting out his smoke, the boatman joins them; away they go!

Turning back to the open door, you are startled to find Biasio standing closely in the dimly lit entrance, patiently waiting and thoughtfully watching you. You blush as your heart rate increases. You can't help but to glance to the stone at your feet as you grin reactively. Looking back up, you see that he is smiling in response to your expression. You are relieved to see that he is not in costume but dressed in dark jeans, a fine charcoal sweater and a crisp dress shirt (a pressed cream collar peeking out at his neck). The clean scent of his cologne, fresh and not at all overwhelming, meets you as you enter the door at his gesture. Feeling his body close to yours, he closes the door behind you.

TURN to page 486.

ARRIVING at the waterside dock at the Palazzo Splendore, both you and Belloza mount a set of marble stairs from off of your gondola, reaching a stone platform that lies before the face of the dwelling. In the dusk, a cheery light illuminates from a large open gate leading into the palace property. Even from the canal, you can hear the dull roar of many voices mixed together in the act of merrymaking, abounding in animated speech and laughter. Walking upon the stone platform from off the waterway, you both enter the gate into a small courtyard at the center of the *palazzo*. Looking up, there are lanterns warmly lit throughout to lead the way. It is an inviting entry, filled with potted outdoor plants and trees, all hearty cold-weather greenery well tended. There are a scattering of marble-topped wooden-legged tables surrounded by chairs and benches covered with stitched fabric. In the center of the courtyard is a water-well for the maintenance of the household. You imagine that during the day, the sun pours in brightly and that this area would be, like most Venetian courtyards, intimate and charming. You'd spend the day away reading books, lounging with confidantes and writing letters here, you imagine. Several of the seated arrangements are filled with costumed guests, chatting amicably with glasses of wine, lit by the early evening glow and candles. On the verge of entry into the ball, your heart quickens with both expectation and nervousness.

Passing out of the opposite side of the courtyard and through an enormous wooden door open wide, you enter a brightly lit marble foyer and into the surge. Immediately, two stewards step forward to greet you and your maid. One asks for your cape should you so wish to relieve it. You take it off gladly and hand it to him, as does Belloza, while the other man hands you both fine Murano glass goblets filled with effervescent wine. Before you there is a massive winding staircase leading to a second floor. Scanning above, you see over 50 people standing, talking, teasing, flirting and playing. To your right, a grand ballroom is evident by the mass of people, the waft of baroque music and the rapid movement at the center of the crowd: dancing! To the left, there is a dining hall opulently prepared with long tables covered in linen, glass, porcelain, candelabra, shiny silver cutlery and bursting flower arrangements like nature's fireworks. Belloza appears entranced, even stupefied, as her eyes dart to either side. Which way to walk first with such excitements to choose from? You grant her leave to explore and then wander on alone.

Advancing slowly toward the dining hall, you bring the bubbly beverage to your lips and smile over a sip of its chilled sweetness. Entering, you find that the dinner must be a formal one where all are seated together at the same time to dine before resuming the dance. You are awed when spying the very end of the grand hall, there is entry into another room and then yet another at the far end. They appear full with guests moving about like bees in a hive, finding honeyed amusement. You slowly stroll all the way down past the long tables lying in wait, pausing here and there to move aside as others pass by in the opposite direction. The way through to the other rooms mimics the Venetian *calli*; too thin for multiple panniers to negotiate all at once.

Entering the next room, you quickly identify a gambling den. The space is filled wall-to-wall with mirrors (tricky for card games you are sure). There are a prolific many fruit trees potted at the four corners of the room, standing as tall as your person: lemons, limes and kumquats. Spread around are at least 10 dark linen covered tables and around them, dozens of guests in the sport of the game. There are chips, cards and coins scattered everywhere joined with the serious faced players and the jovial onlookers. A peal of screams, laughter and cheering ignites one table, some well-played hand and a pile of monies won. Walking through at length to see what is to be found in the next room, you are in awe of all of the masked faces, the expensive gowns and pillared wigs. No matter age or infirmity, under disguise and in the heat of the drink, dance and game, all are young and strong. With such excess, you assume that many are flattened in the daily beat of life with all its normal, banal moments. Perhaps that is why Venetians in this day continue to make the celebrations increasingly grandiose throughout the season, a grappling to keep the festive high, a dream in which the Carnevale *never* ends.

Gaudy but dazzling are the red lips and powdered faces, the full plume of every feather and the bleeding links of rubies on the bosom. There is the glint of a tinkling glass, bubbles rising before a candle's flame. Beauty marks are many. A few brash guests are stuck with dozens of patches like dots of the pox while others display only one velvet mark on a brow or breast. Stockings and bows, lace and curls, ribbons, lashes and luxury abound. Beneath their mesmerizing appearance however, the realities of decay shows in some: rotten teeth exposed in a haughty laugh, black filth under a set of long fingernails, a ratty moldy wig teeming with lice and fleas, a milky set of eyes beneath a half mask, the passing sour breath from the wine drank too many hours on end. For those still fresh and fair, it is their fleeting glory owed to youth and health. Others have death calling too soon due to an illness within that cannot be healed in these days. You are amazed as you pass, feeling yourself like a spy from another time, going unnoticed in the debauched crowd. In this very room the fates of many are settled on account of reckless gambling, drinking and excess. The Carnevale is the very stage for the grasping at life over death, you think. For this night, you'll join into this seething play.

In the room next, you find an intimate concert; you are enraptured. Spread about loftily and resembling a scene from a dream, guests regard a quartet ensemble whining out a beautifully sad piece. An oboe's heightened cry cuts into the listeners in the glow of an enormous fireplace set with candelabra above its mantel. Though human in their tights and breeches, vests and jackets, half masks and coiffures, these instrumental men divinely trigger the audience to ponder their souls; the melody hints at the passion and fleet that is life. Women sitting on comfortable settees watch the musicians intently to the soft whoosh of their painted fans, their ample skirts pooling out in pastel loveliness. Men standing at their sides observe these creatures unnoticed, regarding the heaving breasts, blushed cheeks and feminine inhales; the emotions of all are stirred. There is love and jealousy, lust and want in the warmth of this room.

You see a door leading out into another room to the right which you assume rounds around heading back to the ballroom. You slowly edge past these human statues frozen to the call of the music and walk through to the next place. As you do, there is a cool breeze flowing in from an open double door leading out to a balcony situated above a canal, though not the one you boated in on. You can see that lanterns are flooding the balcony in a warm glow and the glinting of moonlight from off of the flowing water. A dark gondola passes carrying several masked men who you assume are on their way here. This salon is a comfortable sitting room with a scattering of guests resting and enjoying a bit of fresh, salty sea air away from the entertainments. There are couples whispering at each other's necks, ladies chattering with their exciting gossip and men gathered in serious conversation. You wonder how many guests your cousin invited for her ball this evening when ironically, a woman in a gold and sequined sparkling bodice and magnanimously flowing skirt, walks directly up to you.

Dearest! So glad that you have come! I see that you have cast away your mourning clothes and graced my ball with your beauty. I am honored! Though, I am verily disappointed that you chose to take rooms at the Hotel Fato rather than stay with me here where I could have spoiled you. Perhaps you do not feel in need of spoiling with how very rich you are! Come, let us go out onto the balcony and speak a moment. Dinner shall be served in half an hour.

You knew this would be difficult, this cousin is of course a complete stranger and you are unaware of what inquiries may surface while alone with her. How will you maintain this fraud? You try to remember that you must keep up the show of being Countess Fortunato for your very survival. You have no other choice unless you run away and face the dark corners of the streets alone while figuring out why you've been brought back to this time, an option you'd rather avoid. Clearly a wealthy woman with a warm bed is the better part to maintain than a penniless runaway. Following her as though she is a familiar cousin and in as stately a manner as befits a countess, you trail her out onto the balcony.

TURN to page 467.

AS your heartbeat quickens, you feel your brow becoming prickly with cold anxiety; this is very bad. Six months after the passing of the countess's husband, there appears to be some foul play being investigated. You certainly cannot go to the council, as this could prove to be very dangerous. If the countess is guilty of some crime, you surely will not be able to defend yourself against it. You would hardly be able to answer two questions correctly before Belloza, let alone many during an examination by a committee. Even if the countess is guilty of nothing, even if she is innocent and the inquiry is a matter of question on some other within her household, you certainly cannot stand before a judging entity without looking like a strange, amnesia-stricken crazy woman. They would throw you into the Piombi prison with condemned criminals and those lost to insanity and you would wither away in some dark, dank corner, unable to find your way home again. If you never found your way back (a thought that makes you shudder), at the very least you would prefer freedom in the here and now. You cannot go before the council and you cannot be found, of this you are certain. You must sneak out immediately and try to survive the best you can until you can figure out how and why you've been sent into the past, and how to return.

You have almost no time before the countess is to show herself at the Doge's Palace. When they find that you are not present, it will not be long before they send men to find you. You are thankful even that you've eaten a meal and are fully clothed in the correct attire for the times. With hardly a moment to spare, it would have been terrible to run out into the *calli* without so much as a piece of bread in your stomach and dressed only in your underpinnings. Walking to the door of your room, you carefully open it and peek out into the hall. You are certain that Belloza is in the dining room on the first floor, but don't know when she will return. It could be at any moment. Sneaking across the hall to the other rented room, you carefully try the door and are relieved to find that she has left the chamber unlocked. Shame on her for the countess's sake, a thief could have gone in and stolen all, and *will*. You are very glad that she has made this easy mistake on *this* day. Entering in, you softly close the door behind you. Looking around, you find that the room doesn't appear much different than your own, excepting the traveling luggage, clothes and accessories strewn about.

Of one thing you are sure. You don't want to look

obvious out on the streets, like a woman on the run. You are immediately appreciative of the anonymity delivered by the masks that are worn in Venice during the Carnival. You will be able to hide your identity for at least long enough to get away and hide.

There is no time to spare; you must hurry! You rush to a large armoire and swing open the double doors. Within, you find your original gown. The very sight of it makes you nearly burst out into tears! It reminds you of home and how you wish you could blink your eyes this very moment and return. You know that you cannot take the dress with you. To wear it at any point might bring attention to you, you may look a little odd. Riffling through the pockets, you are pleased to find the items that you were carrying when you leapt time. There is your passport, lip balm and some euros. You bundle these treasures up into the linen breakfast napkin that you had snatched off your lap as you rose from your seat moments ago. You then rush to see what else is available, stuffing the bunch into one of the pockets in the skirt of your current dress. Money, you must find money or you'll quickly starve. You search the desk drawers and a standing chest of drawers, nothing. After stumbling over a small valise, empty and hardly bigger than eight shoeboxes altogether, you grab several fresh shifts from the drawers and a simple blue dress hanging from within the armoire. You also seize clean stockings, a pair of embroidered slippers and a full mask painted cream and stuff all the items into the valise. Finding a gold half mask on the writing desk, you pluck it up and tie it into place over your eyes. Lying on the armrest of a plush chair, you find a warm cream-colored cape that falls to your waist and tie it around your neck. It comes with a hood, which you pull up over your head. Entering the powder room you glance in a mirror and find that the simple disguise makes you impossible to identify; you could be any 1 out of 100 women. Also owing to the fact that this morning's attire is not as ornate as evening clothes, you'll be able to move quickly and not draw much attention to yourself. For all anyone would know, you are a shopkeeper's wife rather than a rich countess.

Reviewing the powder room frantically, your eyes finally land on a small lacquered box, which you are certain must hold something of value. Working to open its latch, you find that an impenetrable lock will be keeping you from seeing what is within. Blast! There is simply no time to search the room any further, especially for an infinitesimal key. You'll just have to take the box with you. Clutching it to you, you hear the hallway door to the main room open. It is Belloza returned to her chamber! Hardly able to breath, you are unsure what to do! You could simply waltz out of the powder room and claim that you wanted to take a walk but did not want to disturb her meal in order to get your cloak and mask. However, this wouldn't be the brightest idea as she will be puzzled at why you are carrying out the lacquered box. She might yell for help from the hotel staff and request the doctor back again, setting the hotel astir believing that you've lost your mind with all of your recent erratic behavior. Should anything slow your escape out of the hotel, you'll find yourself face to face with officials come to take you in for questioning.

In an instant, you have slipped behind a painted dressing screen in the corner of the powder room, knocking into and almost tipping Belloza's standing washbasin. Expecting the crash of porcelain and wood as you secret away, you hear only a creaking teeter and then silence. The stand must have steadied itself. Your breathing is heavy and you try with all your ability to pace and quiet it. You swallow and find that your mouth has grown dry and you begin to feel more than a little claustrophobic, being masked and under the weight of a cloak, trapped in a little room. You are truly afraid of being caught and given over to the authorities.

You squeeze your eyes shut and try withal not to move. Even the slightest shift warrants a rustling noise from your layered attire. You focus on slowing your intake and exhale of breaths; slow, slower, and still yet slower. Your eyes open abruptly and you almost stop breathing altogether when you hear Belloza humming merrily and closely too. Entering into the powder room, she sounds to be busying herself with some tidying (affirmed when a wrinkled gown is flung over the changing panels, behind which, you go unmoving). After some more bustling about and singing, you hear her exit far out into the hall leaving her chamber and then her knocking on the door of the countess's rented room. Calling out to her mistress and hearing no response, she enters there as noted by the echo of her voice far off.

This is your only chance. As stealth and quietly as your trembling body will take you, you ease out from behind the large accordion-like panels from the side opposite of the washbasin so as not to bump it again. Holding the box close to your bosom you grab the little valise on your way out, which you left sitting on the floor near the chair. Rushing through the bedchamber you exit out into the hall. Though you do not see or hear Belloza through the open door of the countess's room and assume that she is in the washroom wondering at where her lady has gone, you feel her presence so closely that you fly down the staircase. Never more quickly or more dangerously have you descended a stairway, encumbered by layers of fabric and an asphyxiating corset, half-blinded by mask and hood, carrying weighty stolen items.

Not hearing the maid descending behind you, you try to slow your exit out of the lobby of the hotel so as not to cause notice and walk straight out of the front entrance, determined to escape. As you pass into the courtyard, you make to head out onto the street but immediately come to a halt. There just without on the *calle*, you are startled to see several sober faced, somberly dressed gentlemen with swords at their hips discussing something with yet another man (perhaps an employee of the hotel or a random citizen). They seem to be questioning him. Could they be looking for *you*? Have they come to seek you out so soon? How will you make it out of the courtyard? Looking in the opposite direction, you mark your opportunity. The large wooden door leading out to the waterside entrance of the hotel is wide open and you can see vessels floating on the canal, just as was the funerary gondola the day before. What begins as a fast walk in that direction soon becomes a sprint when you hear Belloza's voice crying out from above!

Contessa? Contessa Ciossa Fortunato! Where are you going? My lady? Contessa Fortunato!

There isn't even time to look behind you. You are certain the men have heard the cries of the lady's maid from the window of your hotel room. You are certain that they'll be in pursuit instantly and you can't so much as pause for a single moment. Running out of the open air and light, into the tomb of darkness that is the pass over the marble dock, you sprint to the canal where your only escape is boating past and at great speed. A stout man in wine-colored velvet breeches, doublet and half mask is rowing quickly and about to pass the dock. You must jump aboard his boat, however dangerous! You must get away!

IF you jump aboard the stranger's boat, turn to page 452.
IF you are too afraid to jump and will find another way to escape, turn to page 463.

LOOKING warily into her eyes not knowing how she will take the truth, you decide that at the very least, honesty is always the right course.

I will tell you honestly. Something happened, something very strange. I am from the future, the twenty-first century. Venice is still as beautiful as ever and Carnevale is still celebrated. I am not from Venice, nor have I ever set foot in Padua. I know that this will sound like madness to you, but I don't even speak Italian and am at a loss to tell you how I am able to do so now and to understand you. You see, I planned a trip to Venice to enjoy Carnival and I only spent one night in the city. When strolling in Piazza San Marco looking for a gondola to take me for a tour, I found myself no longer in my year, but yours. I returned to my hotel, afraid of the things I saw along the way. When I arrived at my room, there was Belloza, your cousin's lady's maid.

Cutting in, Amedea retorts with some impatience.

Yes, I know Belloza. Continue!

You swallow and take a deep breath before beginning again.

Well, she behaved as though I was the countess and I was baffled. Even the room that the countess was renting was the very one I reserved in the future. I

435

wondered how Belloza recognized me as her, but soon saw a portrait that the contessa had commissioned as a gift for you. We look so much alike! I only pretended to be her so that I could bide time until I could figure out how to return home. I don't know how this happened or if even, the contessa is some distant relative and perhaps there is a purpose for this mix-up. It may even be possible that you are my distant relative too, if the contessa and I are indeed of any relation. But that is only a theory. I don't know anything more than that. I swear to you that this is the truth.

Amedea regards you seriously, having listened intently to all that you've confessed. Though not completely at ease, you think that she may actually believe you. Within moments, she speaks.

Well my dear, I guess if you claim that you do not know anything more, we'll have to make you remember! You will tell me where Ciossa Fortunato is, or you will hang to your death in the Piazza. I swear it! Aiuto! Help!! Imposter! Aiuto!

Her commands for aid are so shocking to your trembling body that you drop your goblet; it shatters into thick shards on the marble floor of the balcony. You must think fast or you are certain that her words will come true. No one will save you but yourself! You hear her shouting again and again for help but become deaf to her cries as you look around hopelessly for an escape. If you run back into the *palazzo*, you will surely be retained. Over the side of the balcony and into the canal is the only way. You lean your arms on the balcony's marble enclosure at a height of your waist and consider how far the jump is. It isn't far at all, perhaps only double your height! It will be an easy plummet though you'll have to swim hard to the water's edge and run away before you are caught, as there will surely be a pursuit. After all, Amedea believes you are holding her flesh and blood cousin hostage!

While preparing inwardly for the jump, the duchessa clearly senses your plan from your movements and moves to grab your arm hard to stop you, shrieking even more loudly than before. In this fight or flight moment, you face her and use all your force to wrench her grip from off of your arm, next planning to push her away with enough energy to give you the necessary moment to jump over the ledge. She releases her hold on you as you pry her hand away with all your might. From the corner of your eye, you see the figures of several men running toward the balcony from within the sitting room. You make to push her then, your hand falling at the top of her bodice, causing her to lose balance and step backwards, but not hard enough for her to lose her footing. Pulling your hand away, it entangles in her diamond necklace, the gems cutting at your fingers. It breaks after a painful strain, precious diamonds falling to the balcony's stone floor. They make a sound like the dispersion of heavy raindrops on glass. You look to her face desperately as the fierceness in her eyes increases, the tinkle of raining gemstones full in your ears, both your chests heaving from the fray.

It is in that moment that you are returned, accompanied by the sound of clattering pistachio shells thrown to the stone floor of the Piazza San Marco, the gondolier staring at you expectantly as he crunches. Are you sure you won't take that ride?

THE End.

THE ball! You feel as though you've been waiting to attend a fete like this for as long as you can remember. There is something to be amazed by when one thinks of a truly grand bash. Events like this are so very infrequent in modern times. There are the occasional fund-raising parties, dressy affairs and holiday functions. However, even those are rare and hardly what a thoughtfully planned masquerade ball during the Carnival in Venice, Italy, could ever be.

Arriving at the waterside entrance to the *palazzo* in the dark of the evening, there is a line of three gondolas before yours in wait to drop costumed guests. As each boat pulls up before a small stairway lit by candled lanterns, two men dressed all in white with glittering silver masks greet patrons. As women disembark from their watery vessels, the employed fellows lend them their gloved hands to assist them onto the stone platform leading to the entrance of the palace, and offer them a white rose. The way into the fortress has at present doors open wide, covered by a billowy curtain of sheer white fabric. You can see shadows moving behind it in the glow of a golden light. Your heart rushes with the excitement of the moment as you anticipate your entrance. As your boat stops before the stairs, one of the men helps you to alight and then offers you a flower and a slight bow. Accepting the rose, the other attendant smiles and with a sweeping gesture of one hand and a bow points to the door.

As you arrive before the façade, there is a woman attired in a white gown and sparkling silver mask. Pausing before her, she requests of you the entrance fee, which you gladly proffer. With that, she pulls open the curtain and you are given access. Walking down a short but grand hallway with a few other ambling guests, you admire the architecture immediately. Shiny marble floors, blocks of stone polished out of different colored rock from varied destinations pieced together like a chessboard. There are long tables on either side of the hall, polished marble tops over ornately carved wooden legs painted in gold. They elevate bright candles, white rose topiaries, gold dishes of whole fresh fruit, white rose petals sprinkled liberally, chocolates wrapped in bright foil and gold, silver, red, black and white half masks for anyone who has mislaid their own. You haven't passed into the depths of the estate, but are already stupefied by the glory of Venetian palaces. Looking to the ceiling, there is an enormous painted fresco all along the expanse. Fluffy white clouds floating in a sea of blue sky, cherubs flying lazily aided by gold leaf wings; their flight glimmers in the light of many candles.

Coming to the end of the hall, it spills out into a grand foyer. Four marble pedestals supporting fine white statues are placed with two on each side of the entrance, each figure standing four feet tall. You pause to admire the smooth white stone denoting the forms of Aphrodite in a flowing robe, Poseidon holding his trident, a Satyr with the torso and face of a man and legs of a furry goat, and Medusa with her head of snakes and entrancing smile. To the left of the foyer, there is an enormous ballroom where many people are amassed; music flows out like a scintillating river. To the right, a sumptuous dining room filled with a multitude of round tables so ornately dressed, you wish to immediately bask in its luxury. Before you, there is a monumental marble staircase peeling up both sides to a level above. Under the behemoth staircase, you find a discreet room where silvery masked attendants are accepting capes and cloaks for the evening, safely stowing personal articles as a guest courtesy. You opt to admit your cozy mantle and gloves. Accepting the items, you are told by a female attendant that the lady's powder room is up the winding stairs to the left should you have the need. You ask her also, whether there is a set dining time as the banquet tables appear set to formality. She tells you that in half an hour, you may dine as you please and throughout the whole evening, as there will be a frequently replenished buffet.

Smoothing one hand gently over your person, a gesture to assure yourself that you are ready for entry, you slowly approach the ballroom. You take a deep inhale of your white rose and smooth the petals gently between your fingers as you enter. Gliding into the abyss you are electrified with anticipation, ready to behold a strange, exciting phenomena: a Venetian ball of the Carnevale.

Around the edges exiting out of the foyer sit arranged enormous potted greenery come alive from out of porcelain pots. You spy a man and woman nesting themselves close to several orange trees full of fresh green foliage and low hanging fruit. He is observing the delicate skin of her bosom heaving lightly from without her bodice as she leans in to whisper into his ear. He smiles, pleased with her words meant only for him. Further in, you find that there are people lined in pairs and groups all along the perimeter of the room and facing in to the interior scene and splendor of the dance. Some pool languidly together on long plush benches or gather around on cushioned stools, some stand the circumference of high top tables covered in white linen and littered dreamily with half empty wine glasses, white rose petals and a scattering of shimmery foiled chocolates. Others lean intimately against the intricately designed walls. Your eyes can't help but wander those walls with their ornate wood paneling, elegantly painted eighteenth century landscapes in field and forest and the varied amassing of colorful polished marble.

The ballroom is lit gloriously and entirely by candlelight! Rare few acknowledge today, the mystery and sheer beauty of a candle's glow in this, the day of electricity. Your heart is warmed by the diffusion of candelabra, wall sconces and colossal candled chandeliers, which light the room well enough while keeping it yet in a magical dusky glow. Candlelight flickers deliciously on every part of the scene, casting glimmer and shadow in every place.

The dance floor is flooded with the footfalls of many dancers. The music loftily enveloping all comes from a divine instrumental of the Baroque era, played by an ensemble of 10 musicians at one side of the room.

Like the greeters and attendants of the ball, they too are dressed entirely in white. There are soft cottony gowns with wide panniers and silver ribbons tied around the waists of the ladies and breeches, vests and coats for the men. The glittering silver half masks worn by them all sparkle like diamonds as they gesture fervently at play on their beloved instruments. There is also a sensual background beat accompanying the compositions, which a sound engineer maintains using several technical panels aside the musicians; he is dressed the same. The energy in the room shows that the antiquated and modern can work together harmoniously to create something new.

The scene captures the essence of something otherworldly; the cautious stir of a minuet long forgotten, clinking crystal and the warm press of a perfumed crowd, flickering light and laughter unbidden. The masks are a category of amazement all their own, artistic creations of every conceivable face type constructed out of varied medium. There are thousands of shimmering sequins, scenes of night and day, animals wild and demure and many fully painted faces with long lashes, glossy lips and tears of glass. Some are half, secreting just the eyes and others are complete, disguising one's visage entirely. There is soft velvet and shiny tin, paper mache and coarse fabric, carved wood and delicate lace. This is the house of the mask, a museum of disguise both past and present. Here are all convened: libertines and lovers, ghosts born of the dark and angels exuding the light.

Walking slowly along the edge of the ballroom, your spirits high and your chest heavy with excitement, you take in the splendor of the costumes of this night. The wigs are monumental in all of their glorious fashions. Men and women alike aspiring to the heavens with their cottony bouffants adorned with garish and magical additions: tinsel, stuffed birds, miniature model ships, bows, lace, gaudy gems. Each face is powdered and vainly made up with beauty marks, arched brows, penciled lips and rosy cheeks. And, how could one begin to enumerate the dresses: haughty, desirous, glorious and bold. Some women host panniers so wide, they expand the length of six persons side by side. Yet each of these ladies continues to move in every way elegantly, to your delight. All around are tight corsets, silky ribbons, strung pearls, tall heels and beautiful stitchwork that only could be found presently. The men are refined with expertly tailored tricorne hats, calf-flaunting breeches, lacy linen shirts, cravats and brassy buttons closing up fitted vests and fashionable jackets.

The sight already bursting with extravagance and every unique detail, how can you be even more delighted with each passing entertainer? There is the court jester and his beloved dog donned in a belled collar; his merry yelps bring a jingle. A trio of women garbed as glittered wood nymphs clad in ethereal wings (blue, pink and purple) tiptoe about. There are characters of every sort: a magician, a storyteller, a fire handler and a gypsy who reads palms. Further, what you thought were four life-sized marble statues in one corner of the room are actually muscled men partially swathed in linen, standing or sitting upon solid marble blocks and wearing white paint and talc to look like stone! They appear as such chiseled works as The Thinker, Michelangelo's David, Discobolus of Myron, and Zeus. At intervals, they descend their pedestals to weave throughout the crowd.

At length, the music pauses and all begin to hush one another while glancing expectantly to the furthest end of the room, where constructed is a platform leading off of a door at that place. As the room quiets, anticipation grows within you, though for what reason you are not sure. As with everyone else, you watch and wait until you see what all were expecting: the hostess. The first time that you saw her in the arcade of St. Mark's Square (dressed like the sea and a wild peacock combined), you were impressed. Now however, you are dazzled! Signora Romana Sapienti, the owner of this very estate, enters from the far door and mounts her stage as confidently as a queen in her court. She is dressed in an expansive gown as red as brilliant rubies and in fact, a reflective strand around her neck makes you suppose that stone does indeed adorn her neck, though you are not close enough to identify the gems. You assume also that one of her many party assistants has pinned a microphone to her person, for when she speaks, all can hear. In her Italian tongue she addresses her guests.

Welcome to Venice and the Carnevale and to my home! Dinner is served. Please enjoy the evening!

Repeating her words, a voice you soon detect as coming from the sound engineer translates her announcement into several other languages for the internationally diverse crowd.

You expected a mass exodus to the dining hall but find that this is not the case. The music begins again as

Signora Sapienti steps down from the stage and begins to mingle with her guests. The song has a wild pulse and you know not how the visitors are aware of the dance being called forth, but they do and proceed to execute it with perfectly timed jaunty jumps, planned partnered passes and lined movements hand in hand.

Partly due to a twinge of dinner hunger coming on and partly just out of curiosity of what you'll find in the next room, you make your way into the dining hall. There are plenty of places to sit and you like that despite the marvelous decoration of the room and the delicious buffet you see before you, there is no unease or pressure for formality. One may come and go as they please, eating when they wish, nibbling again as they desire.

After weaving though the tables covered in pressed white linens, shiny silver candelabra and glass bulbs arranged full of fair flowers, you lay your rose down at one place setting at a table positioned to the side of the room and make your way to the buffet. Approaching the superb spread, you pick up a spotless white plate. You find that there is no official line to file down, diners simply approach here and there for a portion as they see what delights them and you do the same. It is almost too grand to process all of the delights before you: herb roasted chicken, sweetly glazed salmon, buttery baked white fish, broiled garlic shrimp, generously sliced braised steak and pink cuts of juicy ham. There is lemony seafood salad with grilled octopus and crab and fresh handmade pasta paired with many a sauce and simmered vegetable. There are rosemary potatoes, golden mashed squash, risotto dressed with asparagus, squid ink spaghetti, marinated sardines and bowls full of oily olives. There are rice dishes, polenta dishes and platters full of thinly sliced carpaccio and sweet soft cantaloupe salad with prosciutto. There are leafy greens with tangy balsamic vinegar and herbed olive oil to dress, accompanied by sweet ripe tomato wedges in orange, red and yellow, sea salt and freshly ground pepper too. There are grilled scallops and calamari served with a squeeze of lemon and lightly steamed, garlicky mussels. Baskets full of freshly sliced Italian bread, simultaneously crusty and chewy, are laid out in abundance with fluffy whipped butter. You are in a gastronomic paradise. Attendants in white dress shirts, white aprons and crisp black dress pants, wait behind the tables to organize and refill amenities as guests deplete any items and as the kitchen sends forth fragrant and steaming new entrees. Even as you make several selections for your plate, more dishes not there a moment before are served. What an opulent feast!

That however, is not all. Coming to the end of the table, your plate set with a meal fit for a noble, you see yet further banquet! Walking lightly toward the spread without any intent of piling any more food on your plate, you see that it is the dessert offerings heaped with sweets: puffy fried dough sprinkled with powdered sugar, tiramisu, soft iced cakes and sweet crisp cookies. There is also a coffee service accompanied by an attendant to make you your favorite style of the beverage: espresso, caffé latte, Americano, ice café or cappuccino. These are just a few of the ways that you may ask for it to be prepared. Back at your table you take your place and laying your dinner napkin on your lap, begin to delight in all that you've chosen. It is delicious; each and every bite is well seasoned and succulent! After a few minutes, a server inquires whether you require a beverage. You ask for a glass of sparkling water and it is not long before a full glass makes its way to you, topped with a slice of lemon. Taking your time, you fully enjoy this special meal. As you take pleasure in each bite you also appreciate the scene as others make their way into the dining room, observing their interactions as they sit together to take part in the feast. Though alone, you are completely content and not at all disappointed to be without the nearness of another. Even without friends and intimate companions to brighten an experience, a woman can find herself in a dream in her own company!

TURN to page 490.

THOUGH you fear the lack of an effective launch and safe landing, you will have to take the only chance of escape that you see. You can now hear the muffled yells of the officials calling out to the contessa and their boots hitting the stones in pursuit behind you. Running to the edge of the dock, you let out a sharp cry as you jump from its slippery edge. Miraculously, you make it into the boat, falling down into the belly with great force. The boat rocks fiercely, sending waves outward from either side of the vessel. The boatman teeters uncertainly and with great surprise as he works to keep his standing body and long oar from falling out into the water. Releasing your grip on the lacquered box and the valise, you look up to the passing dock in terror as you hear the approaching voices. Looking to the boatman, you put your hands up to your ears to silence out the pursuers' commands, as though you can shut out the chase entirely, and search his face pleadingly. There will be only one of two outcomes. Either he will immediately row you to shore and give you up to the men, wiping his hands of this folly. Or, he will continue to row on, putting even himself at jeopardy if you are both caught.

Steadying himself while looking to the men and then back to you, he continues rowing, harder and faster than before. The men who are now standing at the edge of the dock begin to yell even more loudly, demanding the man to pull the boat ashore. As you look around you in the boat, you see that it is not a gondola but rather a very steady rowboat of sorts and that a large pile of rope coiled in the bottom held your fall. Without it, you may have slipped out of the boat. You are very thankful to have landed safely. You could have catapulted into the water over the far side of the vessel or broke an ankle. As the boat picks up speed on account of the brute strength of the rower, you untie and pull the cape from off your shoulders, letting it pool around your sitting body. Looking to the sky, you exhale a sudden and desperate sob that is unexpected even to you. It was not enough to be cast back into a time not your own, where everything around you may be historically familiar yet is alarmingly unknown and where *anyone* could be dangerous to your person, but that you are also to be chased as only a criminal should be. What did the contessa do? Poison her husband? Even as you think the words, you sob harder hoping that she indeed is innocent of *any* crime. You weren't going to wait around and find out. Exhausted, you collapse into your own lap and cover your face with your hands so as not to bring any more attention to the boat and try to collect yourself.

Soon, you feel the boat gliding farther and farther away, pulling faster and faster. You can hear the labored breaths of the oarsman as he works with great effort to take you, a stranger, to safety. To safety, you *hope*. You are too afraid to look up again lest on viewing the side of the canal, you see the men pursuing still along the marble lane aside the water. You sit up and drop your hands to your lap, glancing only to the man. Even through his labored breaths, he kindly whispers a hushing noise, soothing you into being quiet and peaceful as he carries you away. To where, you do not know. After a few turns, the vessel is running along the water very fast indeed and as far as you can tell, there is no one following by foot or by boat. At short length, you are floating out onto the Grand Canal and then the wide-open lagoon. You would ask where you are going, but feel too tired and listless to do so. It isn't long before you are sure that you know. Out onto St. Mark's Basin, a large ship is anchored in the deep. Slowing his laborious rowing, the man stops altogether as the boat rocks atop the waves, the sunlight warming your face. He looks to you as he removes his half mask from his eyes. His face is full of unshaven stubble and perspiration, brown hair falling into his eyes in a wild, natural way. Wiping his face, he drops the mask and looks you straight in the eyes before speaking.

Signorina, I am uncertain why fate has deposited you into my boat. We don't even have time for me to ascertain an answer, as those were Venetian authorities that were following. I recognized one of the men myself. If they had reason to chase, then they have reason to follow. What would you? I can take you far along the shore and drop you. Or you can come aboard my ship, which is ready to sail out into the Adriatic Sea this very moment. I embark, almost this very minute, for my next voyage. I am a spice merchant. You can get safely away from the city and escape by another port. Though, understand that such an exit will be onto more exotic soil than you are accustomed to. What would you do woman?

You are stunned. You hadn't really thought about what might happen next once you jumped. You are also surprised by the handsomeness of the face before you. The wind carries a scent of the man, which is both earthy and spicy. All you can manage is a single question.

Is that your ship?

He nods in the affirmative. Looking to the

enormous vessel and taking a deep breath, you remove your mask as well and gaze back to the merchant. He smiles broadly as he explores your unmasked face.

Please, take me to it then. I am obliged for your rescue and wish to go with you.

THE End.

YOU can't possibly tell her the truth. The Duchessa Frivolo will never believe your time traveling story. Your pulse quickening in your veins, you can feel the thumping of your stressed temples pushing against your mask. You'll try to apply to her heart, woman to woman, if you can. Once you are able to escape the palace, you'll have to get far away and quickly too. There won't be time to go back to Hotel Fato to secure coin or gems from the contents of the contessa's belongings. But there is an emerald necklace strung around your neck (thank you Belloza). Selling each gem off individually, perhaps you could survive long enough to find a solution and return home.

Signora Frivolo, I beg you for mercy. You are wise and perceptive and not at all a fool. I am not from Venice. I am a traveler and a sore gambler. I came to Venezia just three days ago and gambled away the last that I owned and more. The man I owed came to my hotel and threatened my life when I told him that I could not pay. Inspecting me closely, he saw the likeness to the face of your cousin and being a dangerous libertine, said that he had a way for me to pay him back and to fill my own depleted purse. And so, as your cousin walked the crowded streets of the Carnevale without a companion yesterday afternoon, he snatched her and is keeping her, I don't know where. I was to take her place long enough to profit as much as possible from the role, to take all the riches she was traveling with and then more from your palazzo if I could manage it this night. Once my job was done, tomorrow morning at dawn, she would be released and my gambling debt paid. But, I see that our plans have been foiled. He, the contessa's captor, is here tonight. He sits just now in the other room, gambling with your guests. I promise that I never meant for this to become such a serious matter. I will lead you to this man directly so that your cousin may be freed and I will confess all to the authorities. Come, I will take you to him.

You are shocked at your own lies. How did you become such a storyteller? You suppose the only reason you conceived this excuse and so quickly too, is due to the dire misfortune you now find yourself in. Fighting to survive when the world has turned upside down requires a creative will. The duchessa regards you with a look of shock herself, likely at how easily she was able to demand and procure a confession. Standing tall, her head cocked, she laughs nervously and then more confidently as she wraps her mind around all that you have said.

Wondering at your words yourself, you are surprised that she doesn't look horrified. After all, you've confessed a kidnapping! But perhaps, never before having lived in the eighteenth century, you are unaware whether shocking matters are regarded with much surprise (perhaps imposters are as common to the 1700s as car thieves are to the twenty-first century).

Well then! Listen closely. I do not want this situation in a gazeta for all of Venice to read. These harrowing and devilish schemes only bring a stain and gossip to one's house and I'll have none of that. I will instruct several of my servants to follow close and to take the man up to a quiet wing of the palazzo where we will wait for the authorities to guide the last part of this investigation and release the contessa from her captivity. If you do just as I say and if she is found unharmed, I will ask that you are given a less harsh judgment by the Venetian tribunal than this kidnapper will receive. For him, there should be no mercy. Stand by a moment.

For a mere second, you consider jumping over the side of the balcony but are afraid to break a limb on the stones aside the canal directly below. You see that Signora Frivolo is whispering directions to several men of her household who were standing in attendance in the sitting room. Walking back out onto the balcony, she demands that with discretion, you walk through to the gambling room and point out the guilty criminal.

As you pass through the sitting room, gracefully as you can while so nervous, you put down your glass goblet on a table and look over your shoulder. The duchessa is following behind at a distance. Soon, you weave through to the game room and try to stand as close to the great door of the dining hall as possible. Turning into the room, you casually look close to where the duchess and her attendants stand in wait, and select an unsuspecting masked victim for their questioning. The poor fellow! From among a table of men at a game of *faro*, you point to one who appears strong and stout, not chancing that once grabbed, an older fellow might collapse with a strained heart. You wish that you need not point at all, but you must to buy the needed seconds for an escape. You are certain once all is worked out, they will know of your trickery and free your selected target. You extend your arm forward and point. Instantly the men are walking toward your choice and you are out of the room, running down the expansive dining hall, sprinting through the crowded foyer, breathlessly arriving at the waterside entrance off of the canal. Out onto the stone dock, laughter and commotion all around you with the new arrivals just alighting from their gondolas, you look to both left and right for a way out as the waterway is too crowded and there is not time enough to hail a boat.

Due the smallest glimmer of luck, you detect a stone path weaving along the side of the *palazzo* and are able to follow it for a short distance until you find yourself at an alley cutting between other sizeable buildings. It is horribly dark and you can see the shadows of squeaking rats running with you in the lane. You can hear muffled shouts far behind you at the rear of the palace, as well as several reactive and concerned voices from the newly arriving. You run as fast as your feet will carry you, never looking back. Gasping for breath under the strain of your corset, you *run*. Under the shifting mask clinging to your eyes, sometimes impeding your vision, you *run*. Lifting your full and heavy skirts, afraid that each rustling sound of moving fabric will reveal your course, you *run*. Reaching a larger *calle,* weaving between the happy images of affluent partygoers and the stricken faces of street dwellers, you *run*. Over bridges and winding through the maze that is Venice, the way lit by flickering lamplight and the silvery moon high overhead, you *run*. You run until you find yourself at the very edge of the island that is Venice, huffing for your life as your eyes dart wildly over the expanse of the lagoon. Where will you go now? How will you escape? You spy the enormous merchant ships, docked and resting easily in the murky, undulating waves and think you know the answer.

THE End.

YOU are too afraid and cannot jump. Seeing the distance, you are sure that you'll break a leg once you hit the boat. Surely you'll drop your filched possessions or fall into the canal to drown under the weight of your clothing. There isn't much time, but you must find another way. At the very edge of the marble dock, you see that to the right there is nothing but the stonewall of the next building meeting the water. To your left there is a set of marble stairs steeply ascending to a thin lane running parallel to the canal at a height. Looking out over a distance, you find that it will eventually lead you to a bridge spanning over the canal. Hearing the men behind you, accompanied by labored yells and heavily booted footfalls, you dart warily up the stone steps without even looking back, clutching the lacquered box in one arm and the thick wooden handle of the valise in the other. You could ascend and run faster if you were rid of these items. But should you escape, their contents could be very necessary to your survival.

Your breathing grows louder and more strained and your heart races terribly fast like that of a wild rabbit's as you mount to the top of the stairs and scamper along the lane. It is very narrow and you are certain that one misplaced step, one slip of a foot, will bring you plummeting below. You hear the name of the contessa being shouted for, directed to desist her fleeing, the sound close enough to know that the men are not far behind. You must go faster, you tell yourself, and will yourself to run as best you can along the narrow path until it descends some steps on the other side to a wider marble walk. You dash as fast as a frantic deer down the way and turn right, flying up over the bridge.

Running, running, running. You don't look back though you continue to hear the men's voices. Their demands become increasingly muffled, until you cannot hear them at all. You continue to sprint, cutting through marbled squares, weaving the winding *calli*, and flying over bridges. Before long you feel certain that you are far enough away from the Hotel Fato and have taken so many turns, that you will not be immediately found. You step up into a dark and vacant doorway as festively masked revelers stroll by, laughing and throwing confetti overhead, some of it landing on your person as you labor to breath. You feel that at a slow amble, even the pursuers will not recognize you. How many women are dressed the same as you? It was only in the heat of the chase that you needed to create a sweeping distance, so as not to be immediately caught. From here you should be able to blend into the crowd. After your breathing returns to normal, you reenter the flow and continue to wind farther and farther away until you find yourself on the edge of the island that is Venice, the Laguna Veneta stretching out before you. Finding a loose stone in the path at the water's edge, you discreetly pick it up and make your way onto a quiet walk beneath a nearby bridge. First looking around to ensure that no one is watching, you lean down over the lacquered case and strain to smash the catch off of its face. After the second blow, the lock falls off with ease; you are exceedingly glad that it was held to with thin decorative metal and a delicate lock rather than by steel plating. Clearly Belloza kept it secure only to detour the maids at the Hotel Fato from snooping. Opening the box, you find a small leather pouch filled with coin and another velvet bag stuffed full with precious jewelry. You may have just made off with all the gems and gold that the countess brought on her journey from Padua. You drop the chest, now empty and broken, into the canal and watch it sink out of sight. Scanning around you cautiously, you stuff the stolen loot into the pockets in the folds of your skirt and then walk back up to a square overlooking the water. You are determined to buy your way onto a docked vessel, to whatever nearby city it will take you to, using the name you were born with in the twenty-first century to disguise your identity apart from the sought after contessa.

You aren't sure where your escape will lead you, but if you are wise with the gold and jewelry that you've stolen, you are sure to live comfortably for some time. There are many questions left unanswered. How were you transported through time? Is the countess a distant relative or one of your very own past lives? Have you been sent here to learn some lesson or make something right? Perhaps some great spell cast by the contessa (potentially a dangerous and most certainly powerful woman), caused you to switch places with her. Does magic exist? Perhaps she could see into the future to find a look-alike to take her place once she had committed some well-planned crime. But of course it is absurd to believe this woman could be your evil doppelganger, or is it? You may never be the wiser and you may never return home. But there is one thing that *is* certain. You are a very strong woman and determined to survive!

THE End.

BOTH walking out onto the balcony, you and your cousin spend a moment gazing out over the water. As she seems to be about to break the silence, you turn to observe what sort of woman she is. The duchessa is slightly shorter than you and though slim, appears quite fit and robust. However, you are still surprised that she is able to carry the excessive weight of her gown, as it is quite profuse, though certainly befitting the hostess of such a grand occasion. Atop her head is a white bouffant dusted in gold glitter and decorated with white roses and over her eyes is a half mask covered in intricate gold Burano lace. Her face is powdered flawlessly with a hint of gold glitter as blush and a sparkling gold sequin placed at the height of her right cheekbone (a flashy beauty mark). Her bosom is bedecked with a string of diamonds larger than you have ever seen, each stone glinting in the flame of the lanterns, they flash with light at her every breath. She turns to face you and then pauses only to look suspiciously around her before directing a question to you in a hushed, strained manner.

What have you done with my cousin, you evil, conniving doppelganger?

Doom! You'd hoped that things would go better, the greeting started out so deceivingly pleasant. So much for trying to bide time and fit into the situation long enough to find a way home!

You are not my cousin, though I admit that your farce is well played. I'm guessing that you are no more than a clever street performer put up by some foul swindler to play this trick? What a very elaborate plan you must have created in this collaboration. You do look like her! Where is my cousin and what is the meaning of this switch? If you do not tell me immediately, a single scream will bring a houseful onto this balcony and you will be destroyed in moments at my bidding, thrown into the Piombi prison as an imposter. Tell me now!

Sweat starts to bead on your brow and your heart begins to beat as fast as that of a chipmunk who is on the escape from a fierce clawed cat. You feel somewhat faint and your mouth becomes noticeably dry. Still holding the glass goblet, your hand beginning to tremble, you take another sip of wine before speaking. Looking up and into her expectant eyes, facing her defiant glare, you answer.

It is true. I am not your cousin and never meant to deceive you. But I promise that I am no imposter.

Her eyes growing large beneath her lacy disguise with her increasing anger and her tone even more stressed in her throat, she asks,

Not an imposter? How can this be when you are here pretending to be her? I want to know what you've done with my cousin. Do you have an accomplice? Are they here with you right now?

You have two choices. You can tell her the truth and hope that she will believe you. Perhaps she will even help you, which may benefit both you *and* her missing cousin (who you can only assume is in your modern shoes at this time, though you cannot know for certain). Or, you can tell her a lie and try to distract her long enough to make an escape. Which will it be?

IF you tell the truth about your being from the future, turn to page 435.
IF you decide to tell her a falsehood and make a run for it, turn to page 457.

YOU are at a loss as to what to say. You are embarrassed to be caught in a private room of the *palazzo* uninvited. For all anyone knows, you could be a snooping thief. Being found in this manner sends a bad message.

I couldn't help myself, I guess. I was leaving the powder room and as I was walking back to the stairs, I looked in and saw these paintings. This one struck me in particular. The woman who sat for this portrait looks very much like the hostess, Signora Sapienti.

His having approached to stand not far away from you, you regard his stature and secretly delight in his appearance. He is donned in black fitted breeches, vest and jacket, gold buttons glinting in the firelight. There is no makeup on his olive complexion and you are able to see his features clearly, regardless of the black half mask set with reflective gold sequins that hampers your seeing his full visage. Neither is he wearing a wig, revealing a dark head of hair, a gentlemanly cut though somewhat tousled at the moment.

I see. Well, it is neither the lady nor is it her relative, though this painting was certainly an inspiration for the gown she is wearing tonight. If you look closely at Romana's features and compare her with this woman, there isn't a striking resemblance, I assure you. The woman in this painting in fact, goes unknown.

Looking again at the painting, you review it once more and then look back to the stranger. You aren't certain that you believe him, though there can't be a reason why he'd tell you such an inconsequential lie. It is neither here nor there however as you are presently dazed by the cool masculinity in his voice and will soon forget the painting altogether. His words are assured and direct, he seems a confident man. You spontaneously wonder what more honeyed words would sound like coming forth from his handsome lips. You feel yourself blush, absurdly fearing that he may know your runaway thoughts. You better make haste and not overstay the moment.

Oh, yes, well. I'm sorry to have disturbed you. I should not have entered this room without permission. I was just drawn to the beautiful art and felt compelled to take a closer look.

Stepping away in an attempt to leave, he bids you to wait.

Pause a moment, you were not disturbing me. I was taking a break from the crowd, but your presence is invited. Enjoy a turn before every portrait in the room if

*you wish. Or perhaps, take a glass of wine with me and
sit a moment?*

Normally you'd be wary of a situation like this.
However, you feel comfortable enough with the door to
the room open to the hall (in case you need to call out or
split in a hurry). You'll go back to the ball in a few
minutes. You can surely sit a spell, if only to take in the
view of this beautiful man…these beautiful *paintings*.

You are unable to keep the hint of a smile from
creeping up on your mouth but you make every attempt
to curb it. Nodding warmly in acceptance of his offer, he
gestures to two chairs before the fire and moves off to a
table supporting a serving tray. Upon the tray sits a glass
decanter filled with red wine and four delicately etched
crystal wine glasses. Floating to a chair, you take a seat
and spread your full skirt out before you. The heat of the
blaze is delicious! Pouring two glasses, he hands one to
you and employs the seat opposite. You lift your wine
glass to your lips and take a discreet sniff of the heady
potion before taking your first sip; it smells intoxicating
and will likely taste so. Sitting brusquely before you, the
man's presence is palpable. He watches you closely
without making to speak. Though not uncomfortable,
you feel too self-conscious to sit in silence in this man's

company, as he is yet unknown to you.

I was delighted to be among the guests this evening. What a beautiful palazzo and a genuinely awe-inspiring display. I can't imagine all of the preparations required to host so many and in such a thoughtful, diverting way. It will be the highlight in my memories of Venice. May I ask, how do you know Signora Sapienti?

His voice is mesmerizing and his gaze direct as he tells you that they are childhood friends, mainly due to the fact that they are neighbors. His family and hers have been connected for many years. He is the proprietor of the *palazzo* across the canal.

Of course he is. Not that owning a palace could make this man any more attractive, perhaps just a tad more unique. With every second, it is his natural appeal that increasingly affects you. You can't give him all the credit however. Your surroundings all evening may have something to do with how the moment is unfolding. Venice's passionate aura seems to be taking hold over you!

There is something about the silence of a handsome man who is regarding you closely that makes one feel as though they need to fill the silence with entertaining commentary. But as you look him over, thankful for the cover of your half mask, you try your best to encourage your companion to ignite the conversation. You ask him his name and he tells you that it is Giacomo.

Ah, Giacomo! Just like the historic Venetian, Giacomo Casanova?

Yes, he tells you, *just* like Giacomo Casanova. You tell him your name and he tells you that it is a very beautiful one, suitable for a very attractive woman. Though, won't you take off your mask for him? He'd like to see your eyes without it and put a face to the name.

You feel instantly that your cheeks will blush the color of a vermillion tulip and are unsure of what to do next. Compelled to be polite, you set down your glass on a table between you both and carefully untie the laces of your mask, pulling it away from your face, setting it gently on your lap. You feel exposed despite the fact that on any normal day, you never wear a mask. Smiling, you look up unsure of the moment and search Giacomo's face. An approving smile is set on his lips, a look of growing pleasure even. Warmth swirls in your bosom and you look away momentarily, unable to keep his gaze. Taking up your glass again, you take a sip and then boldly, tell him that it would be unfair to leave you uncovered in this way. Won't he remove his mask for you as well?

Continuing to smile, he stands to refill your wine glass though you aren't sure that a few sips gone, warrant the need. Your suspicions are correct. You see that he only filled the glass to get closer to your person when he reaches out a strong hand and for the slightest second, delicately lifts your chin as though to get a full look of you up close. Your eyes meet his as you inhale a fresh, slightly spicy scent, his cologne. Then, stepping to face away from you before the grand fireplace, he unties the ribbons of his mask slowly, placing his disguise upon the mantel top. You can't help but feel expectant and desirous as you watch his hands smooth through his hair before turning around. As he does, you reflexively arch an eyebrow. Before you, there is a *very* attractive man. Trying to look natural, you craft a witty greeting.

Very nice to put a name with a face…Giacomo.

He expresses delight with a quiet, hauntingly sexy laugh and seats himself again, lounging quite comfortably before you with a natural self-assurance. After he takes a sip of his own wine, you both sit in silence for a time observing one another to the crackling of the embers, the shadows from the flames leaping over your faces. At length he tells you a little bit about his life and about Venice, vague details of this and that that only make you want to know more about him and what it's really like to live in this city (especially in a *palazzo*). However, you don't question him too particularly but keep the conversation light. You offer similar details about where you are from and some of your interests. Before long, you are certain that you've been sitting for some time and that the last hour has gotten away from you. You wonder if you shouldn't break away from him now, as it isn't right to dominate any more of his time, whether he looks to be enjoying himself or not. This is when he asks if you'd like to hear a story. Mind you, if he tells you this tale, you'll have to keep the contents of it a secret. Again, you find yourself a little unsure, even a hint nervous. He already presumptuously caressed your face with his fingertips and there has definitely been a hint of flirtation so far, but should you be drawing in to him so quickly? You promptly assent with a nod.

Do you know much about Giacomo Casanova?

You tell him that yes, you've read a bit about him. He was a very interesting man.

Oh yes? How so?

Pondering it momentarily, you offer your view.

I think that he was incredibly intelligent, a very clever man. He was much more than his conquests and scheming plots. From reading some of his journals, all with an interest in eighteenth century history of course, I found that most of his exploits, those women that he enraptured...well, he seemed to truly believe that he was in love with them...most of them anyway. Surely he was the very worst libertine, but I'm not certain he thought himself one. I think he was a rare type of lover. One who loves within all of the parameters of that emotion...beauty and hope, passion too, but also with an ugly selfishness. He so forcefully wanted the love of each of his paramours to be returned, for adoration and ardor to last forever, that he would do anything to try to achieve possession of these lovers entirely.

Looking thoughtful, Giacomo questions you further.

And could you ever desire to be loved by a man like that? One whose love was all-consuming? Someone who would do anything for your love?

With a fading smile, you answer him.

No. I wouldn't want that kind of love. It is reckless. I do not want to be devoured physically and emotionally by any man. To be loved carefully, gently, consistently, is to be loved plenty. I'm sure however, that I would have liked to have observed Casanova from a distance. He was a considerably worldly, intelligent and charismatic man judging by his writings. He was also Venetian. What a remarkable stage for such a passionate individual! Also, he traveled extensively through the European courts during his life. I found his entries of everyday life and his descriptions of the lives of Europe's most renowned nobles, to be fascinating. I too, at present, have a strong interest in seeing more of the world.

Giacomo's watchful stare, as sharply handsome as are his looks, is almost intimidating. Yet, you wouldn't want to move away from him if given the chance.

I see.

He pauses between words long enough for you to feel that you are entranced. You cannot say what has come over you. Certainly looks have never been enough to captivate you, lacking both depth and permanency. There seems to be something more here, in this man. He is refined, likely very cultured and studied; his movements are those of a gentleman's even if the look in his eyes is not.

So, what is this story that I am to keep entirely to

478

myself?

Offering him a delicate, direct smile, he returns the expression. His vision is altogether desirable and you are in anticipation of what secret he may have to tell, especially to you, a stranger. You aren't certain how you feel about a stranger telling you a secret, but you'll make an exception this time. No doubt, it will not be deeply personal, probably just something amusing. Leaning towards you, with a somewhat nefarious expression, he tells you.

Giacomo Casanova allegedly died in 1798. He would have been 73 years old. As you already know, he was an avid traveler, though not all of his wanderings were by desire. He often could not stay in a city, you see, due to some legal conflict, political issue or personal matter causing him trouble, such as a gambling debt or the jealous husband of one of his lovers. Napoleon Bonaparte's army had seized Venice in 1797. In the year of his death, it would have been an impossible blow for any Venetian to be home. At that time, he was living in the Castle of Dux in Duchcov, which is in the Czech Republic, and a city, which accommodated travelers of great wealth and noble heritage. This is where he sat writing these memoirs of which you've said you are familiar. However, I have come to believe that Casanova escaped death while in Dux and in fact, crossed paths with several esteemed nobles traveling abroad from Romania, who stayed a short time at the Castle of Dux and offered him an elixir for eternal longevity.

Giacomo pauses for effect, you believe, and smiles devilishly.

There is a small region in Romania called Transylvania of which I'm sure you've heard, just less than 600 miles away from where Casanova was residing. It is said that they specialize in ancient, immortal potions there and this is the place the travelers hailed from.

As your host lapses to take a drink, you laugh outright (delicately and with pleasure), smiling as encouragement for him to proceed. Your suspicions were correct, an amusing tale indeed!

Ah, I see, Transylvania! Are you telling me that Giacomo Casanova lived on? Perhaps you are insinuating that he is a vampire and is still alive, or undead rather, today?

Enjoying your blithe questioning, he amuses you further.

Undead no. He regained his youth at the first drink

of this elixir, but his heart remained beating as any other man's and he doesn't survive on the blood of innocent victims or shy away from garlic...a beloved staple in Italy...or avoid the sun's healthy caress. He is in fact, quite tan.

You laugh again and then prod further.

On what does he live then?

The response comes immediately.

Love. Without it, the potion will eventually fail him and he will cease to live. He abides in Venice even now...home again in his beloved birthplace. He's been settled back here for well over a century.

You take another sip of your wine and looking over the edge of the glass into his eyes, swallow and then ask smartly,

And what about his grave? Who is in it if not Casanova?

He too takes a drink, the red *vino* glowing crimson in the burn of the fire. Contemplatively, he replies.

No one today knows where that grave is. That is perhaps because it never existed at all.

You brandish away the falsehood with a flick of your hand.

So then, Casanova continues to live eternally, off of

his never-ending conquests?

And you are answered poignantly as a serious expression spreads across Giacomo's face.

No. As you said, he was a man that could experience many parameters of an emotion. One can experience passion out of a great many things...learning something for the first time, focused pursuits, the sensual in enjoying life's daily pleasures. As long as he continues to apply his passion to something that he loves, he will go on. But at the moment, living this extended life alone is not enough and he fears that left in this state, the love he feels for the simple joys in life will quickly dwindle and he will disappear. He needs his muse.

Strangely pensive, yet still exuding a masterful confidence, Giacomo stands and moves again to face the fireplace. His brawny back is to you, his baroque attire and exemplary figure silhouette in the glow.

It's you I've been waiting for. I knew it when I saw you in St. Mark's Square yesterday. I was overwhelmed when I saw you arrive tonight and watched you tour the ballroom...there is something about you. Be my muse.

What? You sit momentarily stupefied as he remains facing the fireplace. His tale is creative for certain. But could this actually be a revelation, a confession? At the very hint of an odd situation, especially alone with a strange man, you'd be out the door. However, you don't feel like you are in any danger despite the man having ended this farce so directly. His behavior conveys that he is telling the truth, yet magic isn't real. Instant and unexplained miracles perhaps happen from time to time, but not one's ability to overcome *death*. What an actor! Wait...did he just say he wanted you to be his muse? You sit unmoving, not sure what will be said next and so break the silence.

You have told me quite a tale Giacomo! It isn't real, but your inventiveness is very impressive!

Still facing the fireplace, he replies.

Of course it isn't real, you lovely creature. During Carnevale, by the firelight, we are to tell each other remarkable stories that excite the senses. Casanova, like any other mortal man, died. He surely sleeps in Dux. Yet, there is a part that isn't story. I would like to become better acquainted with you, if you would allow me the opportunity.

Turning around, a most imploring, seeking look on his face, he asks,

Would you honor me by being my partner in the

dance this evening?

Sheepishly, you admit that you do not know the movements involved with the dances in the ballroom. Their baroque steps, though fascinating, are completely unfamiliar to you. As he moves closer, you feel an unprecedented magnetism toward this man. You would usually keep a careful distance from anyone that you know so little about, but as you look into Giacomo's eyes, you don't feel the need to know more about him at present. Surely you feel comfortable enough to dance with him. You can ask more questions later.

There is no need to worry about the steps. I will be with you and will show you how. I know every step by heart…I must have danced them all in another life. Only, allow me the pleasure of being the only man you partner with tonight. Perhaps it is selfish, but you are too beautiful and I want your company all to myself.

His words sound reminiscent of what Casanova would say and your mind wanders. In the heat of the flame blazing upon the hearth's stone, as you both replace your masks and as he takes your hand to lead you to the ballroom, you wonder if you spoke truthfully about never wanting to be devoured in a reckless, all-consuming love, and whether you may have been wrong about magic.

THE End.

YOU follow Biasio out into the courtyard and into the foyer well remembered from your recent visit. Climbing the polished stone steps and turning down the opposite direction in the grand hallway from where the spare chamber was where you recouped, he leads you to a small sitting room lit by the flame of a lapping fire. The room is inspiring with its marble floor covered in an exotic rug, gilded furniture, comfortable seating and an enormous, ornately dressed window. You immediately walk to it and looking out, see the lagoon from above. Moonlight kisses the crest of every wave in shimmering beauty. You gasp at the view and imagine for a moment what this exact panorama would have been like with a flood of ancient merchant vessels docked in the place of cruise ships and motorboats. No matter the modernity however, no charm is lost to this city, it is eternally glorious.

Not far off from the window is a table thoughtfully arranged: seating for two, a crystal decanter of red wine with two wine glasses, pressed linens, shiny silver cutlery and a vase full of fresh pink peonies. You'd like to plant your face into the fragrant petals, and so you do! Walking over to the table, you lean over the delicious flowers and inhale deeply. After surfacing for air, Biasio appears delighted at your happiness and asks if he can relieve you of your coat. You take it off along with your scarf and gloves and hand them to him, next walking to the fire to warm your hands. Looking around, you enjoy the entire scene. It is an intimate sitting room with bookcases displaying old copies, antiquated oil paintings and a cozy wool blanket lazily thrown over a chaise near the hearth. You could easily spend hours in this room, which makes you wonder with awe at all the more within this enormous *palazzo* there is still yet to explore.

Walking over to a bookcase, you review the titles and marvel at how well the leather bound beauties are kept; not a hint of dust is upon the case that cradles these treasures. Having hung your winter trappings on a coat stand in the hall, Biasio reenters the room and pours you a glass of wine, bringing it to you where you stand. For a time, you speak about your favorite books and these antique copies. Soon moving to the table and nesting into your respective seats, you speak of many other topics: Biasio's family, his commanding home, Venice and the Carnevale. After half an hour, a man courteously knocks on the open door and enters, wheeling in a silver cart full of delectable items. You are relieved to be able to serve yourself, filling your plate buffet style rather than being formally looked after. Something about Biasio also makes you feel comfortable, like you can just be yourself. The idea of a dignified residence and your host's potentially great heritage and wealth don't seem to effect the moment. Biasio's demeanor seems quite natural and relaxed.

Helping yourself to a heaping portion of steamy asparagus risotto, you bite your lip in anticipation of the delicious meal to come, and then gasp as you accidently drop the goopy serving spoon. It rebounds off of the serving cart with a sharp clanking noise and then bounces off of Biasio's shoe. Oops! He laughs outright and asks if you are trying to hint that you don't like his selection of footwear. You laugh too and try to help him by grabbing at a white tea towel hanging on the handle of the cart while still balancing your dinner plate in your other hand. Reaching out, his hand stops yours, guiding you back to standing just before him. Unsure of why he is preventing your assistance (maybe he doesn't want you to spill the rest of your food on him), he looks you in the eyes warmly and smiles. Guiding your free hand, he lifts it to his lips, kissing your knuckles gently. Shy if not momentarily surprised, you can feel a blush coming on as your heart quickens.

You're beautiful.

He tells you, still grasping your free hand firmly. As though out of a dream that could only happen during the Venetian Carnevale, grand booming heard coming from the heavens without turns both your heads in the direction of the great window. And there, the stunning, bursting blooms of a fireworks display begin to light the evening sky with color, dawning the festive night to come.

THE End.

AT your leisure, having finished your delicious meal, you decide to go up to the restroom. You are too full to enjoy cake and coffee at present. You'll just wash your hands and refresh your lip color before another stroll in the ballroom. Breaking off the stem of your white rose, you tuck it behind your ear and exit the dining hall. Ascending the great stairs, you turn to your left at the top as earlier directed by the coat attendant and follow the hall until you see several women exiting from a doorway that you are certain must be the place. Once entered, you are struck by the impressiveness of even the powder room! It has its very own anteroom where a scattering of women are taking their ease on plush chairs and tending to their makeup. There are gilded mirrors and even a heavenly fresco above! There are marble sinks, gold faucets and small, soft towels enough to accommodate the drying of many delicate hands. Silver bowls filled with mints, dainty glass bottles of rose water to mist and refresh one's face and even a complimentary fabric box full of playful beauty marks to apply to your person. You are amused by this added touch and select one tiny velvet black round, pull off its paper backing and apply its tacky side just above your bodice line on your burgeoning bosom. It's an additional feminine touch to your already lovely display!

Once refreshed and back into the hallway, you begin making your way back toward the staircase, smiling to yourself in review of the already treasured hour and a half that you've spent at the ball. An open door catches your notice. Looking in as you approach, you see a warm sitting room mirroring much the same architecture of other rooms: marble floors, gilded furniture, comfortable seating, elegant window treatments, bookcases filled with the covers of old prints and a number of antique paintings of seventeenth, eighteenth and nineteenth century portraits. There is one painting in particular that is noticeable from the doorway and you can't help but to think that the image documented on the canvas looks very much like Signora Romana Sapienti. In fact, though difficult to get a very good view, the gown looks amazingly similar to the one that Signora Sapienti is presently wearing! You immediately make the connection that Ms. Sapienti is likely from the lineage of owners of the *palazzo*. Being the Carnevale in Venice (and obviously of some means) perhaps she commissioned a gown to be made in replication of the garb of a centuries-old ancestor. You are intrigued and would like to get a closer look but know that it isn't appropriate to enter a private room in your hostess' home, one that is not a common area, without an invitation. However, the door *is* open wide enough for anyone to look in. Surely it would do no harm to step inside for a moment to get a closer view of the portrait.

TURN to page 89.

MY New Friend,

I cannot thank you enough for what you did for me. Your selfless act will never be forgotten. Please allow me the pleasure in knowing you better? Won't you be my guest for dinner tonight at seven o'clock? A gondola will pick you up at Hotel Fato's waterside dock at six-thirty to bring you to my home, of which you are already partially familiar. If I am too forward in my invitation, please simply accept this gift and ask the concierge to send away the gondola this evening. I will understand without question and will wish you most well. However, I hope that you will come. It would please me very much.

Fondly Waiting,

Biasio

Opening the larger box first, you find that all of the items that you so hastily left behind are within. Much to your surprise however, every item is dry, clean and restored. Your passport is only slightly wrinkled from the little water pooled in the belly of the boat (which caused Biasio's slip and which you dropped your top layer into), with a bit of ink bleed that is dry but running off from the Italian entry stamp you received after landing in the country. However, it is certainly usable and not worse for wear. All of your paper currency appears brand new. You have a suspicion that someone switched your waterlogged euros for crisp ones. Furthermore, your wig is refreshed, your mask retouched, your gown clean and pressed and your gloves flawless and ironed. Even your loose hairpins are within, tied with a little ribbon. Such care was also taken with your underpinnings, which are neatly folded in the box, clean and freshly scented. It appears as though you'd never trampled on or swam in these clothes at all!

Moving on to the smaller box, you carefully remove the paper and open the lid. Within, you gasp to find what at first appearances, looks to be a diamond pendant on a platinum chain. After closer examination and in reading the trademark stamped on the back of the fine setting, you are relieved to discover that it is something less expensive. However, because you are in Venice it is more special and still quite a luxury. It is a single look-alike gem made out of Murano glass; an artisan crafted, precious stone replica. The crystal looks everything like a genuine diamond and the silvery setting is etched and elaborate. It is a piece that you'd expect to see on a stylish woman; it is very fine. Holding it up to the sunlight bursting in from your window, you are dazzled by its beauty! What a thoughtful gift! Murano, the glass island, is only a short boat ride from Venice and hosts some of the most talented glass artisans in the world. This reputation has been in place in Murano for hundreds of years!

Replacing the necklace into its box, you peek into the paper bag and discover a variety of sweet pastries. Perhaps it is a breakfast peace offering for having been woken so early! Thinking this turn of events over for a spell, you are left with a decision.

IF you accept Biasio's invitation and will meet him at his *palazzo* for dinner, turn to page 413.

IF you will send away the gondola to make room for an alternate excursion, turn to page 405.

YOU are by far experiencing the most bizarre hours of your life. You are cast into a moment of history where you do not belong, are conversing in a language that you normally would not comprehend, with a woman who believes you to be a countess. There is also a plague doctor from out of your nightmares watching you from the corner of the room. You are also afraid to look in a mirror lest you find another woman's reflection peering out at you. Have you lived multiple lives? Were you once a contessa from Padua? Or, have you been thrown into the past and into someone else's life for some mysterious purpose and no longer carry your own face? Is there some other reasonable explanation for this cosmic error, which has lanced the fabric of time?

There is one thing that you do know. You have to carry on the farce of being in control and aware of a life as the countess, or else you could find yourself sampling the scenery of a madhouse in the eighteenth century. You shudder to think of it. What could be worse than finding yourself in another time period and not knowing when or how you'll return to your true life? Incarceration, *that* would be worse and would certainly leave you unable to aid yourself home again. You figure that if there is a reason why you have come here, you might find it while following the same course of action that the contessa had originally planned. Her intention was to visit her cousin's *palazzo* this very night.

Belloza, please send away the good doctor. We have no more need of him. Please pay him for his troubles from our purse. I would like to bathe and eat breakfast in peace without any more talk of illness. Tonight, we shall go to the ball. Please follow through with every preparation.

Bowing thoughtfully, she then hurries the vulture out of the room and into the hall. Bidding him to wait, she crosses over into another chamber which is surely where she sleeps and where the traveling luggage is stored. The room that you currently reside in is simply too tidy for all of a countess's necessary items. Reentering the hall, she hands the doctor a few coins and he disappears, to your great relief. His presence was stiflingly unpleasant as he stood silently in wait for payment. You are for the moment, out of immediate danger.

The day brings with it, many unique experiences. You bathe using an elegant porcelain washbasin, elevated on a wooden stand rather than taking your daily shower. Where your modern bathroom once was, there is now a powder room arranged with a potty-chair, changing screen, vanity table with a cushioned stool, and the washbasin. They are not at all poor accommodations, simply far different than you are used to. After scrubbing yourself with a cloth and clean smelling soap from the hot water poured into the basin by Belloza, you put on clean underpinnings left neatly folded for you on the seat. At the time you woke, you were wearing only the shift from the costume that you went out in yesterday. Presumably Belloza removed what she must have thought was an oddly stitched gown, before pulling you up into your bed after you fainted the previous day.

After slipping into the fresh linen, the lady's maid assisted you into a day dress. She was so kind to first pull the strings of a corset so tightly (quite a new sensation) that you half expected your insides to be rearranged by the end of the day. With moderate panniers in place, you were dressed in a cream colored gown. Sitting to the vanity (and relieved to see *your own* reflection in the mirror), Belloza proceeded to arrange your hair simply without powder, as she expected that you'd care to wait for a more elaborate arrangement that evening.

With a little time to yourself, you enjoyed quite a

delicious breakfast and the reading of a local gazette. You discovered that it is the year 1779 and most certainly, a day in the midst of the grand Carneval. By reading the pages, you quickly got a taste for the local gossip, which seemed to take a primary focus above the more serious news. As you scanned the stories, some made you smile due to their absolute absurdity, such as the story of a Venetian nobleman who claimed that his favorite wig was stolen at the Caffe Florian. He entreated the thief to return it to his address (which he provided) and soon! Other topics seemed to be glossed over with less concern than should be due, such as the mention of a missing shopkeeper's daughter gone three days. The article seemed to imply that the young woman ran off in an elopement rather than blaming foul play (despite the family not believing marriage at the heart of the disappearance). You hoped that she was out of harm's way. Reading further, you soon found announcements for those elite who had come to visit the city. It was there that you saw the name of the very woman whose shoes you are filling.

The esteemed Contessa Ciossa Fortunato arrived in the city Tuesday, settling into the Hotel Fato at two o'clock in the afternoon. Though dressed in the black of mourning and veiled, it is hoped that she will throw off her dark raiment in favor of festivity. It is rumored that she has come to Venice to visit the Duchessa Amedea Frivolo of Palazzo Splendore, her cousin. It is at the Palazzo Splendore where today, the duchessa will throw one of the most anticipated events of the season. The duchessa was recently counted as one of the wealthiest women in Venice. Her esteemed husband the Duca Frivolo died of a ruptured spleen three years ago in a duel with the duchess's rumored lover, Piero Libertino, who even now frequents the Palazzo Splendore. The contessa, said to be more devout to her laureled husband than the latter (the Count Fortunato who passed six months ago from a spontaneous fever), was once known as an avid dancer of the furlana and an insatiable gambler, having won from Doge Alvise Giovanni Mocenigo his favored pet camel on a previous visit to Venice two years ago this month. Donning the black, she is said to have avoided any such pleasures since her husband's last breath. We hope with her recent and noteworthy entry into the city, that she will once again amuse us with her elegance, swift feet in the dance and gambling savvy at the ball at Palazzo Splendore.

You were shocked! Do the writers keep such a keen

eye on the population that it would be printed in the local gazette that the countess had arrived in town? As a piece of toasty buttered bread hung out of your mouth, you thought about the modern day. Yes, newspapers take a more serious tone. However, gossip magazines are *all* about celebrities. Perhaps this is the era in which the lines are blurred in the papers and that noteworthy nobles are revered like celebrities, mentioned alongside the more sober concerns of the day. This caused a moderate amount of anxiety on top of the stress you were already feeling. Not only do you have to try to pretend to be someone who you've never met, but you will also be closely watched by the Venetian paparazzi! You were amused however, to learn that you were now in possession of a pet camel.

After a bit more leisure time, you finally told Belloza that you would be going out for a walk and that she could take a break from attending until six o'clock this evening. She shouldn't worry; you won't do anything alarming or return to faint on the floor again. Covering with a black mantle, mask and gloves, you feel secure in your anonymity. Belloza hands you a handkerchief for your pocket and when you ask her where she keeps your spare coin, in case you wish to make any purchases, she looks at you a little oddly but then goes for some. Returning to the room, she asks if you are sure that you are well enough to go out and you tell her that you are certain. When you ask her why, she tells you that it is strange that you would carry coin, not your usual behavior. All vendors simply bill the purchases to your account here at the hotel, where you write out any payments all at once. Apparently the countess isn't known for making too many street purchases with small change. You tell her that today despite your wealth, some coin for little purchases from the local stalls rather than just the stately shops, will please you. It is a festival after all. She seems pleased as well. From the purse, you take some money and then tell Belloza to enjoy the rest of the loose coins to go shopping with if she so wishes. Telling you that this is too much (you already pay her generously), you tell her that you won't allow her to say no. This is what a holiday is about! Happily, she curtseys as you walk out into the hall, down the steps and out of the hotel.

Out in the courtyard, you hesitantly look to the hotel's waterside entrance where you saw the funerary gondola float past yesterday. However, all that you see today are masked citizens gliding down the canal in the sunlight, cheerfully talking and smiling. Walking out into the maze of *calli*, you spend the next five hours ambling and shopping, grinning and laughing, frowning and watching, all behind your *maschera*. What an active, glorious city! It doesn't take long before you are lost in the *calli* amongst the daily life and merrymaking that is brewing throughout the streets all around you. Even without deeply inhaling, you note that the odors of the city aren't particularly different than they are in the future, but certainly they are stronger and more intertwined with the heightened presence of life less sanitized. Smoke streaming from out of a street vendor's iron grill where he is roasting nuts for sale, wafts acridly before you, momentarily stinging your eyes. You wave it away with your hands as you walk past, watching the hot greasy nuts pop about on a searing iron pan elevated above glowing coals. The pungency of mildew is all around like a damp, chalky press at the back of your throat. It is mixed with the stink of refuse and a hint of urine, all of which you smell in turn as two feral dogs run past your legs yelping at each other in a playful chase. There are crumpled papers, bits of fish bones, crumbling marble pieces, dirtied rags and piles of slop near the open doors of the shops and residences alike (though not in excess and easily walked around). You hate to think that the majority of the contents of the city's chamber pots and garbage are emptied waterside, but this is surely the case. Your best guess is that the waste strewn along the edges of the buildings get swept up by city workers and are eventually dumped into the canals as well.

You can't help but to be a little curious when crossing over a bridge, you observe two courtesans hanging over the side to wave and yell to a gondola full of masked men boating below. They are as colorful as exotic birds in bright red and orange gowns with garishly powdered white faces smeared with rouge. Looking to one, her cream half mask is filthy with greasy prints, besmirched by old makeup. They laugh and wave with abandon, working to entice the crew to dock for a midday romp. They are clearly a set of *cortigiane di lume*, a pair of base courtesans far below the rank of the learned and refined category known as honest courtesans or *cortigiane onesta* (historically more remembered). As one laughs aloud wantonly, they both turn to run to the other side of the bridge as the boat floats under, knocking you firmly. Before even being able to expect an apology, they are on the other side to repeat the attention-getting tactics before their potential customers with even greater fervor.

There are plenty of vendors selling fried treats; you suppose that on festival days all around the world and throughout the centuries, the most unhealthy and greasy bites are the ones most sought-after. There are also sweets for sale: cookies and little cakes, candies too. Pulling off your gloves and stowing them in one pocket, you retrieve a coin and purchase a paper cone filled with tiny fried donuts called *frittelle*, which are rolled in sweet syrup and then sprinkled with sugar. The confectioner thanks you excessively when you refuse the change due from payment. Once biting into one of the custard filled little gems however, you find that it is you that should be thanking him! Nibbling with pleasure and licking the sugar from your fingers, you enter into a *campo* where there is a delightfully uplifting group of musicians playing a happy song on a drum, lute and mandolin. A small group of citizens have commenced before them in a high-spirited dance filled with swinging, hopping, twirling and merry laughter. You stop to observe them for a time, humming lazily to the songs (despite never having heard them before) and cheering on the participants of the frolic. The world seems darker and brighter at the same time, here in this moment of the past. The buildings are not as scrubbed and the streets not as clean. Many of the folks are clearly in want, poor and dirty. The street dogs are wilder and ready to bite if frightened, the noises more blaring and the cries and laughter more passionate. The surroundings are noticeably worn but the colors in the midst, brighter. As though both the starkness and splendor of life are parading in this square, in Venice and throughout the world at this time. The vibrancy of reality is not quieted away, as it so often will be in a future time of emotional temperance. The living is more alive, defiant in the face of fate! The picture before you is the very epitome of hauntingly beautiful and all those before you, are ghosts.

Finishing your treats, you stuff the sugary paper from the donuts into your pocket (not sure where to throw your trash and having the modern sensibility to not litter). You wash your hands in a fountain, cold water flowing out of the mouth of an enormous marble lion with wings. Two little boys in masks and velvet frippery (neither a day over five years old), yell at the lion and stand valiantly before it with wooden swords in hand. One of the two attempts a growl to show his fierceness before the stone animal. You can't help but to laugh with delight. Hearing you, so do they. As you walk away, they turn their swords on one another in a playful duel.

Passing the storefronts in no hurry, you note how the windows from the outside are grimy but within are well-lit places of finery. There is a paper shop with bottles of colored ink, feather quills and tanned portfolios to hold one's most intimate writings. There is another store for gloves of every fine fabric: leather, silk, cotton and velvet. Each pair is worked to softness and dyed every color imaginable, then decorated with elegant beadwork, lace and stitching. There is a perfumery, shelves lined with large glass globes filled with stores of oil and scent. Once your choice is made, small portions of the rich potions are decanted into smaller vials for your wearing pleasure. The very rush of pure floral fragrance is a heady hit as the door of the shop opens and a patron exits. A delicate woman dressed in a grey gown and an enormous fluffy pompadour dusted with silver glitter rising 12 inches up from the top of her head, decorated with sparkling yellow butterflies and two stuffed canaries (poor birds), walks out with an air of extreme privilege. She laughs jovially as her eager and handsome companion (his clothes tailored with the very same fabric as her gown) grabs her bare arm and smells it as if about to taste a delicious morsel. As they walk past you in a hurry, the sweet and exotic scent of jasmine wafts by with them. You are going to a ball this evening, why not enter and choose a fragrance for yourself? You realize that though in the precarious situation of being in another time and unaware of a solution for how to return, you are actually wallowing in the pleasures of the moment. For now, you'll enjoy the backward reflections you've been given and worry about your situation when it becomes necessary.

Pushing past the wooden door of the shop's entrance, you enter to the sound of a vibrating brass bell overhead. Greeting you is a fresh maiden wearing a light blue cotton dress and a crisp white apron pinned around her waist as well as a feminine white linen cap resting on her head of blond curls. Not masked, she smiles happily and her blue eyes show gratitude for yet another customer to greet. Despite the brightness of the day out-of-doors, the shop is hewn out of dark wood within its marble housing and thus in need of its brightly lit glass-ensconced candles, which glow along the walls and counter spaces. The smell of flowers, herbs and spices permeate the small shop. Your nose tells you that the scents are pure rather than manufactured, lacking those chemicals that are so harmfully engineered to create the perfumes of the twenty-first century. There is a long board made of polished wood resting upon the front counter. Carved into it are several hundred circular indentations where glass vials rest easily. In each vial, there is a glass stick for smelling or sampling a droplet of perfume. Behind the counter and nesting over shelves on all sides of the room, there are glass globes, which you assume carry the larger portions of the fragrances available from the testers. Though offering her assistance, you tell the clerk that you'll just take a moment to smell some of the scents available. She busies herself grinding a handful of fragrant seeds with a mortar and pestle. There is every kind of precious oil and perfume that you could ever imagine and their fragrances are unadulterated, lacking laboratory alterations and additives. You are overcome with the thrill of discovery, whiffing one right after the other: peppermint, lemon, clove, juniper berry, cinnamon, orange, rose, sandalwood, strawberry, lavender, myrrh, apple, spearmint. The fragrances go on and on in an endless succession and you are amazed. Too overwhelmed, your eye catches a linen lined basket.

Within are tiny bulbous glass jars sealed with round corks. Attending, the young lady uncorks a sample, calling it honeyed salve, and uses a miniature wooden paddle to remove a pearl sized dollop. Asking for your hand, she pools it into your palm and tells you to smooth it onto the top of your other hand. Doing so, you find that it is a silky cream: soft, clean smelling and a little sweet. You purchase two vials, one for you and one for Belloza, and exit the shop in a flurry of fragrance.

The viral bite gotten from the pleasure of shopping has taken hold. Before you even know what has possessed you, you've entered many a store and purchased a mix of fine items, most having to be billed to your room at the Hotel Fato for future payment. What countess wouldn't do the same? With great satisfaction and sensory delight, you weave in and out of the crowds, buying with abandon. Among your newly acquired purchases are ornately painted and glittering masks, spiced nuts, honey balm, scented handstitched gloves, silk stockings, colorful ribbon, sweet and nutty pastel colored nougat and bite-sized chocolates filled with lemon, raspberry and strawberry cream. Then, there is a glass mirror gilded in silver, a pearl set on a ring of gold and perfumed stationery, scented with rose. There is also the purchase of a kitten, which you sent directly to your hotel room (though tempted to carry it around with you snuggled in a basket). The little white ball of fur was yours the moment you saw her. Why not? With an estate in Padua, she'll find a comfortable plush cushion or two to claw and rule as her throne. You'll request that she is fed as many delectable pieces of fish and meat as she pleases. After all, pets make everything lovely; she was too precious to leave behind! You just hope that if you switch places back with the true countess and any time soon, that she isn't allergic to cats!

With some purchases sent on to your room and others carried, you finally return to the hotel. Bursting into your room, Belloza looks somewhat stunned standing in wait with a mewing furball in her hands, but then quickly sets the kitten onto a soft pillow and relieves you of the excess of packages, placing them about wherever the objects will be made useful. She is quite pleased with several items chosen and gifted to her: honey balm, scented talc, chocolates, tea, a hand-held fan painted with delicate flowers and two exquisitely stitched and scented handkerchiefs. Though visibly elated with the treasure of fine items she has been gifted with, she reminds you that it is past time to begin readying for the ball. You are late beginning your preparations! As it usually takes hours to dress for such occasions and you don't have that much time, you'll have to hurry! You inform her that it will not only be you that attends, but her also. The kitten kneads her tiny paws into her new bed and purrs, and you smile. With bewildered yet happy eyes, Belloza works to help you to prepare while you demand that she too chooses a dress from your own wardrobe and any accessories she wishes! Having been such a faithful companion in your illness of the previous evening and such a dedicated friend for so long, she too will share in the delights of the ball. With this, you both make haste and ready.

TURN to page 419.

WATCHING the apparition, who very much like a live person seems to exhibit embarrassment by his sorrow, makes to brighten his tone.

Forgive me...I don't want to frighten you. I just want to speak to someone again and be heard. It has been so very, very long.

By far the strangest moment you've ever experienced, you feel overwhelmed by this unnatural appearance, but also some magnetism to his emotions. Perhaps this is because they have been pent up for so long, they cause the man's very aura to make your heart reach out to his lost soul. You fail to pound on the door, despite your fear.

My lady, she was so beautiful. Her name was Trisola.

You entwine your hands into your scarf, pulling them up under your chin, working to keep out the cold and subliminally trying to keep out some painful story you must hear.

You appear to be a visitor in Venice, so perhaps you have never heard of the Flight of the Dove?

You nod "no" to his question, eyeing his expressions keenly.

Trisola...I loved her in the year 1759, even some

years before, and I love her now. But I should start further back than that. In the 1500s, about the middle of the century, there was an astonishing stunt performed for the entire city to see in Piazza San Marco. There, is a bell tower. Perhaps you saw the Campanile? It is not the same one of course, but there was one there in the 1500s too. There was an impressive man from Turkey who with daredevilry gave quite a performance. You see, they strung a rope from the top of this campanile to a grand boat moored at the banks of St. Mark's Basin. There also was a rope that passed the balcony of the Palazzo Ducale. The Turk walked up the first rope to the top of the bell tower. Do you believe that madness? The people loved him for it; they were moved by his courage. On the way down, he walked the rope to the balcony and paid respects to the Doge himself. From then on, at the start of every Carnevale, a brave acrobat would prove his valor by performing a similar display.

I am noble born of a very wealthy house. I fell deeply in love with a woman who was not so fortunate. A match would have met with disapproval from my family, but in any case, they never intended for me to marry at all. Through the centuries, Venetian noblewomen were sent to nunneries and noblemen made to remain lifelong

514

bachelors, while only a select one or two of their siblings was destined for marriage. It all comes down to the game of keeping wealth in the family by limiting the lines of inheritance. I could have eloped, snatched my beloved away, far away. I had every resource to carry us out of Venice and live a lifetime on the jewels, gold and finery that I was given as an incentive never to marry. I would never have threatened a brother's succession. But I didn't take her away with me. Instead, I left Venice and went to university in Padua. And though my lady wrote to me, beseeching me to come for her, that she loved me with all the passion that is within a woman, I did not.

Her family was poor, as I have said…entertainers. She had a single brother who was an acrobat. I had not been gone long when planning began for the Carnevale of 1759. Trisola's brother was selected to be the performer that would chance the rope at the opening ceremonies, the act then called the Flight of the Angel. This was a great privilege, I assure you. Altered from the original feat, the performers were now swung down on a rope from a great height wearing angel wings, like ethereal beings in flight. Before a crowd of thousands, and my paramour, at the point when he began his descension, a terrible misfortune happened. Some error provoked him to fall 300 feet from his lofty place, smashing to the stones in the midst of the people. Grieved by the death of a brother, my abandonment, and I suppose the poverty of her family...who would have been rewarded handsomely had there not been an accident...she too took flight from the bell tower, though in the secret of night after climbing its internal stairs to end her life.

Consequently, in the years following they no longer allowed live men to go to such heights for all to see, but rather sent a wooden dove down the rope, which released colorful bits of paper and fresh flower buds; the Flight of the Dove. I felt such guilt from her loss, for having stood firm against a marriage that would not receive my parents' consent. They intended for me to remain unmarried for all of my days to uphold the patrimony. And perhaps I rationalized this as acceptable by believing Trisola's family wasn't good enough for my noble blood. How unjustifiable! I loved her! Had I been an honorable man, I would have come for her and married her before everyone, and then taken her away to make her always happy. Thereafter, every time I watched the descending of that dove, I didn't remember her fallen brother, I saw the bride I could never have. I lived to an old age, bitter and alone. After my time, I remained in Venice as you see before you. Very rarely does anyone see me. But you did. Should I finally let go of her memory, I am sure to leave Venice for my eternal rest. However, I am not ready, not yet.

Standing as still as stone, moved by the apparition's tale, you feel on the verge of a faint, but some inner fortitude encourages you to ask if he is alone in his condition and whether he can't be moved to let go.

There are others who wander these calli, canals, churches and bridges. You might call them ghosts or lost souls, but they are only people who linger because they pine to make a past wrong right, or to understand why such pains met them in life. In time, they will all find their way. Take for instance another of my kind who I see no more. If you might honor me with a little more of your time sweet lady, I can tell you of him.

You assent to his request; despite all you will hear the spirit. Perhaps it will help him to move on.

I remember him because he too was eternally changed after the events of a local festival during the Carnevale: the Festa delle Marie. I had heard stories of what happened from my nonna, all Venetians knew of it. It was in the late 800s that there was a tradition to bless all marriages in Venice on one special day. For that day, there were also chosen 12 damsels, all betrothed. They were to be of lowly birth without means and also pretty, very pretty. They were selected to make a show of the sanctity of marriage and also the profundity of Venice's love for its people. The Venetian nobles paid for these women's dowries and provided for elaborate weddings and marriage banquets. They were 12 fortunate women, though choosing only from the most lovely of maidens was considered shameful to many. In the year AD 943, there was a very unfortunate situation in which pirates abducted the 12 selected brides for that year. The barbarians stormed the celebrations and made off with the beautiful women and all of the noble wealth that they had been given for their marriages. Though horrified that such a breach had occurred, Venetians were swift to act. Pirates should have known not to challenge our city with its undefeated warships. The criminals were pursued and murdered, the brides and their dowries saved.

Sadly, there was one groom who did not trust that his bride would be recouped. He drowned himself in the lagoon on that wedding day, out of pure despair. Who is to know what happened to his beloved, as she in fact returned home. He should have waited, or so he said the many times I saw him wandering near the water's edge in Piazza San Marco, eternally keeping watch for his bride. I don't see him anymore, given he was around much longer than I. Having moved on...or so I believe he has done...he's given me hope that I will desire to do so as well. I'm just not ready, yet. I hope that I have not troubled you for too long. I thank you for allowing me, however unnaturally, to take up your precious time. You look so much like her; like my lost dove. Buonasera, sweet lady.

With that, the ghost vanishes before your eyes, leaving you completely alone with only the sound of rushing water from the canal.

You awake from a shake to your shoulder. Opening your eyes, the sun's early light shines down, excited to show you a cheery new morning. Your body feels achy and cold. A piece of wilted spinach falls out of your hair as you sit up from the strange arrangement you slept in; lying half bent over on your two suitcases, not far from the *bacaro's* trash heap. The green leaf must have blown off the trash to nestle on your head, how lovely. Blinking slowly, you see a man with a healthy (living) complexion. He peers down at you quizzically, though with a smile.

Buongiorno!

You wish the man a good morning as well, your mouth terribly dry. Thankfully, he doesn't ask you any questions, but helps you to pull your luggage into the bar. You are certain that you must look terrible, but take up the offer of a cappuccino before heading out. The warm cup defrosting your cold and throbbing fingers, you sit at a table watching the early morning traffic; Venetians on their way to work and stopping in for their morning coffee. The normality of daybreak's commotion soothes your frazzled nerves. You hardly wish to revisit what transpired the evening before, though somehow, you are not worse for wear. If anything, the transitory phantom taught you something of the power of love.

As you stare off wearily toward the window, taking a smooth and satisfying sip, something white flashes before your eyes. Your brows furrowed, you hardly believe what you are seeing. Two pristinely white doves have flown up from the marble *calle* to land on the awning of the shop across the way. With great attention, you watch the two birds nestle and preen one another in the morning's light. It is too beautiful for words. Setting down your cup and leaving your luggage behind, you walk to the door of the *bacaro* and out into the street. The doves coo to one another in a most soothing way. Your heart is warmed; a repose coffee could never deliver. Within moments, both take flight into the sky above, lit by the glorious pastels of dawn. In that moment, you are sure that no matter how dire and unfair the world might seem, justice and peace will always settle affairs.

With that, you reenter the bar to pay your tab and retrieve your luggage. You are looking forward to the comforts of your hotel! The attendant, who so graciously helped you to rise without judgment, cheerfully holds the door open for you as you leave, and welcomes you to Venice!

THE End.

Venice

66318367R10315

Made in the USA
Lexington, KY
10 August 2017